The Place of Dead Kings

GEOFFREY WILSON

HODDER

First published in 2012 by Hodder & Stoughton
An Hachette UK company

First published in paperback in 2013

1

A CIP catalogue record for this title is available from the British Library

ISBN 978 1 444 72115 7

Typeset in Minion Pro by Palimpsest Book Production Limited,
Falkirk, Stirlingshire

Printed and bound by CPI Group (UK) Ltd, Croydon, CR0 4YY

Hodder & Stoughton policy is to use papers that are natural, renewable and
recyclable products and made from wood grown in sustainable forests. The logging
and manufacturing processes are expected to conform to the environmental regulations
of the country of origin.

Hodder & Stoughton Ltd
338 Euston Road
London NW1 3BH

www.hodder.co.uk

The Place of Dead Kings

This was a good place for an ambush. A very good place . . .

A man nearby gasped. Jack swivelled and saw a porter with an arrow in his chest stagger forward. Blood welled from his wound and soaked his tunic red. He coughed and vomited more blood, then toppled over and splashed into the water.

Suddenly arrows hailed down from the bluffs. Missiles thudded into men and animals, dashed the water and chipped off carts and wagons. Porters screamed, choked, stumbled and flapped about in the river. An arrow nailed one man's hand to a cart. Another speared a porter in the eye. The oxen roared and wrestled to free themselves from their yokes.

They were trapped.

And soon they would all be dead.

By the same author

Land of Hope and Glory

About the author

Geoffrey Wilson was born in South Africa, grew up in New Zealand and then backpacked around the world before eventually settling in the United Kingdom. He studied Hinduism and Buddhism at the University of Canterbury, New Zealand, and has been fascinated by India since travelling there in the early 1990s. He has worked in IT for several years, eventually starting a web development business with three friends.

www.geoffreywilson.net

For my parents, Gail and Harry, and my brother, Edward

Prologue

Saleem al-Rashid scrambled through the tangled woods. The night was so dark he could barely see the way ahead, the forest nothing but a suggestion of interlocking branches. Thick bracken grasped at him, twigs scratched and vines snared his legs.

But he stumbled on. He had to deliver the message to Colonel Drake. And he had to do it quickly.

Artillery fire punched off to his left. He saw the momentary flare of the blasts through the trees.

A round shot whistled overhead, then thrashed through the leaves like a giant bird. Another shot cracked through branches and thumped into the earth. The missiles were falling all around him, but he couldn't see them in the dark, just hear them shrieking and slashing at the forest.

His heart pounded and sweat filmed his face.

Would he be hit? There was no point thinking about it. There was nothing he could do to protect himself anyway. He had to keep running. That was all.

'Allah is great,' he whispered under his breath in Arabic. 'Allah is great.'

'Saleem,' Yusuf called behind him.

Saleem spun round. His comrade stood more than thirty feet back, his eyes wide and his mouth hanging open.

'What is it?' Saleem shouted.

'My foot's stuck.'

Foot's stuck? What was Yusuf talking about? Here they were on an important mission, with shot falling all around them, and

1

now Yusuf had trapped his foot. They would both be smashed to pieces. They wouldn't get the message to Drake. The enemy would overrun them all and march on through Wiltshire—

A ball shredded the foliage directly above. Twigs and scraps of leaves twirled down.

He had to stay calm.

Allah is great. Allah is great.

And he shouldn't think badly of Yusuf. His comrade was a fellow soldier and a fellow Muslim. Saleem's father had always taught him to respect others, to show self-restraint, and to be patient even in the most trying situations. These things were laid out in the Quran, and you had to follow the Quran even in the middle of a battle.

Saleem took a deep breath and hurried back. Yusuf was crouching and frantically trying to pull his leg out from where it was trapped between a pair of tree roots.

Yusuf looked up. A gun rumbled on the far side of the valley. The glare fingered its way through the branches and lit up his face for a moment. His skin was pale and shone with sweat, while his wild eyes darted around constantly as if the enemy were about to appear out of the shadows at any moment.

Yusuf was eighteen, only a year younger than Saleem, but this would be his first taste of combat. Saleem found it strange to realise he was a veteran by comparison. Three years ago he'd fought at the Siege of London, surviving a bombardment worse than that being hurled at the forest now. Remembering this somehow reassured him. Made him feel more like a real soldier. A knight.

'It's all right.' Saleem put his hand on Yusuf's shoulder. 'I'll get you out.'

Saleem bent and investigated Yusuf's leg. The foot had somehow forced its way into the hole and now refused to come free. Saleem stood again, tensed, then slammed the sole of his boot into one of the tree roots. The root shifted a little but not enough. Saleem leant back, then kicked again. The root cracked and Yusuf yanked his foot out, tripping backwards.

'You all right?' Saleem asked.

Yusuf put all his weight on the foot. 'It's fine.' He glanced up and smiled. 'Let's get moving.'

Saleem grinned back. But then felt a twinge of shame. Hadn't he been arrogant in thinking he was a veteran? Did he think taking part in one battle three years ago made him a knight? Did he think he was so much better than Yusuf?

The Quran taught humility – his father had often told him this – and yet he'd let himself get carried away with thoughts of grandeur. He looked down, feeling his face redden.

They set off again, fumbling through the mesh of undergrowth. Saleem's knife-musket bounced on his shoulder and snagged on bushes.

Ahead, a speck of fire streaked down through the canopy and slapped into the ground. A flash lit up the moss-covered trees for a moment, then a sheet of flame erupted from the earth. The roar shook the woods and flying metal screamed in the dark, lashing branches and clipping leaves.

Saleem ducked and pulled Yusuf down with him. He heard a large chunk of metal whirl past overhead.

Yusuf stared at Saleem, eyes even wider than before.

'Shells,' Saleem explained. 'Bombs.'

Yusuf swallowed hard and wiped the sweat from his forehead with his sleeve.

They peered over the brush and saw fire crackling where the shell had struck.

'Come on.' Saleem pulled Yusuf to his feet. 'Keep going.'

They pressed on, clambering up a slight incline while the guns continued to rumble. Further shells hurtled down like tiny comets and smacked into the earth. The bright blasts sent the shadows dancing and the whiplash of metal fragments echoed deep in the forest. Flames hissed as they engulfed trees and spat sparks into the night.

Allah is great.

Saleem's father had taught him those words. Saleem's father had taught him all about praying and worshipping Allah, including the five daily prayers and the proper times for performing them. He'd insisted on the Arabic words being pronounced clearly and correctly, and he'd clipped Saleem on the head whenever he'd made a mistake.

Saleem felt a stone in his throat. His father had died more than a year ago, after collapsing suddenly for no apparent reason. The old man, who had seemed so tall and strong and implacable and stern, was gone. And that left Saleem alone to look after his mother and five sisters.

He reached the top of the slope and came to the edge of the woods. Figures crouched in the undergrowth around twenty yards ahead. For a moment Saleem wondered whether they were enemy troops, but then he saw they wore civilian tunics and hose. They were rebels, like him. Most people called them crusaders, but Saleem could never bring himself to use that term. The word was enough to put many Muslims off joining the struggle. Before he died, Saleem's own father had often told him not to fight for the Christians. But Saleem knew he had to fight. He was an Englishman and he would defend his country.

Saleem ran towards the huddled soldiers. With the trees opening up, he could see he'd reached the summit of the hill.

A scene of terrible beauty unfurled before him.

A grassy slope rolled down to a dark valley, on the far side of which rose a further hill, indistinct against the black sky. An unholy thunderstorm seemed to crackle across the hill's crest. The enemy guns flickered like sheet lightning, streaking the clouds above orange. The deep booms rocked the valleys and gullies. And from somewhere behind, Saleem heard the pounding of the rebel artillery returning fire.

The sky seethed with sparks and flashes. Shells darted across the valley like fireflies on a summer evening, while explosions roared and tore open the night. Specks of flame wheeled overhead.

4

Saleem swallowed, slowed his pace for a second and then ran on.

One of the rebels – a tall man with a musket slung over his shoulder – stood up and shouted, 'Greetings.' Then he glanced at the skullcaps on Saleem and Yusuf's heads and his expression shifted, like the subtle movement of sand on a dune.

Saleem knew that look well – he'd seen it all his life. It was a mixture of surprise, distaste and suspicion. The expression of a Christian seeing one of the old enemies of England.

'We're looking for Colonel Drake,' Saleem shouted.

'Drake?' the soldier said. 'He's with the Amesbury Battalion. About half a mile down there.' He nodded along the line of the forest. 'Why?'

'Got a message from Colonel al-Hasan. Vadula's army is marching on our position. They aren't attacking from the west.'

The rebel forces had been retreating for days as the much larger army of Mahasiddha Samarth Vadula advanced into Wiltshire. Earlier in the day, Saleem had fled with the other rebels to their position on the hill. The rebel commanders had planned to hold the ridge, expecting an attack tomorrow in the west. But as Saleem waited in the east with his comrades in the Muslim Battalion, sentries spied a large party of Rajthanan and Andalusian troops crossing the valley. Vadula had obviously decided on a surprise night-time attack where the rebels were weakest. The Muslims were outnumbered three to one, and had no artillery.

Colonel al-Hasan had hurriedly summoned Saleem and Yusuf and sent them to call for urgent reinforcements from Drake. If they couldn't get word to Drake in time, their Muslim brothers would be overwhelmed and Vadula's forces would sweep across the ridge, attacking the rebels in the flank.

The soldier frowned and cast a wary look at the firestorm over the valley. 'You'd better run.' He looked back at Saleem and a blast lit up his face for a moment. 'If those bastards attack from the east we'll do our best to hold them.'

Saleem nodded. Then he and Yusuf sprinted off down a path that followed the summit and the edge of the woods. At times, he spotted rebel soldiers crouching in groups behind whatever cover they could find. Ahead, in the distance, the slope dipped towards a saddle that was hidden in shadow. Drake and his men must be down there somewhere.

A round shot thumped like a thunderbolt into a tree just ahead of Saleem. The trunk split in half and scraps of bark went flying. A broken branch swung past over his head.

The gunfire was intensifying. Shot and shells swarmed across the sky.

'Down here,' Saleem shouted to Yusuf.

He led the way deeper into the forest, where he hoped they would be at least slightly more protected.

They fought their way through brambles and briars, and all the while a storm of missiles threshed the trees. Explosions glimmered in the darkness and splashed the undergrowth with livid orange. Fires billowed. Twigs, leaves and shards of metal swirled in the air.

For a moment Saleem pictured his mother and sisters cowering together back in his home village, which was barely three miles away. His family would be able to hear the steady stomp of the artillery, probably even see the blasts lighting up the horizon. If Vadula's men took the ridge, they would sweep on towards the village. They would torch huts, rape, loot and kill. And only Saleem could stop them by getting word to Drake.

Allah is great. Allah is great.

His foot struck something. He found himself flying forward and skidding through the leaf litter. He gasped and scrambled back to his feet.

Had he been hit? Was he injured?

No, he felt fine.

Behind him, Yusuf gave a loud shout.

'I'm all right,' Saleem said. 'Just slipped.'

But when he turned, he saw Yusuf had backed himself against a tree and was pointing at something on the ground. Saleem looked down and now he saw what he'd tripped over – a human skeleton. The bones had been completely picked clean, and yet they gleamed a brilliant white, as if they'd just been placed there rather than lying in the forest for weeks.

'It's nothing.' Saleem straightened the musket on his shoulder. 'Come on.' He'd seen skeletons three years ago – many of them. Once he would have reacted in the same way as Yusuf, but not any more.

'But what's that thing?' Yusuf asked.

'What thing?'

Then Saleem noticed something the size of a finger crawl out of one of the skull's eye sockets. It looked like a large ant, except it was made of metal that had a greasy sheen in the dim light. Its head was a deformed mass of feelers and mandibles, with what looked like gills flickering on the side. It emitted a clicking sound, and a faint, shrill hiss.

A chill crossed Saleem's skin. He'd seen something like this before in London. It was one of the Rajthanans' infernal creatures. An avatar.

The beast stood on the edge of the skull, facing Yusuf. It raised itself up and flicked its feelers through the air. It seemed to stay poised for a long time, although it must have only been a second.

Saleem knew well what the thing would be capable of. He'd seen avatars in London kill men within seconds. He had to do something quickly, but he felt frozen, transfixed. He stood still, gazing at that glinting body with the glimmer of a tiny fire beneath the carapace.

Then the avatar squealed and darted forward. It rippled over the skull and shot across the leaf-strewn ground towards Yusuf. Yusuf cried out, but the creature was so fast he had no time to flee.

Saleem found himself moving without thinking, as if possessed

7

by a djinn. He plucked a rock from the ground, bounded forward and flung the stone at the avatar just before it reached Yusuf's boot. The rock struck. The creature shrieked, buzzed against the stone, and splintered into metal fragments. The head spun across the earth, the feelers and mandibles still whirring.

Yusuf yelped and jumped away. He gave small cries and danced from one foot to the other as if to avoid a swarm of invisible beasts.

'It's dead,' Saleem shouted.

When Yusuf continued jumping around, Saleem grasped him by the collar and yelled again, 'It's dead.'

Yusuf stopped moving, his chest heaving up and down. Finally, he managed to say, 'What was it? A demon?'

'A type of demon, yes.' Saleem couldn't think of any better way to describe the thing. It was a monstrous creation of the Rajthanans' black magic. That was as much as he knew. As much as he wanted to know.

'Come on.' He turned to lead the way forward.

'Wait a moment.'

Saleem turned back. What was Yusuf playing at now? 'What?'

'Why are there no guns here?'

Saleem was about to tell Yusuf to stop talking nonsense when he realised that his comrade was right – no shots struck the forest and not a single shell explosion was visible in any direction. The gunfire continued but it was more distant now, coming from the area they'd just travelled through. Without realising it, they'd passed into a part of the forest where there was no fighting.

'I think it's a good sign,' Saleem said.

'Why?'

'Vadula's attacking to the east. Why would he send artillery to the west? He wouldn't, would he? That means we must have come far enough to find Drake. He must be around here somewhere.'

'Suppose so.'

They set off again, Saleem leading the way back uphill. He

knew that once they reached the summit they could follow the edge of the woods down to where Drake and his men were encamped.

They struggled through a thicket. And then the undergrowth cleared and the trees thinned, allowing them to move more quickly. The flashes of the distant artillery filtered through the leaves and provided enough light for Saleem to see the way ahead more clearly. When the scarp tapered to a gradual incline, they began to jog.

A sound crept into Saleem's awareness, sneaking up from beneath the boom of the guns. He stopped dead still and Yusuf ran up beside him, panting heavily.

'What?' Yusuf asked.

Saleem put his fingers to his lips and strained to listen, making out an unmistakeable popping sound, like seeds bursting in a frying pan.

'Musket fire,' Saleem said.

'Vadula's men?' Yusuf asked. 'Here?'

'Don't know. Let's take a look.'

They jogged on, the sound of musket fire growing louder. And now Saleem noticed something else as well – a familiar scent that reminded him of perfume, incense and spice all mixed together. The hair stood up on the back of his neck. It was sattva, the mysterious vapour the Rajthanans used for their black magic.

Sweat ran down the side of his face and his hands felt clammy, despite the chill in the air. The musket bounced on his back, tapping insistently against his shoulder blade. The last time he'd fired a musket in a battle was three years ago. And even then he hadn't shot anyone. Would he have to shoot a man now?

There was a sudden screech beside him. He looked at the tree trunk where he'd rested his hand for a moment and nerves shot through his body.

Another ant-like avatar was perched on the tree near his fingers, clicking rapidly.

He lurched away, skidded on the leaf litter, then regained his footing. He didn't stop to look back, just kept running. He heard Yusuf crashing through the undergrowth behind him.

No more than a minute later, he burst out of the trees and found himself on a grass-covered slope that led down into the saddle he'd spied earlier. At first he was confused about what he saw. A grey-white cloud smothered the bottom of the incline where the forest met the open ground, as though thick mist had descended on that spot alone. Hundreds of tiny shafts of fire stabbed within the cloud and a dense crackling sound floated up the incline.

'What is it?' Yusuf asked.

A cold hand took hold of Saleem's chest. Now he knew what he was seeing. 'Muskets.'

'The Amesburys?'

'Has to be.'

'But Vadula . . .' Yusuf said. 'They were attacking in the east.'

'Looks like they're attacking here too.'

Colonel al-Hasan had believed the enemy were only strong enough to mount an attack in one location. But clearly the Amesburys were fighting below.

And that meant Vadula's forces were stronger than the rebel spies and scouts had reported.

'The reinforcements . . .' Yusuf's voice was soft and shook slightly.

Saleem tightened his lips and nodded. Tears pricked the edges of his eyes.

With the Amesburys engaged in battle, there would be no reinforcements. The Muslim Battalion would be overrun.

And his home village . . . his mother and sisters . . .

'What should we do?' Yusuf asked.

Saleem ran his tongue along the inside of his teeth. He became intensely aware of each groove and furrow, as if studying some fascinating rock formation.

He stared down at the boiling fog of powder smoke.

There was no point returning to the Muslim Battalion, and there were no other rebel forces who could provide reinforcements. He and Yusuf had few options.

Deep down, he'd always known it would come to a moment like this. Ever since he'd signed up with the rebels, he'd known the Rajthanans would eventually come. Although he'd always tried to stay hopeful, to believe the rebels could win the fight, he'd always known they couldn't. After seeing the destruction of London three years ago, he knew the Rajthanans were too strong to ever be defeated.

'We'll go down there.' Saleem nodded towards the battle. 'At least we'll have done our best.'

Yusuf nodded, pursed his lips, stood up straighter and puffed out his chest a little. One of his eyes glinted with moisture as he turned to Saleem. 'Allah is great.'

Saleem swallowed, his mouth so dry it was painful. This was it. Time to fight. He was prepared to die for the cause, but the image of his family cowering in their hut kept flashing in his head. He could only hope Allah would save them. 'Allah is great.'

He went to sling the musket from his shoulder, but then heard a series of shouts nearby. A figure came sprinting over the brow of the hill, fleeing from the battle churning below. It was too dark to make him out clearly, or to hear what he was saying, but his cries were loud and urgent.

Finally, Saleem caught the meaning: '*Run!*'

Yusuf glanced at Saleem, forehead creased in puzzlement.

'Run!' the man shouted again. 'The horses.'

Saleem looked over his shoulder and spotted five cavalry horses picketed about a hundred yards away beside the line of the trees. A wagon and a couple of barrels stood nearby, but there was no sign of any sentries.

'Saleem.' Yusuf's voice was thick. He tugged at Saleem's sleeve.

Saleem turned back. The running man was close enough now

for his green tunic and hose to be visible. He was clearly a rebel. His face was gaunt and he waved his arms about wildly as he shouted.

Behind him, a tide of darkness rushed across the grass. Saleem heard a sharp squealing and sizzling noise, and the smell of sattva was so strong now it stung the back of his throat.

He took a step back and his legs weakened.

Within the moving shadow, he could make out the glint of tiny bodies and feelers. It was a swarm of ant avatars, all racing towards the rebel soldier . . . and towards him and Yusuf.

'We'd better get to those horses.' Saleem's voice was cracked.

Yusuf nodded, his face so pale it shone in the dark.

They spun round and sprinted towards the animals.

The distance had looked so short but now it seemed so far. Saleem felt as though he were running without getting anywhere, as if in a nightmare. Why couldn't he go faster?

He heard Yusuf panting beside him and the cries of the soldier behind. The dense hiss of the avatars grew louder, cutting through the spluttering muskets and roaring guns.

Drake's men must be fighting the beasts. There was no sign of any enemy soldiers in this part of the valley, as far as Saleem had been able to tell. That had to be part of Vadula's tactics – march troops to the east, then hit the west with black magic to prevent any reinforcements being sent.

But the rebels had nothing with which to counter black magic. Only the Rajthanans knew how to control sattva and avatars.

The horses whinnied and trod skittishly as Saleem and Yusuf drew near. Saleem's fingers felt fat, clumsy and far too slow as he unhitched one of the creatures. Finally, he swung into the saddle and looked across the hill.

The running soldier was perhaps fifty yards away, but the mass of avatars was almost upon him. The trilling and clicking was so piercing it made Saleem's ears hum. The sickly sattva scratched his eyes and nose.

Yusuf mounted a mare beside Saleem. 'He's not going to make it.'

Saleem tightened his jaw. Yusuf was right, but what could they do?

The avatars flooded like black water around the soldier's feet, then coursed up over his legs and rushed on to his abdomen. Within seconds the beasts had engulfed the lower half of his body. He cried out and slapped at them as they wriggled over his chest and circled around to his back. But there were so many of them there was nothing he could do to stop them. He screamed as the swarm rushed over his face. The writhing mass now encased his entire body and he staggered forward like some misshapen clay figure.

Then he toppled over.

As he hit the ground, he seemed to smash into pieces. But each fragment was an avatar that went spinning away across the ground.

There was nothing left of the man but fresh, white bones. His skull – completely picked clean – rolled across the earth, with several ants still slithering about it.

Nerves coursed through Saleem's body. 'Ride!'

He slapped and spurred his charger into a gallop. Yusuf yelped and did the same. The horses battered across the grass, hooves throwing up chunks of turf.

Saleem looked back and saw the avatars still racing over the summit. At least the horses were outrunning the creatures.

'What now?' Yusuf shouted.

A good question. Saleem didn't have a clear answer. They'd been about to fight and die with Drake and the Amesburys, and yet now they were in fact riding away from the battle and towards the looming forest. Beyond the trees, the hills led down to the plains . . . and then Saleem's village.

If they turned back, they would most likely die with Drake and his men. That would be the honourable thing to do. On the other hand, if they pressed on as they were, there was a chance they could escape, get back to the village, warn everyone there to flee. They could get word out to the neighbouring villages too – and with any luck save as many lives as possible.

Was it better to flee?

What did it say in the Quran about such matters? What would his father have told him to do?

He had no idea. You needed to be a scholar who'd studied the Quran for years in order to reach a decision. And Saleem was no scholar. He couldn't even read – and, unlike his father, he hadn't memorised large sections of the sacred text.

He would have to decide for himself what to do.

Allah is great. Allah is great.

Now his eyes fell upon a pale line that cut across the hillside – it was a path, leading into the woods and away from the battlefield.

'Down there.' Saleem pointed at the track.

'What?' Yusuf shouted back.

'We'll follow that. We have to warn the villages. There's nothing more we can do here.'

Yusuf glanced back at the avatars fanning over the slope. He shivered, clenched his jaw and nodded at Saleem.

The horses thundered on to the path, charged towards the woods and then rushed through an opening in the line of trees. Shadow slammed over them. The canopy clasped overhead and arcades of tree trunks receded into the gloom. The pounding guns were muffled to a heartbeat and the horses' hooves sent echoes whispering through the leaves.

Saleem noticed that his hands were shaking and his heart was bashing inside his ribcage.

The hiss of the avatars and the smell of sattva had faded. He and Yusuf had got away. Escaped. He felt like laughing or cheering for a moment, but then he remembered his comrades, who were fighting at that very moment. While he was riding away, they were dying.

He tightened his grip on the reins.

Had he really decided to flee just to save his family and the village? Hadn't he, in fact, been afraid all along? Hadn't he wanted to avoid the fight?

How could he ever have thought to call himself a knight?

Yusuf gave a strangled shout. Saleem shot a look at him.

'There's something there.' Yusuf pointed into the black wall of branches flickering past to his right.

Without slowing his pace, Saleem peered into the shadows, listening carefully. At first he noticed nothing, but then made out a faint, cold clicking and smelt a trace of sattva. His skin crawled.

'Ride,' he said to Yusuf. 'Fast as you can.'

The avatars swept from the right, boiling up from the ground and bubbling over the tree trunks, flowing like a cloud shadow on a bright day. Saleem saw the tiny metal beasts scurrying across the branches overhead. Their piercing hiss drowned out every other sound.

Saleem slapped the side of his charger frantically, shouting at the animal to run faster. His horse was quicker than Yusuf's and he started to pull away.

A black pool of avatars spilt across the path ahead. With no alternative, Saleem spurred his charger towards them. The pool darkened and deepened as more of the creatures slipped out of the woods. But Saleem pressed on, aiming for the left side of the track where there were fewer of the creatures. His horse squealed, rolled its eyes and galloped into the mass of squirming beasts, smashing several beneath its hooves.

And then the horse was through, leaving the avatars behind.

Saleem glanced to either side. Were there any creatures on the horse? Any on him? He saw none.

Allah is great.

Yusuf cried out.

Saleem looked back and the ground seemed to drop.

Yusuf was still sitting astride his horse, and the horse was still charging along the path, but both Yusuf and the animal were covered in clumps of avatars. The beasts swirled around Yusuf's legs, streamed over his torso and twined about his neck. He shrieked and swatted a few of them away, but more kept rippling up from the horse's flanks.

Saleem yanked at his reins and circled his charger round. He was about to ride back along the path when he saw the avatars engulf Yusuf's face. Yusuf began a scream, but it was choked off by the creatures surging into his mouth. Both Yusuf and his horse were now completely smothered. The horse stumbled and fell forward, Yusuf tumbling off over its head. As rider and steed struck the ground, the avatars smashed off them, leaving nothing behind but gleaming bones.

Saleem felt a cry boil inside him.

Bile rushed up his throat, but he hurriedly fought it down because the mass of avatars was still hurtling up the track and was now less than ten yards away.

He swung the horse in the opposite direction and spurred away. The dark branches rippled past to either side, the rutted path streamed below and the wind tore the skullcap straight off his head.

Tears welled in his eyes. His face felt hot.

Yusuf.

Loud hissing sprang up to his right. Another wave of avatars flooded from the darkness and shivered over the trees.

There seemed to be no end to the creatures.

He slapped the horse hard, shouted until his voice cracked and repeated the words 'Allah is great' over and over again in his head. He had to escape, had to get to the village, had to save his family.

But the mass of avatars was folding about him like a giant hand.

As the shrill clicking beat in his ears and the smell of sattva wedged itself in the back of his throat, he began to realise he wasn't going to make it.

He shut his eyes and whispered, 'Allah is great.'

PART ONE

1

SHROPSHIRE, 620 – RAJTHANAN NEW CALENDAR
(1855 – EUROPEAN NATIVE CALENDAR)

Jack Casey clasped the pommel of the scimitar hanging at his side. The metal felt cold and reassuring. The weapon had a fine blade, perfectly curved to land a deep cut with minimal effort. It had been forged in the Rajthanan military sword-mill at Christchurch, and you could always trust Rajthanan military blades.

He hoped he wasn't going to have to use it.

He stared at the eleven men standing in a semicircle in front of him. Several bore sputtering torches that flicked sparks at the dark night. Others rested their hands on arming-swords or pistols. They eyed Jack like crows around a lump of meat.

'The girl stays here,' Jack said.

The men's leader, Constable Henry Ward, stepped forward. His face was flat and his eyes were dark as obsidian. His rough beard climbed high on both of his cheeks, but above this his skin was rubbed raw by the cold. He wore a white surcoat bearing the red cross of St George – the mark of the Crusader Council of Shropshire.

Henry's breath misted around his mouth. 'She's a witch. She must return to Newcastle for punishment.'

The young woman gave a muffled whimper. Jack glanced at her standing slightly to the side and behind him, her face shiny with tears, her jaw quivering and her eyes wide as a trapped

19

animal's. The freckles on her skin stood out like pox blisters.

How old was she? Someone had told Jack, but he couldn't remember now. She looked no older than fifteen. A child.

Jack's daughter, Elizabeth, put her arms around the girl, gripped her shoulders tightly and whispered something comforting in her ear. Elizabeth then raised her head, jutted out her chin and glared at Henry and his men as if she could set them on fire with her eyes.

Near to her stood her husband, Godwin, looking particularly ineffectual tonight as he shuffled about and flexed his fingers around the grip of a longsword that was far too large for him. Behind Godwin, in a loose arc, were fifty men and women – almost the entire adult population of Folly Brook village. They carried pitchforks, hoes, scythes and other farming implements, but few true weapons. Their eyes darted about and many shivered, no doubt not just because of the cold.

Jack wondered how far they would back him. He was their reeve and wore the white surcoat of office. But Henry was the representative both of the local lord and the Council. Would the villagers really be prepared to make a stand against him?

Jack turned back to Henry. 'The girl is under my protection while she's in this village. I say she stays.'

The girl had fled from the town of Newcastle-on-Clun two days earlier and taken shelter in Folly Brook with her aunt. Jack knew what would happen if she went back – she would be burnt at the stake, like any other witch. And he would never let that happen. He might live in the native state of Shropshire, where his backward countrymen continued with the barbaric practice, but in Folly Brook, where he was in command, he'd banned it.

Henry paced across the ground in front of Jack, boots crunching on the hard ground. He lifted his chin and stared at the villagers, seeking each out with his eyes, questioning them, testing them.

What kind of calculation would he make? Jack had fifty people on his side, but they were poorly armed civilians. Henry had only ten men, but they were hardened soldiers with swords and fire-arms. The soldiers could win in a fight, but would Henry want the blood of ordinary peasants on his hands? How would he explain that to his commanders?

No doubt Henry was hoping the villagers would simply buckle and give in to his demands. If they did, there would be little hope of Jack preventing the girl being taken.

A line of pain wormed its way across Jack's chest and his breathing became more laboured. His old injury. Why did it have to flare up now? He did his best to hide any sign of weakness in his face.

Henry stopped walking and squinted at Jack. 'What gives you the right to question our age-old customs? We have lived according to these laws for hundreds of years. And yet here you are, in your arrogance, deciding which laws to follow and which to ignore.'

'If something's wrong it doesn't become right just by being an ancient custom,' Jack said. 'We need to change. Learn. We'll never defeat the Rajthanans otherwise.'

'Learn, eh? That's what you do here, isn't it? Learn the secret ways of the heathens. What do they call it? Yoga. Well, I call it something else.' He fixed his gaze on Jack. 'I call it black magic.' A piece of spittle flew from his lips.

One of Henry's men roared and unsheathed his sword, the blade ringing.

Jack heard clattering and rustling behind him. Glancing back, he felt a surge of warmth in his chest as he saw the villagers drawing together and lifting what weapons they carried.

They weren't going to back down. They were still with him.

Jack faced Henry again. 'You raise your arms against common folk?'

Henry scowled and his face reddened. He gripped the hilt of his sword, his knuckles whitening.

Everyone went silent. The only sound was the rustling of the trees.

The wound in Jack's chest tightened and he fought not to wince.

Henry's eyes blazed for a moment, but then he gestured at the soldier who'd drawn the sword. The man stepped back and slid the blade into its scabbard.

'I'll be speaking to Sir Alfred,' Henry said.

'Do so,' Jack said. 'And send him my good tidings.'

Sir Alfred was the leader of the local arm of the Crusader Council. The old man was an ex-soldier, like Jack, and had risen to Sergeant Major in the Rajthanans' European Army. After serving with the Indians for so many years he was more open to Jack's ideas than most. Jack was certain he still had Alfred's blessing.

Henry's face twisted, then he spat, wiped his mouth and turned away. He and his men trudged back across the grass towards their horses, their burning brands dwindling in the dark.

Jack breathed out as a wave of pain swept through his torso. He grimaced. He would have to get back to his hut and meditate in order to get the injury under control again.

'Father.' Elizabeth strode over to him, her long cloak swishing around her. Her nose was red from the cold and her dark hair was pulled back beneath a bonnet.

Jack cleared his throat and quickly suppressed any expression of pain in his face. Despite living with his injury all these years, he'd managed to keep it hidden from his daughter – and almost everyone else.

Elizabeth gazed at the disappearing figures and gave a small smile. 'Didn't take much to scare them off, did it?'

Jack raised an eyebrow. 'Perhaps I should have left them to you?'

Elizabeth flashed him a wider grin, then her features turned more sombre. 'You think they'll come back?'

'We'll deal with them if they do.'

Godwin strutted across the grass with one hand on the pommel of his longsword and the other on his belt, as if he were a lord surveying his castle. 'We saw them off, make no mistake.'

Jack stiffened. Why had Elizabeth married an idiot like Godwin? He nodded at Godwin's blade. 'You sharpened that?'

Godwin faltered and swallowed. 'Yes, sir.'

'Let me see it.'

Gingerly, Godwin drew the sword and handed it to Jack, who inspected it in the faint moonlight. Jack wasn't a swordsman – he'd only been trained to use a musket in the army – but he knew enough about blades to pass judgement. The sword was well balanced, but heavy and cumbersome. He was more used to the Rajthanans' scimitars, which were lighter, faster and designed to be wielded one-handed from horseback. A longsword was largely a weapon for smashing your foe with brute force, while a scimitar was for deft cuts and parries.

The blade gleamed softly – it was well polished. But when Jack passed his thumb along the edge, it drew no blood.

'Blunt.' Jack handed the sword back to Godwin.

Godwin slammed the blade back into its scabbard, lifted his chin and stared into the distance. 'I sharpened it today, sir.'

'Then you made a bloody hash of it.'

'Father.' Elizabeth slapped Jack's arm gently, then turned to her husband. 'Godwin, ignore him. I'll see you back at the cottage.'

Godwin pursed his lips and sniffed. 'Very well. I'll see you there.'

He turned on his heel and strode away, the longsword swinging at his hip. The other villagers were also dispersing and making their way back to the white-walled huts of the hamlet. The young woman from Newcastle was being led away, stumbling as though she felt faint.

'Godwin's a good man,' Elizabeth said.

'I'm happy for you,' Jack muttered.

'He's trying his best.'

'Is he?'

'Father, be nice to him.'

23

'I'm nice.'

'You know what I mean.'

Jack put his hand on her shoulder. The pain was streaking down his left arm now and darkness frosted the lower rim of his vision. He knew he had to meditate soon in order to save himself. 'Let's get inside.'

He walked back with Elizabeth, smarting at the pain but keeping it hidden. He was reeling by the time they reached his small, thatched cottage and he had to place his hand against the wattle-and-daub wall for a moment to steady himself. He strode through the door and entered the single room. A fire smouldered in the centre, the smoke floating up through a hole in the roof. The beaten-earth floor was strewn with fresh straw and his few possessions had been carefully put away in two chests and a wooden crate. A pair of knife-muskets hung on one wall, the ornately engraved metal quivering in the firelight.

He turned to his daughter, who still stood in the doorway. 'Good night, Elizabeth. God's grace to you.'

'Father.' She stepped into the room and the fire tinged her features yellow. Her face was serious. 'Can I talk to you for a moment?'

Another pulse of pain beat in Jack's chest and sweat broke out on his forehead. He needed to meditate. Now. 'If it's about Godwin—'

'No.' She stepped closer. 'I'm pregnant.'

Jack stood up straighter. He'd been expecting this news one day but this had still taken him by surprise. A smile slipped across his face. 'Elizabeth.' He embraced her. 'That's wonderful news.' He looked her in the face again, holding her by the shoulders. 'How long?'

'About three months.'

'And you're sure?'

Elizabeth nodded. 'Mary said it's certain.'

Mary was the village wise woman. She wasn't a Rajthanan doctor, and Jack was sceptical about many of the herbal treatments she prescribed, but she knew about childbirth, having delivered many of the children in the village.

He embraced Elizabeth again, held her tight. Although she was eighteen, she was still his little girl. It was strange and miraculous to think she was going to be a mother. The only thing that darkened his happiness was that Godwin was the father.

His injury flared again and rippled down his left arm. He gritted his teeth until the sensation passed.

He let go of Elizabeth. 'You'd better rest.'

She smiled. 'I'm not ill.'

'All the same. You get back to Godwin. I'm sure he'll want you with him.'

She stood on tiptoes and kissed him on the cheek. 'God's grace to you, Father.' Her eyes went glassy.

'Go on.' He waved her away before things got too emotional.

Once she'd left, he shut the door, leant against it for a moment, pulled back his hair and retied his ponytail.

He shook his head in amazement – he was going to be a grandfather.

Then pain split his chest. He grunted, doubled over and slumped to the ground. Wincing and fighting off the darkness threatening to overwhelm him, he crossed his legs and sat up as straight as he could.

He shut his eyes.

Another wave of pain flooded through him but he did his best to ignore it.

He inhaled and concentrated on the air passing through his nostrils.

'Your mind is like a rippling pool.'

These were the words all the yogins spoke. His drill sergeant had said it to him when he'd first joined the army. His guru, Captain Jhala, had repeated it when initiating him into the secrets of the siddhas, the 'perfected ones' who developed supernatural powers.

The mind was like a rippling pool and it had to be calmed to a still, mirror-like surface, free of thoughts, confusion, doubts, passions, images, sensations. This was the only way to use a power.

The wound in his chest throbbed. He felt himself slipping into unconsciousness for a moment, but managed to pull himself back.

He had to focus. If he couldn't enter the trance, his injury would undoubtedly kill him. He sensed the sattva-fire burning in his chest. Tentacles of blue flame licked around his heart.

He brought to mind a yantra, an intricate, circular design that unlocked a power. He pictured the dense tangle of lines, triangles and curlicues that writhed within the circle, trying to recall every part of the design, every minute shape. He remembered Jhala saying to him, 'You must be able to hold the entire image still and perfect in your mind, without any other thought intruding. Only then will you be able to use the power.'

But this was no simple task. Whenever you tried to keep a yantra steady, other thoughts would inevitably well up, or you found yourself concentrating on a single part of the design rather than the whole.

Memories flickered in his head.

He remembered Jhala the last time he'd seen him, before his old guru had died. Jhala had looked frail and tired after struggling for years with his own sattva-fire injury. Jack's throat tightened. Jhala had betrayed him, had threatened to kill Elizabeth.

Then he saw his wife, Katelin, on her deathbed, her Celtic cross necklace rising and falling with her chest and her weak hand reaching up to him. She'd died eleven years ago, leaving him to raise Elizabeth alone.

And he pictured his old friend William, who'd been a rebel leader and had died at the Siege of London when Jack had betrayed him.

So many dead people.

Finally, he managed to get the yantra squarely in the centre of his mind's eye. It glowed white on a black background. As the pain bubbled in his torso, he held on to the image, fought to keep it in place.

With his mind, he reached out to his surroundings, sensing the soft, grainy throb of sattva all around him. He was in a strong stream – he'd specifically chosen this hut because of the large amount of sattva coursing through it. He drew the sattva towards him and smelted it in his mind, the familiar perfumed scent filtering into his nostrils.

The spirit world drew close.

Suddenly the yantra froze, glimmered, then burst into brilliant light. Fire shot up his spine and radiance roared around him. He felt as though he were hurtling upward into the stars. A grand, holy space opened in his head and the worlds of spirit and matter touched.

He remained in the trance only for a moment. But by the time he released his focus and slipped back to the material world, the pain in his chest had subsided and his breathing had eased.

He'd used a power – a healing power that fought off sattva-fire injuries. Usually it eliminated the effects of his wound completely, but over the past few months the results hadn't been as good. Tonight he still felt the fire crackling near his heart, although it was subdued and no longer as great a threat.

Every day his injury seemed to worsen, and every day his power became less effective.

He sighed and wiped the sweat from his forehead. The embers of the fire throbbed and breathed, holding back the chill of the night. A breeze rustled the thatched roof and shook a loose window shutter.

Wearily, still wincing at the pain, he crawled across to a bed of straw, wrapped himself in a blanket and tried his best to sleep. Beneath his discomfort, buried within him, was the warm knowledge that Elizabeth was pregnant.

Three years ago Elizabeth had almost died. Now she was with him in Shropshire, safe, happy and soon to be a mother.

He clung to this thought as he drifted off.

———❖———

Jack paused before leaving his hut and rubbed his chest through his surcoat. Pain still streaked through him and his breathing was shallow and wheezy. On waking that morning, he'd meditated immediately, but his power had only had a limited effect. Now he felt as if he hadn't used the yantra at all.

But still, he had to get on with the day's work. People would wonder where he was if he stayed in his hut any longer.

He took the deepest breath he could. Would the healing power stop working completely one day? If it did, he would die. And now he wanted very much to live, to protect Elizabeth and his grandchild.

He pushed open the door and squinted in the morning sunlight. 'Sir.'

A voice to his left startled him. His hand reached involuntarily for a weapon, but he wasn't carrying one. He was about to lash out with his fist when he saw it was Godwin, standing close to the door with his longsword drawn.

'What the hell are you doing?' Jack asked.

'Sorry, sir. I wanted to show you this.' Godwin moved the sword in Jack's direction.

'Put that down, you idiot. The next time I find you outside my hut with a weapon you'll be on the end of my boot.'

Godwin lifted his chin and stared into the distance, as if he were some high-minded martyr. 'I sharpened it today, sir. For your inspection.'

'Inspection?' Then he recalled the night before. 'For God's sake. Get out of here. Go and do something useful for once.'

Godwin dithered. Was he expecting something more? Something about the baby?

But Jack was in no mood to talk and instead strode off towards the village green, still wincing at the pain lancing him. What Elizabeth saw in Godwin he would never know. He'd given the lad a chance – he'd tried to be pleasant, tried to understand him, tried to act as a father-in-law should. But the boy was simply a fool and there was no getting around it.

He would have to say something to Godwin about the child at some point, but that wasn't going to be today.

He walked down the rough road through the centre of the village. Tom, the blacksmith, was already at his forge, beating a strip of glowing metal. Mary, the wise woman, waved good morning from the door of her cottage. James, a tenant farmer, nodded as he strode past, his dog yapping around his feet.

For the moment everyone seemed to have forgotten the confrontation of the night before. And everyone still saw Jack as their reeve, still acknowledged the authority of his white surcoat.

He crossed the green, went down to the brook, splashed across the ford and walked through a short stretch of woods. The leaves on the trees were already turning gold, and shimmered in the breeze.

He came out at the secluded glade that contained the hut known by many as the House of Sorcery. It was easy to imagine the building stood apart from the rest of the village because no one wanted to live close to a place where strange, possibly infernal, practices were carried out. But in fact Jack had chosen the spot because it was right in the path of the strongest sattva stream in the area.

A ripple crossed his skin as he passed into the invisible stream. A faint trace of perfume tickled his nose. He shut his eyes for a moment and sensed the sattva flowing around him, tiny whorls and eddies forming about his body.

The stabbing sensation in his chest brought him back to the material world. Forcing himself to ignore the pain, he pushed open the hut's door and entered the dimly lit interior. As his eyes adjusted, the single room came into focus. The window shutters were closed and the only light came from the fire in the central hearth. A large banner displaying an intricate yantra hung across one wall, the image trembling in the firelight. About a dozen young men sat cross-legged on the earth floor, staring up at the design. Two others sat scratching yantras into boxes of wet sand, and a third meditated with his eyes closed.

Jack had 'discovered' all these young men. Most had been sent to him from elsewhere in Shropshire when it became known that he was looking for people who experienced second sight, saw ghosts, or suffered from fits. Many who arrived were simply mad or ill, but a few, a very few, turned out to be sensitive to sattva.

A handful of women had even shown up. That had surprised him and he suspected some might even have been sensitive enough to become siddhas. But it was of course out of the question to train women in the secret arts. It wasn't right to get them involved in something that could be dangerous, especially as his aim was to develop siddhas who could eventually fight the Rajthanans.

Mark, a tall lad who was slightly older than the others, walked across to Jack, carrying a stick he'd taken to using like a drill sergeant's cane as he led the meditations. 'Morning, sir.'

Jack tightened his face as a pulse of pain crossed his chest. 'Any progress?'

'Afraid not yet, sir.'

Jack nodded. It was a long, difficult process training siddhas. It was almost a year since he'd started teaching and so far Mark was the only one who'd mastered a yantra. Jack didn't know why the success rate was so low. Was it normal? Did the Rajthanans face the same problems? Or were his training methods wrong?

The difficulty was that he didn't know nearly enough about yoga. He'd only been given the basic training by Jhala and had only ever seen three yantras – only two of which he'd been able to use. In truth, he was a disciple himself rather than a guru.

A disciple who'd lost his own guru.

'Any of them finished memorising the native yantra at least?' He motioned to the banner strung across the wall. It was the first yantra he'd learnt and the first one he taught his students.

'Not yet.' Mark looked down. It was the same news every morning. 'Stephen's not far off, I reckon.'

Jack rested his hand against the door frame for support. Black specks danced before his eyes. 'Ah, Stephen. Promising lad, I thought.'

'Yes, sir.'

Jack's gaze drifted to the native yantra. It unlocked innate abilities in Europeans, but you could never tell what power it would produce. When Jack had learnt it years ago, he'd been gifted the power to track quarries using the traces they left in sattva. Mark, on the other hand, had gained the ability to find lost animals. Who knew what powers Jack's other disciples might develop?

If only they could progress.

Jack felt sweat beading on his forehead. 'And you, Mark? Anything?'

'No.' Mark picked at a piece of dirt on his sleeve. 'Still trying to memorise it.'

Jack patted Mark lightly on the shoulder. 'It's all right. It's a difficult one. Took me a year.'

Mark drew a sheet of paper out of a pouch and unfolded it to reveal a huge yantra sketched in blue ink. The paper was precious – a rare item in Shropshire – and the Rajthanan pen used to draw the design was the only one in the village. But these were both as nothing to the priceless yantra depicted on the sheet. Jack called it the 'mystery yantra' because he'd never been able to learn its purpose. A strange Sikh called Kanvar had given it to him in London three years earlier, and since then he'd been trying to use it. Despite memorising the design and learning to hold it steady in his mind, it had never given him a power.

He could only hope that Mark would do better.

'This part.' Mark pointed at a particularly intricate piece of the image. 'Can't seem to get it.'

'Yes. Tricky. You'll get there.' Pain punched him in the chest and he couldn't help but grimace.

'Are you all right, sir?' Mark asked.

'I'm fine. I'll be back later.'

'Sir?'

'Carry on with the training.'

He left suddenly, doing his best not to trip over as he walked. He knew Mark would be watching him and he didn't want to show any weakness. If he could just get back to his hut and meditate he could at least hold the sattva-fire at bay for a little longer.

But his chest was so tight he could barely draw in air, and his surroundings seemed overly bright. He stumbled through the trees, crossed the brook and lurched past the green. It was strange to walk through the peaceful village, seeing everyone busy at their tasks, and yet be on the brink of death. It was as though he were suffocating behind a sheet of glass, unable to attract anyone's attention.

But what could anyone do to help him anyway? He had a sattvic injury, and only yoga could treat that.

If only he'd learnt more yantras, then he might have been able to cure himself. But he knew just the three – the native, the mystery and the yantra that healed his chest. Not much to treat himself with.

And not much with which to build an army of siddhas.

His right knee buckled and he almost toppled over. He grasped a tree stump and only just managed to stay on his feet. A pool of blackness passed before his eyes but he blinked and fought it off.

'You all right, sir?' a young girl called Marian asked as she came up the street.

32

'I'm fine,' he muttered.

'You sure, sir?'

He grunted and staggered on.

One step at a time. Keep going. Back to the hut.

He felt as though he were floating, as though he were in a dream. There were houses and trees and fields and hills about him, but they were as real as hallucinations.

He reached his hut, fell though the door and collapsed on the ground. Fighting for air, he rolled on to his back. He heard the sound of children playing in the distance. A sheep bleated and a dog barked incessantly. Tom the blacksmith's hammer tinged and tinged against the anvil.

He tried to sit up, slipped back, tried again and finally got himself into the correct posture for meditation. He closed his eyes and brought up the image of the healing yantra. It circled and danced in his mind's eye, white on black, with intricate, lacy detail. He tried to keep it still but it constantly blinked out of view as other thoughts flooded his head.

Your mind is like a rippling pool.

Darkness enclosed him entirely and he passed out for a moment, only waking just before he slumped to the ground. He stuck out his hand to steady himself and eased back into a sitting position.

The fire in his chest seared him.

He didn't have much longer – he was sure of that. If he were going to live, he must use the power now. He thrust every other thought aside and focused solely on the yantra. Finally, he held it still and complete in the centre of his mind's eye, and the image blasted him with white light.

He slipped immediately out of the trance, expecting the sattva-fire to have been forced back – at least, to some degree.

But there was no change at all.

Damn it.

The pain was as fierce as before and his chest was just as

constricted. He rasped down what air he could. His small hut was hot and oppressive and the sound of Tom's hammer echoed as if down a long tunnel. The children's laughter seemed to taunt him.

He brought up the image of the healing yantra once again, but now the darkness was clutching at him and drawing him close. He tried to fight it off, tried to keep his focus on the yantra. But everything was slipping away.

He was choking.

Was he going to die?

He was certain he would. These past few years had been a temporary reprieve, but the healing power was no longer enough to save him.

At least he'd had a few good years with Elizabeth in Shropshire, and at least he'd been able to save his daughter's life. He thanked God for that.

His only regret was that he would never get the chance to see his grandchild.

2

Bells pealed. Several bells. Two were small and high-pitched, while a third was large and dolorous. The sound was familiar to Jack but he couldn't place it. It seemed to come from the past, from far away, from another world.

Then he recognised it – the call to Vespers.

He opened his eyes and found he was lying on his back and staring up at a shadowy, vaulted ceiling. The ringing bells were close, the sound vibrating in the air about him.

Was he dead? Was this heaven?

Then he felt a stab of pain in the centre of his chest and he knew he was still alive and in the material world.

He sat up. He was lying on a hard cot in what he thought at first was a small church, until he noticed the row of ten other cots stretching away beside him. Most of the beds were occupied by old men who lay huddled beneath blankets.

He was in a monastery hospital.

A blast of pain hit him in the chest and he slid back down. He tried to sit up again, found he was too weak, tried again, and then darkness swirled around him.

He fought to stay conscious, but couldn't prevent himself slipping away.

He woke to the sound of the bells chiming Nones – three o'clock. Chalky light floated into the hall from the window behind his cot and he smelt a trace of frankincense.

His chest still hurt and each breath was a struggle.

'Father.'

He shifted his head and saw Elizabeth standing next to the cot. She whimpered and put her fist to her mouth when she saw his face.

An elderly monk in a black habit stood behind her. The man had a sombre expression and skull-like features. He looked as though he'd just risen from the dead.

Elizabeth knelt beside the bed. 'How are you feeling?'

'Terrible.'

Elizabeth smiled and gave a short laugh. She took his hand and he felt her icy fingers coil into his. Her eyes were watery and he could see she was fighting to hold back the tears.

'Where am I?' he asked.

'Clun Abbey. We found you out cold. No one knew what to do. We brought you here.'

Jack had seen the abbey up on its hill many times but had never visited. It stood about two hours on foot from Folly Brook and the path to Newcastle passed beneath it.

The old monk stepped closer and folded his hands within his habit's sleeves. 'It's good to see you awake. I'm Brother Michael. I've been trying my best to treat you, but I'm afraid no one here understands your ailment. It is beyond our knowledge, I fear.'

'Ah.' Jack eased his head back. 'It's a strange matter.'

'What is it?' Elizabeth's face was creased with worry.

Jack turned his head to Michael. 'Can we speak in private?'

'Of course.' Michael bowed his head and withdrew, making no sound save for the rustle of his clothing.

Jack held Elizabeth's hand tighter. 'Listen, you mustn't worry.'

'What's going on?'

'I was injured. A long time ago, on a battlefield. You know about sattva-fire?'

'Yes. You told me once. It's like magical flames.'

'That's it. The Rajthanans use it in war. I got hit by some once

36

– an accident. It's in here now.' He placed his shaking hand across his chest. 'It'll never go away and once it gets bad enough it'll stop my heart.'

A tear rolled down Elizabeth's cheek. 'But can't you get rid of it?'

'I could. Before. I had a power that held it back. It's not working any more.'

'Why not?'

'I don't know.'

'Then you need another power.'

'I'd need a new yantra for that, and I haven't got one. The Rajthanans have all the yantras and they keep them secret.' He struggled to breathe and sweat burst on his forehead. 'I don't even know if there *is* another yantra that can help.'

Elizabeth gripped his fingers tighter. 'There has to be something you can do.'

'You mustn't worry. It's in God's hands now.'

'No.' Fresh tears trickled down Elizabeth's face.

'Listen.' He reached under his tunic and drew out Katelin's necklace. He held up the cross, with its sinewy designs. 'You remember this?'

Elizabeth nodded and sniffled. 'It was Mother's.'

'She gave it to me before she died. Now, if I go, you take it, you understand?'

Elizabeth shook her head, as if to drive away a nightmare. 'No, Father.'

'You take it, Elizabeth.' He held her hand urgently. 'Promise me that. You take it. And then one day, you pass it on to your child.'

Elizabeth's face creased and she sobbed.

'Promise me this, Elizabeth.'

'Yes.' Her voice came out strangled.

He lay back, sighed as if he were dying, but then managed another breath. He placed the cross down on top of his tunic and let go of Elizabeth's hand. 'I need to rest.'

Elizabeth nodded, swallowing down tears.

He shut his eyes. 'You go.'

'No. I'll stay here.'

A bolt of pain slammed into his chest and he gasped and opened his eyes. Elizabeth trembled and put her hand over her mouth. But then the pain subsided and he closed his eyes again.

Slowly, sleep enveloped him.

***

He woke at different times, often as the bells tolled the canonical hours, dividing the day into orderly segments. He sensed rather than heard the brothers shuffling behind the walls, cleaning, cooking, chanting, working in the gardens and marching to prayer at the allotted times. The monastery was like an enormous heart beating softly.

Occasionally, orderlies came to clean his face and hands and twice Brother Michael bled him, cutting his arm and draining the blood into a bowl. Jack doubted this treatment would help, but there was little point in objecting.

He was aware that Elizabeth was nearby sometimes, and sometimes Brother Michael or other monks visited. He saw Godwin occasionally, standing behind Elizabeth with his hand on her shoulder.

He didn't know how long he'd been lying there. Perhaps it was hours, perhaps days. Sweat plastered his clothes and hair to his skin and each breath was a small victory.

He was surprised he was still alive at all, but knew the end must come soon. He was forty-two, which wasn't a bad age to reach, considering how many battles he'd been in and how close he'd come to being killed during them. It was cruel to be torn from Elizabeth when she was pregnant, but if that was God's will, he accepted it.

No doubt he was due punishment for what he'd done three years ago in London. He'd betrayed his old comrade, William, and now he was getting what he deserved.

He clasped his limp hands together in front of his chest and whispered, 'Forgive me, Lord, for my sins. Forgive me for what I did.'

—✦—

He heard movement near to him and peeled open his dry eyes. His head felt swollen, twice the size it should be. The wound burnt like a hot coal in his chest.

His eyesight was blurred and at first he had trouble making out the figure standing at the foot of the cot. Gradually the shape solidified and he saw an orange, knee-length tunic and a peaked turban.

It was Kanvar – the Sikh who'd given him the 'mystery' yantra.

Questions stirred like ancient dust in his mind. He tried to sit up.

'Father.' Elizabeth was suddenly at his side. 'It's all right.' She put her hand on his shoulder and eased him back down.

Kanvar pressed his hands together and bowed slightly. 'Greetings.'

'What are you doing here?' Jack said.

Kanvar removed his riding gloves. He was still as gaunt as the last time Jack had seen him and his eyes still had a way of boring into you as if all your secrets had been laid bare. Jack had never known the Sikh's exact age, but he looked to be in his late twenties.

'I came when I sensed your illness,' Kanvar said.

'Sensed?' Jack said.

'Through a power. It's not important now.'

Could he trust Kanvar? The Sikh had given him a yantra, and was an enemy of the Rajthanans. But all the same, Kanvar was an Indian – and Jack didn't trust Indians any more. 'What do you want?'

'To help, of course.'

'Why?'

Kanvar shot a look at Elizabeth.

She rested her hand on Jack's shoulder and gazed at him with her brow creased. 'He says he can treat you.'

'You haven't used the yantra I gave you?' Kanvar asked.

'No.' Jack took a rasping breath. Should he even tell Kanvar anything? 'I tried. Many times. It didn't work.'

Kanvar pursed his lips. 'I see. I thought . . . you would be able . . .' He frowned and stared into the distance, muttering in an Indian language Jack didn't understand.

'Kanvar,' Elizabeth said.

The Sikh looked at her, as if startled from a dream.

'You said something about a treatment?' Elizabeth said.

'Oh, yes.' Kanvar sat on the end of the cot and leant forward to stare at Jack more closely. Dim light angled from the windows and silvered one side of his face. He placed a hand on Jack's chest, shut his eyes for a moment and then opened them again. 'The fire is very severe now.'

'My power doesn't hold it back any more,' Jack said.

Kanvar nodded slowly. 'The wound is too great. Your power is no longer strong enough.' He sat back. 'But I have another power that could help.'

'Will he be cured?' Elizabeth asked.

'Maybe.' Kanvar replied without turning. 'But it is dangerous. There is a complex ritual that takes many hours. He could die . . . I could die.'

Elizabeth tightened her jaw. 'Will you do it?'

'Of course.' Kanvar stood. 'I must.'

'Stop.' Jack's voice was cracked. 'I forbid this.'

Elizabeth frowned. 'Father, why?'

'I don't trust him.' He squinted at Kanvar. 'Why have you come now? After three years. Why would you want to help me?'

'You need to trust me.' Kanvar slipped on his gloves. 'I must leave now. We will perform the ritual tonight.'

'I said, I forbid it,' Jack said.

Kanvar stared at him. 'You must live, Jack. It's important.'

Then the Sikh turned on his heel and slipped out of the hall.

Jack looked at Elizabeth. 'The answer is no.'

'It's your last chance.'

'I forbid it. You understand?'

'Yes.' Elizabeth put her hand on his chest. 'Lie down, Father.'

Darkness crept across his vision. He shut his eyes and black water seemed to pour into his head, swill around and drown out all thought and feeling.

'I forbid it,' he managed to rasp before he passed out.

❦

Moonlight through clouds. The glow like breath on glass.

Jack blinked a few times. He was lying on his back, staring up at the night sky and moving along with a jiggling motion. The cold air chilled the sweat on his face and threaded painfully through his lungs. The wound in his chest burnt and throbbed constantly.

He managed to look around and saw he was on a stretcher being carried along a rough road by four men. Dark hills loomed about them and stands of trees were visible beside the track.

He tried to speak but then felt soft fingers touch his hand.

'Father.' Elizabeth was walking beside the stretcher, a cloak over her shoulders and her eyes shining in the pale light.

'What's happening?' Jack asked, voice thick.

'We're going to the village.'

'Why?'

Elizabeth looked away, and then Jack noticed Kanvar loping nearby with his hands behind his back, staring up at the moon, lost in thought.

'No.' Jack tried to sit up but could barely move. 'Take me back.'

'We have to try.' Elizabeth glanced at her feet as she walked along. 'The monks wouldn't allow it in the monastery. Said it was black magic.'

Jack tried to speak, but his voice was too weak and all he could do was feebly raise his hand for a moment. The men bore him on across the moonlit landscape as if he were bouncing gently on air.

The black hillsides steepened and drew closer together. Soon Jack recognised his surroundings. He saw glimpses of the white-walled cottages of Folly Brook and the stone cross near the edge of the village. And then they were passing through the entrance to his hut and the stretcher was being placed on the earth floor.

There was no light in the hut, save for a smoky tallow candle in each corner of the room. The wavering glow turned everyone's faces gaunt and spectral. Incense burnt somewhere and tinted the air with spice.

'You must all leave,' Kanvar said to the small group gathered in the chamber.

The men filed out, but Elizabeth bent beside Jack and grasped his hand again. 'Father, I'll see you soon.'

Jack opened his mouth. He wanted to protest, but when he moved his lips only a faint wheeze came out.

Diamond tears crossed Elizabeth's cheeks.

Feelings surged in Jack's chest. Was this the last time he would see his daughter? For a second he remembered when she was born, when he'd first held her in his arms.

He wanted to say something but couldn't make a sound. All he could do was grip her hand a little tighter.

Elizabeth stifled a whimper, then rose and rushed out of the hut, sobbing.

Kanvar slung his coat from his shoulders, revealing his orange tunic beneath. He shut the door, crouched beside Jack and stared with his fish-like eyes. 'We're ready to start.'

Jack croaked weakly.

'You have to help me with this,' Kanvar said. 'You must not fight it. This is a dangerous ritual. We could both die if something goes wrong.'

42

Jack tightened one hand into a fist. There was nothing he could do. He was virtually paralysed and on the brink of death. He wanted to live, wanted to protect Elizabeth and her child from whatever the world threw at them. But what was Kanvar up to? Why would an Indian risk his life for a European? It made no sense.

'When I begin,' Kanvar said, 'you must meditate and get yourself near to purusha, the spirit realm. You must leave the world of matter, prakriti, behind as far as possible. But do not focus on a yantra and do not use a power. That would be very dangerous. Concentrate on something important to you and move towards the spirit realm.

'Focus on whatever you choose and hold on to that. Do not let your mind wander. Otherwise there is a danger one or both of us will not survive the night.'

Kanvar rose and took two measured steps away from Jack. He then sat, crossed his legs and placed his hands on his knees, touching his thumbs to his index fingers. He looked once at Jack, his features grave and sad in the candlelight. 'Now, Jack. Focus on something important to you.'

Jack swallowed, his throat dry as gravel. He shut his eyes. There was no point in fighting against it any longer. Kanvar was going to go ahead with the ritual regardless and it would be better to help the process rather than hinder it. He would follow Kanvar's instructions as best he could.

What to focus on? In the army he'd always meditated before the regiment's standard, the three red lions running in a circle on a blue background. But he'd given up his allegiance to the army. The Rajthanans had betrayed him – Jhala had betrayed him – and he would no longer meditate before their emblems.

Elizabeth emerged from the mist of his thoughts. He saw her pale face, surrounded by long black hair, with the fire in her eyes that had been there since she was a child.

That was it. He would focus on Elizabeth.

Kanvar began humming and singing words Jack didn't under-stand. Jack knew Rajthani well enough, but Kanvar was using some other tongue. The language of the Sikhs? The secret language of the siddhas?

Kanvar's voice rose gradually from a whisper to a loud chant, the sound filling the hut as it bounced from the walls and roof. It was as though there were many voices instead of one, a chorus that was at times discordant and at other times harmonious.

Jack felt as though he were floating, although the ground was still pressing against his back. It was as if he'd been drinking ale and his bed were spinning beneath him. He focused on Elizabeth's face and did his best to suppress any other thoughts. He studied her features and piercing eyes, tried to hold her image still.

The sattva-fire in his chest boiled and churned, his left arm ached and his heartbeat thumped in his head.

The spirit realm drew closer and he noticed the first prickle of sattva in his nostrils.

Suddenly something clammy pressed against his skin. He jumped slightly and opened his eyes. An eerie mist – like the smoke from a hookah – hovered above his chest. It filtered through his clothing and touched him with cold tendrils. A twisted thread of the mist stretched up from his body, coiled through the dark-ness and clouded around Kanvar's chest.

Jack and Kanvar seemed connected by some strange umbilical cord.

It only took Jack a moment to take in all this, but in that time his meditation was completely broken. The spirit realm receded and the material world swamped his senses. The misty cord tugged sharply at his chest, like the rope on a boat moored on a choppy sea. And with each tug he had the sickening sensation of his mind being ripped out of his head and sucked into the mist. One moment he would be in his body, then for a second he would be outside it, looking into the darkness from within the mist itself. The next moment he would be back in his own body.

Kanvar flung open his eyes. 'No! Meditate! Quickly!'

Jack slammed his eyes shut. He had to still the rippling pool of his thoughts. He pictured Elizabeth again, studying every minute detail of her features, each strand of hair on her head, each fleck in her eyes, each seashell coil of her ears.

The strange tugging sensation lessened and then stopped completely. He was back in his body. Then, slowly, the material world – the world of pain and illusion – began to drift away.

Memories rushed through his head but he did his best to suppress them. He used all his remaining strength to concentrate on Elizabeth. Her face began to glow white on a black background.

The icy mist continued to stroke his chest.

Was Kanvar's power working? Jack didn't feel any better, but he didn't feel any worse either. He was still alive – and that was more than he'd expected a few hours ago. A trickle of hope ran through his body. Maybe Kanvar's power would save him.

The mist pressed harder against his chest and seemed to ooze through his skin. It felt as though cold, liquid steel were gently spreading through his heart and lungs.

Then suddenly the sattva-fire flared. Pain tore through the centre of his body. White spots danced before his eyes, bells rang in his head and he gritted his teeth so tightly he thought they'd shatter.

He couldn't breathe. He couldn't think. The only thing in his world was the agony of the fire.

He couldn't stop himself opening his eyes, and he cried out when he saw the misty cord was now blood red and spiralling like a whirlpool. A gale-like sound engulfed the hut.

Kanvar opened his eyes and stared at Jack. 'No! Meditate!'

Jack closed his eyes and fought to overcome the pain. But the fire seared every part of his body.

He heard Kanvar's voice over the rushing sound. 'You must meditate now!'

He struggled to comply, but it was impossible to blot out the pain and noise. The ground seemed to buck beneath him and his face wept with sweat. The tendons in his neck strained and pulled.

He had to do it. But he couldn't do it.

He saw Elizabeth's face in a flash. Then he heard Kanvar shriek before the sound was swept away by the deafening roar.

He hadn't drawn breath for minutes and would die soon if he couldn't get some air. He heard a sound like a thunderclap and something punched him hard in the chest.

3

Jack jolted and opened his eyes. The meditation was broken and he was nowhere near the spirit realm any longer. He was certain he would die – and perhaps Kanvar too.

But he found himself simply staring into the darkened roof of his hut. His eyes picked out the differing shades of black of the wooden rafters. Weak moonlight trailed down through the smoke-hole. He began thinking, absurdly, that it was about time he repaired the thatching as he could see a gap forming in one corner.

He was alive. And it was silent and still in the room. The roaring sound had vanished and instead he heard the faint rustle of the wind in the trees.

The strange mist that had previously floated about his chest had disappeared.

And more than that, he could breathe. And the pain in his chest was gone.

He took a long, deep breath and the cool air was like a balm. He flexed his fingers, bunched them into fists, released them again. He felt stronger than he had for years.

Then he remembered Kanvar.

He sat up and saw the Sikh slumped to the ground beside the hearth, his eyes wide open and unblinking.

No.

Jack scrambled over. Kanvar lay on his side without making the slightest movement. His face was pale and his mouth hung open as if fear alone had struck him down.

Jack thrust his finger against Kanvar's neck, felt nothing, moved the finger around, and finally found a slow, trembling pulse. He gave a sigh of relief. Kanvar was still alive, but for how long? And what was wrong with him?

Jack didn't pause to consider this any further and instead jumped to his feet, flung open the door and charged out into the night, shouting for help.

———◆———

'He's woken up.' Elizabeth wiped a stray lock of hair from her face.

Jack blinked in the watery sunlight. He was standing in the middle of the village green, on his way to the House of Sorcery. He hadn't expected Kanvar to recover so soon. He hadn't expected him to recover at all. 'When?'

'A few minutes ago. I came right here.'

Jack nodded and strode with Elizabeth back to his hut. Since the ritual, Kanvar had been motionless and seemingly unconscious, although he'd remained alive. For the past day Elizabeth and Mary had been tending to him as best they could, but in truth no one, including Jack, had any idea what was wrong with the Sikh.

Jack pushed open the door and stopped in surprise. Kanvar was sitting cross-legged on the ground in the middle of the room, his tunic straightened, his face calm and his skin no longer wan.

'You're . . . all right.' Jack stepped inside, Elizabeth following him.

'Yes.' Kanvar smiled serenely, his eyes shining.

Jack sensed a smile crawl across his lips. The Sikh might be strange, but Jack owed him his life. All the same, he had many questions and it was about time Kanvar gave him some answers.

He turned to Elizabeth. 'I need to speak to him alone.'

Elizabeth frowned and opened her mouth to protest.

'Elizabeth.' Jack raised his hand.

The creases on Elizabeth's forehead deepened further and she stuck out her jaw. But after a moment she huffed and stepped back outside the door.

Jack turned to Kanvar and folded his arms across his chest. 'Why did you come here?'

Kanvar's smile broadened. 'You still don't trust me?'

'I'll trust you when you tell me what's going on.'

Kanvar bowed his head slightly. 'Very well. But first let me check you. I need to see how effective the treatment has been.'

'I feel fine.'

'But for how long?'

'What do you mean?'

'The power is not an absolute cure.' Kanvar looked down. 'The fire is still within you. I just don't know how severe it is.'

Jack paused. He'd been thinking he'd been cured completely. 'Will it get worse again?'

Kanvar raised his palm to indicate Jack should sit. 'Let me check.'

What choice did Jack have? Kanvar had helped him so far. He would have to trust the Sikh for the moment.

He sat cross-legged before Kanvar, who now shut his eyes, frowned in concentration and placed his hand against Jack's chest. Kanvar hummed softly and the smell of sattva circled in the air. The Sikh was smelting – processing sattva with his mind in order to use a power. As Jhala had often explained to Jack, to use a power you needed both a yantra and sattva. The yantra provided the instructions, and the sattva the fuel.

After around two minutes, Kanvar opened his eyes and stared straight at Jack. 'It's as I thought. The fire remains and it will increase in strength as the weeks pass. Within two months it will be severe once again.'

'So, it'll kill me.'

'I'm afraid so.'

'Unless you use your power on me again.'

'Ah.' Kanvar looked intently at the ground before him. 'That won't be possible. The power can be used on a person only once. After that it becomes fatal.'

Jack's shoulders slumped slightly. What had he thought? That he would be saved so easily?

'I have done what I can,' Kanvar said. 'It is one of the greatest powers I possess. It drives away any ailment, but not indefinitely. The sickness always returns, eventually.'

'Two months . . .' Jack ran his tongue around his mouth. Not long. Enough time to say goodbye to Elizabeth and not much else. The world, which only minutes before had seemed bright and hopeful, now darkened and closed in around him.

'There is one other way,' Kanvar said.

Jack met Kanvar's intense gaze. 'What?'

'The yantra I gave you. You still have it?'

'Of course.' Jack stood, walked across to a chest and retrieved the cloth embroidered with the design. He waved it at the Sikh. 'But I told you. It wouldn't work.'

'Yes.' Kanvar frowned and stared into space. 'I was sure you would be able to use it.'

'You told me. The law of karma says that once you use a power you can't learn another. You're blocked, right? You can memorise a yantra, but you won't be able to use it.'

'Indeed. Except—'

'Except I used a new yantra in London, when I was already blocked.' Jack had been dying on the battlefield, when suddenly the healing yantra had worked and saved him.

'That is correct. You should not have been able to do that. No one has ever done that. The law of karma is absolute.'

'So, how *did* I do it?'

'I don't know.'

'And why can't I do it again?'

'That I don't know either. It is a pity, however. The yantra I gave you would heal you completely.'

'What?' Jack clenched the cloth tightly and walked back to Kanvar. 'You're telling me this would have cured me all along?'

'That is why I gave it to you. It is one of the strong yantras, the maha-yantras. It is known as "Great Health". It will cure any ailment.'

'Why didn't you tell me?'

'What difference would it have made?'

A fair question. There was no point in Jack knowing what the yantra was for if he couldn't use it anyway. And if he'd been able to learn it fully by holding it in his mind and smelting sattva, then he would have instantly found out its purpose.

Jack waved the cloth in front of Kanvar's face. 'All right. You use it, then. Cure me.'

Kanvar looked up at Jack. 'I cannot. For one thing, I have never learnt it. And since I have been using powers for many years I can no longer learn new yantras. Like most siddhas, I am blocked.

'But there is something else. Great Health can only be used to cure your own sickness. No one else can do it for you. You must use the power on yourself.'

Jack gripped the cloth tighter. Each time there seemed to be some kind of hope held out before him it was snatched away. 'Well, that's that, then.' He bunched the cloth into a ball and tossed it aside. 'Two months is all I've got.'

'Jack, sit down.'

Jack pointed at Kanvar. 'I'll be dead in a few weeks. What'll happen to my daughter then?'

'Please.' Kanvar again gestured for Jack to sit. 'Maybe there is still hope.'

'Hope?'

'You broke the law of karma once. Perhaps you can do it again.'

'I've been trying for three years and I can't.'

'There is something about you . . . I cannot explain what it is, but I sense it. I sensed it when we first met.'

Jack sighed. He felt a weight of tiredness on his shoulders. He sat back down in front of Kanvar. 'Whatever ability I might have, it's gone.'

'You must keep trying. If your ability comes back soon you could still be saved.'

Jack rubbed the back of his neck. 'Perhaps. What's your interest in all this anyway? You still haven't told me.'

'I would have thought it obvious. The Rajthanans are the enemies of the Sikhs. Our countries have often fought. I am in England with my other countrymen to . . . investigate the uprising.'

'You're a spy.'

Kanvar smiled. 'In part. I am also here to help the uprising. You saw me and the other Sikhs fighting in London. We will do what we can to assist the English.'

Jack had indeed seen Kanvar in London and for a moment he wondered whether the Sikh had ever suspected him of being involved in William's death. Kanvar had never voiced any suspicion, however, so it seemed he knew nothing.

'Why are you interested in me particularly, though?' Jack asked.

'Oh, I think you are potentially very useful to the English. A siddha, who wants to train other English siddhas. But more than that. Someone who has shown, at least once, an unbelievable ability.'

'I bet you Sikhs would like to learn how I did it.'

Kanvar nodded thoughtfully. 'That is certainly true. I would like to understand this very much.'

Jack stood and brushed the straw from his tunic. 'Well, if you're here to help, there's one thing you can do for me.'

Kanvar looked at Jack intently.

'Don't tell anyone I'm still sick. Especially not Elizabeth. Just say I'm cured.'

'But that is not true.'

'There's no point worrying anyone.' Jack eyed Kanvar closely. 'You keep your mouth shut for the time being.'

Kanvar bowed his head slightly. 'As you wish.'

❖

'Lightning.' Kanvar stood before the pupils in the House of Sorcery, pointing at a new yantra on a banner strung up on the wall. '*Saudamani* in Rajthani. It is a war yantra. Useful against large numbers of troops, but not so good against artillery or avatars.'

The pupils stared at the Sikh with open mouths. Not a single one of them moved or looked away even for a second. Most of the lads had only occasionally seen Indians, and even then only at a distance. Some had never seen an Indian at all. With his brilliant orange tunic and turban, dark skin, loose trousers and knee-high boots, Kanvar was like some exotic bird that had appeared out of legend.

'You should learn this first out of all the war yantras,' Kanvar continued. 'The design is less complex than the others and the operation is simpler. Once you have mastered this, you will be ready to move on to the others.'

Kanvar stepped back from the banner.

'You heard him.' Mark raised his cane. 'Get learning it.'

The lads all sat perfectly still and stared at the banner, concentrating harder than they ever had before. Not only would they be in awe of Kanvar, they would also be tantalised by the prospect of learning a yantra they could fight with. After all, that was why Jack was training them – to fight the Rajthanans.

Kanvar, Jack and Mark stood to one side, watching.

'Lightning,' Mark said. 'We never knew the proper names.'

'No,' Kanvar said. 'I understand the Rajthanans don't teach them.'

'The Rajthanans don't teach Europeans anything other than the native siddha yantra.' Jack pointed at the native yantra drawn on a large sheet of paper lying nearby.

'Ah, yes,' Kanvar said. 'They call it simply "Europa". A unique yantra, in that none have been able to use it, save for Europeans.'

'And why is that?' Jack asked.

'No one knows for sure. It seems somehow particular to these lands.' Kanvar glanced at Jack and smiled. 'In India we like to think we know everything there is to know about yantras and sattva. But once you start travelling you realise there is much more to learn.'

Jack found it strange to hear an Indian say something like that. His Rajthanan officers had always seemed so full of knowledge, so sure of their understanding of the world. 'The Rajthanans told me Europeans couldn't learn anything other than the Europa.'

'That is not true. Europeans can learn any yantra. You have demonstrated that yourself.'

'Yes.' Jack rubbed his chin. 'That's as I thought. So, is there something wrong with the way I've been teaching this lot, then?' He motioned to his acolytes. 'Hardly any of them manage it.'

'I think not. There is no secret to the teaching. It takes a long time to learn a yantra and many don't succeed, even if they are sensitive to sattva. This is true of Indians just as much as Europeans.'

They were interrupted by a young boy from the village who appeared at the door and said to Jack, 'Sir, the men from Newcastle are here again.'

'The Constable?' Jack asked.

'Yes, sir.'

Jack balled one hand into a fist. So, Henry and his men had come back for the so-called witch. That hadn't taken long. Perhaps Henry had heard Jack was ill and thought to take advantage of the situation.

Jack turned to his acolytes. 'Come on, you lot.'

They all marched across the village green, Jack and Mark in front, with Kanvar and the apprentices following in a phalanx. Other villagers were assembling on the outskirts of Folly Brook, near the road to Newcastle.

Jack strode into the group. 'What's going on?'

Tom pointed up the road and Jack made out a man on horse-back. The rider was definitely Henry – Jack could see the large man's black, fur-trimmed cloak and white crusader surcoat. But there was no sign of Henry's henchmen.

Strange. Was it some kind of trick?

Jack had no weapons on him and there was no time now to return to his hut to fetch any.

He heard the hiss of a sword being unsheathed.

Godwin stepped up beside him and held out his longsword. 'Sir, take my blade.'

Jack frowned. He was actually grateful for the gesture at that moment. But he decided against taking the sword. Henry had come alone, so it was only right to see what he had to say for himself first.

Henry dismounted, tethered his horse to a tree and swaggered across the grass. His arming-sword swayed at his hip and an ornate pistol glinted in his belt.

'I've told you before,' Jack said. 'The woman stays here.'

Henry raised his hand. 'Calm down. I haven't come for the girl.' He stopped suddenly, stared at Kanvar and narrowed his eyes. 'A Rajthanan. So, you truly are a traitor.'

'He's not a Rajthanan,' Jack said. 'He's a Sikh.'

'They're all the same. He'll kill you in your sleep if you keep him here, mark my words.'

'He's a friend. And he's been here three days so far and we're still alive.'

Henry wiped his mouth with the back of his hand. His eyes darted about the crowd of villagers. Eventually, he snorted and shook his head. 'You're a strange one, Jack Casey. And you seem to have all these good people bewitched.'

'They accept me as their reeve of their own free will.'

'Aye, that's your story.' Henry paused for a moment, eyes shifting as if he were weighing up his options. 'Very well. If you say the Sikh's a friend I'll have to take your word for it. I haven't come here to argue, in any case. I need to speak to you. In private.'

Jack stood a little straighter. This was a surprise. 'What about?'

'It's a delicate matter.' Henry rubbed his mouth. 'I need your help with something.'

Jack couldn't help grinning at the thought of Henry needing his help. He turned to the small gathering and nodded to dismiss them. Godwin and Elizabeth stayed behind until he waved them off.

'Over here.' Jack gestured to the row of willows beside the brook. There was less chance of them being overheard there.

They walked down the slight incline and reached the bank of the stream. Henry stared at the water for a moment, then squinted at the sky. It was a clear day but a chill hung in the air.

'What's all this about?' Jack asked.

Henry gave a deep sigh. 'Wish I knew myself, to be honest. Sir Alfred asked me to come. We've been getting some strange reports out of Scotland.'

'Scotland?'

'Yes. We have spies, informers, you know. The Crusader Council has to keep an eye on what the Rajthanans are up to.'

'That's wise enough.'

'Aye, well, some of these spies say the Rajthanans are getting worked up over something in Scotland. There's a Rajthanan sorcerer called Mahajan who's set up some sort of kingdom in the wilds. From what we hear, he's broken away from the Rajthanans – become a sort of Scottish chief, they say.'

'A strange thought.'

'Indeed.'

'What does that have to do with me?'

'Well, this is the thing, from what we can gather, the Rajthanans believe this Mahajan is working on some sort of powerful black magic. He's hidden away in a place where no one goes, you see, and he's up to something. The Rajthanans are worried about it for some reason.'

'Any idea what this magic is?'

'No one knows for sure. Some think it's a weapon of some kind. We've heard tales of demons rising up from hell and all sorts.'

'Sounds a little hard to believe.'

Henry raised an eyebrow. 'I thought you of all people would believe it.'

Jack smiled. 'Because I study yoga?'

Henry grunted and kicked a stone into the water. 'You call it what you like.'

Jack stared past the brook and up the slope of the forest-shrouded hill. The greenery was dusted with red and yellow leaves. On the bare summit, an old stone cross watched the valley like a sentinel. 'It's not like you think. Yoga's not about demons.'

'If you say so. You know more about it than anyone else around here.'

'What is it you want from me? I can't tell you anything about this Mahajan. I've never heard of him.'

'No, it's not that. You see . . .' Henry tightened his lips and tapped his boot against a tree root. 'There are some on the Council who wonder about the Grail. Some stories say the Grail was found in the north.'

Jack snorted. 'The Grail's just a legend.'

Henry scowled. 'That's not what the Church says. The Grail came to us in the past to free our lands from enchantment. If we can find it now, then we can use it to throw the heathens out of England.'

Jack shook his head. 'They were saying that in London too, you know. Before the Rajthanans took the city.'

Henry looked at Jack, narrowing his eyes. 'You call yourself an Englishman, but you forsake all our customs. What are you really? An Indian? A half-caste?'

Jack tensed and felt his face flush. 'I'm an Englishman just as much as you.'

'So you keep saying.'

Jack took a deep breath and calmed himself. There was no point getting into a fight over this. 'What is it you want?'

Henry scratched his beard. 'There are some on the Council who wonder if Mahajan hasn't found the Grail. If we go to Mahajan's kingdom, perhaps we could get it for ourselves.'

'I see.'

'If we don't try, there's a risk the Rajthanans could lay their hands on it instead.'

'I thought only the pure of heart could ever touch the Grail. That's what the stories say, isn't it?'

Henry muttered something, then said, 'I don't pretend to know about these matters. I'm a fighting man, not a sorcerer. All I know is that if this Mahajan has the Grail, we need to get it from him. It's our only hope to save our lands and free King John. The Rajthanans are strong, far stronger than us. You know that. But with the Grail, we could win.'

A cold wind ruffled Jack's hair and tugged at his ponytail. The trees on the hillside swayed. 'I still don't see what I have to do with all of this.'

Henry hawked and spat at the ground. 'The Rajthanans are planning an expedition into Scotland to find Mahajan's kingdom. You see, they're taking this matter seriously. We've decided to send a small party to infiltrate the expedition. The Rajthanans will need guides and porters and cooks. If we can get some men in there, then, when they get to Mahajan's lands, hopefully they can take the Grail – or find out what Mahajan is up to, at any rate.'

'How many men are you sending?'

'We can only spare a few. Ten or so.'

'How big is the Rajthanan party?'

'We don't know that yet. The Rajthanans are still planning themselves. Some say a few hundred soldiers might be sent.'

'Ten against a few hundred. Not good odds.'

'The plan isn't to fight the Rajthanans. We'll travel with them, that's all. Scotland's too wild for us to send a small party. We'll find safety in numbers. When we get to Mahajan's kingdom . . . then our men will have to do their best.'

'Sounds risky. You expecting any of those men to come back?'

'Our whole life here in Shropshire is risky. Vadula's army could come at any time. You heard about Wiltshire?'

Jack nodded. Everyone had heard the Rajthanans had taken the rebel enclave and stories of massacres were circulating. He felt a chill as he remembered the Siege of London and the many men who'd died there.

Henry paused for a moment, then said, 'So, how about it, then?'

'How about what?'

'The mission to Scotland. We want you to lead it, of course.'

'Me?'

Henry grimaced and stared at the water. 'It wasn't my idea. Sir Alfred insisted.'

'Why?'

'Like I said, you know about black magic. No one else around here does.'

'You want me to go looking for something I don't believe in?'

Henry's face reddened. 'You may not believe in it, but others do. Why else would the Rajthanans march into Scotland? Why would they bother?'

That was a good point. The Rajthanans would only send a force into the wilds if they had a reason. There had to be something behind the stories about Mahajan, even if it wasn't the Grail.

But all the same, why should Jack get involved? After William had died, he'd promised before God to keep up the fight against the Rajthanans, and he'd done that. He'd spent the past year training siddhas to the best of his ability. He'd done what he could to support the crusade. He didn't have to do more, especially now that he would be dead within two months.

'You really think the Grail's up there in Scotland?' Jack asked.

'I wouldn't know.' Henry looked down. 'It's worth a try. The omens are good. A white hart's been seen in the hills. You heard that?'

Jack hadn't heard, but then he had little time for his countrymen's superstitions. 'You take that as a sign the mission will succeed?'

'Some say that.' Henry gazed up the hill, as if searching for the creature amongst the trees. 'A white hart is rare. It must mean something that one has come now.'

'Look, Henry, I appreciate this offer. Tell Sir Alfred I'm honoured. But I can't go. I have my work here. That's how I can best serve the crusade.'

'Sir Alfred will be disappointed.'

'He'll understand.'

'You afraid? Is that it?'

'You won't convince me like that.'

Henry's face twisted. 'You're a traitor after all. I knew it.'

'If you wish.'

'You don't want us to find the Grail.' Henry's eyes glinted as he pointed his finger at Jack's chest. 'That's it, isn't it? You want us to fail. I see right through you, Casey. You should go back with your Indian friend.' He waved his finger in the direction of the village. 'Go back to the Rajthanans. You're their servant, after all. They've warped your mind.' He tapped his finger against his temple.

Jack held up his hand. 'Henry—'

'Sir Alfred won't be happy when I tell him about this. You can be sure of that.' Henry's lips sprayed spittle. 'You'll be out of here in no time. And you can take your little sorcerers and devils and witches with you.' He pushed back his cloak and flexed his fingers around the handle of his pistol. 'I ought to shoot you now and be done with it.'

Jack tightened his hands into fists. He wasn't carrying a weapon and there was no one nearby who could help. He could probably jump at Henry and knock him back before he had a chance to get out his firearm.

Probably.

His heart spiked. Should he do it? Now?

Henry was breathing heavily, his nostrils flaring. His fingers clasped the pistol . . . and then released it again. He pushed up his bottom lip so that his chin puckered. 'You haven't heard the last of this.'

He turned and marched back towards his horse, his arms swishing to either side of his huge frame and his cloak swirling behind him.

Jack breathed out. It was hard to know how far Henry would take things. He and Jack had been having these confrontations for the past year, with Henry regularly threatening violence, but so far it had always come to nothing. Henry had a short temper, though, and there was no knowing what he might do if he were pushed too far.

Jack strolled back through the willow trees, up the slope and on towards the village. Henry's story was a strange one. A Rajthanan called Mahajan becoming a Scottish chieftain. The Holy Grail. Demons. What to make of it all?

It was best for him to just put it out of his mind. There was little he could do to help. He would soon be dead – and he was no expert in sattva or powers or the Grail. He was just an ordinary siddha.

Or was he?

Kanvar had said he had a special ability. And Kanvar knew more about these things than Jack.

Elizabeth, Godwin and Kanvar stood waiting for him at the edge of the village.

'What did he want?' Elizabeth asked.

'Nothing.' Jack patted her on the shoulder. 'Just the usual complaints.'

'Why did he want to talk in private, then?' she said.

Jack shrugged. 'Forget about him. Come on, let's get back.'

———◆———

Kanvar's horse stood on the edge of Folly Brook, snorting and gouging out chunks of earth with its hooves. The villagers gathered twenty feet away and stared at the impressive, pure-white charger. Many of them had come out simply to marvel at the animal's gleaming coat, straight back and well-formed legs.

Kanvar held the bridle and patted the horse on the neck.

'You really have to go?' Jack asked as he stood beside the Sikh.

'Yes, I must speak to my commander. I have already been here too long.'

'Will you be safe travelling through Shropshire? People will think you're a Rajthanan.'

'I made it here safely, didn't I?'

'Yes. How *did* you do that?'

Kanvar smiled. 'I have my ways.'

'When will you be back?'

'As soon as I can. Within a month. I will teach your pupils more yantras then.'

'A month. Suppose I'll still be here.'

Kanvar patted Jack's arm. 'I am certain you will be. Keep trying Great Health.'

'I will. I don't hold out much hope, though.'

Elizabeth called out as she jogged over from the village, waving her arm.

'You must tell her,' Kanvar said.

'I will.'

'You only have two months—'

'I said, I'll tell her.'

Elizabeth ran up to them and threw her arms around Kanvar, almost knocking him over. 'Thank you. Thank you.'

Kanvar, a little startled, took a step back and Elizabeth released him.

'And you'll come back, won't you?' Elizabeth asked.

Kanvar bowed his head slightly. 'Soon. But now I must go.' He looked past Jack and Elizabeth and waved at the onlookers. Then he swung into the saddle, gave Jack a final parting nod and nudged his horse into a trot. He bobbed away along the track, his bright orange turban shining against the green and gold of the trees.

A cold wind plucked a handful of leaves from the ground and scattered them across the grass. Jack glanced at Elizabeth. Kanvar was right – he would have to tell her soon. But she wouldn't take the news well.

And how would she fare once he was gone? He needn't worry. She was old enough to look after herself now. And she had Godwin, who was better than nothing.

He gazed along the track and saw that Kanvar had almost vanished into the distance.

He would die, but Elizabeth and his grandchild would live on.

4

Jack squinted down the road. It twisted off along Clun Valley, between hills that rolled away to either side. In the distance he made out a column of people on foot, wispy dust rising behind them.

'Can you see them?' Elizabeth asked. She knew her father had uncannily good eyesight.

Jack nodded. 'About a thousand of them.'

A gust of wind tugged at the edges of Elizabeth's bonnet. 'So many.'

Jack stayed silent. A thousand was indeed a lot of people to have walked all the way from Wiltshire, but it was only a small fraction of the tens of thousands said to have fled from the army.

He glanced about him. Along the road, at various points, people from the surrounding villages had assembled to provide what support they could to the approaching refugees. A large contingent from nearby Newcastle stood on a slope on the opposite side of the track. Amongst them was Henry, his hands on his belt and his black cloak flicking in the breeze. Henry cast his eyes down at Jack and his mouth twisted with disgust for a moment before he looked away again.

Beside Jack stood Elizabeth, Godwin, Mark and six others from Folly Brook. They'd brought a mule cart bearing all the parsnips, turnips and carrots they could spare. This wouldn't go far, but it would at least give a few hundred people a decent meal. There wasn't much more Folly Brook could offer.

The refugees began arriving in small groups. Their clothes were dishevelled: hose torn, sleeves ripped, dresses and tunics stained, and bonnets grey with dust and sweat. Their faces were sallow and gaunt, and many had weeping sores or blisters on their exposed skin. A few bore sacks of possessions and one man even pulled a small cart behind him, but most appeared to have nothing more than the clothes they were wearing.

The villagers handed out food as the refugees passed.

A group of five women stumbled over to Jack. Elizabeth and the others offered vegetables, which the women wrapped up in pieces of filthy cloth.

'God's grace to you all,' one of the women said in a wavering voice, her hand shaking as she accepted the food.

The women limped away up the road, their feet bare and bloody, save for one who wore a pair of boots so broken they flapped open with each step.

Jack felt Elizabeth grip his arm.

'We should take them back to Folly Brook,' Elizabeth said.

'And what about the rest of them?' Jack motioned to the column of people further down the road.

'We should help some of them at least.'

'Your father's right.' Godwin put his hand on Elizabeth's shoulder. 'We can't help them all.'

Elizabeth narrowed her eyes and shot her husband a withering look. He coughed, lowered his arm and suddenly became interested in his boots.

The refugees streamed on, a thin haze of dust drifting around them and the wind dragging at their tattered clothing. The groups became larger and clusters of as many as thirty people staggered past. Parents carried their children on their backs and a few old people, who'd somehow survived, limped past using branches as walking sticks.

Jack stared into the distance and could only just make out the end of the train. He and the others from Folly Brook had already given away half their vegetables, and there were more than five hundred refugees still to come.

Then he thought he recognised someone in the crowd. Someone he'd known three years ago.

No, it couldn't be. He was imagining things.

And yet . . . he found himself hunting through the throng once more, just to be sure. His gaze settled on a young man striding up the road with an elderly woman and five girls. The women were Mohammedans – Jack could tell immediately by their head-scarves and loose black dresses. But it was the young man who interested him most. Jack made out the lad's white skullcap, locks of ginger hair and thin beard. He knew that face. There was no mistaking it.

Saleem.

Jack whispered a prayer under his breath. The boy had lived. Thank God.

Jack had met him on his way to London three years ago. They'd travelled together and eventually reached the city, all the while Jack pretending to be a crusader, when really, at that point, he was hunting William. He'd locked Saleem in a cellar when the Rajthanans attacked London. He'd done it to save the boy, but Saleem wouldn't see it that way. No doubt Saleem would view him as a traitor. And Saleem wouldn't be far wrong about that.

Jack stepped back and turned his face away from the road. What to do? He wanted to greet the lad, but what would Saleem's reaction be? Would he call Jack a traitor in front of everyone? Jack couldn't risk that. It didn't matter if he were publicly shamed – in many ways he deserved it. What mattered was Elizabeth. He didn't want life made difficult for her after he was gone.

'Back in a moment.' He set off down a short slope towards the woods nearby.

'Where're you going?' Elizabeth asked.

'Just have to sort something out,' he said, without turning.

He strode into the trees, walked a few yards and then paused, leaning against an elm.

He shook his head slowly. Look at him, skulking around in the forest like a coward. Saleem was just a young man. Jack should be prepared to face him. But he had no choice.

'Father?' Elizabeth came walking down the slope.

He set off along a track that snaked through the trees. After he'd gone a hundred yards or so, he stopped and looked back. There was no sign of Elizabeth. She must have given up and returned to the cart. He would wait here for a few more minutes and then head back himself. Saleem was bound to have gone past by that point.

He gazed up at the branches criss-crossing above him and smelt the mouldering leaves underfoot. There was no nagging pain in his chest, no shortness of breath. He felt better than ever. It was hard to believe he'd be dead in two months.

After around five minutes, he turned and went to head back up the track.

He stopped dead still and felt a tremor of nerves.

Saleem was standing on the path directly in front of him.

The boy had changed over the past three years – he was thinner, taller and his face had become more angular. But his wide eyes and wispy beard were the same. He clenched and unclenched his hands, while his bottom lip quivered as if he were holding back tears.

'Saleem.' Jack took a step forward.

Saleem pointed a finger at Jack, his hand shaking slightly. 'I thought it was you. Don't come near me.'

Jack opened his hands to show he wasn't carrying a weapon. 'Calm down, my friend.'

Saleem's jaw shivered more rapidly. 'I trusted you. You tricked me.'

'I didn't trick you. I just wanted to save you.'

'We should've both been fighting.'

'And then we'd both be dead. Look, the Rajthanans were already in the city. There was nothing you or I could have done to stop them. Sometimes it's best to retreat and fight another day.'

'You could've run away if you wanted. But you should have let me make *my* choice.' Saleem beat his fist against his chest.

'You were young. I did what I thought was right.'

'You were a coward.'

Jack looked at the ground. He wasn't a coward, he was worse than that. He'd betrayed the crusade and betrayed his friend. He'd never told anyone the truth, not even Elizabeth. Perhaps he should have. Perhaps he should tell everyone now, confess his sins before he died.

Jack ran his fingers through his hair. 'It's not as simple as you think.'

'Seems simple to me.'

Jack glanced into the woods. If he didn't confess now he never would. 'You remember William Merton, the rebel leader?'

'Of course.'

Should he continue? What about Elizabeth?

He paused for what seemed a long time. Finally, he said, 'William used to be my friend, back when I was in the army. I went to London to kill him.'

'What?' Saleem blinked. 'Why?'

Jack sighed. 'My daughter, Elizabeth. The Rajthanans had captured her. My old commander, Jhala, said he'd execute her if I didn't give him William. He sent me to bring back William, dead or alive.'

'And you agreed to that?'

Jack stared into Saleem's eyes. 'What would you have done?'

Saleem gritted his teeth. 'You killed him, then.'

'No. The Rajthanans did. But I let them do it.'

'You stood by while William Merton was murdered.'

'I had no choice. They would have killed my daughter.'

'What would the people around here think if they knew that?'

'Probably burn me at the stake.'

'Perhaps I should tell them.'

'Can't say I don't deserve it. But I hope you won't. Truth is, I'm ill. I'll be dead in a few months. But my daughter has to live here with these people. I don't want her to suffer because of me.'

Saleem paused and his eyes flickered. 'Is all this true?'

'Every word.'

Saleem's eyes went glassy again. His whole body slackened, as if all his strength had drained away. He looked down at the leaf litter. 'You were a traitor all the time.'

'Suppose so. But I support the crusade now. I'm a true Englishman.'

Saleem jabbed the toe of his boot into the soft ground and studied the mark it left.

'We all have to make hard choices sometimes,' Jack said.

Saleem nodded, and when he looked up Jack saw a grey tear running down one of his cheeks. 'I did something wrong too.' Saleem's voice came out high-pitched and he struggled to continue.

Jack raised his hand. 'It's all right. You don't have to—'

'No.' Another tear coursed down Saleem's cheek. 'I want to tell someone. There was a battle in Wiltshire. The Rajthanans were marching in. I should have stayed to fight but I ran away. My village was nearby and I had to warn my mother and sisters.'

'You ran away to save your family?'

'Yes.' Saleem sniffled and wiped his eyes with his sleeve. 'But I was relieved too. I wanted to live. I was a coward.'

Jack walked over to the lad. 'You had a hard choice to make and you made it. Those women on the road are your family?'

Saleem nodded, his eyes bloodshot.

Jack placed his hand on Saleem's shoulder. 'Then you saved them.'

Saleem put his hands over his face and sobbed, his shoulders shuddering. 'I saw my friend die. There were creatures. I thought they'd kill me too but I just got away . . . And then we were walking for so long. Days and days. There were soldiers and bandits and we had to hide sometimes and we had no food.'

Jack's throat tightened. Suddenly he saw Saleem for what he really was – a poor, lost lad. Jack didn't know why he'd been so anxious about seeing the boy again.

He gripped Saleem's shoulder more firmly. 'It's all right. You did well. You made it here with your family.'

Saleem nodded and managed to hold back the tears. 'But what now? We've got no food. Where will we go?'

'Don't worry about that. You'll get help here.'

'Mother's weak. She can't take much more.'

Jack patted Saleem's arm. He quickly made up his mind about something. 'I have an idea. Come with me.'

———◆———

A bonfire crackled and tossed sparks into the night. A large iron cauldron stood in the flames, the lid clattering as the pottage inside puffed like an avatar.

Jack warmed his hands as he crouched nearby on the grass. About half of Folly Brook had congregated in a circle about the flames. Elizabeth and Godwin sat with Jack, while Mark and another lad from the House of Sorcery huddled nearby. About a hundred yards away, the white-walled huts of the village shivered in the firelight.

'They're coming.' Elizabeth pointed at Jack's hut.

Seven shadows appeared from Jack's doorway and bustled across the grass. As they came closer, the light filled in their features, and Jack could see Saleem, in his white tunic, herding his mother and sisters. The women stayed close to each other as they walked and shot nervous looks at the villagers. They'd refused to come out at first, but Saleem had clearly convinced them in the end.

Jack stood and waved his arm. 'Over here.'

Saleem led the way across to Jack, but the women sat down in a tight group a few yards away, half concealed by the darkness. They held hands and kept their eyes down, whispering to each other.

Saleem shrugged at Jack. 'They aren't used to eating with men.'

'It's all right,' Jack said. 'At least *you* come and have a seat with us.'

It hadn't been as simple as he'd thought to show hospitality to Saleem and his family. He'd forgotten how difficult Mohammedans could be. But he kept any irritation to himself. Saleem was a good lad and Jack would do anything he could to help him.

Saleem sat cross-legged between Jack and Elizabeth. 'I can't thank you all enough.'

'How's your mother?' Elizabeth asked.

'A little better. It's a light fever. At least she can rest now.'

'You let us know if she gets worse,' Elizabeth said. 'Mary can take a look at her.'

Tom the blacksmith, who was serving as cook tonight, lifted the lid of the pot with a cloth, stirred the contents, sniffed the rising steam and then turned to Jack and nodded.

'Right.' Jack stood and clapped his hands. 'Everyone listen.'

The villagers quietened and looked up at their reeve.

Jack smoothed the rumples in his white surcoat, the material gleaming in the firelight. 'I won't bore you with a long speech. But I'm sure you'll all join me in welcoming our guests from Wiltshire.' He gestured to Saleem. 'I have here Saleem and his family. We also have Guy and Faith staying with Mary.' He pointed across the fire to two further refugees. 'And Tom has taken in Roland.' He motioned to an old man in ragged clothes. 'They've come a long way and faced many hardships. I'm sure everyone will do their best to help them while they're here. God's will in England.'

'God's will in England,' murmured the small gathering.

Jack sat down and the villagers began talking amongst themselves again. Tom spooned pottage into bowls and handed them around. It was simple fare – barley, peas and beans – but it was the best Folly Brook had to offer.

Saleem gulped down the steaming food and emptied his bowl in less than a minute. Jack grinned and waved over Tom, who refilled the bowl.

Godwin finished his food and shifted on his haunches so that he was facing Saleem. 'So, you fought the Rajthanans.'

Saleem lowered his spoon and looked up. 'Yes.'

'What was it like?' Godwin asked.

'Leave him, Godwin,' Jack said. 'He'll talk about it when he wants to.'

'It's all right.' Saleem placed his bowl on the ground. 'I don't mind. I can tell you what it was like. Terrifying. The Rajthanans are led by Mahasiddha Vadula. Suppose you've heard of him.'

'We have,' Godwin said. 'An evil man, they say.'

'Yes.' Saleem picked at the grass. 'It seems that way. We heard lots of stories in Wiltshire before the army came. They say things are bad in the Rajthanan lands. Vadula's men are cruel and the people are treated like slaves.'

Jack had heard this before – similar stories had made their way to Shropshire over the past few years. After Vadula had taken London, and imprisoned King John in the Tower, he'd been appointed Raja of All England and had immediately carried out brutal reprisals. Suspected crusaders were hanged, villages were torched and whole communities were forcibly moved to work in other parts of Europe. The oppression continued to the present day, with all English people living in fear of Vadula's soldiers.

'We planned for a long time in Wiltshire,' Saleem said. 'We always thought Vadula would come one day. But there were so many soldiers. And Vadula had black magic . . .' Saleem paused. The fire spluttered and popped. 'We couldn't hold them. I managed to get back to my village, but most of my friends didn't make it.'

Everyone sat in silence for a moment.

Wind buffeted the fire and sent smoke and sparks trailing into the dark. Elizabeth shivered and drew her knees closer to her chest.

'Enough,' Jack said. 'Let's stop this talk. This is supposed to be a celebration.'

'Aye,' Mark said. 'We've got food and friends. What more could we want?'

The villagers began talking again, but more quietly than before. The night seemed colder now and the dark was like a heavy weight, pressing in on them from all around.

'Constable Ward told me to tell you particularly, Master Casey.' The young squire stood in the open ground near the House of Sorcery, his thin hair pushed around by the wind. He glanced at the building, as if a demon could leap out of it at any moment.

'Go on.' Jack folded his arms across his chest. What could Henry want with him now?

The squire swallowed. 'It's the Rajthanans, sir. Vadula's planning to march on Shropshire.'

Jack paused for a moment. The light seemed to dim slightly. He'd known this day would eventually come but it was still a blow. 'Henry's sure about this?'

'Seems so, sir. The Council got word the other day.'

'How long before they get here?'

'Four months. The army's still gathering in Worcestershire. They're waiting for reinforcements from Europe.'

Jack nodded. If the Rajthanans were waiting for reinforcements it could certainly be four months before they marched.

It wasn't hard to understand why Henry had sent this message. Normally, there would be no reason for him to advise the reeve of a small village. Clearly, he was trying to pressure Jack into joining the expedition to Scotland. Perhaps he was testing Jack too, trying to see whether Jack really was as loyal to the cause as he claimed to be.

'Tell Henry I'm grateful for his message,' Jack said.

'That's all, sir?'

Jack frowned. Had the squire been told to expect something? 'What more do you want?'

'No, sir.' The squire paled. 'I didn't mean—'

'Go on. Get out of here.' Jack waved the lad away.

The squire scurried off and Jack turned back to the House of Sorcery. Mark stood in the doorway, his face gleaming white. How much had he heard? Jack would tell him the news anyway. The rumours would spread quickly through Clun Valley and it was only a matter of time before everyone knew.

The Rajthanans were coming. Vadula was coming.

5

Jack walked with Brother Michael down the aisle in the centre of the monastery library, the monk's habit rustling in the silence. To either side of them stood lecterns and shelves clotted with books. Monks sat hunched as they studied manuscripts, while the slightly sweet and fruity scent of ancient parchment hung in the air.

'Here it is.' Michael stopped, reached up to a shelf and took down a heavy tome. The chain attached to the front cover clinked as he lowered the book on to a lectern.

He looked at Jack, his face gaunt and his eyes shrouded in folds of grey skin. He prodded the book with a thin finger. '*The Annals of the Holy Grail*, written by the Good Knight Sir Bartholomew. There are only five of these in existence.'

Jack stared at the ornate leather cover. This was the first time he'd ever sought wisdom in a book, given that he couldn't read a word of English, or any other language. 'Thank you for this.'

Michael stared at him for a moment, as if deciding whether or not to proceed. Then he opened the cover and leafed through vellum pages inscribed with Gothic text and fading illuminations. Finally, he stopped at a page with an illustration of a shining, golden chalice sitting on a table covered in a white cloth.

'The Grail?' Jack kept his voice low so as not to upset the quiet.

'Yes.' Michael touched the edge of the page. 'Some say it is a sort of goblet, like this. Others call it a platter or a tray. There are different theories.'

'Does it say anything about its powers?'

Michael turned a few more pages, the parchment crackling. 'Ah, yes. Here it is. The Grail is said to possess great healing properties. Sir Bartholomew recounts how it cured one of the kings who guarded it. The king had a deep wound inflicted through some kind of magic, and it would never heal. But then Sir Galahad discovered the castle that housed the Grail – Corbenic was its name. When Galahad touched the Grail, the king was miraculously healed.

'There's more. The Grail, in a sense, had the power to heal the whole land. Britain was in the grip of a sort of curse back in King Arthur's day. The countryside was sick. But the Grail . . .' Michael paused in reverence. 'The Grail cured the land.'

'What about war? Was the Grail a weapon?'

Michael gazed into Jack's eyes. 'This is a question many have asked.'

Michael turned a handful of further pages and stopped at a picture of a set of armed knights standing on a hilltop. At the base of the hill gathered a mass of men brandishing scimitars and wearing flowing robes and turbans. 'The Battle of Garrowby Hill. This was where King Edward V made his final stand against the forces of the Caliph of England. At the same time as the Caliph's men came up the hill, a knight called Sir Oswin discovered Castle Corbenic once again. Like Galahad, he was completely pure of heart, and therefore he could touch the Grail. When he did this, a power flowed out from the Grail. This aided King Edward's army and they defeated the Caliph.'

'How did the power help?'

'The book doesn't say exactly. Sir Bartholomew writes: "The power was with them and so Edward's army that day was victorious." That's how he describes it.'

'The power was with them? What does that mean?'

'No one is certain. These things happened more than two hundred years ago.' Michael turned the page and revealed an illustration of a man, surrounded by winged angels, floating in the sky. Michael smiled for a brief moment – the first time Jack had seen him smile. 'Sir Oswin, taken up to heaven by the angels after he touched the Grail. The same happened to Galahad. They both went directly to our Lord.'

'Does the book say where the Grail Castle is?'

Michael frowned. 'No. The exact location of Corbenic is not important. Only the pure in heart will ever find the Grail. Unless you are pure, you could pass right by the castle and not see it.'

'I heard it was in the north.'

Michael folded the book closed. 'Ah. That comes from a small manuscript called *The Tale of Sir Oswin*. It relates the journey of Sir Oswin to Corbenic and the adventures that befell him along the way. There is a passage that refers to him travelling in the north of Britain. Shortly after that, he finds the Grail.'

'Where exactly in the north?'

'It doesn't say.'

'You have the book here?'

'No. There is no copy anywhere in Shropshire.'

'So, the Grail could be in Scotland?'

'That is possible, I suppose. Then again, it might not be.'

Jack stared at a shaft of sunlight, watching motes of dust weave within it. 'There seem to be more riddles than answers.'

'That is true. It always seems to be the case with the Grail. As Sir Bartholomew says, it is mysterious and elusive.'

⎯⎯◆⎯⎯

Jack paused on the hilltop and glanced over his shoulder at the imposing stonework of Clun Abbey. A pallid sunset tinted the walls and the bell tower golden. He turned and gazed across the valley coiling away below. Knots of trees bordered the river and lines of rising smoke marked out where the villages stood. The shadows were deepening and smothering the bottom of the valley.

Was the Grail real? Were any of the stories about it true? The Church might believe in it, most of his countrymen might believe in it, but Jhala had told him the tales were nothing more than myths. Jhala had lied to him, though. His guru had said Europeans couldn't develop any powers beyond those of the Europa yantra, and that wasn't true. Jhala had also told him to use the first power he'd learnt, which had led to him becoming a blocked siddha. Could he trust anything Jhala had told him any more?

He should have asked Kanvar about the Grail. Perhaps the Sikh knew something. But Kanvar was gone now and wouldn't be back for several weeks. If he even came back at all.

Jack's eyes wandered across the valley and over to his right, where the hills rolled away into the lands of the Lord of the Marches. The mad Welsh ruler was said to be even more cruel than Vadula and a willing puppet of the Rajthanans. So far he'd left the Crusader Council alone, but what if the Rajthanans marched into Shropshire? Would he join forces with the army?

Jack gazed into the south, squinting as the last of the light pierced his eyes. Down there, miles away in Worcestershire, Vadula's army was massing. The Mahasiddha had gradually been annexing native states where the crusade was still strong. Leicestershire was gone, so was Warwickshire, and now Wiltshire too. It looked as though Shropshire would be next.

Clun Valley seemed surrounded by enemies. How long could it hold out? Weeks? Days? His people weren't strong enough to withstand an onslaught by the Rajthanans. He'd always known that. But he'd hoped that somehow they would find a way to defend themselves.

He pulled his hair back and retied his ponytail.

He'd seen what the Rajthanans were capable of. He'd been at the Siege of London. And he'd heard the stories about what had happened afterwards, with scaffolds erected in every quarter of the city and bodies left dangling for the crows.

Vadula would show no mercy to the crusaders of Shropshire.

For a moment Jack had a vision of Folly Brook burning, but he pushed the thought quickly out of his head.

He remembered the day he'd made a promise to William. To atone for his sins, he'd made an oath to continue the crusade as best he could. Had he done enough? He'd been training siddhas, but that was all. Should he be doing more? If William were here now, what would he expect Jack to do?

With his thoughts still swirling, he set off down the hill. The dusk thickened and shadows shrouded the forest to his left. Folly Brook was two hours' walk away and it would be dark by the time he got back. He and Saleem were staying temporarily with Elizabeth and Godwin, while Saleem's mother and sisters slept in Jack's hut. Elizabeth would have already lit the fire and would probably be wondering where he was.

He walked more quickly, following the path as it wove its way down the incline. He felt fit and well, but he was aware that the sattva-fire still throbbed softly in his chest. He would most likely die before the Rajthanans arrived, and then Elizabeth would be left on her own to face the invaders.

Damn his illness.

His illness . . . Brother Michael had said the Grail was a healing power. It had cured the king with the mysterious wound. Could it heal sattva-fire injuries? Was that possible?

He shook his head. Look at him, clutching at vain hopes and fanciful tales. There was no Grail. If there were, the Rajthanans would have found it years ago. Jhala hadn't lied.

Something flickered in the woods to his left. He froze and was instantly a tracker and a soldier once again. Was someone following him?

He crouched instinctively, despite the fact that he was completely exposed on the slope. He peered into the tangled shadows of the forest, but saw nothing.

Had he been mistaken? Was it a trick of the light?

But then he spotted the flicker once again, a white will-o'-the-wisp that slipped between the tree trunks and then vanished. He stared harder, focusing his abnormally good eyesight on the place where the shape had been.

And then he saw it, still for a moment in the forest – a white hart.

The ghostly creature turned and gazed at him for a second, before it bounded off into the shadows, visible for a moment, then fading to a white shimmer, then vanishing completely.

———◆———

'I'll do it.' Jack tossed his knife on to the table in front of Henry.

Henry widened his eyes and pushed aside his plate of chicken. He stood, wiped his greasy fingers on his tunic and offered his hand to Jack.

Jack clasped Henry's palm and shook.

A grin slid across Henry's lips. 'Sir Alfred will be pleased.'

'I have some conditions, though.'

Henry narrowed his eyes. 'Conditions, you say.'

Jack stepped over to the open window and gazed out at the bailey of Lord Fitzalan's castle. A couple of men-at-arms were training with swords, and a laundress was washing sheets and tablecloths in a trough. The outer wall loomed ahead and the giant square-shaped keep rose to his left.

He turned back to Henry. They were in the refectory, which was empty save for a row of trestle tables. A hookah stood in one corner, but it couldn't have been used for months as there was no tobacco to be found anywhere in Clun.

'I want to choose the men who'll come with me to Scotland,' Jack said.

'Very well. We have some volunteers already, but you can take whoever you want.'

'Good. And I want to appoint a temporary reeve for Folly Brook.'

Henry rubbed his beard. 'It's not your right to do so. The Council chooses the reeves.'

80

'This is just for while I'm away.'

Henry took a deep breath. 'I'm sure it can be arranged.'

Jack looked back out of the window. The sky was heavy with dark cloud and the cold pressed against his cheeks. 'One last thing. There'll be no witch burnings in Folly Brook.'

Henry went silent. When Jack turned back, he saw the man's face was contorted and reddening. Henry gritted his teeth and, seemingly with a great effort, nodded. 'As you wish.'

'Then you have a deal. When do we leave?'

———❖———

'The Grail?' Elizabeth stood beside the hearth in her hut. 'You said it wasn't real.'

Jack ran his fingers through his hair and took a further step into the room. 'I'm not so sure now.'

'When are you going?'

'In a week.'

'A week? No.'

'I have to.'

A tear crystallised in the corner of one of her eyes. 'Why?'

'The Rajthanans are coming. We need something to fight them with.'

'Yes – your siddhas.'

'That won't be enough. There're only a few of them, and most of them haven't even learnt a power yet.'

Elizabeth dabbed away the tears with her sleeve. 'Why does it have to be you?'

'No one else knows about powers. Look, there's something I haven't told you.'

'What?'

Jack looked at the earth floor. 'Kanvar couldn't completely cure me. I still have the fire in my chest. In less than two months it'll kill me.'

'No.' Fresh tears welled in Elizabeth's eyes.

'But there's still hope. The Grail heals wounds. You remember the story. The king with the wound that wouldn't heal.'

'Yes.' She gazed hard at Jack. 'You think—'

'Maybe. I don't know. It's worth a try.'

She nodded. 'You're right.' Then her brow furrowed. 'In the story, Galahad was taken up to heaven. And Oswin.'

'That might not be true.'

'You just said the story *was* true.'

Jack thought quickly. 'Parts of it could be true.'

She put her hand to her mouth. 'What if you find it, and—'

'Elizabeth, I don't have all the answers. But the Grail was always supposed to be on the side of God. If it exists, it'll help me. I'm sure of that.'

She looked down. 'Why do the cursed Rajthanans have to come?'

He stepped over and took her by the shoulders. 'Listen, you need to be strong now. For the baby.'

She bit her bottom lip and nodded.

Jack drew out the cross necklace and held it up. 'Mother's always with us. Watching over us.'

'I still miss her sometimes.'

Jack fought back the tears. 'I miss her too.' He put the necklace back under his tunic.

She dried her eyes with her hand. Then she looked up at him with so much cold defiance he was startled for a moment. 'We'll fight the Rajthanans.'

He felt a flush of pride. That was the thing about Elizabeth. She might face setbacks, but she would pick herself up and stride ahead again with absolute determination.

He didn't know what he would do without her.

─────※─────

Saleem stumbled as he tried to keep up with Jack's long strides.

Jack stared straight ahead and kept up his pace as he crossed the village green. 'I said no.'

'But I want to come,' Saleem said.

'You need to stay here with your family. Look after them.' Saleem had been through enough and Jack wasn't going to take him on a probably doomed mission to Scotland.

Saleem stopped walking. 'I could tell everyone about William.'

Jack paused and turned round. 'If you do that it'll only hurt Elizabeth.'

'I need to make up for what I did.' Saleem's voice came out high-pitched and choked. He stared at the ground, his eyes glassy. He clenched and unclenched his hands.

'You don't need to make up for anything.' Jack's voice was softer now. 'You did your best.'

'But I ran away. I left my friends to die.'

'Sorry, it's still no.'

'Then I'll follow you.'

Jack shook his head. 'You don't give up, do you?'

'I have to do this.'

Jack rubbed the back of his neck. He'd already chosen his party and he didn't need anyone else tagging along. But at the same time he understood Saleem. Wasn't Jack also, in a sense, going to Scotland to atone for his sins? Wasn't he trying to make up for what he did to William? 'This journey is suicide. You know that?'

'I heard you're looking for the Grail.'

'There's no guarantee we'll find it. We'll probably all be dead in a month.'

'I still want to come.'

Jack sighed. Why was he getting so soft these days? 'All right.'

Saleem smiled broadly, his cheeks going red. 'I won't let you down.'

<hr />

The mare spluttered and stomped. Jack grasped the bridle and patted the animal a few times to calm it.

'When will you be back?' Elizabeth was standing beside him.

He found it hard to look at her, but forced himself to turn. Her skin was grey in the early morning light and the mist that had descended on the village swirled behind her.

'Not sure,' he said. 'Before the Rajthanans get here.'

'But there's less than two months—'

'You stay strong.' He squeezed her arm, then glanced towards Folly Brook. The cottages were indistinct blocks of shadow. Figures emerged from the haze – most of the village had come out to see him off. Saleem walked with his mother and sisters, and Godwin strode across the grass, wearing his longsword for some unfathomable reason.

'Listen . . .' Jack frowned as he searched for the words. He had to say this quickly before the others arrived. 'I know you said you'd fight. But, if the Rajthanans do come before I get back, you take Godwin and go. Run. Anywhere.'

Elizabeth shook her head slowly. 'We'll stay here and face them.'

He gripped her arm tighter. 'Think of the baby.'

'I am. I want my child to live in a better world.'

He was about to say more, but the villagers were within earshot now and he knew there was little he could do to convince Elizabeth anyway. As always, she would make her own decisions.

Godwin walked over to them and stood with his hands on his belt and his head raised, staring into the distance. 'Good luck, sir.'

Jack nodded slowly and eyed the small crowd gathering about him. There was sturdy Tom, old Mary, Mark and the other acolytes from the House of Sorcery. He met the eyes of each in turn. To his left, Saleem – the only other person from the village coming on the journey – was slinging saddlebags across the back of his own horse and saying goodbye to his family.

Jack faced the villagers again. 'I'm proud to be your reeve. I'll be back in a few months, but in the meantime I've decided to appoint a temporary replacement.' He took his folded white surcoat out of a bag on the side of the horse. 'Godwin.' He offered the surcoat to his son-in-law.

Godwin gasped and stepped back.

Jack thrust the coat towards him. 'Go on.'

Godwin swallowed, stood up straighter and solemnly took the folded cloth. 'Thank you, sir.' His voice shook slightly.

Jack looked back at the villagers. 'Godwin's in charge now. I'm sure you'll all do your best to help him.'

Tom started clapping, and shortly after that everyone else joined in. Godwin sniffed and puffed out his chest. And then it was as if a spell had been broken and the villagers bustled around Jack, hugging him and wishing him well, some with tears in their eyes. Jack said farewell to each of them in turn. Finally, he shook Godwin's hand and gave Elizabeth a hug.

'Thank you for Godwin,' Elizabeth whispered in his ear.

Then he swung up on to the mare, glanced at Elizabeth and felt his throat tighten when he saw her forlorn face. He looked across at Saleem, who was also now up on his horse, his mother and sisters crying in a huddle nearby.

Jack nodded to the crowd. 'God's grace to you all. God's will in England.'

Then he turned his horse and set off into the mist at a canter, with Saleem keeping up the pace beside him.

PART TWO

6

'Not far now, sir.' The man from Dun Fries pulled the hood of his cloak tighter about his head. The rain streamed down the folds in the cloth and dripped from the rim. 'Just over that hill.' He pointed to where the dirt road rose to pass over a saddle between two low, barren hills.

Jack shivered as he walked alongside the man. The rain was seeping through his heavy tunic and even the doublet underneath. 'How big is the party?'

'About a hundred soldiers, I heard. Hundred porters too. Maybe more.'

'You sure they're still looking for men?'

The man shrugged. 'Don't know. You'll find out soon enough.'

Jack stared ahead through the shafts of rain. The droplets pummelled the ground, turning it to sodden muck. The landscape was empty and grey, save for a few twisted trees that had already lost most of their leaves.

The Rajthanans had better still be looking for men. Jack and the others had to be on that expedition into Scotland. Otherwise there was little chance of them making it all the way to Mahajan's kingdom.

Jack glanced back. Saleem and the eight other crusaders from Shropshire were trudging up the slope behind him. They all looked tired and grim in the silver dawn. It had been a long journey up to Dun Fries and they'd arrived later than planned to find out the expedition was due to leave shortly.

'Do you know where this expedition's going?' Jack asked the man from Dun Fries.

89

The man's eyes flickered beneath his hood. 'I might know something. Then again, I might not.'

Jack understood, drew out a penny that flashed in the dim light and handed it across. He'd already paid the man a penny to lead them to the Rajthanan camp.

The man slid the coin into a pouch. 'Heard they're looking for a Rajthanan sorcerer called Mahajan. They say he's gone mad. He's living up in Scotland now.'

None of this was news to Jack. He hoped he was going to get more than this for his money. 'Where in Scotland?'

The man shrugged his cloak tighter. Steam misted about his mouth. 'A place called the Land of Mar.'

'How far away is that?'

The man grunted. 'Don't know. No one knows. No one's ever been there, that I know of anyway. Scotland's a wild place. Not many go more than a few miles over the border. Most of it's uncharted. I once saw a Rajthanan map and I can tell you, most of it was empty white space.'

'This Mahajan seems to have gone there.'

The man lifted his top lip for a moment, as if snarling. 'If Mahajan's even real.'

'Real?'

'Well, sometimes I wonder. You hear rumours, but how much of it do you believe? No one's ever seen Mahajan. No one's ever been to Mar. No one even knows whether Mar exists for real.'

'The Rajthanans seem to think it's real.'

'Well, they don't know any more about Scotland than the rest of us . . . Here we are.'

They'd reached the top of the saddle and below them the road zigzagged down a scarp. Spread out along the base of the hill, indistinct in the haze, were knots of carts, ox wagons and pack mules. Men swarmed about the vehicles, loading supplies and equipment. Other porters coursed down the slope, lugging boxes, crates, chests, sacks and furniture from a camp at the summit.

Along the top of the hill, Jack made out white army tents shivering in the wind. Towards the centre of the camp, the regiment's standard snapped and tugged at a flagpole, and nearby stood the large striped marquees of the officers. Further off, on the edge of the camp, rose a sixteen-foot-high bronze statue of the elephant-headed god Ganesh. The rain drooled over the rotund figure, giving the metal an oily sheen. The statue's four arms, raised like writhing snakes, were dark against the turbulent cloud.

'I'll leave you to it, then,' the man said. 'You lot are mad, if you ask me. But that's your business.'

'Mad?' Jack said.

'Scotland's full of savages and demons and all sorts. You'll be lucky to get out alive. You'd be best to turn round right now and go home.'

'Seem to be quite a few men down there who aren't afraid.'

The man snorted. 'They're all desperate. That's the only type that would go on a journey like that.'

'Thanks for the advice.'

'Only trying to help.' The man adjusted his cloak and then shuffled back towards Dun Fries.

'Cheerful fellow,' said Andrew, a black-haired man in his early twenties. He was one of Henry's men, but Jack had taken a liking to him and agreed he could come along.

'Aye.' Jack glanced at Saleem. The lad looked tired and pallid, his skullcap soaked and sticking to his head. But his lips were pressed together tightly and his jaw was firm. He appeared determined to see the mission through. Jack glanced at the others, who looked just as set on continuing as Saleem.

Good. He'd chosen these young men well.

He patted the satchel hanging at his side and felt the hard curve of the rotary pistol concealed within. Henry had lent him the precious weapon, along with a powder flask and a handful of bullets. He was the only one of the group carrying a firearm, although the others all had concealed knives.

'Right,' he said. 'Let's get down there. God's will in England.'

'God's will in England,' his men repeated in unison.

They followed the road down the slope, splashing through the mud. As they neared the bottom, Jack heard the oxen moaning, the mules braying and the porters shouting and cursing as they laboured. He made out two giant Rajthanan vehicles, plus around fifteen native carts and wagons. That was a large number for an expedition of this size. The party was not travelling light.

'You there!' A stocky sergeant marched across the slope towards them, swinging his arms wide as if they were too muscular to hold any closer to his body. 'Get out of here!'

'We're here for work,' Jack shouted back.

'Work?' The man strode up to Jack. Deep lines creased his face and a white scar shone on one of his cheeks. His left eye was lazy and half closed, but the other was wide open and scrutinised Jack intently. 'We don't need anyone else.'

Jack couldn't place the man's guttural accent for a moment. Then he recognised it – Saxon. He'd met Saxons plenty of times in the army. For the most part they were vagabonds and pirates who'd been forced into the military to escape the hangman's noose. And as they were Mohammedans, they had an instinctive hatred of Christians.

'We'll work hard,' Jack said. 'You can count on us.'

'Work hard?' The Sergeant stepped closer and looked up – he was a few inches shorter than Jack. 'You work for me and you'll work hard all right. Old Wulfric's a hard taskmaster. Old Wulfric won't let anyone laze around.'

'Good.'

Sergeant Wulfric stared at Jack with his good eye, while his lazy eye flickered beneath its swollen eyelid like a cockle in a shell. Finally, he nodded slowly. 'There is one thing.' He pointed up the slope at the huge Ganesh statue. 'That needs to come down here.'

'We'll do it.'

Wulfric wiped his nose on the back of his hand. 'All right. You move that and you're hired. One penny a day each. Paid when we get back from Scotland.'

'Fine.'

Wulfric led them up the incline, dodging the numerous porters still hauling supplies down to the road. Men were dismantling the tents and packing them away, but the standard – a white horse on a red flag – still flapped in the wind. The rain beat on Wulfric's cloth hat and trickled down to the shoulders of his blue tunic. His loose grey trousers were soaked, and mud speckled his boots and puttees.

Jack glanced up at the tangled form of the statue. How much did it weigh? Three tons? More?

It would have been easier to take a wagon up to the top of the hill and load the statue there, but he could see why Wulfric had chosen not to. Most of the slope was reasonably gentle, but the last few feet at the bottom were too steep for oxen.

'Why are they taking that thing anyway?' Andrew nodded at the statue, keeping his voice low.

'The Rajthanans pray to Ganesh when they're travelling,' Jack said. 'He's said to remove all obstacles.'

Jack had often seen his officers worshipping the elephant-headed deity before setting off on a journey. But his regiment had never hauled along a large statue like the one above.

'Bloody heathens,' Andrew said.

'Shut it,' Jack hissed.

As they climbed higher, Jack spotted a striped awning standing near the statue. Beneath the canopy, five Rajthanan officers sat cross-legged on ornate cushion-seats, puffing on hookahs. From time to time they pointed down the hill or observed proceedings through spyglasses.

Rajthanans.

It was three years since Jack had last seen a Rajthanan. He'd served them for most of his adult life, but while he'd been in

Shropshire they'd become a distant, almost unreal, enemy. Now here they were again. Officers, just like the ones he'd known in the army.

Behind the officers, on the back wall of the awning, hung portraits of two stern-faced Indian men wearing jewelled turbans. Jack recognised one man instantly – the Maharaja of Europe. The other he assumed must be Mahasiddha Vadula.

Wulfric reached the statue and patted the base. 'Right. Get on with it.'

Jack squinted up. Rain bounced and danced as it struck the figure. It would be no easy task to move the statue, even with ten of them lifting.

He turned to Wulfric. 'We'll put it on its side. Tie ropes around it and slide it down.'

'Slide it?' Wulfric narrowed his good eye. 'Can't slide it. No, no—'

'Sergeant Wulfric.' One of the Rajthanans stood up and came to the edge of the awning. He was a young man – in his late twenties or early thirties – with a thin moustache that was waxed into curls at the ends. He wore the scarlet turban of an officer in a Saxon regiment and the moon-clan insignia was embroidered on his blue tunic. He spoke in Arabic, the common language of the European Army. 'Did that man just say he was going to slide the murti down the hill?'

'No, Captain Rao,' Wulfric said in Arabic. 'I mean, yes. But I was just about to tell him—'

'The murti must be treated with respect. I won't have it sullied.'

'My mistake,' Jack said in Arabic. 'We'll carry it, sir.'

Captain Rao stared at Jack. He pressed a handkerchief to his nose and grimaced as if he could smell something disgusting. 'Why is this boy speaking to me, Sergeant?'

'Scum.' Wulfric slapped Jack on the arm with a short leather strap. 'You don't speak to the Captain, see? You speak to me if you need to speak.'

Jack felt his face grow hot. He would have happily punched Wulfric in the face, and Captain Rao too while he was at it. But he had to stay calm. He couldn't jeopardise the mission. 'I understand . . . sir.'

'Right, then. Get on with it,' Wulfric said.

One of the Rajthanans in the shelter laughed and said in Rajthani, 'Leave them, Rao. The Sergeant will deal with it. You can't reason with these natives.'

Jack glanced past Rao and saw the man who'd spoken – a slightly flabby lieutenant with a smooth, round face.

'He's right,' said another man. 'Come back.'

Jack paused for a moment. This second man had thin features, a hawk-like nose and a carefully trimmed moustache and goatee. He wore a purple tunic and turban.

The uniform of a siddha.

Jack hadn't considered that a siddha might be sent with the expedition, but it made sense. Only a siddha would know how to deal with Mahajan or understand what it was he was up to in Scotland.

Wulfric grunted. 'I said, get on with it.'

Jack turned to the statue. Metal poles had been slotted through holes in the base and poked out on all sides. These would make the figure a little easier to carry, but it was still going to be a challenge.

'Right, lads,' Jack said. 'Spread out. Wait until I say to lift.'

Saleem and the others took up positions around the statue, bent down and gripped the poles. Jack stood in front of the figure, directly beneath the coiling trunk.

'Lift!' he shouted.

They all heaved as hard as they could. The statue was even heavier than Jack had imagined, but they somehow managed to raise it from the ground. Jack's neck tendons strained, sweat popped on his forehead and his fingers ached as they clasped the pole.

'Right,' he said. 'Move.'

They staggered down the slope, each of them grunting, groaning and gasping. The statue dipped slightly to one side, but they managed to rebalance it.

'Careful, Sergeant,' Rao called from the awning. 'They'll drop it.'

'Slow down, scum.' Wulfric strapped Jack across the back. 'Drop that and you'll get a hundred lashes.'

Blood rushed in Jack's ears. Now he really did want to hit Wulfric. If he weren't holding the damned statue he was sure he would.

'Slowly!' Jack shouted to his comrades.

They eased their pace and did their best to keep the statue steady. Jack's arms felt as though they were being pulled from their sockets. He trod carefully on the muddy ground, only too aware that if the statue fell forward it would crush him instantly.

Saleem gasped, slipped and let go. The statute listed to one side and was about to topple over.

'Hold it!' Jack yelled.

Somehow the rest of them managed to keep the heavy weight upright.

Saleem scrambled back to his feet and got into position again, wailing, 'Sorry. Sorry.'

They continued down the slope and reached the final, steeper section. They inched their way now, planting their feet cautiously. Jack's hands felt as though they were on fire and he was certain he would let go at any moment. But he wasn't going to let the bloody statue beat him. He wasn't going to let Wulfric or Rao or anyone else beat him. He would get that cursed statue down the hill if he had to carry it by himself.

And then they were at the bottom of the slope.

'Over here!' Wulfric guided them to one of the huge Rajthanan ox wagons. 'On that. Lie it on its side.'

Jack stared at the wagon. It was going to be hard to lift the statue up on to the back while simultaneously lowering it on to its side.

But they had to do it.

Faces twisting at the strain, Jack and the others manoeuvred themselves into position and began to tilt the statue down. It went well at first, but then the huge figure began to roll to the left.

'Careful, scum!' Wulfric strapped Jack on the back.

Jack clenched his teeth. He was going to kill Wulfric one day. 'Move it to the right!' Jack bellowed to his comrades.

With a strangled growl, he tried to roll the statue back into place. White pain shot up his arms and he had to shut his eyes for a second in order to blank it out.

But the metal was slippery and for all their efforts the figure continued to slide.

It was going to fall.

Jack grunted and roared. Damn the statue. Damn Wulfric. Damn the Rajthanans and their stinking empire.

Then a man charged through the rain, slammed into the side of the murti and got his arms underneath it.

'Gently, lads!' he shouted as he heaved.

The man must have been enormously strong, because the statue immediately began to ease back to the right. Soon it was in position again and with a final shove they slid the figure on to the wagon, the oxen stomping and groaning.

Jack bent over, put his hands on his knees and panted heavily. He felt a hand on his shoulder and looked up. It was the man who'd helped to load the statue – he was a giant, with wild ginger hair and a thick beard. His eyes twinkled like a fox's. 'You all right, wee man?'

Jack nodded, still trying to get his breath back. He stood up straight again and glanced around for his men. They were all leaning against the side of the wagon, exhausted but smiling, save for Saleem whose face was ashen.

'All right, scum.' Wulfric stood with his hands on his hips. 'You lot can stay. But you'll be looking after that statue. You'll unload it every night and load it back again in the morning. If you drop it or damage it you'll each get a hundred lashes. Understood?'

Jack and the others nodded.

'Good. Now get that statue covered and tied down. Quickly now. Old Wulfric doesn't like lazing about!'

The porters took less than an hour to pack away the remainder of the army camp. Then, at a barked command from Sergeant Wulfric and a blast of horns, the column of men, animals and vehicles ground into life and marched, trod and trundled up the road. Rain battered the carts, channelled over the wagon covers and smeared the backs of the oxen and mules. Men called instructions to each other, animals moaned and wheels churned the mud.

Jack, Saleem, Andrew and the others strode behind the wagon containing the statue, while a driver cracked a huge whip above the eight pairs of oxen. The figure of Ganesh had been covered in canvas and secured with chains, but the wagon creaked and sagged under the great weight.

The tall man who'd stopped the statue from falling walked nearby.

'Thanks for your help,' Jack said.

The man grinned broadly, his eyes glinting in the dim light. 'It was nothing.'

Jack offered his hand. 'Jack Casey.'

'Robert.' The man took Jack's hand in his meaty paw. 'I'm the cartwright for this journey.'

'Keep moving, scum!' Sergeant Wulfric marched up and down the column. 'Don't laze about, you hear!'

One man slipped and clung to the edge of a cart to stop himself falling.

'Watch your feet, scum.' Wulfric strapped the man on the arm. 'Get on with it.'

'Charming Sergeant we have there,' Jack said to Robert, keeping his voice low.

Robert chuckled. 'Och, you've only seen the half of it. We've been working for him since yesterday. We're all sick of him.' He spoke with a thick, unfamiliar accent and some of the words he used Jack couldn't even understand.

Jack craned his neck to see over the heads of the men in front. He was near the rear of the column and there were at least a hundred porters, along with animals and carts, stretched out before him. Beyond the baggage train, the European soldiers marched in an orderly formation, with knapsacks on their backs and knife-muskets at their sides. They wore standard blue caps and tunics, while their officers, who rode alongside on horses, all had scarlet turbans. A drummer beat time as he strode at the rear of the group.

Jack pointed at the troops. 'Saxons?'

'Aye,' Robert said. 'Call themselves the 7th Native Saxon Infantry.'

Jack wiped the rain from his eyes and made out three figures on horseback at the head of the party. Staring hard, he identified Captain Rao, holding a black parasol above his head to protect himself from the rain. Beside him rode the rotund lieutenant, also with a parasol, and behind them came the man in the purple uniform.

'What about the Rajthanans?' Jack asked. 'What are they like?'

'Keep themselves to themselves for the most part,' Robert said. 'They've hardly spoken to us. Captain might be a wee bit inexperienced, though.'

'What makes you say that?'

'Just heard it. His first assignment, they say.'

'What about that lieutenant riding with him?'

'Parihar's his name. Heard he's an old friend of the Captain's.'

'And that man behind them?'

Robert squinted. 'Him? They call him Siddha Atri.'

Jack rubbed his chin. So, this Atri was indeed a siddha. Jack would have to watch him carefully.

A shudder ran through Jack's body. They'd passed into a powerful stream of sattva, and he caught a whiff of the perfumed scent.

A ripple of unease passed back through the men as the baggage train rounded a hill. Jack noticed porters talking agitatedly to each other and pointing up the road. The smell of sattva became even more overpowering and mingled with a suggestion of coal smoke.

Jack turned to Robert. 'What is it?'

Robert just nodded ahead. 'Look.'

They passed around the side of the hill and a shallow basin opened up to their left. The land looked as though a battle had pounded it. What must have once been a forest had been reduced to scorched stumps. The grass and undergrowth had been burnt to ash and small fires dotted the ground despite the rain. Dim figures moved in the murk, as if rising up from the mud. Jack made out gangs of men digging with spades, driving poles into the earth or hauling up the few remaining trees. Rajthanan soldiers whipped the labourers with crops if they paused for even a moment. Near to the road, a giant European soldier was flogging a man chained to the side of a cart.

'What is this?' Andrew made to move towards the basin, but Jack held him back.

'Mills,' Robert said quietly. 'They're building new ones. Those men are traitors. Captured by the army.'

'Crusaders,' Andrew said.

'Shut it,' Jack hissed.

There was nothing they could do to help the men, but Jack understood what Andrew was thinking. He was thinking it himself – out there, toiling beneath the whips and crops of the Rajthanans, were his brothers, his comrades, his fellow freedom fighters.

In the past, when he'd been a loyal subject, he'd thought the empire was a force for good. Jhala had often told him the Rajthanans had brought dharma to Europe, and Jack had believed him. But before him he saw the true face of the empire. It was like a giant mill that sucked in people and land and sattva and ground them all into pieces.

Cold determination flooded through him. If the Grail existed, he would find it and use it against the Rajthanans.

Or die trying.

A metallic howl split the air. Smoke blasted from the side of the road and a giant shape, about the size of an elephant, reared up. With its claws, feelers and quivering mandibles, it looked something like a lobster, but its body was constructed entirely of black iron studded with rivets. Rain steamed as it struck the creature's carapace and deep within it, just visible through the joints in its thorax, roared a red fire.

The porters cried out and stumbled to the other side of the road or ran ahead to get past the beast. One man shrieked and sprinted up the barren slope to the right, clambered to the top and disappeared over the ridge without looking back even once.

'Lord Jesus.' Andrew crossed himself.

'Stay where you are,' Jack shouted to his men. 'It's just a transport avatar.' He sounded confident, but he'd learnt even transport avatars could be dangerous and he kept a wary eye on the creature.

A driver in a grey tunic and turban rushed across to the avatar and tapped it on the side with a stick. The beast grumbled and a jet of steam whistled from its side. Then it raised itself up on its hind legs for a moment, exposing an underbelly riddled with tubes and pistons, before it spun round and crunched back to the earth. It ambled off, the driver following and continuing to tap it with the stick.

'Keep moving, scum!' Wulfric paced alongside the column. 'Anyone who stops again gets fifty lashes!'

The men pressed on past the desolate basin. The scent of sattva remained intense, and Saleem raised his sleeve to his face so he could breathe through the cloth. Jack patted the lad on the shoulder and gave him a grim smile. No doubt Saleem was remembering their encounters with avatars three years ago.

Finally, the road bent away from the basin, the sattva faded and the men's unease seemed to lift. The porters walked with more confidence and a few even laughed and joked.

Robert shivered. 'Evil place.'

'That's true enough,' Jack said.

He stared ahead through the sheets of rain. The road snaked off across a dismal heath and into a line of hills.

'You know how far it is to Scotland?' he asked Robert.

'Not far.' The big man grinned. 'The border's three hours away, at the most. All this land used to be part of Scotland, before the Rajthanans got here a few years ago.'

Three hours. Good. They were making progress. Each step forward was a step towards Mahajan's kingdom and whatever secrets it held.

Jack caught snatches of singing. The soldiers were belting out Saxon marching songs, and while their voices were harsh and guttural, there was something uplifting about the sound.

He remembered singing himself as he and his army comrades marched along. He smiled as he recalled one of his regiment's favourite tunes.

> There was a girl from London town
> With tits as white as snow
> For the price of just one penny each
> She'd put them both on show!

He grinned a little wider and the cold and rain seemed to fade away. The Saxons continued chanting, but in his head the English song ran on and on.

There was a girl from Newcastle
With an arse like a ripened peach
If you bought her booze she would happily
Let you give that arse a squeeze!

From out of the past, the voices of the men from his regiment seemed to swirl about him, soft at first, but then rising to a loud chant. William was beside him. And all the others who'd died in battle. They were marching along with him. All around him. So many of them.

Ghosts.

7

Misty drizzle cloaked the land. Rain dripped from the branches of the hunched trees and puddles smeared the fields. The sodden ground sucked at the men's boots as they walked, while the cart and wagon wheels slashed the mud. Occasionally Jack heard the spectral cry of a seagull overhead, but this became less frequent as the expedition left the coast behind.

After three hours, the ground began to rise and undulate, and the hills swelled ahead.

'That's it,' Robert said. 'We're in Scotland.'

Jack looked around. He couldn't see guards or a border post of any sort. 'How can you tell?'

Robert grinned and his eyes shone. 'A Scot always knows when he's come home.'

'A Scot?'

Robert grinned more widely. 'Aye. Did you not realise?'

Jack mumbled that he hadn't. He glanced at the big man, who wore a worn tunic, hose and old boots. The only thing notable about him was his height and his unkempt hair and beard. He looked no different from an ordinary Englishman. 'I thought . . . you'd look—'

'Like a wild savage?' Robert opened his eyes wide, as if he were crazed.

That is what Jack had thought. He'd been posted to the Scottish border years ago with the army and he'd even seen Scots bandits in the distance. But they'd always fled when he and his platoon had pursued them.

Robert chuckled. 'No, you're thinking of the tribes to the north. Here in the south, near the border, we're little different from you English.'

Jack stared ahead into the grey haze. He didn't know much about Scotland. During his posting to north-east England, he'd learnt almost nothing about the lands beyond the border. Scotland had always seemed a place of mists and secrets. A place he was unlikely ever to travel in.

'This Land of Mar,' he said. 'How long will it take us to get there?'

'Now there's a question.' Robert scratched his beard. 'No one knows precisely because no one knows exactly where it is.'

'Great. How are we going to get there, then?'

'See that man?' Robert pointed to the head of the column, where an indistinct figure now walked alongside Captain Rao's horse. 'He's a guide. Another Scot. He'll lead us as far as he can. But after that we'll have to ask the local tribes for directions.'

'Sounds as though it's going to take weeks.'

'Aye. It will. I heard the Rajthanans are estimating two weeks. But that's just a guess.' His teeth flashed in the dim light. 'That's if we even make it at all.'

Two weeks? Jack went silent. That was longer than he'd hoped. In Shropshire they'd estimated a week, but that was based on information in ancient manuscripts, which could well be inaccurate.

There were only four weeks left before Kanvar's cure wore off. At the moment he felt well enough, but the sattva-fire was always there, quivering in his chest whenever he stopped to think about it. And he would grow weaker as the end of the two-month period drew closer.

He stared across the windswept landscape.

He remembered Elizabeth on the night she'd come to his hut and stood in the doorway and told him she was pregnant. Then he found himself picturing Vadula's army massing in Worcestershire.

He shook his head to dispel these thoughts.

Your mind is a rippling pool. Still it.

Keep your thoughts focused on the task. Keep your feet on the road. Keep marching forward.

＊

They trudged on through the remainder of the morning. From time to time carts appeared ahead and pulled over to allow them to pass. The hills steepened and funnelled them into a gloomy valley. Dark fir forests, blurred by curtains of rain, swirled over the slopes.

At midday, they paused for lunch and porters set up an awning for the Rajthanans on a low mound. The officers sat at a table and their Rajthanan batmen served them food. Captain Rao was silent most of the time. When he glanced at his surroundings, he crinkled his nose and pressed a handkerchief to his face, as if the landscape produced a foul odour. Lieutenant Parihar talked constantly, often waving his arms to emphasise whatever points he was making. Siddha Atri picked carefully at his food with his long fingers and from time to time gazed out at the rain-logged fields.

After lunch, they marched for half an hour before Jack spied a huddle of buildings near the road. He made out a low stone wall surrounding long wattle-and-daub structures and ten or more tents. A handful of figures moved around the compound, and further back a transport avatar crouched beside a wooden shed. The beast appeared inactive – no fire was visible within it and it sat with its legs folded beneath it and its head hanging limp.

'Rajthanans.' Robert lowered his voice. 'They're prospecting for black magic, I heard.'

'Sattva?' Jack said.

'Aye. That's what they call it. You know about it, then?'

'A little.' What Robert had said made sense. Jack had noticed numerous sattva streams since they'd crossed the border and no doubt the Rajthanans were keen to exploit these rich reserves.

Robert put his head closer to Jack. 'I heard the sattva's running out down south.'

Jack almost stopped walking. Running out? Could that happen? 'Where'd you hear this?'

Robert drew back a little. 'In Dun Fries. Word gets around.'

Jack swept the damp hair from his eyes. Was this true? He'd never heard of sattva running out, but perhaps it was possible. Jhala had often described sattva as a 'fuel'. And fuel burnt as you used it. It didn't last for ever.

As always, there seemed to be so much about sattva and yoga that he didn't know. Jhala, supposedly his guru, had kept him in the dark, no doubt on purpose, and Jack hadn't had enough time with Kanvar to ask all the questions he would have liked.

The countryside closed in around them. The hills rose higher and the valley narrowed. Firs swarmed up to the road and loomed over the train of men and animals. Arcades of tree trunks stretched away into the murk in all directions.

The road faded to a rough track. Carts no longer came along the path and Jack saw no sign of human habitation, save for a few roadside stone crosses decorated with Celtic designs.

At one point Robert stared into the hills and said, 'This is as far north as I've ever been. We're truly in the wilds now.'

As the light began to fade, and afternoon crawled towards evening, the trees thinned and occasionally Jack noticed tiny villages crouching in the distance. Once, he spotted a shepherd with his flock, but otherwise the Scots kept themselves hidden. No doubt they would be wary of the army, which would be a strange sight so far north of the border.

The rain eased and finally two Saxon horn blowers blasted the command to halt. The column trundled into a meadow and the porters began unloading the carts.

'I'll see you shortly,' Robert said to Jack. 'We're off to buy sheep.' He opened a satchel to reveal about twenty boxes of matches. 'Hard to get these around here.'

Jack watched Robert and a couple of other porters stride towards a distant hamlet. Then he turned back to the wagon, where the statue was still covered and bound by chains. 'Right. Let's get that off.'

Jack and his men struggled, swore, strained and sweated, and finally unloaded the statue. They heaved it over to the edge of the camp and thumped it down in the grass. The figure brooded in the twilight and gazed into the distance. Campfires sent dull gleams dancing across its surface.

With that task complete, Jack and the others helped to set up the Rajthanans' tents. Jack and Saleem carried a writing desk into Captain Rao's two-storey marquee. Saleem gasped at the lavish interior, and even Jack, who was used to Rajthanan opulence, was surprised at the luxury on display. A rug decorated with intricate designs covered the floor, paintings depicting battles and hunting scenes hung on the walls and ornate oil lanterns swung from the roof. Cane and mahogany furniture dotted the chamber: chairs, side tables, cabinets and display cases. A brocaded curtain on the far side of the room hung slightly open to reveal further chambers deeper within and a set of wooden stairs led to the upper level.

A Rajthanan batman ordered them to place the desk in a corner. Then, as they left the marquee, a cry went up on the far side of the camp.

Saleem frowned. 'What was that?'

Jack touched the satchel hanging at his side and felt the pistol press against his hip. It was good to know he had a weapon, but there was no time to load it now.

He heard further shouts. 'Come on. Let's take a look.'

They jogged around the outskirts of the camp, dodging the guy ropes of the tents, and came to a stretch of open ground. A flock of sheep milled about on the grass, along with a dozen small black cattle.

Robert and the two porters who'd been sent to find food stood beside the animals, while Rao, Lieutenant Parihar, Wulfric and several Saxon soldiers stood nearby. Further soldiers and porters were arriving, forming a small crowd.

Rao pointed at the cattle and shouted, his voice high-pitched and cracking, 'I won't have it!'

'We bought them with our own matches, sir,' Robert said. 'They were for us to eat. We didn't steal them.'

'I don't care who you bought them for, you pink imbecile. They're sacred. I won't have beef eaten in my camp. Not by anyone.' Rao spoke English well, despite his strong accent.

'Sorry, sir,' Robert said. 'We didn't know.'

'He's insulting you.' Parihar put his hands on his hips. 'Look at his eyes.'

'You're right.' Rao glared at Robert. 'Insolence.'

Robert frowned. 'Sir?'

'Challenging me, are you?' Rao's voice came out shrill. He turned to Wulfric. 'Arrest them, Sergeant. They shall be flogged.'

Jack had seen enough. He knew exactly what the problem was – he'd seen this scene played out many times before.

He pushed his way through the gathering. 'Wait.'

Rao looked at Jack and mouthed words silently, as if so shocked he couldn't think what to say.

Parihar's face darkened 'What did you say, boy?'

Wulfric strode towards Jack, his face clenched like a fist.

But Jack held up his hand and spoke to Rao, 'Sir, there's been a misunderstanding. It's our custom to look our superiors in the eye.'

Rao frowned. 'What?'

'We Europeans look at our superiors. At least, a bit. This man isn't insulting you. He thinks if he looks away you'll think he's lying.'

Jack had had to explain this many times to new arrivals from Rajthana. When he'd been a sergeant he'd often had to instruct the young subalterns sent to the regiment.

'Scum.' Wulfric grasped Jack's tunic. 'You'll be flogged for—'

'He's right.' Siddha Atri slipped out of the shadows, stroking his beard with a spidery finger.

'Look, Atri,' Parihar snapped in Rajthani. 'Rao's in command—'

'Wait.' Rao raised his hand to silence Parihar, then spoke to Atri in Rajthani. 'Is this true?'

'Indeed.' Atri gave a vague smile. 'European soldiers learn not to meet their officers' gazes. But this man probably didn't know.'

Rao's jaw worked for a moment and his eyes flickered from Jack to the cattle. Finally, he turned to Robert and said in English, 'Very well. There'll be no flogging. But I won't have beef eaten in this camp.'

'That's understood now, sir,' Robert said.

Wulfric grunted and released Jack's tunic.

'But if it happens again you *will* be flogged.' Rao crinkled his nose and held his handkerchief to his face. 'Now get these animals away from the camp. The smell is abominable.'

<hr />

'You want some beef?' the cook asked as he lifted the lid of the three-legged pot standing in the campfire.

'What?' Robert looked up, his jaw dropping. Then he noticed the glint in the cook's eye and a smile slid across his lips. 'I should pop you one for that.'

Everyone around the fire snorted with laughter. Jack chuckled softly, along with Andrew and the rest of the men from Shropshire. Saleem was the only one who was silent – he sat with his knees drawn up to his chin, staring into the flames as if transfixed.

'Cheer up, Sultan.' Robert slapped Saleem on the back. 'It was only a joke.'

Saleem smiled feebly. Robert had taken to calling him 'Sultan' as he was the sole Mohammedan amongst the porters, but Saleem didn't seem to mind.

At Rao's command, the cattle had been driven back to the village. Robert had then invited Jack and his men to share a meal with him and his work gang.

'Sorry, everyone,' the cook said. 'It's pottage. No beef. No pork neither.'

As the cook spooned the stew into bowls, Robert leant closer to Jack and said, 'Thank you for before, wee man. Thought I was in for a beating.'

'No need to thank me.'

'You seem to understand these Rajthanans.'

'A bit.'

'I can't make head or tail of them. No beef. And that statue.'

'They're a strange lot, that's for sure.'

Jack heard a snarl behind him. He turned to see Wulfric staggering from the darkness and into the firelight. The Sergeant swayed unsteadily and Jack caught a whiff of ale. Wulfric appeared to be drunk. This was surprising for a Mohammedan, but Jack had known many Saxons who weren't particularly devout.

Everyone went silent and the only sound was the crackling and spitting of the fire.

Wulfric's good eye flitted over the group, like a fly searching for a place to land. His bad eye shifted beneath its heavy eyelid and the scar on his cheek glowed white. Finally, his gaze rested on Jack. 'Ah. There you are.'

He took a few uncertain steps forward. 'Hiding here, are you, scum? Well, I've found you.' He sniffed the air. 'Old Wulfric can always smell them. Old Wulfric will always find them.'

'Just eating our dinner, sir,' Jack said. How was he going to defuse this situation?

'Dinner, eh?' Wulfric stumbled to the fire, lifted his leg and smashed his foot into the pot, almost falling backwards in the process. The pot toppled into the fire, the pottage spilling out and hissing amongst the embers. Sparks flickered in the dark.

'I'm warning you.' Wulfric swung his arm to take in the whole group sitting about the fire. 'Old Wulfric is watching you.' He turned to Jack, blinking and trying to focus. 'Old Wulfric is watching you too. I won't have some English filth causing trouble. No, I won't have you meddling.'

Jack stared back at Wulfric. His satchel sat next to him, but the pistol was still unloaded.

Wulfric bent his knees and leant in close so that Jack could smell the ale on his breath. 'Old Wulfric will have you one of these days.'

Jack's heart beat harder. What would Wulfric do next?

Then the Sergeant lurched upright again, gave the fallen pot a final kick and stumbled away into the darkness, muttering unintelligibly to himself.

They marched for eight days, passing through the valley and then heading north across the open plains and rolling countryside beyond. The air grew colder, but there was little rain and at times a pale sun blinked through gaps in the cloud.

The native Scots continued to avoid the party, although Jack often saw them in the distance: men out hunting with dogs, women walking across fields with pots of water on their heads and children hiding and watching from behind patches of gorse. The villages at first appeared little different from those in England. But after the first two days, they changed. The huts became small and often circular, with dry-stone walls and roofs covered in green turf. The surrounding fields consisted of narrow ridges that rippled like water across the hillsides.

As the days wore on, the party settled into a routine. In the morning, a horn blower would sound the call to wake. The Rajthanans would perform their ritual – their puja – sitting cross-legged before the Ganesh statue. The Saxons – joined by Saleem – would pray in unison. And the porters would pack away the Rajthanans' tents. Jack and his men would heave the statue on to the back of the wagon. Then the party would march for hours, stopping only occasionally to rest and water the animals. At midday, the batmen would serve lunch to the officers as they sat under the awning. After that, the column would set off once again and they would travel until dusk. Some of the porters would then wash themselves as best they could, don white livery and act as servants for the Rajthanans. Others were paid by the Saxons to cook dinner. Jack and his men would unload the statue and place it on the edge of the camp, as if to keep watch overnight.

Siddha Atri often rode off from the column and Jack saw him standing on hilltops, observing the landscape through a complicated-looking spyglass set up on a tripod. Sometimes Atri and his batman would disappear for much of the day and at other times he sent porters to plant flags on distant slopes. Jack asked Robert what Atri was up to, but the big man merely shrugged. He had no idea either.

Jack did his best to find out more information about the expedition. He talked to Robert and the other porters, but no one knew anything of note. They'd all been told they were going to Mar to find a Rajthanan called Mahajan. That was it.

Jack tried to snoop around near the Rajthanans' tents in the evenings. He heard scraps of conversations in Rajthani, but nothing of interest. When he realised Wulfric and the Saxons were becoming suspicious, he stopped.

The land buckled the further north they travelled. The Scottish guide, a wiry man almost as tall as Robert, led the party ever deeper into the knotted countryside. He often clambered far ahead, pausing on outcrops to get his bearings and scout the way ahead.

As the ground became more treacherous, the oxen struggled to pull the statue. Two of the wagon's wheels broke and had to be replaced by Robert and his gang, who seemed as confident repairing Rajthanan vehicles as native carts.

On the morning of the ninth day since leaving Dun Fries, Rao summoned everyone to a clear patch of ground just outside the camp. He stood on top of a boulder, his scimitar hanging at his side and a rotary pistol in a holster attached to his belt. The wind shuffled his tunic and from time to time he placed a handkerchief over his nose and breathed through it.

He spoke in Arabic and then repeated himself in English. 'Men, I have been informed by our guide that we are now passing into more dangerous territory. The tribes north of here are not like those to the south. They will not have seen army troops before. We will be as strange to them as they are to us.

'There is no need to fear them necessarily. Should they attack, we shall deal with them swiftly. Their primitive weapons will be no match for our muskets. But be on your guard.'

The men were dismissed and within half an hour the column was moving out once again, the vehicles rattling along the crude track.

For the whole of that day, they saw not a single other person. The natives, if they were anywhere at all, remained hidden. Siddha Atri still occasionally rode away from the party, but he remained closer than before and always within eyesight.

A wall of dark mountains appeared in the distance, rising above the foothills. The wind blowing down from the slopes contained a trace of ice.

'The Highlands,' Robert said. 'Never thought I'd get to see it.'

'And Mar's up there somewhere,' Jack said.

'Aye. Somewhere in there.'

Pain wormed across Jack's chest. It was faint, but stronger than it had been for weeks. Kanvar's cure would wear off in less than three weeks now and the injury was getting worse.

In the late afternoon, as shadows clutched the landscape, the ruins of an ancient castle appeared ahead, rising like a giant claw from the summit of a hill. The outer wall had crumbled in several places, revealing an inner bailey overgrown with grass and weeds. Two broken towers poked above the wall and slabs of half-buried stone lay scattered across the slope.

Wulfric called a halt and the soldiers and porters set about making camp on a stretch of grassland at the base of the hill. After unloading the statue, Jack stood staring up at the castle for a moment. Twilight had set in and the broken stonework was indistinct against the blue-black sky.

'A strange sight, don't you think?' Robert had walked up beside Jack.

Jack nodded. 'I've been thinking about it. Since we got to Scotland we've seen no large towns, no castles, no monasteries, no cathedrals. Just tiny villages. And then there's this castle up there. What's left of it anyway.'

'Aye. There were once castles in Scotland. There were kingdoms in the lowlands, just like in England. But the kingdoms fell apart long ago. The castles crumbled. There's nothing left now but ruins.'

Jack had never heard this. 'Why did the kingdoms fall?'

Robert shrugged. 'Couldn't tell you. I'm no scholar. Can't even read.' He frowned. 'A monk did tell me once that when the Moors came, we Scots were cut off from everything else. We weren't Mohammedans like the rest of Europe. We weren't part of England. We were left on our own. And our kingdoms withered and died . . . That's what this monk said anyway.'

Jack was silent. The wind gave a reedy moan as it whipped across the hillside.

It was strange to think that once kings, queens, knights and courtiers had inhabited the castle. Perhaps at the bottom of the slope there'd been a town, with people in it who lived a life similar to the English.

And yet now it was all gone. Forgotten.

'Look!' one of the porters shouted.

'I see it,' another cried out.

Porters and soldiers scurried to the edge of the camp to see what was going on. Jack and Robert picked their way around the tents and arrived at the bottom of the hill, where a small crowd had gathered. Several porters were pointing excitedly up the slope.

Rao, Parihar and Atri strode over from the direction of the officers' marquees.

'What's going on?' Rao asked Wulfric.

Wulfric pointed up into the darkness. 'Look, sir. Up there.'

Jack stared hard, but even with his abnormally good eyesight he saw nothing at first. Then he noticed a dark shape moving about halfway down the scarp. Further to the left was another shape. Then another.

About fifty hunched figures were creeping down the incline. As they came closer, the firelight picked them out and a murmur rippled through the crowd below.

'Lord Shiva!' Rao said.

The figures were men, but they looked more animal than human. Their hair was long and matted, their beards wild, and grease and dirt streaked their faces. They wore huge brown cloaks that were as shaggy as bearskin, and simple tunics that reached to their knees. Their legs were bare and their shoes were nothing more than roughly sewn animal hide.

Most of them held spears, but a few carried bows and arrows. Crude amulets hung from chains about their necks, the metal clinking and rattling as they moved.

A few of the Saxons slung their knife-muskets from their shoulders and pointed their weapons up the slope. The approaching natives froze, crouched and spoke softly to each other.

'Put your muskets down,' Rao said.

The soldiers looked back at Rao, confused.

'Down!' Wulfric shouted.

The men flinched and lowered their weapons.

The natives spoke further, then began descending the slope again. They approached as tentatively as cats. When they were about a hundred feet from the bottom of the hill, they halted. A tall man, who appeared to be the leader, handed his spear to another then crept ahead with his hand outstretched, palm open, as if to show he wasn't carrying a weapon.

'Talk to him,' Rao said to his Scottish guide.

The guide wove his way to the front of the gathering and stepped slowly up to the tall native. The guide spoke in a strange language, his voice slipping between being soft and harsh, as if he were whispering and clearing his throat in turn. Both he and the native then squatted on their haunches and talked some more. During the conversation, the guide drew something from a bag and handed it to the native.

Finally, the guide stood and called across to Rao. 'He says he is Chief Morgunn mac Ruadri vic Cannech of the Grym tribe. He comes in peace and grants you permission to pass through these lands. In exchange he wanted fire sticks.'

Rao frowned. 'Fire sticks?'

'Matches, sir,' the guide said. 'He says he's heard of them but never seen them. He knows of the land of the Mar tribe. He says it's to the north, but far, many days. He also says the lands north of here are dangerous, full of hostile tribes.'

The soldiers and porters shuffled and murmured on hearing this.

Rao held up his hand. 'Enough. You will give me a full report in my tent. Tell the Chief that we thank him for his permission and we wish him and his tribe good health and long lives.'

The guide nodded, squatted and spoke again to the Chief, who replied with a few words, then slipped back to his men. The natives crept quickly back up the slope and in less than a minute had slid away into the dark.

'Hostile tribes?' Saleem said as they walked back to the other side of the camp.

'That's not all the Chief said.' Robert's expression was sombre.

'What?' Jack came to a stop. 'You understood?'

'Aye,' Robert said. 'He was speaking Gaalic. I ken it well enough. Some people speak it in the south too.'

'What else did he say, then?' Saleem fidgeted with the hem of his tunic.

Everyone in the small group – Jack, Saleem, Andrew and a few of the other porters – stared at Robert.

The big man licked his lips and scratched his beard. 'He said we must beware Mahajan. He's heard Mahajan's a demon who's risen from the mouth of hell. His men have taken over Mar and are spreading their power to the neighbouring lands. They carry the sign of the skull on their chests.' He pressed his hand to his breast. 'They are evil. They torture and kill people. He said we must not go to Mar. We must turn back and go home.'

Everyone went silent. Saleem swallowed so loudly Jack could hear it.

Jack glanced up at the ruins at the top of the hill. The outer wall was like a row of broken, rotting teeth. 'Well, I was told only desperate men would come on this journey. We must all be desperate.'

The men chuckled. As Jack had hoped, his words had eased the mood.

'Aye.' Robert grinned. 'We must be mad. But if I'm going to be mad I'd rather do it with you lot than anyone else.'

8

——◆◆◆——

The call to rise drifted across the camp, the horn's sound frail and uncertain as it echoed in the empty valleys. They all woke. The Rajthanans did their puja before the Ganesh statue and the Mohammedans prayed in rows, standing, kneeling and prostrating themselves in turn. Then they all ate breakfast and packed away the camp. Within an hour and a half they were off once more, marching deeper into the Highlands.

The day was clear, save for a few blotches of cloud, but the air was cool and a chill wind whispered down the slopes. The hills swept like great waves about them, while the higher mountains gathered ahead, the tallest peaks dusted with snow and veiled by mist.

The Scottish guide led them to the north-east, following the directions given by the Chief of the Grym tribe. They spent most of the morning meandering along a narrow gully until the ground sloped up towards a pass. The guide led them up the scarp, following a thin track as it snaked into a forest of birch trees that had lost most of their leaves. The ground was in turns rocky and slippery. Tree roots reached into the path, tripping and hindering them. The carts and wagons bounced over the uneven ground and the animals battled to haul the heavy loads.

The sounds of the wheels grinding, men shouting and oxen bellowing was loud, but seemed to fade quickly into the enormous silence of the valley. When Jack glanced around, he saw no sign of movement. Everything seemed still, smothered by the silence. It seemed, at that moment, as if the party were the only living things on earth and were toiling away across a deserted landscape.

Within an hour, the oxen and mules were exhausted, shivering and often losing their footing. Wulfric ordered a rest stop when they reached a short stretch of flat ground. Porters walked the horses in circles to cool them and watered the oxen and mules. Atri took the opportunity to climb up on to a boulder, peer at the surroundings through his spyglass-like contraption and write notes in a journal. His Rajthanan batman and a pair of porters stood nearby, waiting to pack away the instrument.

What was Atri up to? Jack still had no idea.

Andrew groaned and lay on his back. 'This bloody journey never ends. Let's just call this spot Mar and then go home.'

The others from Shropshire chuckled at this.

Jack noticed Saleem had pulled off one of his boots and was rubbing his foot through his hose.

'Blisters?' Jack asked.

Saleem nodded and winced. Then he quickly said, 'But I'm all right. I can keep going.'

Jack slapped Saleem lightly on the back. 'Don't worry. Happens to all of us. Those blisters will hurt like hell for a day or two, then they'll burst and harden and your feet will be tougher than ever.'

Saleem smiled slightly and stared at the ground. 'I was remembering when we walked most of the way to London.'

'You see, we made it then. Through worse than what we're facing now.'

Saleem went quiet and picked at the burrs stuck to his hose.

'You thinking about Charles?' Jack asked.

Saleem nodded.

Charles had been their companion on the way to London. The young man was from the same village as Saleem and had died during the siege. Saleem had told Jack he'd carted the body home for burial after the battle.

Jack crossed himself. 'He was a brave man, Charles. He'd be proud of us now, I reckon.'

Saleem paused, then said softly, 'We'll do it, won't we? We'll find Mahajan and save the rebellion.'

Jack stared through the mesh of branches and up the grass-covered slope beyond. He'd already told Saleem the mission was mad and they would probably fail. Was there any point repeating that now?

'You worried about your family?' Jack asked.

Saleem nodded glumly, eyes watering a little.

'We're all worried. That's why we'll do our best. There's a true path laid out ahead of us. All we have to do is find it and keep marching along it.'

The words seemed to have the right effect because Saleem's gentle smile spread across his lips again.

They were Jhala's words.

Was it strange for Jack to quote his old guru? Now, when he was fighting the Rajthanans? When Jhala had betrayed him?

Jhala, of course, had been referring to dharma, which defined your role and duty in life. Jhala had often tried to explain the concept to Jack, but struggled as there was no matching word in English. Finally, when they were resting during a march, Jhala had come up with a comparison – dharma was like the road ahead of you. It is the rightful path. All you have to do is keep walking down it.

'My father used to say something like that,' Salem said. 'He told me only those who follow the Right Path are Allah's faithful. I've always tried to follow that path.'

Jack was about to reply when the sound of falling rocks cut him short. He leapt up and spun round, along with the Saxons, who grasped their knife-muskets.

Peering through the branches, he made out a cliff face in the side of the hill about a hundred yards away. A stream of dust, stones and small rocks was bouncing down the precipice. Within a few seconds, the rockfall was over, the dust blew away and silence swamped the valley once again.

Strange.

Jack searched the hillside, but saw only grass, heather and clots of gorse. There was no sign of movement.

The Rajthanans were staring at the slope through their spyglasses and muttering amongst themselves. Finally, Rao called Wulfric over, and then the Sergeant bellowed to the party, 'There's nothing there. On your feet. Break's over.'

The entire expedition stood reluctantly and pressed on up the slope. The rocks dotting the path became larger and both animals and men tripped on them constantly. The incline steepened and the oxen drawing the statue's wagon struggled with the load. Often Jack and the others had to push the vehicle to help the animals. Soon they were all panting and covered in sweat.

'I'm starting to hate that bloody statue,' Andrew muttered.

Jack nodded, but said, 'Keep your voice down.'

Then the wagon stopped suddenly. There was a thud, followed by the groan of bending wood. The wheel nearest Jack buckled and snapped, flinging splinters in the air. He stumbled back and covered his face as a chunk of wood whirled past. When he opened his eyes he saw that the side of the wagon was jammed against a boulder. The wheel had completely shattered and the vehicle was listing to the side.

Robert walked up from behind, rubbing his beard. 'Doesn't look good. That your fault, Sultan?' He grinned and winked at Saleem.

He crouched down and studied the smashed wheel.

'What's going on?' Wulfric zigzagged downhill, jamming his boots into the ground to avoid slipping.

'Wheel's broken, sir,' Jack said.

'Replace it.'

'Can't do that.' Robert stood up. 'We've got no more spares. The load's too heavy on that wagon. Keeps breaking wheels.'

Wulfric's face creased and his good eye quivered. 'Fix it, then. Get on with it.'

'We can't fix that here,' Robert said. 'We'd need to forge a new rim.'

Wulfric's face tightened further. He stepped over to Robert and stared up at the big man. 'Listen here, scum. You fix that thing right now or I'll have you flogged so hard the whip'll be tickling your liver.'

'Why have we stopped?' Rao had walked down from the head of the column.

Wulfric stepped away from Robert and snapped upright. 'Wagon's broken, sir. Just fixing it.'

Rao looked at the ruined vehicle. 'How long is that going to take?'

'We can't fix it, sir.' Jack knew enough about wagons to know what Robert had said was true. 'We don't have a travelling forge.'

Rao glanced at Jack and pressed his handkerchief to his nose. This was the first time he'd paid any attention to Jack since the incident with the cattle. After a second, he looked back at Wulfric. 'Is this true, Sergeant?'

'I . . . They should be able to, sir.'

'It's impossible,' Jack said.

Wulfric looked at Jack as though he were about to stab him. 'You fix that thing now, or—'

'Sergeant, do you have any idea what you're talking about?' Rao asked.

Wulfric's fingers coiled into fists. 'I'm not a cartwright, sir.'

'Right then, who *is*?'

Robert stepped forward. 'That's me, sir.'

Rao drew a breath through his handkerchief. It wasn't clear whether he recognised Robert. 'Can you fix this wagon?'

'No, sir.'

'I see.' Rao turned back to Jack. 'Move the murti to another wagon.'

'The others are quite overloaded, sir,' Jack said.

Rao rolled his eyes. 'Am I surrounded by idiots? Just get rid of anything unnecessary.' He turned to walk back up the slope.

'Sir,' Jack said. 'Can I make a suggestion?'

Rao turned and gave a long sigh. 'What?'

'We leave the murti behind. Pick it up on the way back.'

Rao's nostrils flared. He pointed his finger at Jack, still holding the handkerchief, which fluttered in the breeze. 'Listen here. I won't put up with any insolence.'

Jack made sure he neither looked away nor stared straight into Rao's eyes. 'Sorry, sir.'

'Bow down to me,' Rao said.

Jack paused. It was a long time since he'd prostrated himself before an officer.

'Now!' Rao said.

Jack felt his face darken. What right did Rao have to order him about?

But now was not the time to take a stand. He clenched his teeth, lowered himself and lay flat on the ground.

'Good,' Rao said. 'Never question my orders again.' He turned and trudged back uphill.

Jack stood up and dusted the earth from the front of his tunic.

Wulfric stood beside the wagon, his face twisted and eye glowing white. 'I'll have you, scum.' He pointed his finger at Jack. 'I'll have you. Old Wulfric doesn't forget. Old Wulfric always gets his man.'

Jack didn't respond. It was best not to antagonise Wulfric any further.

Wulfric glared for several long seconds, then barked, 'I want that statue moved in ten minutes! Get on with it!'

Jack and the others sprang into action. The second Rajthanan ox wagon was the only other vehicle large enough to carry the statue. But it was laden with furniture.

Jack gestured at the vehicle. 'We'll empty it.'

'Are you joking?' Robert said. 'You saw what the Captain said about the statue. He won't agree to us throwing that stuff out.' He pointed to a trio of smaller carts. 'We'll unload those and move the furniture there.'

Jack stared at the carts. They were weighed down with sacks. 'What's in those?'

'Barley,' Robert said. 'For us porters.'

'Food? Isn't there something else?'

'Nothing else our masters will agree to.'

Jack hesitated. Robert was right. Food for porters wasn't important. Neither the Rajthanans nor the Saxons would give a damn if they went hungry.

He gritted his teeth. The expedition was carrying far too much baggage. Rao was mad to want to drag a statue and so much furniture through the wilderness. Jhala would never have made this mistake.

But there was no point trying to fight against the Captain's wishes.

He swallowed down his irritation and nodded.

They emptied the carts, moved the furniture and finally heaved the statue across to the large wagon, which squeaked and groaned as the heavy weight was laid across it.

Robert scratched his beard. 'Don't know how much longer that's going to last.'

'It had better last,' Jack said. 'We don't need any more trouble.'

The driver gave a cry and cracked his whip high above the oxen, which lumbered forward. Like a rambling caterpillar, the entire column edged on up the hill.

They came out of the trees and on to a bare slope where the wind combed the grass and heather. The canvas coverings on the wagons crackled and tugged, and a scrap of material tumbled through the air as it was whisked away. Saleem had to hold on to his skullcap to stop it blowing off, and finally gave up and put it in his satchel.

The slope was even steeper now and the officers had to dismount and lead their horses by the reins. They all trudged wearily up the last few yards and finally reached the summit.

Jack stopped for a moment and gazed back the way they'd

come. They were much higher than he'd realised and he had a clear view of the gully they'd travelled along earlier. In the distance, the knotted foothills rolled away towards the blue line of the horizon.

When he turned to face forward again, he saw mountains massing in all directions. Below him, a scarp slid down into a convoluted landscape of valleys and ravines. Secretive forests nestled in crannies and streams twisted along clefts.

'Keep moving!' Wulfric shouted. 'Anyone who stops will be flogged!'

The party wound its way downhill and by the time they reached the base of the incline, the late afternoon shadows were sweeping across the valley.

They trudged on for around twenty minutes and then the column ground to a halt.

'What is it?' Saleem asked.

Jack frowned. 'Don't know.'

He stepped away from the track and saw that Rao, Parihar and Atri had paused beside a hollow between two low mounds. The Rajthanans dismounted and walked down into the depression, followed by their batmen, Wulfric and two other Saxons.

'Let's take a look,' Jack said to Saleem, then turned to the others. 'You lot wait here.'

He and Saleem walked to the head of the party and over to the lip of the hollow, where a few of the Saxons had gathered and stood looking down. At the bottom of a short slope was a circle of cairns. On top of each pile of stones stood an oddly shaped rock worn smooth by river water. In the centre of the circle, a rough stone cross jutted from a further cairn.

Jack had never seen anything quite like this, although he was reminded of the standing stones in Wiltshire and other parts of England. With the cross in the centre, this place was obviously some kind of shrine.

'Look at this.' Parihar lifted up one of the smaller river-worn rocks and snorted. 'Savages.' He tossed the rock into the grass.

Rao put his handkerchief to his nose, as if the stones were exuding noxious fumes.

Parihar slapped his hands together to shake off the dirt. 'Let's go. There's nothing here.'

Rao nodded and set off up the incline with the Lieutenant. Atri remained for a moment, studying one of the cairns and writing something in his notebook.

Wulfric put his boot against the cross. Egged on by his laughing comrades, he kicked the cross over and it tumbled into the grass.

Jack tensed. Wulfric shouldn't have done that. And Parihar shouldn't have thrown the stone aside. It was a sin to damage a shrine and he wondered how the natives would react.

'Come on,' Wulfric barked at his men. 'Get back. We're moving out.'

The Saxons trudged back up the slope and Jack and Saleem returned to the baggage train.

The column once again trundled forward, the shadows thickening all about them. After half an hour, the horn blowers called a halt and they made camp on a stretch of grassland beside a stand of trees.

Jack and his men unloaded the statue and set it aside from the rest of the camp. Afterwards, Jack stood for a moment, hands on hips, staring at the figure squatting in the gloom. It was strange to see it rising from the meadow, the forest and mountains behind it. It looked wrong, a scrap of civilisation in a vast wilderness untouched by human hands.

<hr/>

Jack and the others ate with Robert and his work gang. Jack half expected Wulfric to try something, but the Sergeant stayed away from the porters' section.

As they all prepared to sleep, cloud flooded the sky and Jack detected the coppery scent of moisture in the air. To shelter from any overnight rain, he and his men lay in a line beneath the wagon – there was only just enough room for them all to fit.

Jack was at one end, next to Saleem. The boy fell asleep quickly, but Jack lay awake despite being exhausted from the day's march. He glanced at Saleem's pale face, barely lit by the trace of moonlight. The lad's brow was slightly creased, as if a dream were troubling him.

He looked so young.

Had Jack been right to bring him along? But Saleem had wanted to come, had wanted to absolve himself of his guilt. Who was Jack to deny him that?

A gust of wind worried the canvas lying in the wagon above. The dry branches of the trees cackled.

Jack shut his eyes. Sleep. He had to sleep.

But then a bolt of pain struck him in the chest. He gasped and opened his eyes. The sattva-fire crackled within his ribs. It was the most severe attack he'd had since Kanvar had cured him.

He shut his eyes again and ground his teeth as he fought to stay silent. He didn't want to wake Saleem and the others, didn't want anyone to know he was weakening.

The pain came in waves, from a throbbing ache to searing agony.

Stay calm. Breathe deeply.

Should he try the Great Health yantra one more time? Kanvar had told him not to give up, but after failing for so many years it was hard to have much hope.

He breathed deeply several more times, tried to block out the pain and did his best to bring the yantra to his mind's eye. The design came to him in fragments, first one section, then another. He fought to hold it still, but the pain kept intruding on his thoughts.

If the yantra worked now, he knew exactly what would follow. The knowledge of how to use the power would rush into his mind. Within an instant, he would know everything there was to know about the power. And then he would have a choice – either use the power immediately, or hold back. An unblocked siddha might hold back at this point in order to remain pure. But of course, for Jack there was no choice. He had to use the Great Health power as soon as he could.

He sensed the air grow colder, heard a hush of rain and smelt wet earth. Drops drummed on the wagon, the sound echoing in the space beneath the vehicle.

There was a moment of intense quiet, when his surroundings seemed to fade away, and the yantra sat still and perfect in his mind.

And then . . . nothing.

Damn it.

The yantra hadn't worked. Would probably never work.

And now the pain came rushing back, twisting and knotting in his chest. He tightened his jaw, grasped clumps of grass in each hand and tried his best to muffle his gasps.

He would have to wait it out. He wouldn't die tonight – he wasn't bad enough yet. But the pain could last for an hour, maybe more.

To distract himself he thought of Elizabeth. So long as she was safe he had nothing to worry about.

His mind flickered and danced between memories.

He saw Katelin on her deathbed, Elizabeth as a child, William in the Tower of London moments before his death, Jhala the last time Jack had seen him in Poole.

Then for some reason his thoughts settled on the day he'd left home to join the army. It was winter and the bare trees were cracks against the white sky. He walked along the path from his parents' cottage, the only place he'd ever lived. His father had died of flux six months earlier and without him it was difficult for the family to pay the rent. The local lord was threatening to evict them and the only way the family could survive was for sixteen-year-old Jack to join the European Army.

Jack took a deep breath as he walked along the path. He knew his mother was standing in the cottage's doorway. He wanted to look back at her one last time, but he couldn't bear to see her sad face again.

He took another deep breath. He wouldn't look back. He would keep walking up the road, keep trudging forward and eventually get to Bristol and the nearest army barracks.

The road curved to the right and the forest thickened on either side. Soon the cottage would be out of sight. If he were going to look back, he had to do it now.

But he didn't. He just kept walking around the bend.

He stopped for a moment. Even if he looked back now he wouldn't be able to see the cottage. The cold pressed against his face. A crow squawked in the distance.

He'd done it. He'd left.

Now there was nothing stopping him from marching all the way to Bristol.

9

A cry rang out across the camp.

Jack woke instantly and sat up so quickly his head smacked into the underside of the wagon. He winced and spluttered a curse.

Two further cries drifted over the tents.

Rubbing his head, he rolled out from under the wagon and into the grey morning. He felt groggy and disorientated, but at least the pain in his chest had gone. He stumbled to his feet, slipping a little in the mud.

Drizzle had enveloped the landscape and the mountains were no more than dark blurs.

He heard several further cries from the far side of the camp.

'What's going on?' Saleem scrambled away from the wagon, his eyes wild and a knife in his hand.

'Put that away.' Jack nodded at the knife. 'Might just be more Scots. Let's take a look.'

Saleem hid the knife beneath his tunic, but he kept looking around as if some enemy would appear at any moment.

Andrew and the others crawled out from under the wagon, and Jack led them all towards the shouting. Other porters and soldiers were also rising, hurriedly pulling on trousers and unpiling muskets.

Jack reached the edge of the camp and spotted soldiers gathering near the line of the forest. Most of them were staring at something on the ground, while the rest were pointing their muskets in the direction of the woods. He ran across to them and slowed when he saw what they were looking at. Lying in the slick grass, pale and still, were two Saxon soldiers in full uniform. One had an arrow in his neck, blood clotted around the hole where the missile had entered. The other had three arrows jutting out of his chest.

They must have been on sentry duty overnight.

Sergeant Wulfric arrived and his top lip curled into a snarl when he saw the bodies. He looked at the dark woods, as if the trees themselves had killed the men.

Rao, Parihar and Atri hurried across the meadow, straightening their tunics and buckling on their scimitars. When he saw the corpses, Rao crinkled his nose and shoved his handkerchief over his face.

Wulfric crouched and stroked the feather flights on one of the arrows – they were crudely stitched to the shaft with thread. He looked up at Rao. 'Scots.'

Rao pressed his handkerchief harder against his face and shot a look at the trees.

Parihar drew his scimitar, the metal singing. 'We'll teach these savages a lesson.'

Rao waved his hand vaguely in Wulfric's direction. 'Sergeant, cremate the bodies. We need to get moving from here.'

Wulfric stood still. His forehead rippled, as if a variety of different emotions were passing through his head. He opened his mouth, shut it again and finally said, 'Cremate, sir?'

'The Mohammedans bury their dead,' Atri said to Rao in Rajthani.

'Oh.' Rao frowned, waved his hand again at Wulfric and said in Arabic, 'Bury your dead as you will.'

———•———

By mid-morning, the expedition finally set off into the swirling drizzle. Dark shapes loomed out of the mist before them, condensing into trees, knolls and boulders. The shadowy mountains crowded to either side. To Jack, near the back of the column, the front half of the party were apparitions. The Saxons marched silently, no longer singing in their peculiar tongue. The Rajthanan officers rode alongside on their horses, hunched in their overcoats and staring repeatedly at the surrounding slopes. Rao and Parihar were faint blots in the distance, their black parasols hovering above their heads.

The satchel swung at Jack's side as he walked. He'd found a quiet spot and loaded the pistol before they'd set off. He had a feeling he might need the weapon sooner rather than later.

Why had the savages killed the sentries? Because of the shrine?

Wulfric and Parihar were idiots. They shouldn't have desecrated the sacred place. They'd put the whole party in danger and made the journey to Mar more difficult.

Without meaning to, Jack found himself gripping the edge of the satchel tightly. Rao, Parihar and Wulfric – all fools that he had to obey for the time being.

Saleem looked pale and his face was greasy from the rain. He constantly glanced around him. No doubt he was expecting an arrow to come whistling out of the fog at any moment.

It was hardly an unfounded fear.

In an attempt to distract him, Jack said, 'Bloody rain.'

Saleem nodded, but stayed silent, his lips pressed together tightly.

'Does it ever do anything *but* rain in Scotland?' Andrew said.

The others from Shropshire chuckled and even Saleem managed a smile.

They pressed on along the valley until midday, the soft rain continuing to float around them. Jack noticed they were constantly passing through strong sattva streams, many wider than two hundred yards. Clearly, much of Scotland was rich in sattva.

They stopped for lunch, and then the guide led the way uphill. At first the incline was gentle and the carts and wagons rolled easily over the grass, but then the slope steepened and turned rocky. Boulders protruded from the earth and patches of scree covered the ground. The vehicles' wheels squealed as they juddered over the loose stones.

It became so steep the Rajthanans were forced to dismount. Jack and the others had to push the wagon to help the oxen. Several times a wheel jammed in a crevice and they had to lift the vehicle over the obstacle.

'Where's this guide taking us?' Andrew said. 'Does he have any idea?'

The men laughed, but Jack had real doubts. *Did* the guide know which direction to take? Was he lost?

Then the underside of the wagon thudded into a boulder and wedged itself tight. The oxen bellowed and gouged the earth with their hooves, but they couldn't drag the vehicle forward. The driver cracked his whip, but the animals were still unable to move the wagon.

Jack cursed under his breath. Not again.

He crouched, peered under the vehicle and saw that the rock was jammed tight against the axle and one wheel – but, thankfully, nothing was broken.

He stood up again. 'Right, lads. We'll have to lift it.'

'You lot again.' Wulfric strutted down the slope. 'Get that thing moving.'

Jack and his men took up positions around the wagon. When Jack yelled 'Lift!' they all yanked up, grunting and twisting their faces. Jack wrenched as hard as he could, the tendons in his arms aching and his neck muscles snapping taut.

But the wagon didn't move.

Jack released his grip. 'Wait, lads. Something's caught.'

He crouched and peered under the vehicle again. It was dark and he couldn't make out what was holding the wagon down. He went to slide underneath for a better look when he felt a strap across his back. It didn't hurt but the surprise made him jump.

'Get on with it, scum,' Wulfric said behind him.

Jack paused.

That was it. That was bloody it.

It was as though a pool of oil had been lit inside him.

He swivelled round, straightened and took two quick steps towards Wulfric. 'Do that again and my boot will go right up your arse.'

Wulfric narrowed his eye and a smile stretched across his lips. 'Didn't like Old Wulfric giving you a slap?' He struck Jack lightly on the chest with the strap and smiled even wider.

Jack's hand shook. His head felt hot and full of blood.

He mustn't hit Wulfric.

'Coward, are you?' Wulfric said. 'Afraid of Old Wulfric?'

Although Jack couldn't see them, he sensed the other men watching. Everyone was silent. The only sound was the snuffling of the animals and the soft rush of the wind.

'Come on, scum,' Wulfric said. 'If you want to fight—'

Jack heard a crunch, followed by the screech of wood. He spun round in time to see the wagon's backboard fly apart, sending splinters tumbling through the air. The chains, which had been attached to the board, flew up and the statue slid off the back, canvas and ropes flapping about it. Jack's comrades flung themselves out of the way, Saleem rolling to the side of the track just in time.

Except for Andrew.

The statue slammed into his chest and pummelled him to the ground. He lay pinned, the top of his torso and head poking out from under the metal figure, but the rest of his body underneath.

No.

Jack rushed across to the statue. At the same time, the oxen, now free of the heavy load, sprang forward, wrenching the wagon over the boulder.

Andrew was alive, but he was gasping for breath and his eyes were glazed. A rock partially supported the statue, but a large part of the weight was pressing down on the lad. He moved his arms feebly like a crushed beetle.

Christ.

'Here!' Jack shouted. 'Everyone. Move this thing!'

Within seconds, Saleem and the others clustered around the murti. Robert roared and slammed into the side of the statue, the canvas cover buckling. They all lifted, their feet skidding. Saleem fell and splashed in the mud. The rain bathed them in beads of moisture.

Jack heard a shout of surprise, glanced up and saw a strange sight. One of Robert's gang had let go of the statue and now stood with his hand on the side of his head. The shaft of an arrow poked out of his ear. He looked almost comical for a moment, a jester performing an act, but then blood pulsed between his fingers and drooled down his neck. He staggered, toppled into an awkward sitting position and gave a long moan.

Another arrow hissed through the rain and disappeared overhead.

'Savages!' Wulfric shouted.

A swarm of arrows now flickered about them, bouncing off rocks, impaling the ground and hammering into the sides of the carts. It was as though the sky were raining sticks. Missiles thudded into several more men. One porter, with an arrow in his chest, stumbled into the gloom, crying out for the Lord to save him. Other men lay writhing and moaning on the ground.

Jack glanced down at Andrew, who was still and pale.

Was he alive? There was no time to check.

'Move this bloody statue!' Jack rammed his body into the side of the huge figure. The others joined him, despite the arrows dancing around them.

Blood roared in Jack's ears and his heart bashed in his chest. He wouldn't let Andrew die. They had to move the statue. Had to. He'd allowed the young man to come on this journey and it was his responsibility to keep him safe. And it would be wrong, unjust, for anything to happen to Andrew.

An arrow slapped the canvas and bounced over Jack's head.

Barnabas, one of the Shropshire lads, gasped and fell back with a missile in his mouth.

Christ. They had to move that statue quickly.

'He's dead,' Saleem shouted.

Jack looked down. Saleem was crouching, his finger pressed to Andrew's neck. Andrew lay still, eyes wide and mouth open, as if he were staring at something in horror.

Jack squatted, pushed aside Saleem's finger and felt for a pulse. Nothing. The lad was gone. There was no doubt.

Damn it.

An arrow whispered between Jack and Saleem's faces.

Saleem froze for a moment, but Jack grasped him and yanked him over to a small hollow beside a boulder. Robert crashed down next to them and the other men scrambled to find what little cover they could.

'Over here!' Wulfric blew a whistle. 'Two lines!'

About fifty soldiers had scrambled to the back of the column and now arranged themselves into two rows facing out towards either side of the track. At Wulfric's command, they loaded and fired. The weapons crackled, flame and white smoke jetting from the barrels. Arrows still hailed down. A couple of soldiers lurched back with shafts in their chests.

A horn blower somewhere further up the hill sounded the alarm, although it was hardly necessary.

Jack grasped the satchel still hanging at his side. Should he draw his pistol and help? If the situation got worse, he would, but at the moment he didn't want to reveal to Wulfric and the Rajthanans that he had a weapon.

An arrow struck the ground nearby, slithered along the stones and stopped near his feet. Another speared a puddle and stood there quivering.

Wulfric blasted his whistle several times and barked the commands to reload.

In unison, the soldiers placed their muskets butt-down on the ground, plucked cartridges from their ammunition pouches, bit them open, poured the powder down the barrels and stuffed in the balls. They then rammed down the bullets with their rods, retrieved percussion caps from their pockets and pressed these on to their weapons' nipples. They moved fluidly, oblivious to the noise and confusion about them, even when three of their number fell to arrows.

Finally, they raised their muskets and blasted into the drifts of rain, the clouds of smoke blurring them completely for a moment.

Rao, Parihar and Atri came skidding down the track, their scimitars swinging wildly at their hips.

'Can't see them, sir,' Wulfric said. 'They're hiding all around us.'

Rao and Parihar snapped open spyglasses and stared through them. An arrow hopped along the ground and struck the side of Rao's boot. The Captain jumped in fright, but the missile hadn't harmed him.

'We can't shoot them like this,' Parihar said in Rajthani to Rao. 'We'll have to get the men up there.'

Rao nodded and ducked as an arrow whizzed overhead, although it was far too high to hit him.

'Sergeant,' Parihar said to Wulfric. 'Split the men up. Deploy knives. Get up there and sort these savages out.'

Wulfric blew his whistle and barked at his men, waving also to those who were still further up the slope. He grasped his musket and slipped out the catch so that the knife clacked into place. 'Allah is great!'

'Allah is great!' the soldiers repeated.

With a roar, Wulfric charged up the slope to the right of the track, about half the men following, all of them snarling and shouting in Saxon.

Parihar drew his blade, which flickered in the dim light, and held it above his head. He bellowed and sprinted up the incline to the left, the remaining soldiers scrambling after him.

Clouds of arrows continued to batter the party. One plunged into a mule, which brayed and ran off between the rocks, its load spilling off. Several wounded porters crawled across the ground. Others fled down the track, most of them picked off by the savages' missiles.

An arrow struck the rock above Jack's head and snapped in half. He glanced around for somewhere better to hide, but there was nowhere nearby.

Rao and Atri scuttled under a mule cart. Arrows bounced off the vehicle and jammed into the wood. The mule bucked and stomped, but a driver crouching beside it held it in place.

An eerie wail drifted across the valley. At first it seemed like the cry of some strange bird, but as it grew louder Jack recognised it – pipes. The minstrels in England had a variety of different pipes, but none made a sound quite like this. It was harsh and discordant, and set the hairs on the back of his neck quivering.

Jack glanced at Saleem – his eyes were wide and his skin was grey. Jack put his hand gently on the lad's shoulder for a moment.

Then he caught the sound of chanting, just audible over the skirl of the pipes and the cries of the Saxons. The savages were shouting in their strange tongue.

'It's a war cry,' Robert said. 'Can't understand it all, but I can catch a few words.'

Jack listened carefully. How many savages were there? It was hard to tell. The cries bounced around the mountains and valleys. Was it a few hundred? A few thousand?

The mule driver collapsed to the ground, an arrow in his neck, and the mule squealed and scrambled up the slope, the cart clattering behind. Rao and Atri, still lying on the ground, were suddenly exposed. Rao flung his hand over his turban, as if that would somehow protect him. Atri swung up into a crouch, but an arrow slammed into his chest. The siddha tried to stand up, slipped back to his knees, and then fell forward until he was on all fours.

'Use a power!' Rao screamed in Rajthani.

'No,' Atri shouted back.

Rao grabbed Atri beneath the arms and began dragging him to the side of the track. Arrows pierced the ground all around them and smacked against the rocks.

'Use a power,' Rao shouted again.

Atri grunted. 'Must stay pure. The Brahmastra—'

An arrow thudded into Atri's stomach and he groaned.

Rao glanced at the wound and pulled more frantically.

Atri's eyes rolled white. He began mouthing words silently. Feebly, he raised one arm and a bulb of blue, translucent flame flickered around his hand and trickled down his wrist.

The men crouching beside Jack all gasped.

'Black magic.' Robert crossed himself.

It looked as though Atri were about to summon a ball of sattva-fire. But then he shut his eyes, dropped his arm and slumped forward.

Rao shouted, dragged more urgently and finally got the limp siddha over to a boulder beside the track. He shook Atri, as if he could wake him, but it was obvious the siddha was dead.

What had Atri said?

Must stay pure.

Jack understood. Atri must have been a pure siddha, one who'd never used a power and so remained unblocked. Atri had stopped himself from becoming impure even when he'd been hit by an arrow.

He must have been saving himself for something.

And what was that Rajthani word? *Brahmastra.* Jack had never heard that before and had no idea what it meant.

Suddenly the arrows stopped. The chanting and the pipes vanished. Robert, Saleem and the others looked about in surprise.

Then Jack heard shouts and screams. A couple of muskets cracked. Clearly, the Saxons had found the Scots and attacked.

Jack risked standing and looking gingerly over the top of the boulder. He couldn't see far through the drizzle, but he made out the dark smudge of a forest further up the slope and, before that, figures running about in the open ground. He couldn't tell who were Saxons and who were Scots, nor who had the upper hand. But he guessed the Scots were fleeing, as the shouting was subsiding already and no further shots were fired.

Robert stood beside him. 'Looks like it might all be over soon.'

Jack nodded. Then he spotted Gareth, one of his comrades from Shropshire, sitting next to a rock less than ten feet away. The lad's head lolled to one side and there were five arrow shafts sticking out of his torso.

Jack scrambled to Gareth's side. But of course he was dead.

Another comrade down.

Andrew, Gareth and Barnabas. Gone.

10

———✦———

'I don't know the right words . . . what the priest would say.' The old porter removed his woollen hat and fiddled with it. 'All I know is they were our comrades and now they're gone and all of us here, I'm sure, hope they're smiling down at us from heaven.'

The man paused, then began saying the Our Father in Latin. The other porters, who'd congregated around the mass grave, mumbled along to the prayer.

Jack looked down into the pit. The twenty-one porters who'd died in the attack lay draped over each other like fish dumped on the deck of a boat. His three dead colleagues were somewhere in the pile, but they must have been near the bottom as he couldn't see them.

Porters began shovelling dirt into the hole. The earth dashed over the dead men's faces and bodies and limbs, and gradually the corpses were covered over.

Jack crossed himself. It was inevitable that some of his group would die on this journey, but that didn't make it any easier. Was there anything he could have done to save them? Was there something he could have done better?

No, he was sure he'd done his best.

Saleem stood nearby, his eyes red and watery. Next to him, the five remaining lads from Shropshire all stared solemnly into the grave.

Jack crossed himself again and looked up the hill. The drizzle had cleared, but the light remained dim and silver. All colour was bleached from the grass, the mud, the lifeless trees.

The bodies of hundreds of natives lay scattered across the slope. According to Wulfric, the Saxons had faced up to a thousand savages, although most had fled as soon as the soldiers charged at them. Judging by the number of arrows that had been fired at the party, a thousand was probably an accurate estimate.

About a hundred yards away, the Saxons had congregated around a cluster of graves – twenty soldiers had perished in the fighting. To the left of the Mohammedans, on the track, around fifteen soldiers and ten porters who'd been badly injured were being helped on to mule carts. The wounded faced a long journey back to civilisation. They would have to pass through dangerous territory, with no more than a handful of porters to accompany them. It was unlikely many would make it.

Jack's gaze drifted further up the hill to where three funeral pyres blazed. The yellow flames were brilliant in the midst of the drab landscape. The smoke from the damp wood trailed off to the right and blended into the ash-coloured clouds. Within the fires, invisible from this distance, lay the bodies of Siddha Atri and two batmen.

The remaining Rajthanans stood silhouetted before the fires. There were now only six of them left: Rao, Parihar, two lieutenants and two batmen.

Jack could just make out the red blot of the Captain's turban and he found himself clenching his jaw. Andrew had died because Rao had insisted on dragging a giant statue through the wilds. The Captain was a fool and had no idea how to command an expedition.

And what about Barnabas and Gareth? They'd been killed by savages, but why had the Scots attacked? Probably because Parihar and Wulfric had destroyed their shrine. Those two should have shown some respect for a sacred place. Their actions had cost the party dearly.

He wanted to leave the expedition, taking his men with him.

But if they did that, the savages would slaughter them within hours. They would never make it to Mar on their own.

For the time being, they had to stick with the party.

But once they got to Mar, they would break away as soon as they could.

Jack and Saleem tramped between the rocks towards a pile of sacks that had slipped from the back of a mule. The animal had run about two hundred yards before the load had fallen off and Jack and Saleem had been sent to recover as much as they could.

'What's that?' Saleem pointed at a lump lying amongst a cluster of thistles to the left of the sacks.

Jack frowned. Maybe it was some further piece of baggage. 'Let's take a look.'

They strode over to the thistles and Saleem gasped when they saw the shape was a Scot. At first the man looked dead, but then his eyelids flickered open. He had a tangled mop of ginger hair, a thick beard and skin so pale it seemed to glow against the black mud. He wore a filthy, shaggy cloak that was wrapped about his body like a shroud and his feet were bare, the soles covered in a crust of yellow calluses. Incredibly, the man seemed to have survived in this climate without boots.

There were two bullet holes in his chest and the blood had spread and hardened into two circles on his cloak.

The Scot's eyes focused as Jack and Saleem looked down. He reached out to them with his hand and opened his mouth as if to speak, but only a low hiss came out.

'Out of the way.' A Saxon strode across the slope. He slung his musket from his shoulder and released the catch, the knife snapping into place. He stood over the Scot, paused for a second, then slammed the knife into the man's chest. There was a squelching sound as the blade slid into flesh and a line of blood squirted up.

'Come on.' Jack drew Saleem away. There was no point staying to watch, and it would do no good to plead for the man's life either. He would have died soon from his injuries anyway. It was kinder to kill him quickly.

They walked over to the baggage. There were too many sacks to be carried all at once, so they each lifted one, staggered back to the track and loaded them both on to a cart. As they turned to head back up the hill, Jack caught a voice nearby saying that word again: *Brahmastra*. He stopped and made out men speaking in Rajthani.

'You go on,' he said to Saleem. 'I'll catch up in a minute.'

Saleem trudged off, while Jack ducked down behind a row of boulders – he didn't want anyone to notice him eavesdropping. Staying crouched, he scrambled along the line of rocks, reached a gap and peered around the corner.

Rao and Parihar were sitting on a slab of stone. The Lieutenant was polishing his scimitar with a cloth, while Rao was staring glumly at the ground.

'We can't turn back now,' Parihar said.

'Without Atri . . .' Rao shook his head. 'We won't be able to deal with Mahajan or the Brahmastra.'

Parihar lifted his blade and admired his handiwork. 'We still have swords and firearms. Always been enough for me.'

Rao pressed his handkerchief to his nose. 'Wish I had your confidence.'

'Look, my friend. We've come this far. We're close. It won't look good if we give up. Let's at least find Mahajan and see what he's up to. If we can't deal with him, fine, we'll turn back and report our findings.'

Rao nodded slowly. 'I suppose you're right.'

'You have Atri's notes?'

Rao patted a satchel sitting on the rock beside him. Jack recognised the black leather bag – he'd often seen Atri retrieving his notebook from it.

'Right.' Parihar stood and sheathed his scimitar. 'What's your decision, Captain?'

Rao put away his handkerchief and sighed. 'We'll carry on.'

'Excellent. You've made the right choice.'

Rao stood and the two men set off back towards the track.

Jack turned and leant against the rock.

Atri's notes. They must contain something important if Rao and Parihar thought it necessary to hold on to them. Jack would give anything to know what. But it would be difficult to get his hands on the notebook – and, in any case, he wouldn't be able to read the writing.

And the Brahmastra? What was that?

Brahma was a Rajthanan god. In Rajthani, *astra* meant some sort of weapon, as far as he could remember. That was interesting. Brahma's weapon. Was that it? Was that what Mahajan was working on?

Jack rubbed his forehead. So many questions and so few answers.

⬥

The statue swayed as the wagon bounced up the rocky slope. Jack and his men had secured the murti with chains and ropes, but none of them dared walk immediately behind.

The party was silent. No one spoke unless they had to, and when they did, they kept their voices low. Even the animals seemed quieter.

The column was smaller than before. Only sixty-three Saxons marched uphill, followed by just under seventy porters and a diminished number of carts, wagons and pack mules. And the men looked tired and dishevelled. How would they fare if the savages attacked again?

Saleem shivered and stared out at the hills. 'You think they'll come back?'

'The Scots?' Jack shook his head. 'Think they've been scared off for now. They won't have seen muskets before.'

All the same, Jack found himself scouring the area for any sign of movement. He wasn't as certain as he sounded.

They were all exhausted by the time they reached the top of the scarp and Saleem was stumbling and panting. But as they continued down the far side of the hill, a cool breeze revived them and Jack was certain he could sense everyone's relief as they left that desolate battlefield behind.

They made camp beside a long, narrow lake. The wind had strengthened in the late afternoon and now whistled across the open ground. The soldiers struggled to erect their flapping tents, and porters wrestled with the yards of canvas that made up the Rajthanans' marquees.

As Jack was helping Robert and his gang build a fire, Wulfric appeared from the semi-dark.

Jack stood up straight. What now?

Wulfric grunted, but hardly gave him a second look and instead cast his eye over the group of porters. His gaze finally settled on Robert and a couple of his gang. 'You three. Come with me. They need help with the officers' dinner.'

Robert glanced at Jack.

'Come on!' Wulfric shouted. 'The officers are hungry.'

There was little Robert and the others could do but agree, and they loped off after the Sergeant.

Jack was puzzled. The officers' dinner? Normally only Rajthanans served officers. Unless they'd been blessed by a Rajthanan priest, Europeans were considered too impure to cook food for the higher jatis. Still, there were only two Rajthanan batmen left alive now and no doubt they would be stretched trying to prepare meals for the officers.

Jack and his men ate with the remainder of Robert's gang. The supply of barley was running low and they made only a thin broth rather than hearty pottage.

As they finished eating, Robert and his comrades appeared from out of the darkness, sat quickly and demanded their share.

As Robert slurped his meal, Jack asked, 'So, what happened to you?'

Robert looked up and grinned. 'Och, they're mad, those Rajthanans. We had to help the batmen with dinner, but we weren't allowed to touch any food. All I could do was wash pots and knives, throw away scrapings, that sort of thing.' He shook his head and took another spoonful of food. 'Mad.'

They sat around talking for a few minutes and then silence settled over them. Jack thought again about the three Shropshire lads lying buried in this strange land. No doubt the others would all be thinking of their own fallen friends.

Jack glanced out into the dark. He made out the sentries' lanterns dotted around the perimeter of the camp. The lights seemed small and fragile in the vast night.

A gust of wind moaned and Saleem's eyes widened.

'You think they're out there?' Saleem asked.

Jack paused. The savages might well be out there, but it was best not to think about that.

'We'll be all right.' He took a final look into the pitch black pressing all around them, then pulled his hood over his head and stood. 'Let's get some sleep. It's been a hard day.'

⸻

The sound of a musket shot rolled across the valley.

Jack's heart jumped and he bolted to his feet. The crack of the firearm seemed to echo in his head before trailing off into a whisper.

'What was that?' Saleem sat up, his eyes faint glints.

The other five Shropshire lads also leapt up from where they'd been sleeping.

The thin sliver of the moon was blacked out by cloud and Jack couldn't see more than a few feet ahead of him. Squinting, he made out the huge blot of the Ganesh statue. To the left of that, sentry lanterns wove about in different directions.

Another shot rang out, followed by shouts.

'Savages.' Saleem reached for his hidden knife.

Jack grabbed his arm. 'Wait.' He squatted down. 'All of you, wait.'

The others crouched beside Jack and stared at him intently, their faces pale moons in the dim light. Saleem was breathing heavily and Jack noticed the lad's hand was shaking slightly.

The shouting continued but no further shots were fired.

'We'll stay here for the moment,' Jack said. 'If we're attacked we'll defend ourselves. Stay close to the wagon so we don't get split up in the dark.'

His comrades nodded seriously and they all sat with their backs to the vehicle.

A whistle blasted and Jack heard Wulfric bellowing orders. Dim figures rushed about the camp, only visible as they flickered past the white tents.

Saleem gave a loud yelp and sprang away from the wagon.

Jack's heart flew. He wrenched the pistol from the satchel and spun round.

'God's cause, will you calm down.' Robert's bushy head was poking out from underneath the wagon. He must have crept across from where he'd been sleeping.

Jack exhaled and grinned.

Robert crawled out and gave Jack a curious look. 'Quite a weapon you have there, wee man.'

'Aye.' Jack put the pistol away. 'And I'd appreciate you keeping quiet about it.'

'Don't you worry.' Robert's eyes twinkled. 'I'll keep your little secret to myself.'

'Is it the savages?' Saleem motioned to where the lanterns were still bouncing about in the dark.

'No, Sultan.' Robert's forehead creased. 'Some of the lads have run off.'

'Run off?' Jack peered into the dark. Were they mad? They

weren't soldiers, but they could still be shot for deserting. 'How many?'

'Ten or so,' Robert said. 'No more than that.'

The darkness seemed to thicken as Jack stared into it.

Only ten men? That was a desperate move. Even if they escaped the camp, the Scots would easily pick them off.

Wulfric's whistle blew several more times and after a couple of minutes a horn blower sounded a series of notes.

'What's that about?' Robert said.

'It's the call to assembly,' Jack said. 'Come on.'

They stood and walked towards the centre of the camp. Even with his exceptional eyesight, Jack found it difficult to pick his way in the dark. He tripped on a guy rope at one point and Saleem stuck his foot in a pot.

They found a congregation of Saxons and porters standing in the open space around the flagpole. Several soldiers carried lanterns, which sent light swaying across the grass. Wulfric stood in the middle of the group. He'd obviously dressed in a hurry as his tunic buttons were undone, he wore no cap and he hadn't tied on his puttees. A lantern lay tilted at his feet, the light casting his face skull-like.

With one hand, he gripped the hair of a corpse, holding it up in a sitting position.

The dead man was a porter – Jack recognised the man's face, although he'd never spoken to him. The man's eyes stared into the distance and his arms hung limply at his side. Blood encrusted the front of his tunic.

'God almighty,' Robert whispered and crossed himself.

Jack sensed the men about him bristle. Porters murmured to each other and glared at Wulfric.

'This is a traitor.' Wulfric shook the head of the dead man. 'You all look at him. This is what happens if you try running off like a coward. Don't think you can get away. Old Wulfric has his eye on each one of you! Old Wulfric will hunt you down if he has to himself!'

The porters were sullen as they packed away the camp in the pallid dawn. Few spoke and when they did, it was only to mutter about the events of the night before.

Robert and his two comrades were summoned to help prepare the Rajthanans' breakfast. When he'd finished, Robert bounded back to where Jack and the others were still at work. 'There's a rumour going around,' he said. 'Only five of the deserters were killed last night. Five got away.'

'Could be true.' Jack stared into the thicket of trees the men had apparently run into. 'The soldiers wouldn't want to chase them too far at night. We only saw one body.'

'Aye,' Robert said. 'An unburied body.'

The others present grumbled at this. Wulfric had decreed that the deserters would receive no burial rites and said their bodies had been dumped in the forest for the crows to feed on.

With breakfast finished, and the camp packed away, the column moved out once again. As before, silence seemed to oppress the party. The men only spoke when necessary, the Saxons didn't sing and Jack spotted many men glancing nervously into the surrounding hills and mountains. The doleful tick of the drummer's beat drifted over the party.

At midday they paused for lunch. Porters set up the awning as usual and Robert was instructed to aid the batmen. Jack and his men ate a spare meal of barley soup. Supplies were running low and they hadn't seen a single village to trade with since they'd reached the Highlands.

If the natives would even want to trade.

In the afternoon, they wound their way higher into the mountains. A cold wind spiralled down from the snow-dusted peaks.

The line of fire in Jack's chest came and went. It was never more than a throbbing ache, but it was a reminder of what was to come.

There were just over two weeks left before Kanvar's cure faded.

How accurate was Kanvar's estimate? Could Jack die sooner? Later? Could he have another month?

He drew his hood tighter about his face as the breeze plucked at it.

As they descended from a high saddle, a skirl of pipes twisted down from the mountainside. The hairs stood up on the back of Jack's neck and Saleem gasped and scurried to hide behind the wagon.

One of the soldiers fired his musket up the slope and the pipes went silent.

'Keep moving!' Wulfric shouted. 'Don't stop, you idiots!'

The drivers cracked their whips and shouted at their animals. The oxen kicked up clods of earth and the pack mules trotted more quickly, their loads swaying on their backs. The Rajthanans paced up and down the column on their horses, surveying the mountainside through their spyglasses.

After around fifteen minutes, they finally left the open ground and zigzagged down through a birch forest. Jack felt relieved to reach the relative cover of the trees. Finally, in the late afternoon, the guide led them into a wide valley where high grasses waved in the wind. The ground was soft and even, and they made good progress. But after thirty minutes the wail of pipes rolled down from a mountain to their right.

Jack searched the heather and scrub on the slope, but saw no sign of movement. Saleem bit his bottom lip and fiddled with his sleeve.

'Don't slow down!' Wulfric bellowed.

The sound of the pipes continued to swirl down. And then further pipes began squealing from the other side of the valley. The two drones rolled around the hills and seemed to beat like a weapon against the party.

They all marched as quickly as they could. Jack's legs ached with tiredness but he hardly noticed. Looking around the valley he could see they were horribly exposed. There was almost no cover, and if the natives decided to fire arrows at them they would be in a difficult situation.

The cries of the pipes spooked the animals and the mules often shied or bucked. The oxen drawing the statue wagon roared, grunted and at one point tried to bolt. They were only stopped when two drivers yanked at the yoke of the front two animals.

After an hour, the pipes suddenly fell silent. Jack kept thinking he heard a trace of the squealing, but when he listened closely he realised he must have imagined it. The sound had definitely vanished.

'Thank God almighty,' Robert said. 'That was giving me a headache. And I'm a Scot!'

The porters nearby chuckled, but Jack was still wary. He squinted at the slopes and although he still saw nothing, he couldn't believe the natives had given up. They might well be watching the party at that very moment, discussing what to do next.

By the time dusk thickened, the party was still in the valley and still just as exposed as before. But as it was too dangerous to travel in the dark, they were forced to make camp out in the open.

The wind whipped the campfire as Jack sat slurping his thin broth with the others. On the far side of the camp, the two remaining batmen scurried back and forth between the cooking enclosure and the dining tent, carrying covered silver thalis, goblets and bowls full of food.

'Officers are still eating well,' muttered one of Robert's gang.

'We should be out hunting for food,' another said.

The first man lowered his spoon. 'We should be running.'

'Keep your voices down.' Robert nodded in the direction of a pair of sentries standing about twenty yards away. 'That's dangerous talk. You saw what happened to the last lot who tried that.'

'If we don't try something we'll be dead in days anyway,' the man said.

A glimmer in the distance caught Jack's eye. 'Whatever you do, I wouldn't go anywhere now. Look.' He pointed at the light.

The group shifted on their haunches and stared into the pitch black. A yellow glow flickered high up from the ground. It looked as though it were floating in the sky, although it must have been on a mountainside. At first Jack thought it was a bonfire, but then, as he stared harder, it coalesced into a distinct shape.

A cross.

On fire.

A murmur rippled through the small group.

'God's cause.' Robert tugged at his beard. 'What are they playing at?'

Disquiet spread across the camp and porters and soldiers pointed up at the eerie light. Wulfric blew his whistle several times and ordered further soldiers to take up positions as sentries. The Rajthanans stood in a small group outside the dining tent, peering into the darkness through their spyglasses.

Jack glanced at Saleem, who was staring at the distant fire without blinking. Jack patted the lad on the shoulder and whispered to him, 'You stay strong. We'll just keep our feet marching along the right path.'

Saleem swallowed and nodded, but Jack wasn't sure whether his words had given him much comfort this time.

The savages were out there in the dark. The savages were watching and waiting.

11

A wall of mist surrounded Jack. He paused for a moment and stared into the swaying fronds. The soldiers' tents were pale blurs and the officers' marquees red smears. The world beyond the camp was invisible, the white fog completely blotting out the valley, trees, hills and mountains.

He shivered from the cold and returned to the task at hand – securing the statue. He was standing on the back of the wagon, pulling a section of rope tight over the canvas-covered figure. The other porters were packing away the camp and stamping out cooking fires.

As he tied the rope to the sideboard, he heard Robert calling out behind him, 'Hey, you lot! Come quick!'

Jack looked around and saw the big man running out of the haze. As usual, Robert and his comrades had been helping to prepare the Rajthanans' breakfast.

'What is it?' Jack asked.

Robert stopped near the wagon, panting. 'One of the lads is in trouble. Come on.' He turned and set off into the fog again.

Jack leapt to the ground and jogged with Saleem and the others over to the Rajthanans' marquees. A small crowd of porters and soldiers formed ahead in the mist. As Jack drew nearer, he saw four Saxons holding on to a porter to prevent him from fleeing. The man was one of the two who'd been helping Robert in the cooking enclosure.

Wulfric stood in front of the porter, his hands balled into fists. Rao and Parihar had abandoned their breakfast, left the awning and now stood nearby.

'Scum!' Wulfric bawled. 'Dirtied the officers' food. Ruined it.'

The trapped man's face was slightly flushed and his eyes were shiny. He looked ready to fight if he had to, but for the moment he held himself back. 'I didn't touch the food, sir.'

'Didn't touch it!' Wulfric's eye opened wider. 'Don't need to touch it. Your shadow, see. Even your shadow's filthy.'

Jack understood instantly. Even a European's shadow, if it passed over a Rajthanan's food, could defile it. The man must have walked too close to the awning without realising it. Bad luck, as there were barely any shadows at all in the dim light.

'Didn't know anything about shadows, sir,' the man said.

'Too late.' Wulfric stepped closer. His head was bare and his bald scalp shone faintly. 'You've done it now.'

Parihar spoke to Rao in Rajthani. 'He'll have to be flogged.'

Rao looked at the porters crowding around him and pressed his handkerchief to his nose. 'Is that wise?'

'You have to treat these natives firmly,' Parihar said. 'It's the only thing they understand.'

Rao hesitated, then nodded. 'Very well. Go ahead.'

Parihar put his hands on his hips and addressed the gathering in English. 'This man is found guilty of intentionally defiling an officer's victuals. He is hereby sentenced to be flogged.' He turned to Wulfric. 'Sergeant, three hundred lashes.'

Wulfric gave a slow grin, rolled up his sleeves and spoke to the soldiers restraining Robert's comrade. 'Tie him up on one of the wagons. I'll do this myself.'

A murmur of disquiet flickered through the crowd. Most of the porters had by now congregated near the awning. All the Saxons had massed behind Rao and Parihar.

Jack's heart beat faster. Three hundred lashes was a severe punishment. The man would barely be standing after that and would need hospital treatment. He wouldn't be able to wear clothes on his back, let alone continue marching.

The gathering of porters muttered and drew closer together,

blocking the way to the rest of the camp. Robert stood near the front of the group, glaring at Wulfric.

Wulfric looked into the crowd and narrowed his eye. 'Out of the way, scum.'

The porters didn't move. They stared back with eyes that were tired but determined. Their clothes were tattered and filthy, their faces were haggard, but they weren't prepared to back down.

Jack was pleased the men were standing up for Robert's friend. But how was this going to end?

The soldiers shuffled into a loose row facing the porters. Those who had their muskets to hand snapped out the knives.

There were around sixty porters, all unarmed, save for a few who carried kitchen knives or rocks. They faced sixty-three trained soldiers, some of them armed. It would not be an even fight and the Saxons would undoubtedly win. But it would be a bloody scrap.

The mist swirled about the two opposing groups, hemming them in, as if this one spot were now the only place that existed in the world.

Wulfric took two steps towards the porters. He stood alone, facing them all, eyeing the front row of men one by one. He spoke in a slow, cold voice. 'I said, out of the way.'

The porters shifted and fidgeted. Some glanced at each other. But none moved.

A batman jogged over to Rao and Parihar and handed them pistols. Parihar took a weapon, pointed it into the air and fired. The crack reverberated across the valley.

Several of the porters flinched, but they remained where they were.

Parihar's nostrils flared and he puffed out his chest. 'Insolence.'

Jack could see this was heading towards a disaster. He had to do something.

'Captain Rao.' He stepped out from the crowd of porters. 'There's no need for this, sir. This man made a mistake. He's not familiar with your customs. He meant no harm.'

Parihar turned to Jack, his eyes flashing. 'That is no excuse, you pink bastard.'

'Sir, please.' Jack kept his eyes on Rao. 'We're all stuck out here in the middle of nowhere. We have to pull together. Otherwise the savages will have us. If you spare this man, we porters will go back to our work.'

Jack was uncertain whether he really could make this promise. He didn't speak for all the porters, but he suspected they would be happy to avoid a fight so long as their colleague wasn't flogged.

Rao pressed his handkerchief harder against his face, as though he'd smelt something particularly disgusting.

'How dare you speak to the Captain like that,' Parihar said.

'That's it.' Wulfric strode towards Jack, pointing his finger. 'You've said enough now. I'm going to do what I should have done a long time ago.'

'Wait.' Rao lowered his handkerchief. 'Leave him, Sergeant. He's talking sense. There's no point us fighting amongst ourselves.'

'You can't show weakness,' Parihar said in Rajthani. 'You have to show them who's in charge.'

'And get us all killed?' Rao replied.

'They'll back down as soon as we kill the first few of them,' Parihar said.

Rao stood still. His fingers gripped the handkerchief tighter. His eyes flicked from the porters to the soldiers to Jack.

Jack said a Hail Mary in his head. He prayed Rao would make the right decision.

Finally, Rao inhaled sharply and addressed the crowd. 'Listen to me. I will release this man on the understanding nothing like this ever happens again. But see here.' He pointed at the porters, the handkerchief dangling from his hand. 'You are all to obey me when I command you. Any further insubordination will be punished severely.'

The Saxons released Robert's comrade and stepped away from him. The man circled his shoulders, twisted his neck and straightened his tunic, as if he were a proud lord who'd been manhandled by commoners.

The porters all visibly relaxed, their shoulders slumping and their faces softening.

'Come on, lads,' Robert said. 'We've got work to do.'

The gathering broke apart and the men trudged off to continue packing away the camp.

Jack breathed out and realised his heart had been thumping furiously. That had been a close thing. Thank God Rao had seen sense and hadn't listened to that idiot Parihar.

Wulfric, however, stood nearby with his hands on his hips, immobile even as the porters, soldiers and officers drifted away. His single eye bored into Jack, unblinking, still and cold as the moon.

It was late in the morning by the time the expedition set off. The mist had thickened and they found themselves marching through whorls of heavy fog. Ahead of Jack, the column blurred and vanished. Knolls and copses reared up out of the murk, then disappeared as he went past. At times he felt as though he were walking through a dream.

The mist was cold as metal and left a film of moisture on his face.

The relief he'd felt that the incident at breakfast hadn't spilt over into anything more serious quickly faded. The party might have held back from fighting itself, but it was unlikely the savages had left, and it would be impossible to see them coming in the mist. Of course, the haze would hinder the natives as well, but this was their land, they knew the territory.

At least he had the loaded pistol with him, hidden, as always, in the satchel.

Shortly before midday, the mountainsides drew closer, becoming darker in the mist. As the valley narrowed, the men were forced to trudge along a shallow river, skidding and sliding on the wet rocks. The wagon wheels ground against the stones and sprayed water.

The slopes steepened until the party was passing through a gorge. Sheer cliffs rose on either side, while the river churned in between. The white rapids were phosphorescent in the dim light and the rushing sound echoed in the confined space.

Jack looked up. The drifts of mist obscured the cliff tops. This was a good place for an ambush.

A very good place.

He shivered. They were being watched. He was sure of it, even though he couldn't see anyone up there. He had a tracker's sensitivity to his surroundings and an army scout's understanding of dangerous terrains.

It was madness to march through a place like this.

He had to do something.

'Wait here,' he said to Saleem and the others.

He waded forward, the water swilling about his knees. He edged himself past the oxen pulling the statue wagon, smelling the thick scent of the animals' wet hides. Then he dodged around the men, beasts and vehicles of the rest of the baggage train.

When he was about halfway to the front of the column, with the Saxons just visible ahead in the fog, he spotted Wulfric.

He pushed his way through the stream and shouted over the gurgling water. 'Sergeant!'

Wulfric seemed not to hear and didn't turn round.

Jack slipped on a rock, steadied himself, and floundered forward until he was right behind Wulfric. 'Sergeant! We have to turn back. We'll be attacked—'

Wulfric whirled round and slapped Jack in the face with his leather strap. Jack slid back. His cheek stung but he was startled more than anything.

'It's time I taught you a lesson, scum.' Wulfric stepped forward and swung his strap again.

Jack reacted quickly and raised his left hand to protect himself. Wulfric's arm slammed into his. Both of them slipped and had to step back to rebalance themselves.

Wulfric's eye gleamed in the dim light. His face, damp from the mist, glistened like limestone. He beckoned with his finger. 'Come here.'

What was Wulfric playing at? He wanted to fight now? When they were all probably in danger?

Jack felt his face go hot. Wulfric was an idiot. A bloody-minded idiot. All Jack wanted to do at that moment was punch the Sergeant in the face.

Someone up ahead cried out. More shouts followed.

Wulfric frowned and turned.

Jack stared into the mist and made out soldiers darting about in the small space of the gorge. Were the Saxons under attack?

Wulfric strode forward through the bubbling water, swinging his arms wide from his body.

Then a man nearby gasped. Jack swivelled and saw a porter with an arrow in his chest stagger forward. Blood welled from his wound and soaked his tunic red. He coughed and vomited more blood, then toppled over and splashed into the water.

Suddenly arrows hailed down from the bluffs. Missiles thudded into men and animals, dashed the water and skipped off carts and wagons. Porters screamed, choked, stumbled and flapped about in the river. An arrow nailed one man's hand to a cart. Another speared a porter in the eye. The oxen roared and wrestled to free themselves from their yokes.

Jack crouched down instinctively, although with the arrows coming from all directions there was little point. He snatched a look at his surroundings. The cliffs were steep and there was nowhere beneath them to take cover.

They were trapped.

And soon they would all be dead.

Behind him, he heard the crackle of muskets and smelt the

acrid scent of powder smoke. The Saxons were retaliating, but there was little hope of them hitting any of the savages while they were hidden by the mist.

An arrow whistled past in front of Jack's face.

His heart hammered and the fire flickered in his chest.

What to do?

His only thought was to get back to Saleem and the others and then get the hell out of the gorge.

Still crouching, he sloshed his way back downstream. The baggage train had come to a standstill and the porters were either flailing about in the water in their attempts to flee or cowering beneath wagons and carts. A team of oxen bolted and stampeded straight at Jack, arrows sticking out of their backs like pins. He leapt to the side as the animals and wagon careered past.

He waded forward again, dodging bobbing corpses. By now many porters had come to the same conclusion as him. They pushed and shoved as they fought to get back to the end of the gorge. Jack caught an elbow in his ribs, then someone yanked his tunic so that he almost fell. Grunts and cries surrounded him.

The sound of pipes and war cries floated through the mist.

Arrows streamed down, picking off men. And now even rocks and stones plummeted into the gully as the savages hurled whatever they could at the column. A large slab slapped the river next to Jack and sprayed him with water. Another smacked into the head of a porter, flinging out blood and splinters of skull.

The water boiled and turned bright red.

Ahead of Jack, a wagon and a team of oxen had tumbled on to their sides. Several of the animals were dead, but the others thrashed and groaned as they struggled to free themselves, the water frothing about them. Jack swerved out of the way and stumbled on.

Someone pushed him from behind. He slipped, tried to grasp a man nearby for support, missed and splashed into the river. He rolled out of the way of the rushing crowd, grabbed a rock jutting out from the cliff and hauled himself back up again. He was drenched, but worse than that, his pistol would have been soaked and was unlikely to fire now.

Damn it. Just when he needed a weapon.

He surged ahead again and finally found Saleem crouching beneath a slight overhang in the rock face. The lad's features were frozen in fear and his eyes were rimmed with red.

But he was alive. Thank God.

Jack squatted and grasped Saleem's shoulder. 'Where are the others?'

Saleem's bottom lip trembled and he nodded at the water beside him. Jack looked across and saw two of the lads from Shropshire floating in the river, arrows in their torsos and clouds of blood drifting around them.

Christ. Two more of their little group gone.

He shut his eyes, clenched his teeth. It was hard to see young men die so easily. But they'd believed in the crusade and done what they thought was right.

He was proud of them.

He opened his eyes again. 'What about the other three?'

Saleem looked down. 'They ran off. Said they'd had enough. I wouldn't go with them.'

Jack pursed his lips. He couldn't blame the three lads for fleeing. It'd been brave of them to come even this far.

'Jack!' a voice called behind him.

He spun round and saw Robert bounding through the river.

The big man crouched. 'We're all getting out of here.' He nodded towards the end of the gorge. 'The Saxons are being slaughtered. We'll all be dead if we stay here.'

Jack grasped Robert's sleeve. 'You sure about this?'

'You're not staying here, are you?' Robert said.

'I have to.'

Robert scowled. 'You're mad.'

Jack sighed. He didn't want Robert to go. The big man had

been an asset on this expedition and, more than that, he'd become a friend. But Jack understood his decision.

Jack smiled. 'We always knew it was a mad journey.'

'Aye.' Robert's eyes twinkled and his beard creased as he gave a wide grin. 'We did that.'

'You be careful. It'll be a hard journey back.'

'Better than what you'll be facing.'

That was probably true. 'God's grace to you, then.' Jack slapped Robert on the shoulder.

'And to you, wee man.' Robert put his hand on Saleem's shoulder. 'And you too, Sultan.'

The big man stood, blocking out most of the light for a moment, then loped away into the mist, the river bubbling around him. The fog broke apart as he passed, and then slid silently back together again.

'The arrows have stopped,' Saleem said.

Jack glanced around. It was true, no further missiles fell in this part of the gorge. All the surviving porters had fled. Corpses, arrows and scraps of canvas drifted in the swirling water. A lone pack mule stumbled about, as if in a daze. Carts stood abandoned and riddled with arrows. One of the oxen yoked to the fallen wagon still squealed and lashed the water with its hooves.

From further up the gorge, Jack heard the stutter of muskets, shouts and the ring of steel. He frowned. It sounded like hand-to-hand fighting.

The last thing he wanted to do was go upstream and find out what was going on. But what else could he do? If there was any chance of the party surviving, any chance of them still travelling to Mar, he had to make sure he was with them. He couldn't turn back now when he was so close.

He looked at Saleem. 'You go with Robert. Quickly now. You can catch up with him.'

'What?' Saleem looked as if Jack had slapped him in the face. 'No. Not this time. I'm not running away.'

'Robert was right. It's mad to stay here. I have to go on. But you need to live. Get back to Shropshire. Look after your mother and—'

'No.' Saleem bashed the water with his fist. 'You left me behind in London. I won't let you do that again.'

Christ. Saleem was being an idiot. Jack didn't have time for this. He grasped Saleem's tunic. 'You want to die? Is that it?'

'Do you?' Saleem glared at Jack, his gaze unwavering. He was panting hard and his jaw was tight.

Jack searched Saleem's eyes. He couldn't see a single trace of hesitancy there. The lad had made his mind up and Jack would have to accept it. He imagined Saleem would follow him wherever he went anyway.

He let go of Saleem's tunic. 'All right. If that's what you want.'

'It is.'

Jack's throat tightened. Feelings, hard to place, welled in his chest. He wanted the lad to be safe, but at the same time wanted him to follow his conscience.

It was similar to the way he felt about Elizabeth.

'Good lad.' He patted Saleem lightly on the shoulder.

He opened his wet satchel and pulled out the pistol. The weapon was damp and slick. He reached back into the satchel, took out the cap tin and checked the caps. At least they'd stayed dry. He pressed fresh caps on to two of the nipples, pointed the pistol in the air and pulled the trigger. The hammer clicked down and the first cap gave a bang, but nothing else happened. He cocked the hammer, which rotated the cylinder, and fired again. Still nothing. As he'd thought, the powder was wet.

Damn it.

He would have to pull the bullets out and clean the weapon before he could use it again. But that could take fifteen minutes or more, and he had to get moving immediately.

He tossed the pistol back into the satchel, fished out the brass flask and tipped a little powder into his hand. The grey-black grains were dry. At least he still had powder and bullets, even if he couldn't use them at the moment.

He needed another weapon.

He shot a look around at the floating bodies and detritus. None of the porters were likely to have been carrying firearms or anything more than a dagger. He turned to the corpses of the two Shropshire lads. They'd both had knives on them, and that was the best he could hope for at the moment.

He grasped one of the bodies and was aware of Saleem staring at him as he felt under the sodden tunic. He felt an edge of cold steel – there it was. He slipped out the knife, held it up for a second and wiped it on his sleeve.

He looked upstream. The cliffs and the frothing river receded into the mist. Shouts, cries, chimes of metal and the occasional burst of a firearm reverberated between the bluffs, but he couldn't see anything through the fog.

'Right, then.' He glanced at Saleem. 'Let's get going.'

Saleem nodded and drew his knife.

Then they both stood and strode out into the river.

12

Jack and Saleem splashed through the burbling water, avoiding the drifting corpses and animal carcasses. They passed a couple of porters who were still alive but groaning and lying half submerged in the river. Saleem hesitated, but Jack grabbed his arm and pushed him forward. The men were severely wounded and there was nothing anyone could do to help them.

Jack slowed as they passed the vehicle carrying the Ganesh statue. The oxen were all dead and lying on their sides. The animals were peppered with arrows and gouged by wounds where they'd either gored each other or smashed themselves against the cliff. The wagon was tilted and wedged against the rock face, the wheels on one side lifted out of the water.

The statue had partially slid off the back and the base now rested in the river, the current swishing around it. The giant figure was still wrapped in canvas, but one arm, holding a stylised axe, had slipped out between the folds in the material.

Jack paused for a moment. They'd toiled for weeks to cart the murti through the wilds. Andrew had died because of it.

What a waste.

And all because of bloody Captain Rao's stupidity.

A man screamed up ahead, the cry suddenly cut short.

Jack forged on through the rapids. They passed several dead Saxons, then clambered up an incline where the water guttered down in a series of shallow waterfalls. Then suddenly they'd left the gorge, the cliffs opening out to slopes that were indistinct in the mist.

They found themselves standing in a pool that came up to their knees. In every direction, both in the pool and around its edges, Saxons tussled with savages. Only those nearby were clearly visible – the others were shadow puppets behind the mist. Men shouted, steel rang and now and then muskets blasted, the flashes momentarily lighting up the haze. Pipes wailed in the distance.

Jack only had a moment to take all this in before he heard a shrill cry to his right. He turned just in time to see a savage leaping at him. The man's eyes were wild and his bearded face was twisted with fury. His arms were outstretched and in one hand he held a crude knife. His cloak fluttered like wings behind him, while his legs and feet were bare. Jack caught a glimpse of an emblem on his chest, but had no time to take it in.

Jack's heart shot into his throat. He spun to the side, slammed his knife upwards and slashed the savage's side. At the same time, the man smashed into his shoulder and knocked him backwards.

The savage smacked into the water, while Jack staggered back a few paces until he regained his footing. The man surged upright again, but he was now clutching a red wound in his abdomen. Dripping, he glanced at his injury and then glared at Jack. His cloak flopped open, revealing the insignia stitched to his chest.

A white skull on a black background.

The savage shrieked and dived at Jack.

Christ. The man seemed to have no fear.

Jack slipped easily to the side, swung his knife straight up and skewered the man in the gut. The force of the man's weight knocked Jack backwards and he splashed into the water. He gasped, jumped back to his feet, went to swing the knife again, and then saw the savage lying face down in the water, blood circling out from him.

Saleem was standing rigidly in the pool, shifting his grip on his knife and staring wide-eyed at the dead man.

'Over here.' Jack waded to the edge of the pool. They had to get out of the melee. The Saxons could deal with the savages as far as he was concerned. There was no reason for him and Saleem to get involved unless there was no other option.

They hauled themselves on to the rocky bank and clambered up a steep slope covered in trees and thick undergrowth. Saleem went first, with Jack just behind. The ground was muddy and covered in fallen leaves. Both of them slipped to their knees a few times. Jack grasped a bramble bush by accident and winced as the thorns impaled his hand.

Then something grabbed his ankle and yanked him back. He fell, slid downhill a few feet, twisted over and saw the grinning face of Sergeant Wulfric.

Wulfric's cap had fallen off and his bare scalp glistened with moisture. Dirt streaked his tunic and trousers and what look like blood splattered one of his sleeves, although he appeared unharmed. In one hand he held a red-stained scimitar, which he must have picked up when an officer dropped it, but he didn't appear to have any other weapons.

In a voice like cold honey, he said, 'There you are, scum.'

Jack shook his foot in an attempt to free it. 'What're you playing at?'

Wulfric gripped the ankle firmly. 'No, you don't. Old Wulfric's been waiting for this.'

Jack still held the knife in one hand. Had Wulfric noticed? He tensed his fingers around the handle. 'You'll be shot.'

Wulfric grinned even wider, exposing a row of yellow teeth. 'No one's going to miss one filthy Englishman.'

Wulfric raised the scimitar behind his head. His single eye blazed.

Jack kicked but couldn't free his leg. His heart battered in his chest. He was going to be hit. There was no way out of it.

Then a rock slapped Wulfric in the face. The Sergeant grunted, let go of Jack and staggered backwards. Blood gushed from his nose and ran over his lips. He grunted more loudly and put his hand to his face.

Jack scrabbled out of Wulfric's reach and twisted round to see Saleem standing a couple of feet up the slope. The lad's eyes were frozen wide, his bottom lip quivered and he was panting so hard his shoulders rose and fell with each breath.

'Run.' Jack's voice was cracked.

Saleem clambered back uphill on all fours. Jack followed, slipping, grappling with vines, and grabbing at twigs and bracken.

He heard a roar behind him and the snap of breaking branches. Wulfric was following.

His heart stuttered and his breath was short. He could hear the Saxons and savages fighting, but the sounds were distant, coming from another world. The only thing on his mind was the task of clawing his way up the slope.

He trod on a loose stone, which skidded away from under his boot. He lost his footing, slid down and dug his hands into the soil to stop himself falling further. He managed to ram his foot into a tree root and use that to propel himself forward again.

But something tugged at his ankle for a second and wrenched him back.

He heard Wulfric growling right behind him.

Christ.

Rather than make the same mistake as last time, where he'd lain helpless at Wulfric's feet, he instead swung round and let himself plunge back. He saw Wulfric standing directly beneath him. The Sergeant widened his eye when he saw Jack flying towards him. Jack hit Wulfric in the chest and the Sergeant let out a loud wheeze. They both tumbled down, rolled a short distance and jolted to a stop against a bush.

Jack landed face down and got a mouthful of dirt.

Wulfric roared, scrambled to his knees and swung the scimitar wildly. Jack ducked and the blade whistled over his head, shredding the leaves of a shrub. Wulfric stuck out one leg to brace himself and sliced the blade downwards. Jack rolled to the side and the scimitar thumped into the mud.

Now Jack saw an opening. Wulfric's side was exposed as he knelt with his scimitar stuck in the ground. Wulfric went to lift his weapon again, but Jack shifted his grip on the knife, leapt and thrust the blade into the Sergeant's flank. The knife slipped easily through cloth and skin and into the wet flesh beneath.

Wulfric looked down and saw the knife stuck into his abdomen. He snarled and jabbed backwards with his arm, raising the scimitar at the same time. His elbow smashed into Jack's mouth. Pain flooded Jack's face, darkness puffed before his eyes and his ears whined. He stumbled back, still holding the knife, which was now slick with blood.

Wulfric's face seethed and his eye flared brilliant white. He whirled round, swinging the scimitar, but the attack was far too high and Jack easily ducked out of the way. The blade whacked deep into a tree trunk.

And then it was stuck.

Wulfric growled and struggled to pull the blade free. But it was wedged in firmly.

Jack pounced immediately, knocked Wulfric to the ground and clambered on top. Without pausing for a second, Jack rammed his knife into Wulfric's chest. Wulfric wheezed and his eye opened so wide Jack thought it would pop out. The Sergeant raised his arms to fend Jack off, but the strength seemed to have gone out of him and he could do no more than flail uselessly.

Jack stabbed Wulfric repeatedly in the chest, blood flicking all around him. Finally, he stopped. Panting hard, he stared at Wulfric's face. The Sergeant, amazingly, was still alive, although only just. He tried to lift his head and glared back at Jack.

'Scum,' Wulfric whispered. Then his head dropped back and he gave a final sigh as the life went out of his bulbous eye.

Jack crossed himself, wiped the sweat from his forehead with his sleeve, turned to the side and spat dirt from his mouth.

There was nothing good about killing a man. Even a man like Wulfric. Jack wasn't proud or pleased. He just felt numb and dazed.

He lurched up, stuck the knife in his belt and grasped the scimitar. He yanked and wriggled it until the blade finally came free.

Good. At least he had a better weapon now.

He looked up the slope and saw the gouges in the earth where he and Wulfric had slid downhill.

There was no sign of Saleem.

It was good that the lad had kept running, but it was going to be difficult to find him now. He went to shout Saleem's name but then paused. The gully had gone silent. He no longer heard cries, musket shots or pipes, only the distant gurgling of the river.

Strange.

Then he noticed voices off to his right. It sounded like several men talking.

Someone suddenly cried out, 'No.'

Jack went cold and the ground seemed to drop an inch. That last voice was unmistakeable.

Saleem.

Jack gave an involuntary hiss and struck off through the mist in the direction of Saleem's cry. The sound hadn't come from further up the slope, but instead almost at the same level as him.

He went as quickly as he could, but at the same time tried to make as little sound as possible. In an instant he was an army scout and a tracker once again. His feet found the stable spots of ground and avoided the twigs and loose stones. All his senses quivered into life and he took in every tree branch and shrub about him, searching for the telltale signs of movement.

After about a minute he heard the voices again, but this time they came from below. He crouched and concentrated on the sound. There were three men – or was it four? And they were speaking in the strange tongue of the savages.

Saleem gave another muffled shout.

The lad was still alive. Thank God.

Jack stared hard into the mist, but couldn't see further than forty feet at the most.

He set off down the hill. The voices grew louder and now he could also hear the crunch of the men stepping on leaves. They were close, perhaps only sixty feet away.

His breath shivered and his heart trembled. He couldn't make a mistake now, couldn't make a sound. He didn't have a plan yet, but whatever he did, the element of surprise would be key. He flexed his fingers around the scimitar's grip, his palms so wet with sweat he was worried he'd drop the weapon.

He paused for a second and took a deep breath.

He had to get himself under control. How many times had he crept up on enemy forces when he was in the army? Countless times. So why was he faltering now? He had to focus, just like the old days. Fears about Saleem might be coursing through his head, but he had to block these out.

Your mind is a rippling pool. Still it.

Now he heard more voices. The men seemed to have met further savages and were speaking rapidly to them.

He crept downhill, crouching and trying to stay behind the thickest clumps of undergrowth. Within a few seconds the mist parted enough for him to see the silhouettes of around twenty figures standing at the bottom of the hill. He froze, ducked behind a thorn bush and strained to make the men out more clearly.

Most of them were savages – he could tell by the distinctive shape of their long cloaks. But with them were three other men who wore tunics and trousers, and a further figure who was on his knees.

Jack tightened his grip on the scimitar. He sneaked further down the slope in order to get a better look. He stepped on a pile of leaves and winced at the loud crackle they made. But none of the savages reacted – they were too busy talking amongst themselves.

On Jack stalked. One step at a time. Slowly. Cautiously.

Then he trod on something soft and heard a yelp beneath him. His heart jumped and he leapt back, doing his best to stifle a gasp.

For a second he had the strange thought that he'd stepped on a dog. But when he looked down he saw the truth.

Cowering in the undergrowth, pointing a pistol up at Jack, was Captain Rao.

Jack blinked a few times. What the hell was the Captain doing here?

Rao's hand shook as he held the pistol, sweat beaded on his forehead and there was a look of almost comical terror on his face. His chest was going up and down so rapidly Jack thought he might pass out.

'It's me,' Jack hissed. 'Put the pistol down.'

Rao frowned and raised his other hand to help steady the weapon.

'For Christ's sake.' Jack squatted down. Rao didn't look as though he were about to shoot. He didn't look capable of doing anything at that moment. Jack decided to ignore the pistol for the time being and nodded at the figures down the hill. 'What's going on?'

Rao kept the firearm trained on Jack. His eyes quivered. He frowned, went to speak and then closed his mouth again. He gripped the pistol tighter, gritted his teeth and finally lowered the weapon. 'They've got Lieutenant Parihar.'

Jack parted the branches of a bush and peered down. He was close enough now to make out the figures at the bottom of the hill. Fifteen savages stood in a group. Beside them were two Saxon soldiers and Parihar, who all had their hands tied behind their backs. Saleem was kneeling on the ground, his hands also bound. Jack could see the lad's ginger hair and beard clearly.

Saleem.

Jack felt dizzy for a moment, but quickly pulled himself together.

He studied the savages more closely. They carried spears and bows, and wore the usual shaggy cloaks and tunics. But they all bore the white skull emblem on their chests. Jack was also surprised to see that one of them, a giant with black hair tied in a topknot, had a longsword at his side and a chain-mail shirt

174

under his cloak. Over the chain mail he wore a black surcoat, on which was also emblazoned the white skull.

'Where's everyone else from our party?' Jack whispered.

'Everyone else?' Rao's eyes shone wildly. 'They're all dead.'

Christ. 'All of them?'

Rao nodded. 'I think so. I saw many fall.'

Jack tightened his jaw. There might still be a few survivors hiding like him and Rao. But it didn't sound as though there could be many. 'My friend's down there too. We have to free them.'

'Free them?' Rao's eyes widened even further. He wrenched out a perfumed handkerchief, pressed it to his nose and inhaled.

'We can't just sit here.'

'But there must be hundreds of them down there.'

Jack cast his eye about the gully but couldn't see far in the mist. He made out more savages standing near the edge of the pool and noticed flickers of movement further away.

Hundreds? That could well be right. The savages wouldn't have risked attacking unless they had sufficient numbers.

Jack's eyes fell upon Saleem again. He couldn't see the lad's face, but he could imagine the sorry expression that must be on it.

What should he do? Rao had a pistol but no scimitar. He had a scimitar, but couldn't risk taking the time to clean and dry his own firearm. There were only two of them, against fifteen savages. And as soon as he and Rao attacked, the rest of the horde would fall upon them.

But what else could they do but attack?

They would have to creep down the slope. Then, when they were close enough, Rao would shoot as many savages as he could, while Jack would rush at them with the scimitar and free the captives. Then they would all have to run up the hill as quickly as they could and hope for the best.

Would that work?

Probably not.

Jack glanced at Rao. The Captain was so jumpy Jack wasn't sure that he would be able to shoot straight. Had he ever even shot anyone before?

Rao drew another deep breath through his handkerchief and whimpered. 'Look, they're moving.'

What? Jack pushed aside the leaves in front of him. The savages had been joined by about thirty more of their tribe. The new arrivals had been collecting Saxon muskets and now carried them on their backs in bundles, like firewood gathered from a forest.

Saleem was standing, and the savages were pushing him, Parihar and the two Saxons forward. The group began jogging off up the valley. A stream of further savages followed. Jack couldn't tell exactly how large the party was, but scores of men swept past immediately below and he could see the faint trace of many others moving across the floor of the gully.

Pipes wailed somewhere and several savages gave wild cries.

Jack shivered slightly.

The savages were leaving.

And they were taking Saleem with them.

PART THREE

———◆———

13

Jack sat back against an oak. The mist swirled between the black trees in every direction he looked. He felt as though the breath had been knocked out of him.

How was he going to free Saleem now?

'Where are they taking them?' Rao whispered.

'Not sure.' Jack tapped the pommel of the scimitar. 'I could make a guess, though. You notice the emblem they were wearing on their chests?'

'A skull or something like that.'

'Didn't that old chief tell us that was Mahajan's sign?'

'What?'

'At the ruined castle. When the natives came down the hill.'

'Oh, yes.' Rao lowered his handkerchief. 'I remember now. He said Mahajan's men were killers who were attacking the lands around Mar.' Rao's eyes widened and he stared at Jack. 'Then we're close to Mar.'

'Looks that way.'

Rao narrowed his eyes and looked downhill. 'You think they're taking Parihar and the others to Mahajan?'

'Could be. If they're not going to kill them first.'

Rao shot a look at Jack, then frowned and tightened his grip on the pistol.

Jack shut his eyes for a second. What to do? He didn't care about Parihar, didn't even care about the Saxon soldiers. But he couldn't abandon Saleem. And he wouldn't give up on finding Mahajan. The crusaders in Shropshire were counting on him succeeding.

Elizabeth was counting on him.

He sat forward again. 'We'll follow the savages and wait for a chance to free our comrades.'

Rao frowned. 'Follow them?'

'What else can we do?'

Rao licked his lips. 'We'll go back to Dun Fries. Get help there.'

'Dun Fries? That'll take weeks.'

Rao's cheeks flushed. 'Now, see here. I'm in charge of this expedition. You must do as I say.'

Jack felt his face grow hot. Do as I say? Did Rao really think he could order him around now? By rights, Jack should punch the Captain in the face and leave him there.

But instead he took a deep breath and calmed himself. There was no point in the two of them fighting at the moment. They had to work together.

'Listen,' Jack said. 'Our friends could be killed. We can't waste time going all the way to Dun Fries. We have to do something now.'

Rao stared into space, his nostrils flaring and his eyes glistening. Finally, he said, 'All right. We'll follow them. But you'll do as I say, you understand?'

Christ. Jack felt his face getting hot again. He gritted his teeth and said slowly, 'As you wish.'

'Sir.' Rao fixed his gaze on Jack. 'As you wish, *sir*.'

Jack took another deep breath. 'Don't push your luck, sir.'

They crept through the trees and down to the floor of the gully. By now all the savages had left, but corpses lay scattered across the ground and the groans of the dying drifted through the mist. A Saxon coughed, moaned and tried to drag himself across the rocks beside the pool. But he couldn't get far and collapsed again after a few seconds.

Rao grimaced and put his handkerchief to his nose.

To Jack's left, the numerous tracks of the savages stood out in the soft ground and led off up the gully. Jack wanted to follow the trail as soon as possible, but he also wanted to make sure he and Rao were properly armed.

He glanced at the Captain. And now he noticed that Rao still had Atri's satchel hanging from his shoulder. The Captain had lost his scimitar, but had made sure he kept Atri's notes. Interesting.

'You got any more bullets?' Jack asked.

'With my horse.'

'Better get them. And any other weapons you can find.'

Rao nodded and set off around the side of the pool. Jack scoured the bottom of the gully for muskets. He trod around bodies and looked under discarded knapsacks, blankets and canvas sheets. All the while, the thought of Saleem beat insistently in his head.

He saw at least thirty dead Saxons, but many more savages – perhaps three hundred. In some places the natives lay piled on top of each other, no doubt having been killed in droves by the firearms.

But he found no muskets. The savages appeared to have taken them all. Did they know how to use them?

After a couple of minutes, he gave up and instead grabbed a knapsack. He tipped out the contents and stuffed a box of matches and a bag of army biscuits back in. He found a water canteen and a couple of blankets and shoved these in too. Finally, he transferred the pistol, powder flask and other equipment from his wet satchel to the knapsack.

As he swung the bag on to his back, he heard a groan nearby. He looked around and saw a Saxon slumped under a tree. The man's stomach was a red mess and his skin was pale and covered in sweat.

'Water,' the Saxon said hoarsely.

Jack spotted a canteen on the ground and carried it over to the soldier. As he approached, he almost choked on the stench of excrement. The man's bowels must have been cut open. He handed over the canteen and the man nodded in thanks. Jack wished there was something more he could do to help, but there was no chance of the Saxon surviving.

'Good luck,' Jack said, then jogged back to the other side of the gully.

Rao stood beside the pool, staring at the floating bodies.

'Find anything?' Jack asked.

'No.' Rao looked up. His face was stiff and his eyes were raw. 'They're all dead. Officers, batmen, soldiers. Even the horses have been slaughtered.'

Jack understood what Rao must be feeling. But all the same, they didn't have time to stand about talking. 'How many bullets do you have left?'

Rao waved his pistol. 'Just the six in here.'

'Right. I've got eighteen. That'll have to do.'

Rao stared glumly at his pistol. 'We're going to fight hundreds of savages with this?'

'Not just that.' Jack fished his own pistol out of the knapsack. 'Got this too.'

Rao frowned. 'Where did you get that?' He then stared at the bloody scimitar stuck in Jack's belt, seeming to only notice it for the first time. His eyes widened. 'And that? That's an officer's blade.'

'Calm down.' Jack hurriedly put away the firearm. Maybe it hadn't been a good idea to show it to Rao. 'The pistol belonged to my father. He was in the army.' He patted the scimitar. 'This I just found on the ground.'

Rao looked at Jack sideways, pursed his lips and finally said, 'I see. Shouldn't you at least clean that blade?'

'No time. We have to go now.'

Rao searched Jack's face for a moment. Then he relaxed his shoulders and slid his pistol into its holster. 'Very well. Let's go.'

They ran up the gully, leaving the pool, the dead and the dying behind. The knapsack bounced on Jack's back but he barely noticed it – in the army he'd marched for days and even fought with a knapsack on his back. The scimitar swung at his side and the knife was still tucked into his belt.

He glanced at Rao. The Captain ran stiffly, as if he were trying to maintain some level of decorum. His overcoat was unbuttoned and flapped open at times to reveal his blue uniform beneath.

The savages' footprints were easy to make out in the black soil and their rough hide shoes left distinctive markings. Their tracks were spread out across the ground – they hadn't been running in any kind of formation.

After half an hour, Jack and Rao reached the head of the gully and scrambled up a bare slope. The mist began to clear and the surrounding hills came into focus.

Rao fell behind and Jack paused beside a rock to wait for him. The Captain was sweating and panting heavily by the time he caught up. He slung off Atri's satchel, slipped off his coat and bent double, trying to catch his breath.

Jack pulled out the water canteen, took a swig and offered it to Rao. 'Here.'

Rao raised his head and frowned, his chest still heaving.

Jack waggled the canteen. 'Go on.'

Rao swallowed and licked his lips, but still didn't reach for the canteen.

Then Jack understood. Of course. He'd been away from Rajthanans for so long he'd forgotten. 'I see. Don't want to share water with me.'

Rao's eyes flickered. 'You're an insolent native.'

Jack snorted, looked away and took another gulp of water. 'Up to you.'

Rao hesitated, then grasped the canteen out of Jack's hand, wiped the opening with his sleeve and drank by pouring the water through the air to purify it. He didn't let his lips touch the container. He drank for several seconds, taking large gulps so that his Adam's apple rolled in his neck.

'Calm down,' Jack said. 'Don't drink it all.'

Rao handed back the canteen. He glared at Jack but didn't say anything further.

They pressed on up the incline. When he reached the summit, Jack stopped again to let Rao catch up. He peered down the far side of the hill and saw a slope descending to a wide valley. Shreds of mist still floated about the valley floor, but he could see patches of the ground beyond.

Suddenly he drew his breath in sharply. He could make out the black specks of the savages charging up the valley. There looked to be four hundred of them at least.

He shrank behind a knoll. Rao was still toiling up the slope and Jack waved for him to keep his head down. Rao stooped, ran up the last few feet and flopped down beside Jack. He panted, winced and pressed his hand to his side.

Jack pointed over the knoll. 'They're in the next valley. If we go down now they'll see us.'

Rao nodded, still struggling to get his breath back.

Jack grinned. 'You need to do a bit more training, sir.'

Rao scowled at him, swallowed and pulled out his handkerchief, which he breathed through, as if the perfume could somehow revive him. After a few seconds, he put the cloth away, felt about in his satchel and drew out a spyglass. He rolled over and eased his head around the side of the knoll.

'Careful,' Jack said.

'I know what I'm doing.' Rao raised the glass to his eye. 'Yes. I see them.'

Rao handed over the glass and Jack peered down. The floor of the valley reared up before him in vivid detail. He searched until he found the savages – they were running and leaping over rocks and gorse bushes, their cloaks billowing behind them. He hunted for Saleem and the other captives, but it was difficult to see clearly with the mist partially obscuring the valley. Eventually he gave up and handed the glass back to Rao.

'Still too risky to go down there.' Jack looked to his right to where a fir forest swept down a mountain all the way to the valley floor. 'We could go through that. We won't be spotted in there.'

Rao stared at the trees through his spyglass. 'It'll slow us down.'

'It'll slow us down waiting around here too.'

Rao nodded, and they struck off across the scarp, keeping below the line of the summit. Once they reached the woods, they jogged down in an angle towards the bottom of the valley. The sharp scent of the fir trees wafted around them and they skidded on drifts of fallen needles.

From time to time, Jack stopped, climbed a tree and checked the valley through the spyglass. The mist had cleared completely now and the running natives stood out clearly against the yellow grassland. Each time he looked, they were further away, and finally, after an hour, he could no longer see them at all.

He shinned down the tree trunk and jumped the last few feet. 'The savages are out of sight. We'll go straight down from here. I have to find the trail again.' He looked up and saw that the pale sun was hanging low in the sky. 'It's about three o'clock. It'll be dark in an hour.'

Rao drew a watch from his pocket and flicked open the silver lid. 'Remarkable. You're right. Quarter past three by European reckoning.'

'Wouldn't be much of a tracker if I couldn't tell the time by the sun.' Jack started down the slope.

'Tracker?' Rao slipped a little as he followed.

'Aye. That's what I used to do.'

'Before you were a porter?'

'That's right.' Jack realised he would have to be careful what he said. He had to keep his story straight, otherwise Rao might start to get suspicious.

There was no reason for him to talk much to Rao anyway. The

two of them had been thrown together temporarily, but the Captain was the enemy. In another situation they could be shooting at each other.

Within half an hour, they reached the base of the valley and Jack scanned ahead with the spyglass. The savages remained out of sight and the shadows were thickening fast.

Jack ran towards the middle of the valley, determined to find the trail before nightfall. Rao puffed and wheezed, and soon fell behind. But Jack didn't stop until he spied footprints in the earth before him. He crouched, parted a clump of heather and saw the unmistakeable tracks left by the savages' shoes. He stepped forward a few paces and saw further prints, and then more still. These were definitely the right tracks.

Rao had slowed to a walk.

'Hurry,' Jack shouted. 'They're well ahead of us.'

Reluctantly, Rao started running again and was weak and drenched in sweat by the time he reached Jack. But Jack didn't let him rest for a moment and instead led the way on along the trail.

Dusk soon settled over the valley and the air grew colder. Jack could still just make out the savages' tracks, but it would be impossible to see them once the light faded completely. The only way he could follow the trail in the dark was to use the Europa yantra, his tracking power.

How would using the power affect him? Without Kanvar's cure, the effort would have killed him. But what about now, when the cure was still effective? If nothing else, using the power would tire him out and he was already weary. Further, he would have to reveal to Rao that he was a siddha. That was going to take some explaining.

He would wait until it was absolutely necessary before risking going into the trance.

Darkness swamped the countryside. The moon was a thin streak behind the clouds and the ground turned pitch black.

Finally, he stopped, crouched and studied the earth.

Rao halted and lay on his back, gasping for breath.

Jack stared hard at the ground, but even with his uncannily good eyesight he couldn't make out the trail.

He rubbed his forehead. He would have to use Europa now. There was no other way . . .

Then he noticed a glint out of the corner of his eye. He lowered his hand and peered into the darkness. Straight ahead, further up the valley, he spied twinkling lights.

Fires.

'Get up.' He stood and retied his ponytail.

Rao groaned and pulled himself upright. 'What?'

'Over there.' Jack nodded at the glimmering lights.

'Oh, yes. What is it?'

'Could be the savages' camp. Or a village. Come on.'

They set off towards the lights and half an hour later they were close enough for Jack to make out at least forty campfires spread out across the valley floor.

He halted. 'We need to be careful. There could be sentries about.'

Rao nodded. 'You think it's our savages?'

'Could be.'

'Who else could it be?'

Jack shrugged. 'Maybe there are other tribes around.'

'Other tribes? Those savages have been following us for days. It must be them.'

'I'm not so sure about that. Those savages we fought a few days ago – they weren't wearing the white skull, were they?'

'Weren't they?'

'No. I saw one of them.'

'So, they were a different tribe, you think?'

'Maybe. Tribes usually stick to their own areas. I reckon we've left the lands of one group and then come across this next lot.'

Rao stared into the dark, his eyes reflecting the distant firelight. 'Just our luck.'

'We need some cover if we're going to get closer. I reckon we'll still find woods over there.' He pointed to the mountainside on the right side of the valley. It was impossible to make out the slope clearly, but from what he'd seen earlier he was certain the forest extended this far.

They ran across the grass and the black presence of the mountain loomed ahead, traces of snow illuminating its peak. As they drew closer, Jack spotted the dark, jagged lines of fir trees.

He led the way into the woods and followed a rough animal track as it wound along the base of the mountain. The forest was silent save for the distant hooting of an owl and the rattle of dry branches in the wind.

After twenty minutes, he clambered up a tree and saw that the campfires were now only three hundred yards away. He slid back to the ground and led Rao to a nearby ridge that was free of trees. They crouched behind a mass of tangled brambles and stared across the valley. The campfires were clearly visible and Jack could make out dim figures moving about the flames.

Rao peered through the glass. 'It's them. I can see a white skull.'

Jack took the glass and bright flames immediately leapt up in front of him. He moved the glass around until he saw savages sitting warming themselves before a fire, their faces tinted yellow and their eyes dark beads in their bearded faces. He searched further, discovering more fires and more savages. He spied the tall man in the mail shirt strutting across the camp. And finally he found what he was looking for.

Saleem, Parihar and the two Saxons.

They all sat together near the centre of the camp. Jack couldn't see their faces clearly, but Saleem's ginger hair and Parihar's scarlet turban were unmistakeable.

'Found them.' Jack handed the glass back to Rao. 'In the middle of the camp.'

Rao stared through the glass. 'I see them.' He looked at Jack, a tight smile on his lips and moisture in his eyes. 'Alive. Poor Parihar.'

As far as Jack was concerned Parihar was an idiot. But he understood how the Captain must be feeling. 'You know him well?'

'Parihar?' Rao cleared his throat and his voice shook slightly. 'Yes. Since we were children.'

'Ah. I didn't realise. Don't worry. We'll get them back—' Jack froze mid-sentence. His heart quivered. He stared into the trees off to the left.

'What is it?' Rao asked.

Jack put his finger to his lips and pointed to where a dark figure was slipping slowly between two wizened birches. As the shape left the shadow beneath one tree, Jack could see it was draped in a large cloak and carried a spear.

A savage was moving stealthily through the undergrowth not more than ten yards away.

14

'Shiva,' Rao whispered. 'You think he's seen us?'

Jack stared at the dim figure. 'Not sure. Stay still.'

The savage slid behind a fir tree and paused for around a minute. Then he sneaked forward towards a clump of bushes.

Jack kept low behind the brambles. He could hear Rao's shivery breath next to him. He hadn't had time to reload his pistol yet – he'd been in too much of a hurry to keep up with the savages. If they were attacked, he would grab Rao's firearm. He didn't trust the Captain to shoot straight.

The savage paused behind the bushes, crept uphill a couple of feet, then squatted beneath a tree. He sat there for at least ten minutes. Jack's knee ached, but he didn't dare move into a more comfortable position.

Finally, the savage stood quickly and flitted away into the dark like a sprite.

Rao breathed out. 'What was that about?'

'Think he was just scouting around. We'll have to be careful. There could be plenty more about.'

Rao shivered and glanced into the black mesh of the woods. The wind rustled the branches overhead.

'It'll be too dangerous to go down there now.' Jack gestured to the camp. 'We could be spotted.'

'What should we do, then?'

'We'll have to wait until morning. Then keep following.'

'Keep following? That's your plan?'

'You got a better one?'

Rao pursed his lips, but didn't reply.

Jack led the way uphill. He crept as silently as he could and from time to time stopped and listened for the telltale sounds of someone following. He heard nothing, but this reassured him less than it might have. The savage he'd seen earlier had moved stealthily through the forest. The man clearly knew this country-side well. He'd probably spent his whole life hunting and tracking in woodland like this.

Jack reached a moss-covered boulder that bulged out of the slope. At the base of the rock was a hollow that would provide a small amount of shelter. It was the best place he'd seen to make camp. And what was more, when he turned, he could see the savages' fires below through a gap in the trees.

'We'll stop here,' he said.

Rao frowned. 'Here?'

Jack rubbed his chin. The hollow didn't offer much protection from the elements, and they couldn't risk lighting a fire.

He hunted around nearby, found a few fallen branches and propped them against the boulder to form a simple bivouac. Then he grasped armfuls of leaves and twigs and laid them across the branches. He glanced at Rao at one point and saw the Captain just standing there in the shadows, fidgeting with his handkerchief.

Jack knew there was no point asking Rao to help. The Captain would never have camped without an enormous tent and would never have so much as sullied his hands to collect firewood.

Once he'd finished, Jack slapped his hands together to dust them. He nodded at the bivouac. 'There you go.'

Rao pressed his handkerchief to his nose and breathed in sharply. 'Wonderful.'

They both clambered in and sat in the mottled darkness. The scent of wet leaves and fresh earth hung about them. Rao looked around with his face twisted, as if he'd been forced to eat excrement. He put his hand on the ground, then lifted it again and shook off the dirt. He tried resting his other hand against the boulder, but he pulled it back when it touched the moist moss.

Jack fumbled in the knapsack and pulled out the bag of dry rations. He stuck a biscuit in his mouth and offered the bag to Rao, who crinkled his nose in disgust and turned his head away.

'Suit yourself.' Jack took a bite of the hard, flavourless biscuit and softened it with a swig of water from the canteen.

If Rao wanted to starve himself, he was welcome to.

Rao sniffed and stared at the distant lights, hugging his knees to his chest. He looked so utterly miserable Jack even felt sorry for him for a moment.

'You have to eat something.' Jack offered Rao the bag again. 'Look, I'm not even touching them.'

'What's your name?' Rao's voice was sharp.

Jack chewed his biscuit. Rao didn't know his name? He hadn't thought about it, but of course there'd been no need for the Captain to know anything about him. Jack had been just one of a hundred porters.

He put the biscuit on his knee, wiped his hand on his hose and offered it to Rao. 'Jack.'

Rao looked at the hand and frowned.

'It's our custom,' Jack said. 'It's a greeting. We shake hands.'

Rao tightened his lips and took a sniff through his handkerchief.

Jack snorted and took away his hand. 'Fine.' He picked up the biscuit and bit into it. 'Don't touch me, then.'

Why was he even wasting time talking to Rao? The Captain was just a temporary ally.

He shot a look at the satchel, which the Captain still kept pressed beside him. Jack would have to find out what was in that bag. But not now. First he had to free Saleem, and he still needed Rao's help with that.

'I will have a biscuit,' Rao said.

'Changed your mind, have you?' Jack tossed over the bag.

Rao gingerly slid open the drawstring, sniffed the contents, wrinkled his face and finally pulled out a biscuit. He winced, shut his eyes and took a bite. He chewed for a few seconds, opened his eyes, and gulped some water to help wash the biscuit down. He took another bite.

'Not so bad when you're hungry, are they?' Jack slipped another biscuit from the bag and munched on it.

'Can't believe I'm eating this.' Rao sighed. 'Guess I'm so polluted now it hardly matters.'

'You need to forget about pollution and all that. We're stuck out in the wilds.'

'I suppose you're right. I'll have to go through weeks of blessings when we get back, no matter what I do now.'

'Weeks? Seems a long time.'

'That's the way it works. No other Rajthanans will come near me until I'm pure again.'

Jack knew something of the Rajthanans' complex purity-and-pollution customs, but little of the detail. 'Can't say I understand all that.'

'No, I suppose not. No need for you to. You're a native. Things are more simple for you.'

Simple? Was living like a slave in your own country simple? But Jack didn't bother contradicting Rao. The Captain was fresh from Rajthana and had no idea what life was like for ordinary English men and women. There was no point trying to explain it to him.

They chewed in silence and drank the remainder of the water.

'I'll keep first watch,' Jack said. 'You sleep.'

Rao untied his turban, sweeping the material around and around his head and then folding it neatly and placing it in his satchel. His head – with its short bob of hair pulled back into a knot – looked naked and exposed without its covering.

'I can't believe I'm going to sleep without doing my puja,' Rao said. 'I can't believe I'm not even going to brush my teeth.'

Jack handed over a blanket. 'Never brushed my teeth once in my life.'

'Shiva.' Rao lay back and pulled the blanket over himself. 'I really have come to the end of the earth.'

Rao rolled on to his side, while Jack stayed up, wrapped in his own blanket.

The scent of sandalwood, rose and other perfumed oils permeated the bivouac. Jack had smelt this many times before – the Rajthanans constantly coated themselves in ointments and lotions. They rubbed their hair with a concoction they called 'champoo' and they had the odd notion that you should wash yourself entirely every day.

It was a strange situation. Jack had never slept in close proximity to a Rajthanan. It was unthinkable. Even when Jhala had led Jack's platoon across the wilderness, he'd always slept apart from his troops. And Jhala had been closer to his men than most officers.

Rao shifted, the leaves beneath him crunching.

It must be an even stranger situation for the Captain. Lost somewhere in a world of savages.

Jack stared out at the glinting fires. How was he going to rescue Saleem? He'd tried to sound confident in front of Rao, but he had no idea how they were going to do it.

He shouldn't have let Saleem come along. He'd said no at first, but then he'd wavered. Even back in the gorge, when they were under attack, he should have insisted Saleem go with Robert.

Damn it.

Then he sighed. There was no point in dwelling on this now.

Rao breathed slowly and deeply. He seemed to be asleep.

Good. Maybe he'd run faster tomorrow if he got a good rest. If he couldn't keep up, he would become a liability. And in that case, Jack would have to leave him behind.

Jack reached around for the knapsack. He was finally going to clean out the pistol as best he could. But then a shaft of pain impaled his chest. He shut his eyes and tried to wait it out, but it quickly grew worse. He gasped and lay back. His eyes flashed white and he gritted his teeth. He didn't think he could bear the torture for much longer.

Then the pain ebbed slightly and he took a raspy breath. Rivulets of sweat coursed over his face. He took another breath, tried to meditate enough to at least block out the full force of the pain. He concentrated on the air passing in and out of his nostrils. Fought to still his thoughts.

But another blast struck him. He tensed every muscle in his body and choked back a shout.

For a second he was certain he would die, but then the pain subsided again.

His injury continued to flare and fade in agonising pulses. He didn't know how long it went on for, but it seemed like hours. He shut his eyes and tried to blot it out. His thoughts spiralled. He saw Elizabeth in Folly Brook, Katelin on her deathbed and then Saleem huddled beside a fire in the savages' camp.

Finally, one memory beat so insistently in his head he couldn't think of anything else. He was sixteen years old and standing before the army barracks outside Bristol, after having walked all the way from Shropshire.

'I want to join up,' he told the guard at the gate.

The guard sent for the Sergeant Major, who marched across the beaten-earth courtyard, looked Jack up and down and said, 'Come with me.'

Jack followed, marvelling at the Sergeant Major's smart blue and grey uniform. The brass buttons on the man's tunic shone, his black boots gleamed and there was not so much as a speck of dirt on his clothes. He was apparently an ordinary Englishman, but he looked as grand as an earl, or even a king.

Would Jack himself look like that soon?

The Sergeant Major took him into a long building with wattle-and-daub walls and a stone floor. An Englishman in a grey tunic approached and explained that he was a surgeon. He asked Jack to remove his tunic and undershirt, then listened to his chest through an ear trumpet, examined his teeth, stared into his eyes and told him to breathe deeply a few times.

When the surgeon nodded approvingly, the Sergeant Major told Jack to put on his clothes again and then led him across a parade ground. They reached a bungalow with a veranda across the front. Jack followed the Sergeant Major up the steps and into a dimly lit room.

The first thing he noticed was the cloud of aromatic tobacco smoke. The second was the scent of perfumed oils. The smell was luxurious – as if he'd entered a palace, rather than a small office.

Behind a desk, puffing on a hookah, sat Captain Jhala. He was in his early thirties at the time and his face was free of the lines and furrows that would come to dominate it in later life. He wore a red and white turban that shone in the haze and a blue tunic that had a sun emblem embroidered in great detail on its left side.

Jhala drew on a pipe, exhaled the smoke slowly and sat forward. His dark eyes twinkled as they studied Jack.

The Sergeant Major said a namaste and nudged Jack in the side.

Jack looked up, uncertain what he was supposed to do.

'Go on.' The Sergeant Major pressed his hands together again in demonstration. 'Namaste.'

Jack copied the Sergeant Major, put his hands together in front of his chest, as if he were praying in church, and said, 'Namaste.'

The word felt strange in his mouth, like an exotic sweet. He had no idea what it meant.

'You're supposed to bow as well,' the Sergeant Major snapped.

'It's all right.' Jhala scraped his chair back and stood. 'He'll learn.'

Jhala walked around the side of the desk and came closer, the scent of perfume growing stronger. He stood in front of Jack with his hands behind his back. 'How old are you, boy?'

'Sixteen, sir,' Jack said.

'Ever used a musket?'

'No, sir. But I want to try.'

'Good.'

Jhala picked up a piece of cloth from the desk behind him and held it up. The material was blue and emblazoned with three red lions running in a circle, as if trying to bite each other's tails.

'This is the standard of our regiment,' Jhala said. 'It represents the English, who have hearts of lions.'

Jack stared at the standard, unsure whether he was supposed to respond.

'Are you a lion?' Jhala asked.

'Yes, sir.'

'And will you fight to the death to defend this?' Jhala waved the cloth.

Jack wasn't sure that he would, but he was certain what the reply should be. 'Yes, sir.'

Jhala gave a slight smile. 'Good.' He placed the cloth back on the desk and nodded to the Sergeant Major. 'Take him to the store and find him a tunic. And get his hair cut – it's a filthy mess.'

<hr />

Jack opened his eyes. Daylight filtered through the interwoven branches, twigs and leaves of the bivouac.

It took him a moment to realise what had happened.

He'd fallen asleep. While on watch. One of the worst things a soldier could do.

Christ. He couldn't believe it, but the pain had been bad during the night. He must have been momentarily knocked unconscious and then drifted off. At least he felt fully recovered now.

He scrambled up. What time was it?

The air was cold and the rheum in his eyes felt frozen. His breath misted about his mouth and coiled up towards the roof of the shelter.

Outside, the world had been painted white. A thick layer of

197

snow swept across the ground and collected in the branches of the trees. Pale cloud smothered the sky and a few flakes still twirled to the ground.

Where was Rao? The Captain's side of the bivouac was empty, although his satchel still leant against the rock.

Jack stuck his head out of the shelter and immediately saw the Captain crouching nearby, his turban and coat speckled by flakes.

Rao grinned. 'Ah, you're up.' He dug his hand into the snow and raised a clump. 'Amazing.'

'Never seen it before?'

'Not this thick.' Rao shook the snow from his hands.

Jack looked up at the sky. The faint smear of the sun was only just peering over the hills.

Rao clicked open his pocket watch. 'Eight o'clock.'

Jack rubbed the back of his neck. At least it wasn't too late. Hopefully the savages wouldn't have—

He sat still for a second, then lurched out of the shelter and gazed into the distance. The floor of the valley was a sea of pure white with no distinguishing features. There was no sign of the camp, no sign of anyone at all.

The savages had gone.

No.

Jack struck off down the slope, wading through snow that came up to his knees in places.

'Where're you going?' Rao said. 'Wait.'

But Jack didn't wait. He had to get down into the valley and make sure he could pick up the savages' trail.

He floundered through a thick drift, brushed against a branch that dusted his head with flakes and slipped over completely at one point. He heard Rao huffing and puffing as he followed.

He reached the bottom of the hill and charged out of the cover of the trees. The wide, white valley reeled about him and the wind sent snowflakes swirling and dancing. He was panting by the time he reached the place where he estimated the camp had been. The snow was as unblemished as fresh cream. Not even an animal had crossed it.

Damn. The savages must have set off either before or during the snowfall. Their tracks were completely covered and impossible to follow.

He turned in a full circle, scanning the countryside in all directions. The snow had rubbed out any distinctive features. The white ground blended with the white sky, so that it was impossible to tell where one ended and the other began.

There was no sign of the savages anywhere.

Rao arrived, gasping for breath.

'You have the spyglass?' Jack asked.

Rao drew the glass from his coat and Jack gazed through it, searching the featureless landscape. Apart from a hawk sailing far above, there was no sign of life anywhere.

Damn.

He kicked a knot of snow and sent flakes flying.

Damn. Damn.

'What is it?' Rao asked.

'We've lost them,' Jack said. 'We've bloody lost them.'

15

A trickle of pain worked its way across Jack's chest. He took a deep breath of icy air. He was going to have to use the Europa yantra. And that meant revealing to Rao he was a siddha.

He cupped his hands, blew into them and rubbed them together. 'Look, Rao . . . sir. There's something I haven't mentioned yet. I was in the European Army. A long time ago.'

Rao's eyebrows shot up. 'Really? I didn't . . . Why didn't you mention it?'

'There was no reason to.'

Rao rolled his tongue in his mouth. 'Fair enough. What regiment?'

'The 2nd Native English Infantry.'

'Hold on.' Rao's eyes narrowed. 'I heard they mutinied three years ago.'

'That was long after I left,' Jack said quickly. 'I quit nine years before that.'

Rao frowned. 'All right. If you say so. Why are you telling me this now?'

'Because I'm going to have to use a power to find the trail.' Jack took another deep breath. 'A siddha power.'

Rao took a step back. 'You're a siddha?'

'Sort of. I'm a native siddha. I have an innate power. I learnt how to use it in the army.'

Rao rubbed his moustache. 'I see. I've heard of it. But it's very rare.'

'Not as rare as you might think in Britain. We grow up with strong sattva here. It's something to do with that.'

Rao stared hard at Jack. 'Who are you? Really?'

'I am who I say I am. I'm just a veteran who has a special ability.'

'Then why aren't you still in the army?'

'I just . . . I had to leave.'

'That's it? You just had to leave.'

'Look, we're wasting time. We have to—'

'This is all very strange. We're attacked by Mahajan's savages, but somehow you survive. You convince me to come with you. Now we're alone in the wilderness, and you tell me you're a siddha. That is very strange.'

Jack sighed. 'Perhaps. But there's nothing more to it—'

Rao drew his pistol and pointed it at Jack. His eyes were shining and the snow whirled about his head. 'Why did you leave the army? I demand to know.'

Christ. Rao was an idiot.

Jack tightened his jaw. He shouldn't have brought the Captain along – he was more trouble than he was worth.

'Put that away,' Jack said.

'Not until I get some answers.'

'What are you going to do? Shoot me? How will you find Parihar then?'

Rao's hand shook as he held the pistol.

Surely the fool wouldn't fire. Jack had run down the hill so quickly he'd left the knife, scimitar and pistol behind in the bivouac. He had nothing to fight with, other than his fists. Rao had taken a few steps back and was now about ten feet away. He could shoot before Jack had a chance to cross that space.

A rotary pistol was hardly a powerful firearm, but at short range it was deadly.

'All right, I'll tell you why I left,' Jack said. 'I was hit by a sattva-fire ball.' He tapped his chest. 'Got me here. It burns all the time. I wasn't well enough to stay on.' This was close enough to the truth, without going into detail.

'I see.' Rao tightened his grip on the pistol. 'Where's your proof?'

Jack took off his tunic, undid his doublet and pulled down his undershirt enough to expose the livid red scar on his chest.

Rao stepped a few paces closer and peered at the wound. 'Oh. That does look serious.'

Jack pulled on his tunic again. 'Satisfied now?'

'Why didn't you just tell me all this?'

'It's my private business.'

Rao paused to consider this. 'It's still all very strange.'

'Look, if I was going to harm you I would've done it by now, wouldn't I?'

'That is true.'

'Put the pistol down, for God's sake. We have to get moving. The savages will be far ahead of us now.'

Rao nodded slowly. 'I suppose you're right.' He lowered the pistol. 'You've done nothing wrong so far.' He put the pistol in his holster.

Jack immediately leapt forward, tackled Rao and knocked him backwards. Rao cried out and fell into the snow, Jack landing on top of him.

Jack smashed his fist into Rao's face. Rao scrabbled at the holster. He got the pistol out, but Jack knocked it out of his hand and it went flying into the snow.

Rao wailed, his eyes wide. Blood trickled from his nose. 'Don't kill me!'

Jack grabbed Rao's tunic at the collar. 'I'm not going to kill you. But I will if you point a pistol at me again.'

Rao's eyes widened further. He swallowed and nodded.

Jack let go of the Captain, retrieved the pistol and stuck it in his belt. He marched back towards the bivouac.

Snowflakes swished in front of his face.

It had felt good hitting Rao. The idiot deserved it. Jack didn't care any more what happened to the Captain. He was going to get his things and then he was going after Saleem. Alone.

Rajthanans. Why had he ever served them? Ever followed their orders?

He must have been mad.

He skidded and lurched uphill through the snow and reached the boulder. He crawled into the shelter and grasped the knapsack.

Then Rao's satchel caught his eye.

Atri's old satchel.

He lifted the bag's flap, peered inside and found a notebook and a few large sheets of folded paper. He crackled open one of the sheets and saw wriggling lines, symbols and marks that looked like writing. He couldn't understand any of it. He then flicked through the notebook and saw scratches of tiny writing and what appeared to be diagrams. He recognised the script as the secret language of the siddhas, even though he couldn't read it.

Damn. None of this helped him. He still had no idea what Atri had been doing. Or what Atri had known about Mahajan or the Brahmastra, whatever that was.

And the only person who could help him with any of this at the moment was Rao.

He heard the crunch of footsteps in the snow behind him. He shoved the notebook back in the satchel, grabbed Rao's pistol and the scimitar, and turned round.

The Captain stood about twenty feet away with his arms apart and palms open. His nose had stopped bleeding and he'd wiped his face clean. 'I'm sorry.'

Jack stood, pistol in one hand and scimitar in the other.

Rao's eyes were moist. 'You're right. I was asking a lot of questions that were none of my business. There's no reason for me not to trust you. All you've done so far is try to get our colleagues back.'

Jack hadn't expected Rao to be so contrite. He jabbed the

scimitar into the snow, where it stood like a roadside shrine. 'Glad you've seen sense.'

Rao rubbed his nose and winced as his fingers pressed a sensitive spot. 'I hope we can put this behind us.'

'Do you now?'

'What more do you want? I've apologised.'

'You can also apologise for killing my friend, Andrew.'

Rao frowned. 'What are you talking about?'

'My friend died when that bloody statue of yours fell on him.'

'Oh. Yes, I remember, a man was killed. A wagon broke.'

'That man was my comrade.'

'I'm sorry, but it's hardly my fault. It was an accident.'

'An accident that wouldn't have happened if we hadn't been carting that thing halfway across the wilderness.'

Rao's cheeks flushed. 'Now see here. I've apologised to you and all you can do is insult me. The murti was necessary. We had to have the blessing of Ganesh.'

'Didn't help us much, did it?'

'How dare you insult the god.'

'I'll insult him all I want. You were a fool taking that statue. And all that furniture. You can't travel in the wilds like that.'

Rao pursed his lips and his dishevelled moustache stretched. He puffed his chest out for a moment, but then exhaled again. His shoulders sagged. 'You could be right.'

'I know I'm right.'

Rao's eyes went glassy. 'This was my first command, you see.'

'Thought as much.'

'In Rajthana I was told . . . well, what does it matter now?' Rao sighed, sat on a rock and rubbed his forehead. 'I've made a mess of things.'

Again, Jack was surprised at Rao's reaction. The Captain was prepared to take some criticism from a native. There weren't many Rajthanans like that.

'Shiva, what am I doing?' Rao put his face in his hands.

Jack almost felt sorry for Rao for a moment. But only for a moment.

What now? Was he going to let Rao come along with him? Was the Captain going to be more of a help than a hindrance? Two men were better than one in a fight. And Rao might be able to explain the writings in Atri's notebook.

Jack made a quick decision. 'That's enough. You need to buck yourself up now. We have to keep going.' He strode over and offered Rao his pistol back.

'Oh.' Rao raised his eyebrows. 'Thank you.'

'You need something to defend yourself with,' Jack mumbled. 'Now get up. We need to get our things and go.'

'You might have to clean out that pistol.' Jack sat on a rock near the bivouac, preparing to clean his own firearm.

Rao patted his pistol, which was now back in its holster. 'It's loaded already.'

'It's been in the snow. Powder might be damp now.'

'You think so?'

Jack walked across, took the pistol and pointed it out towards the valley. He pulled the trigger and the hammer clicked down. The cap sparked, then . . . nothing. He tried again. Still nothing.

'See.' Jack handed back the pistol. 'Clean it out.'

Jack sat back on the rock and wrenched the bullets out of his pistol with the screw tool. When he'd finished, he handed the screw over to Rao, whose own tools were either lying back in the gorge or taken by the savages.

'We need hot water to clean out the barrels,' Rao said. 'We'll have to make a fire.'

'And what'll we boil the water in?'

'Ah.' Rao rubbed his moustache. 'True. We don't have a pot.'

'There is one way. But you're probably not going to like it.'

'What?'

Jack picked up the empty water canteen, turned away and loosened his hose. He began urinating into the canteen.

'Ergh,' Rao said. 'What are you doing?'

'Piss is a great cleaner. Trust me.'

Jack fastened his hose again, put small wooden pegs into his pistol's touch holes and poured urine into the six barrels. He passed the canteen over to Rao.

'Shiva.' Rao wrinkled his face and pressed his handkerchief to his nose.

'It's the only way,' Jack said.

Rao grimaced, took the canteen and poured urine into his pistol's muzzles. He turned his face away to avoid the steam rising from the liquid.

Jack put his hand over the end of his pistol and shook the weapon up and down, swilling the urine in the barrels. He looked across at Rao. 'Come on.'

With a look of supreme disgust, Rao put his hand over his pistol and shook. He went pale, as if he were about to throw up.

They both poured the urine out into the snow and repeated the process a few times. Rao gagged at one point, but managed to hold back the vomit.

Once the barrels were clean, they dried the pistols with rags and reloaded with greased patches and bullets. Jack used snow to wipe down the scimitar, then shoved the blade, the knife and the pistol into his belt.

'You all right?' Jack asked.

Rao nodded, colour returning to his cheeks.

Jack couldn't help grinning at Rao's discomfort. 'Right, then. Let's get back to the trail.'

———◆———

Jack sat cross-legged on the frozen floor of the valley. The white landscape stretched away from him in all directions. A faint breeze fluttered the edges of his tunic, but the snowfall had stopped.

Rao stomped his feet to keep himself warm while he waited nearby.

Jack shut his eyes, took several deep breaths and tried to calm his mind. Worries about Saleem beat in his head. Was the lad still alive? Was he strong enough to keep going? But Jack couldn't let these concerns distract him.

He concentrated on the cold air flowing into his nostrils, hitting the back of his throat and chilling his lungs.

The storm in his head receded.

Good. He was getting himself under control.

He focused on the Europa yantra, the intricate details appearing before him on a black background. The design circled slowly and he fought to hold it still.

He sensed the grainy texture of the sattva about him. He was in a medium stream, which was better than nothing. He reached out with his mind, dragged the sattva towards him and began smelting, the sattva exuding a sweet scent as it was processed.

He sensed the spirit realm draw close. A heavy brightness weighed upon him.

Focus on the yantra. Don't let it slip.

Your mind is a rippling pool. Still it.

The fire in his chest flickered and pain streaked through his body. But he ignored it. He wasn't going to let his injury put him off his task.

The yantra locked into place and he held the entire image in his mind without any other thoughts intruding. The design shimmered and then burst into dazzling light.

Warmth flooded through his body, cathedral bells and angelic singing seemed to clamour in his head and suddenly he was in the centre of a vast, interconnected lattice.

He flung his eyes open. The white ocean of snow rolled away from him. Wavelets and swells, with blue shadows, scudded across the valley floor.

He looked down. All about him, strings of lights glowed

through the snow, as if hundreds of lanterns had been buried beneath the drifts.

Trails in sattva. And judging by their size and shape, they were the markings left by the four hundred or so savages.

He leapt up and Rao jumped slightly at the sudden movement.

'Spyglass,' Jack said, and Rao handed it over.

Jack snapped open the glass and peered through it. The luminous trails coursed away down the valley, becoming no more than pinpricks in the distance. He stared harder and noticed the tiny lights curving gently to the right more than a mile off and flowing up over a range of hills. He memorised the point where the trail rippled past a stand of trees and then allowed himself to slide out of the trance.

Pain jabbed at his chest and his breathing was shallow. But he felt better than he'd expected. Kanvar's cure was still holding.

He handed back the glass. 'I've got the trail.'

Rao stared at the ground ahead and frowned. 'I can't see a thing.'

'Trust me. Let's go.'

—♦—

They jogged through the snow, kicking up flakes behind them. Their breath frosted about their mouths and ice collected in Rao's moustache. Their footsteps were the first to mark the pristine snow.

They reached the hills and clambered up the slope towards the copse Jack had seen earlier. A herd of deer stood in the distance and watched them warily.

At the summit, they rested and munched a few dry rations. Jack checked the bag and found there were only ten biscuits left. They would have to hunt for food if they couldn't catch up to the savages soon.

They took it in turns to scan the ground ahead through the glass. Jack saw further mountains and buckled valleys carpeted in snow, but no sign of the Scots.

He sniffed. He caught the sweet aroma of sattva and a shiver crossed his skin. They were in a strong stream – a good place to enter the trance.

He meditated again and soon spied the wide trail running down the slope and into a forest. He grasped the knapsack and led Rao downhill, remaining in the trance so that he could keep his eyes on the tracks. The incline was steep and they had to zigzag in order to stop themselves slipping. Sweat blossomed beneath Jack's tunic and his breath was short and raspy. The trance suppressed his discomfort, but he was only too aware that he was growing weaker.

They reached the forest and paced down between the black, leafless trees. The branches clenched together over their heads and roots snaked out of the snow in front of them. Jack kept his eyes firmly on the glowing tracks speckling the ground ahead.

After around ten minutes, he spotted a distinctive set of holes in the snow. He ran down to them and crouched for a better look. They were the telltale tracks left by the savage's shoes. Glancing around, he saw further footprints interspersed between the trees.

He looked up at Rao and grinned. 'Found the trail again. They must have got this far before the heavy snow stopped.'

Rao paused for a moment, then swallowed and said awkwardly, 'Well done.'

Jack skipped out of the trance. Tiredness swamped him and the pain quivered in his chest. But after a brief rest he felt well enough to continue.

They wove their way between the trees and down to the floor of a narrow valley. The tracks were so clear in the snow even Rao was able to follow them.

After an hour, Jack stopped when he saw Rao was lagging behind. While he waited, he trudged down to a nearby brook, cracked the ice, washed out the canteen and filled it with water.

Rao slowed to a walk, plodded over and sat on a rock. His face was red and he was wheezing. Jack offered him the canteen, but he crinkled his nose and turned his face away. 'You can't drink from that now.'

Jack shrugged and gulped down some water, which tasted fine. Rao scooped up a handful of snow and sucked on that instead.

A thin howl cracked the silence, echoing between the slopes.

Rao jumped up and rested his hand on his holster. 'What was that?'

The howl struck up again, joined by another and then a third. The cries were eerie, but Jack knew what they were.

'Wolves,' he said.

Rao frowned. 'What?'

'Like big dogs.'

'Oh.' Rao searched the scarps. 'Yes, I've heard of them. It's the strangest sound.'

'They'll leave us alone. Come on.'

They pressed on, following the black potholes left by the savages' feet. The wolves stopped wailing after a few minutes and all Jack could hear was the crisp crunch of his and Rao's boots in the snow. As the afternoon wore on, the cloud congealed and darkened overhead, a chill wind whipped through the valley and flakes began to circle down again.

'It's damn cold,' Rao said when they stopped for a break. He pulled the collar of his overcoat tight about his neck. He'd put on riding gloves, but had nothing warmer to wear. Flakes dusted his turban and shoulders and ice was crystallising in his moustache again.

Jack shivered. The breeze whispered through his tunic and the cold pressed against his hose. He lifted his hood over his head. 'We'd best keep moving. Only way to stay warm.'

The wind strengthened and tossed the snow around them as they jogged on. Jack's nose and cheeks were rubbed raw and he pulled his hands into his sleeves to stop them going numb. Blinking flakes out of his eyes, he saw the savages' footprints were filling up with snow. Soon they would be smothered completely.

Several wolves bayed from somewhere high up to the left. The sound cut through the whistling wind and even Jack felt the hair stand up on the back of his neck.

Rao shuddered.

'It sounds worse than it is,' Jack said, trying his best to be reassuring.

'What's that?' Rao pointed into the woods.

Jack stopped and stared. At first he saw nothing, but then spotted a grey shape flicker between the trees about a hundred yards away. Another shape followed and then three or four others. They seemed to appear from nowhere and then slip away again into the swirling haze.

'Wolves?' Rao asked.

Jack nodded. 'Looks like it.'

The cries continued to wheel about them and the wind turned into a gale, blasting them with ice and dashing snow in their faces. They could no longer run and had to trudge ahead, leaning into the squalls. The cold stung Jack's ears and face.

Soon the wail of the wind blotted out the wolves' howling. But the ghostly creatures still flitted through the woods, appearing up ahead, then to the left, then the right.

Jack wondered whether they were encircling him and Rao.

The light dimmed, but Jack couldn't tell whether this was due to the storm or the lowering of the sun. He'd lost track of time and the savages' trail was completely covered over. He would have to meditate again if they were going to continue. But was it wise to continue now with the wolves following them and the temperature plummeting further by the minute?

He shouted to Rao over the wind, 'What time is it?'

'What?' Rao cried back.

'Time?' Jack said more loudly.

Rao plucked out his pocket watch and squinted at it, wiping flakes away from the face. 'Half past three.'

'We should make camp. It'll be dark soon and the storm's getting bad.'

'Where?'

Jack glanced around. Nowhere in sight offered much shelter, but he spotted the dark blur of a line of hills about half a mile away. There might be rocks or an overhang there that could provide some degree of protection.

'We'll try over there.' Jack pointed towards the slopes and forged his way to the right through the deepening snow. Ice encrusted his eyebrows and his lips went numb. Every inch of his skin trembled from the cold.

They couldn't last much longer out in the storm like this. They would freeze to death.

Jack paused beside a tree to catch his breath. When he looked back, he saw Rao was more than a hundred yards back and almost obscured by the snowstorm.

Christ. The Captain was walking so slowly. It would be dark by the time they reached the hills at this rate.

Finally, Rao caught up and Jack noticed that his eyes had a blank look and he gazed about him as if he couldn't understand where he was.

'You all right?' Jack shouted.

Rao started, as if he'd just noticed Jack, then seemed to become more alert. 'Fine, yes. Just cold.'

Jack led the way forward again into the lashing wind. After ten minutes, Rao cried out and Jack spun round to see the Captain lying on his side. Jack waded back and crouched down.

'Just fell.' Rao gasped and raised himself on his arm. 'I'm all right.'

But Rao looked pale and his teeth were chattering so loudly Jack could hear them.

Jack didn't like the look of this. He'd seen men die from the cold several times when he was in the army. It came in stages. A man would become delirious, lose all his strength and even will to continue. Then he would fall unconscious and eventually slip away.

Jack scoured the surroundings. He had to find shelter for Rao. Now.

He spied a wide, twisted oak with roots that formed a series of hollows at its base. That was the best place on offer at the moment.

'Come on.' Jack offered Rao his hand. 'Not far now.'

He heaved Rao up and supported him as they limped over to the oak. He eased the Captain down in the lee of the tree, where he was protected from the worst of the storm. Rao's eyes closed and his head lolled to the side. Jack slapped him in the face a few times and his eyelids half opened.

'You stay here,' Jack shouted. 'I'm going to build a shelter.'

Rao didn't respond, but he held his head straight at least and didn't close his eyes.

Jack stumbled out into the blizzard, searching the ground for branches. The gale pulled at his tunic, flicked snow in his eyes and moaned in his ears. He spotted two large branches leaning against a rock, picked them up, then saw a further branch half split off from a birch and floundered across to it. He wrenched the branch free, turned and then jumped slightly when he saw a wolf standing about ten feet away. It had appeared so suddenly it was like something from a dream. Its grey-white fur rippled in the wind and it stared at Jack with yellow eyes.

Jack kept his eyes locked on the beast as his hand crept towards the pistol.

But then the wolf turned and padded away into the reeling snowflakes.

Jack breathed out. But he didn't wait around any longer. If the wolves were becoming less wary, Rao could be in danger.

He waded back towards the oak and made out the Captain still hunched between the tree roots. The pale form of a wolf prowled up and down around twenty feet away from the prone Rajthanan.

No.

THE PLACE OF DEAD KINGS

Jack tried to run, but the snow dragged at his legs. He surged forward, shouting in an attempt to wake Rao.

The wolf crept closer to the Captain. Another loped out of the white murk and sat watching.

Jack dropped the branches, wrenched out his pistol and fired into the air. The loud crack cut through the wind. Both wolves jolted and sprinted off into the woods.

He scooped up the branches and trudged forward again. He heard a growl to his left, spun round and saw another wolf stalking him. He fired at the creature. But this time the pistol spluttered, crackled and kicked hard in his hand. All the bullets shot out at once.

Christ. A chain fire. Despite their benefits, rotary pistols were prone to accidents.

He'd missed the wolf, but it slunk off anyway. Turning back, he saw the two wolves circling Rao again. But there were no bullets left in his pistol, and no time to reload.

Damn it.

He shouted, dropped the branches and tried to rush forward.

Then he sensed movement out of the corner of his eye. Instinctively, he swivelled and saw a wolf bounding straight at him.

Everything seemed to slow down. He saw the creature flying silently and gracefully across the snow, its eyes fixed on him. It leapt and sailed in his direction. He could see its nose and fangs in great detail. He dropped the pistol and reached for the scimitar.

But he was too slow.

The wolf smacked into his chest with more force than he'd thought possible. He flew backwards and smashed into the snow. The wolf thumped down on top of him.

It paused for a second, then opened its jaws, snarled and lunged at his face.

214

16

Jack cried out, swung his arm and smacked the wolf in the head. The beast's maw was knocked to the side for a moment, but it immediately forced its jaws straight back towards him.

His heart bashed in his ears.

He grasped the wolf's matted fur and tried to drive its mouth away again. But the creature was strong. He felt its neck and shoulder muscles rippling beneath his hands.

There was only one possible outcome to this struggle.

His only hope was to get the knife out of his belt, but that would mean letting go of the beast's head with one hand at least.

Would he be able to stab the wolf before it could rip his face off?

Sweat streamed across his forehead. He stared straight into the creature's mouth. Strings of saliva stretched between its fangs and its hot, stale breath blasted his nostrils. His arms screamed at the strain of forcing the creature back.

He couldn't hold on for much longer. He had to do it now.

He released his right hand, grasped at his belt and ripped out the knife.

The wolf lurched forward and its teeth pressed against his cheek. The reek of its breath was overwhelming.

He slammed the knife up into the creature's belly and felt hot blood splash over his hand. The wolf yelped and jerked its head back. He drove the knife up again, and then a third time.

The creature gave a high-pitched squeal and rolled off him. It tried to flee, but its back legs gave way and it was forced to drag itself along, smearing bright blood on the snow.

Heart still crashing in his ribs, Jack sprang to his knees and saw the two wolves still skulking close to Rao.

'*No!*' he shouted.

He scrambled across to the Captain. His sudden movement startled the wolves and they backed away. But soon they came prowling back.

Rao's eyes were closed and his lips were blue, but his chest was going up and down.

Thank Christ he was still alive.

A pistol. Jack needed a pistol right now. The wolves were mere feet away.

He shoved his hand under Rao's coat and hunted around for the holster. His fingers were so numb he could barely feel anything.

Christ. It was taking too long. He wasn't going to find the damn thing.

Then his fingers touched metal. He ripped out the pistol, swung round and pulled the trigger, praying the weapon would fire. The hammer smacked down and the pistol spat smoke and flame. He missed both wolves, but they both shot off into the trees immediately.

But for how long? He had to get a fire started quickly. That was the only way to keep the animals at bay.

And keep Rao alive.

He shook the Captain, but got no reaction. He slapped Rao in the face until finally he opened one eye slightly. Rao's eyeball shifted around, as if he were drunk.

'Hold on,' Jack said. 'Don't fall asleep. You understand? Don't fall asleep!'

———◆———

Jack's eyes burnt with tiredness. He hadn't slept for hours and had no idea how late it was. Perhaps it was after midnight, perhaps later. But he wouldn't let himself rest. He had to keep an eye on the wolves still creeping out in the shadows, and he had to keep tending the fire. If it went out, the beasts were sure to advance again.

A trickle of dirt fell on his head. He glanced up, but saw that the bivouac he'd cobbled together from branches, twigs, damp leaves and earth was still holding and retaining most of the heat from the fire at the entrance.

Rao lay against the tree, right beside the flames. Jack had wrapped him in both of the blankets. The colour had come back to his face and his lips were no longer blue. But he'd been sleeping for a long time.

Jack reached across and touched Rao's cheek. It was no longer icy cold – a good sign.

The Captain groaned and his eyes crept open. Another good sign. Maybe he would survive after all.

Rao looked around blearily and finally focused on Jack. 'Ah. You're still here.'

'You think I'd leave you?'

Rao swallowed. 'I don't remember . . . Where are we?'

'You fell. I made camp for the night. You were too weak to go on.'

'Ah.' Rao edged his head around and stared at the fire. 'I had a strange dream.'

Jack grinned. 'You were lost in Scotland?'

Rao managed a weak smile. He shut his eyes and struggled to summon the strength to continue.

'You should rest,' Jack said.

Rao opened his eyes again. 'No . . . In my dream I was back in Rajthana. I'd never left. Never come to Europe.' He turned to look at Jack again. 'But you were there.'

'Me?' Jack snorted. 'In Rajthana?'

'Yes, you were there. And you'd come to tell me something. That my father had forgiven me . . . Isn't that strange?'

'You were delirious. The cold gets to you like that.'

'Jack, can you do something for me?'

'What?'

'If I don't make it, can you get a message to the barracks at Dun Fries.'

'You *are* going to make it.'

'But if I don't. Will you promise?'

'There's no need—'

'I beg you.'

Jack sighed and rubbed his forehead. Rao seemed confused. Maybe he hadn't recovered much after all. 'Very well. I promise.'

Rao shut his eyes. 'Good. Tell them at Dun Fries to write to my father to tell him that I died trying my best to make him proud. To atone for what I did.'

Atone? What for? Jack was curious, but knew this was hardly the time to ask further. He put his hand on Rao's shoulder. 'I'll do it.'

'And . . . write to Kumari Reena Chamar. Tell her that I . . . always loved her.' Rao grimaced as if in pain and squeezed his eyes shut even tighter.

'You need to rest now.'

Rao sighed and went limp.

Christ. Was he dead?

But then Jack saw the Captain's chest was rising and falling. He was only sleeping.

With any luck, he was dreaming pleasantly of Kumari Chamar.

❦

Birds chirped high in the trees and sunlight washed through the branches. The snow shone as if it were polished.

Jack trudged, slipped and skidded through the swollen drifts. The sky was sharp blue, with only a few puffs of cloud, the storm having spent itself during the night.

He stopped for a second in a shaft of light, revelling in the warmth on his skin. He hadn't slept at all – he'd had to stay awake to guard Rao. It had been a bad night, but it looked as though the Captain would pull through.

He pressed on, his arms about a clump of wood. He hadn't dared go far from the fire during the night, but now that it was morning he felt confident enough to venture a little further.

The old oak and the bivouac appeared ahead. He halted in surprise.

Rao was standing with his hands on his hips, stretching his back. He grinned. 'There you are.'

'You're looking better.' Jack plodded over to the shelter and dumped the firewood.

Rao breathed in deeply. 'I feel fantastic, to be honest.'

Jack poked at the fire with a stick and threw on a few branches. 'Didn't look so good last night.'

'No.' Rao squatted down beside the flames. 'Look, I can remember bits of it. It seems I owe you my life.'

'You weren't that bad.' Jack busied himself by throwing more sticks into the fire. Rao didn't need to thank him. They were enemies who'd been thrown together. That was all.

And yet, Jack had to admit he was glad Rao had lived. It would have been hard to watch a man freeze to death.

'I saw those wolves,' Rao said. 'I remember that.'

'Do you?'

'I would have been done for.'

'Don't worry about it.'

'And I want to say sorry.'

Jack looked up. 'What for?'

Rao cleared his throat. 'Your friend. Who died. Because of the murti.'

Jack paused. He appreciated these words from Rao. It seemed the Captain had been thinking about their argument yesterday. 'Look, I might have . . . gone a bit far. It was an accident.'

'An avoidable accident. I thought we needed the god's blessing, you see. That's how we do it in Rajthana.'

'In case you hadn't noticed, this isn't Rajthana.'

'Indeed. I have a lot to learn. And I will learn.'

'You just get your strength back up. You'll need it.'

—◆—

Rao paused for a moment as they trudged up a scarp. 'It's quite something, isn't it?'

'Aye.' Jack stopped and looked around.

The land appeared bewitched. The fresh snow blanketing the slopes glittered in the sunlight. Icicles hung from trees and rocks, while the distant mountaintops gleamed like enamel.

Rao took a deep breath. 'Yes. Quite something.'

Jack started walking again. 'Come on.'

Rao had been like a man transformed during the morning. He strode forward with boundless energy, often marching ahead of Jack. It was astonishing to think he'd almost died during the night.

A trace of pain crackled in Jack's chest. It had started earlier when he'd meditated to pick up the trail again and continued even now that he'd left the trance. But it was more than just his chest. His breathing was shallower than usual and his legs felt leaden. Marching uphill through the snow sent perspiration beading on his forehead and trickling beneath his clothing.

There were only twelve days left before Kanvar's cure wore off. Just twelve days.

How far ahead of them were the savages now? Hours? Half a day? More?

And what would he and Rao do when they caught up anyway? There were still only two of them. And now they only had seven bullets between them. He'd had to fire several more rounds during the night to scare off the wolves, and now neither of them had a fully loaded pistol.

In part to stop himself brooding, Jack asked, 'What do you know about Mahajan?'

'Mahajan? Not a lot.'

'But your commanders must have had some information.'

'They didn't know a lot either. No one does. Mahajan's said to be a powerful siddha, but he's worked on his own for years in different parts of the world. Some say he was expelled from the siddha order in Rajthana, but they've denied that. Others say he was asked to leave because of his dangerous experiments. Still others think it was internal politics.' Rao gave a half-smile. 'Who knows? The siddhas are secretive and follow their own rules.'

'What kind of experiments was he doing?'

Rao shrugged. 'No one told me. Atri was supposed to be the expert.' Rao paused after mentioning the dead man. 'That didn't work out, obviously. Atri was going to deal with Mahajan. My assignment was just to get him there.' Rao slid his coat open and tapped the moon-clan insignia on his tunic. 'You see, I'm a military man. I don't know about technical matters. That's for the priest jatis.'

Jack eyed Atri's satchel. Rao might not be technically minded, but he'd still kept the siddha's notes. And he hadn't mentioned the Brahmastra. He knew at least a little more than he was letting on.

'So,' Jack said, 'what are we going to do if we come across Mahajan now?'

Rao rubbed his moustache. 'I've been wondering that myself. Nothing, I suppose. We've no need to fear Mahajan, I don't think. He's a Rajthanan not a savage. He'll treat us decently, I'm sure. We'll have to find out what we can about him and then report back to Dun Fries. There's nothing else we can do.'

'You sure he'll welcome us? He sent those savages to attack us.'

Rao chewed his lip. 'We don't know he sent them. Maybe these savages don't follow his orders after all. Perhaps they acted on their own initiative.'

Jack went to speak, but stopped himself when something caught his eye. He frowned. Was that what he thought it was?

He pushed his way through the knee-deep snow to his right, holding out his arms to steady himself. Ahead of him, the slope folded down into a grove. As he drew closer, he became certain about what he'd seen.

'What is it?' Rao called.

'Tracks,' Jack said.

In front of him, hundreds of punctures in the snow showed where the savages had been.

Rao clambered across the slope. 'How far ahead are they?'

'Hard to say. You can't easily tell how old tracks are in the snow.' Jack squinted up at the sun. 'What time do you make it?'

Rao clicked open his watch. 'One o'clock.'

'It stopped snowing just before dawn. I reckon they'll have sheltered for the night in those trees over there. That means they left after sunrise. Around eight o'clock.'

'So, they're five hours ahead of us.'

'At the most. As best I can tell.'

'We can still catch up to them.'

'Aye. That we can.' Jack went to follow the trail, then halted and stared at the ground about ten feet away.

'There.' Jack's voice was hoarse. He scrambled across the slope, kicking up white clouds behind him. He sank to his knees and studied the snow more closely.

It was just as he'd thought. Four sets of boot prints. One left by a short man, the others by taller men with longer strides.

No savages wore boots.

Rao struggled over to Jack. 'What now?'

Jack pointed out the prints. 'Our friends.'

'You sure?'

'Sure as I can be.'

'So, they're alive.' Rao slapped his fist into his left hand and gazed up the slope, as if he would see the captives there.

'They were alive this morning.' Jack stood again and dusted the snow from his hands. 'Maybe we'll free them yet.'

17

Wind blew down from the mountains, whipped up the snow and spun it into eddies. Flakes splattered Jack in the face and the cold seeped through his clothes and into his skin.

'It's coming down hard again.' Rao shivered and hugged himself.

Jack looked up. Rao was right – swarms of snowflakes were tumbling once more from the clouds. He could still see the savages' tracks ahead of him, but within a quarter of an hour they would be smothered.

Damn. When would the weather clear? He and Rao had had a good morning and made excellent progress, but now, with the snow setting in, they would have to find shelter again.

He glanced at Rao. He couldn't risk a repeat of last night.

Rao must have understood his thoughts because he managed a tight smile and said, 'I'm fine. Much better than yesterday.'

Rao looked well enough so far, but Jack wondered about himself. His leg muscles ached and his chest was tight. Shooting pains jabbed his torso, bad enough for him to have to shut his eyes and concentrate for a moment to blot them out.

They plodded on for half an hour, the wind building, the flying snow thickening and the late afternoon light starting to fade. Finally, Jack had to admit that the tracks had completely vanished. He would have to go into the trance again, but he knew that would weaken him further.

He was about to stop, when Rao pointed at a stand of trees to the left and said, 'Wolf.'

Jack squinted, blinking flakes from his eyes. A grey-white

shape flitted within the woods, followed by several others.

'Those damn things just keep following us,' Rao said.

'They're hungry.' Jack drew his pistol. He was going to have to use a precious bullet. 'I have to meditate again. I'll scare them off first.'

He blasted once into the air and most of the wolves vanished instantly. A few remained, however, prowling up and down and watching with their yellow eyes.

Jack fired twice more, the wind kicking the acrid smoke straight back into his face. Finally, all the wolves slipped away. But now he had no bullets left.

All they had was Rao's weapon.

He scanned the area for somewhere sheltered enough for him to meditate. A fir a few yards away looked suitable, but then he noticed black marks in the snow near to it.

Tracks?

He started off towards the tree, Rao following close behind. As he drew closer, he could see the indentations were human foot-prints, slowly being buried by snow, but still clear.

A shiver ran up his spine. He didn't like the look of this.

Rao peered at the ground. 'Savages?'

'Yes.'

'Good, then we're still on their trail.'

'No. Look, there're only a few footprints. Must have been only two men.'

'So, they separated from the main group?'

'Looks that way. But there's something else.' Jack crouched and studied one of the marks more closely. 'These tracks are fresh. Can't be more than fifteen minutes old. Otherwise they'd be covered by now.'

'Fifteen minutes?' Rao's moustache stiffened and he cast a wary look around him. 'That means they could still be nearby.'

'Exactly.' Jack stood and gazed into the blizzard. He couldn't see much beyond two hundred yards. Were there savages watching from the dark knots of trees? From the dim scarps? From the tops of bluffs?

'We should keep going,' Jack said.

'What about the trail?'

'They were heading up this valley.' Jack pointed ahead. 'The hills are steep, so I reckon they'd keep going straight. I say we press on. I'll check the trail later.'

Rao nodded and they forced their way ahead through the rising snow. A wolf bayed in the distance and the temperature dropped. Jack shuddered and his legs almost gave way a couple of times. Rao was stumbling and skidding too.

Neither of them could keep going for long. But they had to get out of the valley and find somewhere to hide.

They entered a particularly powerful stream of sattva, so strong the scent scratched Jack's nose and the back of his throat. They'd been passing through strong sattva for days, but the streams were becoming even more intense the further they travelled into the mountains.

Mahajan had chosen a good place for yoga, or whatever it was he was up to.

Within twenty minutes, they reached the head of the valley. The scarps to either side were sheer, rocky and virtually impassable. The only clear way ahead was up through a pass between two mountains.

'Should you check the trail now?' Rao shouted over the wind, his overcoat flapping about him.

'Not yet. I want to get out of here.' He pointed at the pass. 'We'll go up there first.'

They started up the slope, ploughing through the snow. The wind shrieked down and blasted them with gritty flakes that stung their faces.

Twice Rao fell, but both times he swung himself up again straight away.

'You all right?' Jack asked.

'I can keep going.'

Halfway up, Jack began to think he'd made a mistake. Both he and Rao were tiring fast, and the sattva-fire clenched his chest. If there were savages around, they were hardly likely to attack in this weather – even they would have to find shelter.

All the same, now that he and Rao had come this far, it would be better to continue to the summit. At least from there they would be able to see more of their surroundings and with any luck spot somewhere to make camp.

They passed into another powerful stream. The whirling sattva made Jack dizzy. His foot slid out from under him and he toppled over, getting snow in his face. He twisted himself round and tried to get up, but his arms were too weak to support his weight. He slid down again and lay on his back in the knee-high snow.

Rao's face appeared above him. The Captain held out his hand and Jack grasped it and let Rao heave him back on to his feet.

'Can you keep going?' Rao shouted.

Jack thought about it. His legs seemed able to support him. Pain forked across his chest, but it wasn't bad enough to stop him walking. Too tired to speak, he nodded and pressed on up the scarp.

They passed out of the sattva stream, but the pain still throbbed between Jack's ribs. At least now they were almost near the summit. The icy gale seared Jack's face and nose, but that wasn't going to stop him. He just had to reach the crest of the hill and then he would see shelter somewhere nearby. He was sure of it.

Just keep going. One step after the other.

A great slab of pain thumped him in the chest. He lost his breath completely. He slipped, held out his arms in an attempt to steady himself, slid again and fell forward into the snow.

A blanket of darkness spread over him. He tried to stay conscious, but he was slipping away.

The last thing he remembered was the snow pressing against his face.

He felt so cold it was as if he were encased in ice. It was pitch black, but that was because his eyes were closed. He was sure of that.

He was alive. He flexed his fingers and although they felt frozen, they moved. Yes, he was still alive.

'Jack.' Rao's voice came from far away and was garbled, as if he were speaking underwater.

Jack tried to open his eyes but the effort seemed impossible.

'Jack,' Rao called again.

Jack tried once more and this time managed to prise his eyelids apart.

Rao was squatting in front of him, dusted with snow, his eyebrows and moustache caked in ice. His face was grim, but a half-smile slid across his lips when he saw Jack stir. 'Shiva. I thought you were gone.'

Jack looked around and saw stone to either side and above him. He was lying in a shallow cave formed by an overhang in a rock face. But the recess was so small his feet stuck out of the entrance. The wild wind screamed and dashed snow in every direction outside.

He was wrapped in a blanket, but this did little to keep him warm. He looked at his hands and saw they were a translucent white.

'What happened?' he asked.

'You passed out. I dragged you here.'

'Where are we?'

'Near where you fell. I couldn't get you far. This was the best place I could find.'

Jack tried to sit up, but the sattva-fire flared in his chest, the force of it so strong it knocked him back against the rock. He grimaced, gritted his teeth and tried again, fighting through the pain. But his arms were weak and he couldn't move more than a few inches.

'You rest.' Rao put his hand on Jack's shoulder.

'It's too cold.' Jack's voice was no more than a whisper. His misty breath coiled up from his mouth, as if his spirit were already leaving his body.

'I'll get firewood. You stay here.'

Jack struggled once more to move. He didn't want to stay where he was. He had to get up. He couldn't let Saleem down.

But it was hopeless. He couldn't move.

Darkness rushed over him again. He fell down and down into a black pit.

He heard the wind moaning. The sound ebbed and flowed, sometimes deafening, sometimes soft.

Someone was shaking him. Someone was shouting.

It took him a great effort to slide open his eyes. Rao was crouching in front of him again and gesturing at a small fire.

'Sorry I took so long,' Rao said. 'I had to go a long way for wood. Right down into the next valley.'

The flames licked along the branches and the smoke hovered in the small space. Jack tried to crawl towards the fire but managed to move only a few inches. Seeing the problem, Rao used two branches to shift the half-burnt wood and embers closer.

A subtle patch of warmth spread across the lower part of Jack's leg. He raised his hands and felt the barest trace of heat on his palms.

Was the fire going to be enough to keep them warm? It was growing dark outside, and with night setting in the temperature would drop further.

'We can't stay here.' Jack's voice was hoarse.

'Can you walk?'

Jack tried to wriggle his legs but they seemed virtually paralysed. A wave of pain swept over him and he shut his eyes until it passed.

'Looks like we'll have to stay where we are,' Rao said. 'I don't think I can drag you down this mountain. You'd probably die of cold if I tried.'

The wind howled.

Rao was right. Jack could see that, despite his dizziness and confusion. His only hope was to warm up and recover enough to be able to move again. But how long would that take? All night? And would he even survive the night stuck up on the mountain?

'I have to get more wood.' Rao upturned the knapsack and emptied the contents. 'I'll take this so I can carry more.'

'Wait.' Jack reached up weakly with his hand. 'The cold out there could kill you.'

'I'm all right.' Rao edged backwards to the cave entrance. 'I owe you this.'

Jack went to say that Rao owed him nothing, but the Captain had already slipped out into the blizzard.

Jack sighed as another bolt of pain shot through him.

Would he still be alive when Rao came back?

Would Rao even make it back?

He tried to get Katelin's necklace out from under his tunic, but couldn't find the strength and instead clutched it through his clothing. As he slipped away, he saw Elizabeth back in Shropshire. And the thought that at least, for the moment, she was safe spread warmth through his frozen limbs.

<hr>

Rao shook him awake. He opened his eyes and stared at the Captain as though through a film of gauze. The pain in his chest was fierce, but he didn't feel cold at all now. He imagined he was blissfully warm for a moment, but then realised he was just numb.

Rao was panting and his eyes were wild. 'I saw people out there.' He swallowed and tried to catch his breath. 'Savages.'

Savages? Jack remembered them. But he didn't care. They were irrelevant. What did it matter if they were creeping about nearby? What did it matter if they killed him and Rao?

He stopped this train of thought, blinked a few times and managed to concentrate.

'I saw wolves.' Rao grasped Jack's sleeve. 'I fired to scare them off but they kept coming. I had to use up all the bullets. Then, as I was coming back, I saw figures. Savages. Out in this weather. Can you imagine?'

Jack felt tiredness swamp him. He wanted to plan what their next move should be. What should they do if the savages approached? But he didn't have the strength. He couldn't think straight.

'I don't know if they saw me,' Rao said. 'I ran back here. At least I got this.' He patted the knapsack, which had a few branches poking out of it.

Jack shut his eyes and felt himself drifting away again. Everything seemed so difficult and tiring. So impossible to deal with.

It was strange to think that he was now incapacitated and probably dying, with Rao trying to save him, when last night the opposite had been the case. God's will was unfathomable sometimes.

He forced his eyes open again. He'd made a decision and had to tell Rao. But was he strong enough to speak?

Rao was busy trying to relight the fire, which had died while he'd been away. The matches kept blowing out and he was cursing in Rajthani.

'Listen.' Jack's voice was a thick whisper.

Rao leant across. 'What is it?'

Jack raised his hand and tried feebly to grasp Rao's coat. 'You go on.'

'Go on?'

'Leave me here. I'm done for.'

Rao sat back. His icy moustache straightened. 'I will not leave you.'

Jack shut his eyes, tried to summon the strength to continue.

He had to make Rao see sense. He opened his eyes again and his vision was even more cloudy now. 'You'll die if you stay here. Too cold. You won't last the night.'

'There are savages out there. And wolves.'

'You have to take a chance.'

Rao's eyes moistened and he touched Jack's shoulder gently. 'Now you close your eyes and sleep. I'm going nowhere. I won't leave a comrade here to die.'

Jack's eyelids slid down. It was too hard to continue. Rao was an idiot if he stayed. But there was nothing Jack could do about it.

<hr />

Jack woke and the cold on his face and hands burnt. His chest throbbed and there was a sour taste in the back of his throat. He glanced across and saw Rao huddled beside him under a blanket. The Captain's face was pale, his lips were tinged blue and his eyes had a slightly glazed look.

Even in his confused state, Jack could tell it was bad.

He looked towards the entrance of the cave. The fire had gone out, leaving just grey coals. The storm still raged outside.

'The fire,' he managed to say.

'What?' Rao leant in closer.

Jack took a deep breath and tried to speak more loudly. 'The fire.'

Rao eased himself back and shut his eyes for a moment. 'Ran out of wood.'

'Go.'

'I won't go.'

'Get wood, then. We'll freeze.'

'No more bullets . . . No more strength either . . . Don't know if I can walk even.'

Christ. They were both going to die of cold. Unless the wolves or savages got them first. 'I'm sorry. You should have gone.'

'I wouldn't do that.' Rao put his gloved hand on a folded piece of paper, which looked as though it had been torn from Atri's notebook. 'I wrote a final letter. In case anyone finds us.'

Jack closed his eyes. It seemed beyond improbable that anyone who could read would ever find their frozen bodies up on the mountainside, but he didn't want to say that. What was the point? Rao was probably well aware his note was unlikely ever to be discovered anyway.

Jack thought he might have drifted asleep but he wasn't sure. At any rate, when he opened his eyes Rao was still sitting beside him, fingering his letter.

'Who did you write to?' Jack asked. 'Your sweetheart?'

Rao nodded.

'You due to get married?'

Rao shut his eyes and winced. 'No.'

'Why not?'

Rao opened his eyes and his bottom lip trembled. 'My father forbade it.'

'Ah.' Jack didn't have enough strength to say anything further.

'She's from a lower jati, you see. Unclean. Our . . . friendship was bringing shame on the family. Pollution. When she got pregnant my father told me I had to leave her or be expelled from the jati. I couldn't bear it, so I agreed.' Rao's eyes brimmed with tears. 'I left her.'

'The child?'

Rao raised his hand weakly and brushed the tears from his eyes. 'She lost the child, I understand.'

'So, you joined the army?'

'Father insisted. Sent me away to avoid the shame.' Rao sighed. 'I never wanted to be in the army.'

'What . . . *did* you want?'

Rao was silent for a long time. 'A poet. I wanted to be a poet.'

A poet? Christ. Jack felt like laughing, but all that came out was a wheezy cough.

Rao seemed to understand Jack's response and managed to give a small smile. Then he shut his eyes and leant his head back against the rock. 'I've made such a mess of things.'

Jack tried to say something more but couldn't manage it. Darkness embraced him and the sattva-fire bubbled in his chest. The storm roared outside, but the sound and the cold didn't trouble him any more.

He felt calm. He accepted his fate.

———◆———

Voices. He heard voices nearby.

He opened his eyes, tried to see through thick rheum and made out a brutish face with a shaggy beard and wild hair.

A savage.

A twinge of fear ran through him, but less than he would have expected. He felt as though he were watching himself from a great distance, as if he'd already slipped over completely to the spirit realm.

A second savage appeared beside the first.

As far as Jack could tell they were both wearing heavy cloaks and carrying spears. They spoke to each other in Gaalic.

Was Rao still alive? Jack wanted to find out, but didn't want to move his head and so alert the savages.

Better they thought he was dead.

He noticed his scimitar lying beside him. He could grab it and attack, but he doubted he had the strength. Once he moved, the savages would know he was alive and kill him.

But wouldn't they soon realise he was alive and kill him anyway? They would crawl into the cave and check him more closely. What would they do then? Stab him? Worse?

The savages were still speaking to each other.

He would have to do something. He couldn't just lie there and let them slaughter him – and Rao too, if he were still alive. He would sit up, grab the scimitar and shove it into the nearest savage's chest.

233

At least he would die fighting.

He counted to three in his head, grunted, groaned and tried to sit up. But it was as though he were strapped in place. He couldn't move his back more than an inch away from the rock.

The savages jumped in alarm and shouted. One of them scrambled into the cave.

Black pools spread before Jack's eyes. He was going to pass out again. There was nothing he could do about it.

So this was it. He would meet his death on the end of a savage's spear.

He no longer fought to stay awake. It was best that he passed out now.

He heard more shouting.

Soon it would be over.

PART FOUR

18

⬥

The guns had stopped, the mortars were silent and no shells exploded. Occasionally, in the distance, Jack heard the pop of a musket, but near to him, in this part of the battlefield, the Slavs made no sound at all.

He sat on the fire step, leant back against the wall of the trench and glanced up at the stars scrawled across the night sky. The smell of the wet earth was all but blotted out by the traces of powder smoke still hanging in the air. He'd got used to the smoke and its sulphurous scent during the long months of the Slav War. He'd run through great, choking clouds of it, felt it burn his eyes and the back of his throat. He'd marched over battle-scarred fields that still reeked of it. He'd fallen asleep with the scent clinging to his clothes. The smell seemed to seep into everything and followed him around wherever he went.

He shut his eyes for a second. He was sure he wouldn't forget that smell for as long as he lived.

A man screamed. A series of moans followed. Then another man, perhaps less than fifty feet away, sobbed.

Jack opened his eyes and shivered. Now that the guns were quiet, he could hear the cries of the wounded. The fallen men had been lying on the shell-pocked field beyond the trench since a failed attack the day before. They would have been crying out all night.

'Bastards!' one man shouted. 'Pull me back there. Bastards! Get me out!'

William, sitting beside Jack, removed his cap and ran his fingers through his thin hair. 'Poor sod.'

Jack shivered again. It was hard to listen to the cries, but the officers had forbidden any of them to help the wounded. The Slavs would fire on anything that moved on that dismal plain.

He glanced down the trench. In both directions, the other men from the company sat huddled on the fire step. A few had thrown blankets over themselves and were trying to sleep, while others rubbed their hands or stamped their feet to fight the cold and the tension. One man was repeating his prayers and crossing himself over and over again. The soldiers' faces seemed more gaunt than even a few hours ago, as if the knowledge that at dawn they would have to go over the top had drained the blood from their skin.

In the distance, the trench snaked away to join other trenches that stretched back for half a mile, worming between dugout shelters, earthworks, fascines, gun emplacements and shell craters full of water, eventually reaching the hospital tents, baggage carts, cavalry pickets and officers' marquees. A whole teeming city of thousands of soldiers had been moulded from the mud as the campaign wore on.

A man lying on the battlefield cried out repeatedly for his mother.

'Wish he'd bloody give it a rest,' old Sergeant Watson said.

The men sniggered and even Jack couldn't stop himself snorting. It was a cold-hearted joke but it lightened the mood. Gallows humour was the only kind available in that bleak field outside Ragusa.

William put his cap back on and secured the strap beneath his chin. He gave Jack a grin. 'I'll wager a shilling I'm the first to reach Ragusa Tower.'

Jack smiled back and shook his head. He was always amazed at the way William managed to keep his and everyone else's spirits up. He was twenty – only a year older than Jack – and yet he seemed like a veteran, as if he'd been through battles many times before, rather than experiencing them for the first time like everyone else in the company.

'A shilling?' someone said. 'My pound says I'll be first.'

Jack jumped at the sound of the voice. Captain Jhala had walked up from a side trench as they'd been talking. Jack leapt to his feet and did a quick namaste, William doing the same.

Jhala beamed. 'At ease, men.' He rested his hand on the pommel of his scimitar. The brass buttons on his tunic shone in the faint moonlight. 'They say there'll be no rain tomorrow. The weather's on our side.'

'Then I'll have no trouble getting to the tower first, sir,' William said.

Jhala chuckled. 'We'll see about that, Private.'

A dying man shrieked in the darkness and they all fell silent for a moment. A soldier a few feet down shook so hard Jack could hear his teeth chattering. The man who was praying said the Latin words of the Our Father even more loudly.

Jhala seemed to quickly take stock of the situation. 'Men! Listen, all of you!'

The hundred and fifty men of the company shuffled to their feet, clasping their muskets to their sides. Men from other companies, sitting further along the trench, peered to watch as well.

Jhala paced up and down as he spoke. 'At first light we'll get the signal to advance. We face a fierce foe. But there is no need to be afraid. The Slavs will crumble before us. That is for certain. We have right on our side. We are following our dharma. There is a true path laid out before us.' Jhala met the eyes of the men as he walked past. 'We each must follow our true path. All we have to do is keep our feet marching along it. One step at a time.'

Jack felt a tingle in his spine as Jhala spoke. He squared his sagging shoulders and gripped his musket more tightly.

The cries of the fallen seemed to fade and no longer troubled him. He was no longer worried about running at the Slavs. He was no longer afraid of the shot and shells and musket balls. He couldn't even smell the powder smoke.

He would go over the top of the trench when the time came and charge along his true path.

Following his dharma.

And following Jhala.

———◆———

Jack heard men talking softly. He was lying on his back on hard ground. His eyes were closed.

He listened carefully to the voices. He didn't understand the words, but they were clearly speaking Gaalic.

He felt a quiver of anxiety. The savages were near to him, just a few feet away. Were they debating what to do with him? Were they planning how to kill him?

Where was he? He couldn't remember anything since he'd passed out in the cave. Was he still in the cave? He didn't think so, because he felt warm. Deliciously warm, in fact. The smell of smoke was strong and the faint crackle nearby could only be a fire.

He was warm and dry and lying beside a fire. If the savages wanted to kill him, they weren't in a hurry.

Should he open his eyes? Would they attack him then?

He tried flexing his fingers. He could move them easily. He tried wriggling his toes and that posed no problem either. The pain in his chest had vanished. He felt well and strong.

If there was going to be a fight, let it be now, when he was in good health.

He opened his eyes, but didn't yet move and simply stared straight up. He saw stone above him. For a second he thought he must still be in the cave after all, but then realised he was looking at a low, domed ceiling made of irregular dry-stone blocks that were blackened with soot. He was in some sort of hut or shelter.

The voices continued.

The savages hadn't noticed him yet.

He would have to move soon. He would jump up, rummage

for a weapon and do what he could to defend himself – and Rao, if the Captain were still with him. He would have to be careful, though. The crude ceiling looked low and he wasn't sure that he could even stand up straight beneath it.

He shut his eyes and listened intently to the voices. The men sounded calm, as if they were talking idly to each other. How many were they? He concentrated for a minute and picked out four separate voices.

Four – he could fight four men, but it would be difficult. The small space would hamper his movements. But then it would hamper those of his assailants as well.

He began counting down from three. Nerves shot through his body and his heart thudded.

This was it. He had to do it now.

Then he heard movement beside him and the voices suddenly stopped. He heard a gasp and recognised a new voice – Rao's.

He flung open his eyes and sprang up, stooping beneath the low ceiling. He felt faint for a moment and darkness whirled around his head. A trace of pain threaded through his chest and his legs trembled. He wasn't quite as well as he'd thought.

But the curtains of darkness quickly receded and he saw he was in a tiny, beehive-shaped hut. A fire flickered in a central hearth, casting a ruddy glow over the uneven walls. Thick smoke wafted through the chamber, filtering only slowly out of a tiny hole in the ceiling.

Four savages squatted beside the fire. Their hair and beards were matted and wild. They wore plain, knee-length tunics and their heavy cloaks lay piled in a corner of the room. Their spears leant against a wall and their knives were stuck in their belts, but they didn't reach for their weapons. In fact, they weren't preparing to attack at all and instead sat strangely still, their mouths hanging open and their eyes wide as they stared at Rao.

Rao sat beside Jack, blinking in surprise. His turban had been removed and his hair was dishevelled and awry. His moustache bristled crazily on his top lip and his blue tunic was smeared with dirt. But he appeared well and unharmed.

Rao glanced at Jack. 'What on earth is going on?'

'Don't know.' Jack crouched down again.

One of the savages said a few words and flung himself to the ground, as if in supplication to Rao. The other three crossed themselves several times and continued to stare wide-eyed at the Captain.

'What are they playing at?' Rao asked.

Jack rubbed his chin. He wasn't sure, but he was starting to get an idea. His eyes darted across the savages. 'English? You speak English?'

The men glanced at each other and muttered. Finally, one of them, a tall man with a crooked, aquiline nose, said, 'Little bit. I go south of mountains once. Long time ago.'

Jack grinned. Thank God at least one of them could understand some English. He pressed his hand to his chest. 'I'm Jack.'

The savage frowned.

'Jack.' He tapped his chest a few more times, as if that would help. 'My name is Jack.'

'Ah.' The man smiled and pointed. 'Jack. You Jack.'

Jack grinned wider. 'That's it. And this is Captain Rao.'

The man gazed at Rao and gave a sigh, his eyes shining. 'Cap-tain Rao.' He sounded the words out carefully.

The other three savages repeated the words several times, crossed themselves and bent their heads in reverence. 'Cap-tain Rao. Cap-tain Rao.'

Rao frowned and said to Jack, 'What are they doing? It's as though they think I'm their guru.'

'Something like that, I reckon,' Jack said.

The tall savage turned to Jack again. 'You come from under mountains too? With Great Shee, Captain Rao?'

Jack thought quickly. Under mountains? He recalled childhood fables about magical folk who dwelt beneath the earth. Even his superstitious countrymen didn't believe such stories any more, but these savages might still take them seriously.

Interesting. This situation could play out well for him and Rao, but they had to be careful.

'Yes,' Jack said. 'Both of us come from under the mountains.'

The savage spoke to his comrades and they all gave gasps of awe and bowed their heads down again, muttering and chanting.

'We are honoured that you and the great Rao are here,' the savage said. 'We believed for long time a shee with brown skin would come. We hoped and prayed. Now the Lord has granted our wish.'

'What on earth is all this about?' Rao asked Jack.

'Listen,' Jack said in Arabic. 'Be careful when you speak English with this lot. That big one understands enough to know what we're saying . . . Now, it looks as though they think you're some kind of magical being called a shee.'

'But . . .' Rao spluttered. 'That's preposterous.'

'Maybe, but you'll need to play along. I reckon it's the only reason we're still alive. Soon as they find out we're not from under the ground we're finished.'

'But Mahajan will see through that.'

'I'm not sure these are Mahajan's savages.'

'What?'

'No white skulls on their chests.'

'Oh, yes. That's true.' Rao sat back on his haunches. His eyes were wide and glistened in the firelight. 'How can I play along, then? What do I do?'

'I don't know. Just . . . act like someone from another world.'

Rao crinkled his face. 'Another world?'

'Just do what you can.' Jack turned back to the tall savage. 'You. What's your name?'

The man raised his head. 'I am Cormac.'

'Right then, Cormac. The great Captain Rao wants to know where we are.'

243

'Mountain of the Spirits.'

Jack rubbed his forehead. He was going to have to be more specific with his questions. 'Are we anywhere near Mar?'

Cormac grinned. 'Aye.' He pressed his hand to his chest. 'We are Mar.'

'You're . . . I see. You're from the Mar tribe.'

'Aye, we are Mar.'

'All right, then. Do you know a man called Mahajan?'

The savages all drew their breaths in sharply, crossed themselves furiously and muttered amongst themselves.

'Do not say his name,' Cormac said. 'It can bring curse. We call him Demon. That is what he is.'

'Mahajan's a demon?'

'Aye. He rose up from hell.'

'I heard he was the ruler of these lands.'

Cormac lowered his head and his voice turned into a low growl. 'It is true. He rules our lands. With help of the Cattans.'

'Who are the Cattans?

Cormac looked up again and there was a fire smouldering behind his eyes. 'They wear white skull.' He gestured to his chest. 'They come from other side of mountains. They old enemy. We fight them for long time. But then, Demon come. He gives Cattans fire weapons and black magic. Then they take our lands.'

'I see. So . . . none of you Mar follow the Demon?'

Cormac sat a little taller and lifted his chin. 'None will fight for Demon. Only Cattans evil.'

'What is all this about?' Rao spoke Arabic. 'I'm losing the thread of it.'

'Not sure,' Jack said. 'But it sounds as though Mahajan's thrown his lot in with some local tribe called the Cattans. He's used them to take over Mar.'

Jack faced Cormac again and said in English, 'These Cattans, did a large party go past here recently?'

Cormac's forehead rippled with confusion.

'Uh, large party.' Jack opened his arms to indicate size, but then stopped when he saw that was just adding to the confusion. 'Many men. Many Cattans. Going past here.'

'Ah.' Cormac nodded. 'Aye, many Cattans go past. Many, many.'

'Four of our friends were with them. Captives.'

Cormac looked puzzled again.

'Uh, taken.' He put his wrists together as if they were tied and mimed trying to separate them. 'Captured.'

'Cap-tured. I ken this word. No, we do not see captured. We keep away from Cattans. Dangerous.' Cormac put his hand to his forehead, as if protecting his eyes from the sun. 'We see them from long way away.'

'I see. You didn't get a good look. Kept your distance.'

'Aye.'

'And do you know where these Cattans are going?'

Cormac discussed this in Gaalic with his companions, then turned back to Jack. 'We think they go Place of Dead Kings.'

'Place of Dead Kings? Where's that?'

'Where Demon lives. It is bad place now. Devils and evil there.'

'Right, so they'll be taking our friends to Mah . . . the Demon.'

'Not ken about friends. But Cattans go over many places. Over Mar. Other places. Then go back Place of Dead Kings. Always go back Place of Dead Kings.'

'The Cattans travel around. Like war parties. Then they go back to the Demon?'

'Aye, make war. Take sheep and cattle. Take land. Kill people. Then go back. Demon tells them what to do.'

Jack glanced at Rao, whose eyes were even wider than before.

'Looks like Mahajan's set himself up as quite the little king around here,' Jack said.

Rao swallowed. 'How many Cattans do you think he has? Thousands?'

'It must be a lot if he could spare several hundred to attack our party. Cormac said something about fire weapons too.'

'Firearms? You think the Cattans can use them?'

'They didn't have any when we met them. But they knew what muskets were, didn't they? They knew to take them.'

'Savages with muskets. Quite a daunting prospect. All the same, I still think if I can talk directly to Mahajan I can reason with him. Why wouldn't he give us Parihar and the others and let us be on our way?'

'Hope you're right about that.'

'What else can we do?'

Jack scratched the back of his neck. 'We don't have a lot of choice. You're right. We'll have to get to Mahajan's hideout and do our best.' He switched back to English. 'Cormac, can you take us to the Place of Dead Kings?'

Cormac crossed himself and bowed his head. 'Will take you there. In time. But we wait. Storm very bad.'

Jack paused. Now that he listened carefully, he could hear the wind moaning outside and whining between the cracks in the stone. In the wall behind him, he noticed a rudimentary door that was made of branches bound together with rope and interwoven with dry bracken.

'I'll take a look.' He stood and walked, hunched over, to the door. At first he pushed against the wood, but then realised that, of course, the door had no hinges and was nothing more than a covering that was unattached to the walls. He lifted the door and shifted it to the right.

The wind screamed and blasted him with cold air. He stared out into a night alive with white flecks. Thick snow blanketed the ground and glowed faintly as it stretched off into the darkness.

Cormac was right. They couldn't risk going out in that. And what was more, he still felt light-headed, his legs shook and the pain in his chest was a constant throb. Rao didn't look all that well either.

Jack shunted the door back into place and waddled back into the warmth. Despite the crudeness of the hut, it retained the heat well. The Mar might not be particularly advanced, but they knew how to survive in this hostile land.

He wiped the specks of snow from his face and said to Cormac. 'All right. We'll wait for the storm to pass. But after that, we must get to this Place of Dead Kings.'

19

Jack stood outside the hut and searched the hills and valleys below with the spyglass. Snow still carpeted the ground, but it was a clear day, the sun was shining and no snow had fallen for hours.

'Can't see any sign of the Cattans.' Jack handed the glass to Rao. 'Must be far ahead of us by now.'

Rao gazed at the surroundings.

Jack stretched his back. His muscles ached all over and a twinge of pain still troubled his chest. But he felt stronger now that he'd slept for the night and eaten some of the savages' oat porridge.

He glanced back at the hut – it was little more than a pile of stones with turf growing on the roof. Cormac and his three companions crawled out of the low entrance and stood staring at Rao, their eyes wide. They muttered to each other in Gaalic and watched every move the Captain made.

Rao noticed he had an audience, lowered the glass and frowned at Jack. 'What are they doing?'

Jack saw the savages gesturing at the glass and he asked Cormac, 'You seen one of those before?'

Cormac shook his head. 'It is magic? Of the shee?'

Jack couldn't help smiling. He said to Rao in Arabic, 'Tell them it's magic. For seeing far away.'

Rao's brow furrowed deeper. 'I'm not sure about all this. Is it really wise?'

'Go on. You have to show them your powers.'

Rao muttered under his breath, then offered Cormac the glass. 'Here. Take a look.'

Cormac recoiled and his comrades gasped.

Rao looked at Jack for help, but Jack just grinned.

'It won't hurt you.' Rao offered the glass again. 'It's good magic. It'll help you see far away.' He pointed into the distance. 'Far away. You know?'

Cormac gingerly took the glass. Rao encouraged him by miming raising the tube to his eye. Cormac grunted, lifted the glass and gave a gasp. He lowered it instantly, a look of shock on his face, then he raised it again and stared for several seconds. He spoke excitedly to his comrades and they each took a turn looking through the tube.

Jack's grin widened. He still remembered staring through a glass himself for the first time and being stunned to see distant objects suddenly rear up before him.

The Rajthanans had many marvels. He couldn't deny that, as much as he might hate the empire.

Cormac bowed his head before Rao and handed back the glass. 'Oh Great Shee with the brown skin. You truly have powerful magic. We have seen with our own eyes how you can see far away. Weather now is good. We must take you to our village.'

'Village?' Jack stood up straighter. 'We need to get to the Place of Dead Kings, remember?'

'Village first.' Cormac grasped the sleeve of Rao's coat. 'You come village, Great Shee. You see Chief. Then go Place of Dead Kings.'

'Hold on, Cormac.' Jack stepped over and stood beside Rao. 'We thank you for your hospitality, but we have to get a move on. The Demon has our friends.'

'Aye.' Cormac tugged harder at Rao's coat. 'Village is on way. Village first.'

'I don't think we have much choice,' Rao said to Jack. 'Sounds as though this village is in the right direction anyway.'

Jack sucked on his teeth. He didn't like the idea of a delay, but they had to rely on the Mar to find Saleem and Parihar now. It might take him half a day or more just to locate the Cattans' sattva trail again, if he even found it at all.

Perhaps he could tell Rao to insist on being taken to Mahajan immediately? But he wasn't sure that was such a good idea. For the moment the savages were in awe of Rao, but he didn't want to push things too far.

He nudged the snow with his boot. 'Very well. The village first. Then the Place of Dead Kings. But we must go quickly. There's no time to waste.'

The Mar didn't run, they flew, darting, gliding and bobbing as deftly as swallows. They took giant strides, their feet instinctively finding the flat and stable patches of ground. They slipped around boulders and trees, leapt over rabbit holes, and dodged gorse bushes. Their feet kicked up clouds of snow and their cloaks fluttered behind them.

'Shiva.' Rao puffed and wheezed as he jogged beside Jack. 'How do they keep going like that?'

The Mar were more than fifty yards ahead again – Jack and Rao had continually fallen behind during the three hours they'd been travelling.

Rao stopped, bent over and tried to catch his breath. His face was red and perspiration speckled his forehead despite the chill in the air. 'Can't go on.'

Jack paused and called to the Mar. 'Hey! Wait!'

The Mar turned and came loping back. Their legs slipped gracefully in and out of the snow. Jack was amazed that they wore no hose, and although their naked skin was in constant contact with the snow, the cold didn't seem to trouble them at all.

'What problem?' Cormac asked.

'The Great Shee wants to rest,' Jack said.

Cormac glanced at the gasping Rao and frowned.

'The Great Shee needs to think about a few things,' Jack said quickly. Maybe it wasn't good for a shee to look weak.

Cormac nodded, seemingly satisfied with this explanation. The Mar squatted on their haunches, resting their spears beside them. Jack noted that although the weapons were basic, they had steel tips that looked as though they could do plenty of damage.

Cormac fiddled with the amulets hanging about his neck. Jack had already noticed that the Mar wore many of these charms, including wooden crosses woven with coloured threads, metal and bone figurines, clumps of dried herbs and white quartz pebbles. When they were resting, the Mar constantly fingered these necklaces and muttered what seemed to be prayers under their breaths.

Jack slung the knapsack to the ground and sat on a rock. He still had the scimitar jammed into his belt, but he'd put the knife and both pistols in the bag. The firearms were useless at the moment as neither he nor Rao had any bullets left.

He drank from the canteen and handed it to Rao, who now had no hesitation in gulping down some water.

When Rao looked sufficiently rested Jack said, 'How far is it to the village, Cormac?'

'Not far,' Cormac replied.

Jack rubbed the back of his neck. It was tricky to get the right answers out of the savages at times. 'How far exactly? How long will it take us to get there?'

'By the time sun over there.' Cormac pointed to a spot a little above the mountains to the west.

'Late afternoon. We should get going again, then. The Great Shee is ready.'

Cormac frowned, glanced at his comrades, opened his mouth to speak and then shut it again. He fidgeted with the wooden cross about his neck. 'Great Shee wants leave now?'

'Is that a problem?'

Cormac toyed more feverishly with the cross, the other amulets

251

clinking as they knocked against each other. He nodded over Jack's shoulder. 'But crow is there.'

Jack turned and saw a crow sitting in the branch of a twisted tree about thirty yards away.

'Crow bad sign,' Cormac said. 'We wait for sun in middle of sky now.'

'Midday?' Jack squinted up at the sky. Noon was about half an hour away. 'We have to wait until then before we move? Because we saw a crow?'

'Aye. Must wait. Otherwise bad luck. Much bad luck.'

Jack exhaled sharply and glanced at Rao, who shrugged and said, 'I could do with a longer break, to be honest.'

Jack grumbled and took another gulp from the canteen. Another delay. And all the while the Cattans were drawing closer to Mahajan's hideout – if that was even where they were headed.

A shaft of pain jabbed his chest and he winced, hunched his shoulders and did his best not to show the others he was suffering.

At noon, they finally set off again. As before, Cormac led the way, his comrades running and leaping beside him. Jack and Rao did their best to keep up, but continually fell behind. The hot sun blazed in Jack's eyes and his undershirt stuck to his sweating back. But at least the snow was melting, which made the going easier.

Cormac, noticing that Jack and Rao were unable to keep up the pace, called frequent rest stops. At around three o'clock he announced that the village was nearby and sent two of his comrades on ahead.

They pressed on, the snow melting further and leaving patches of ground completely clear. They ran down to a narrow river, where Cormac paused, mumbled a prayer and crossed each of them three times.

'What's all this about?' Jack asked.

Cormac gestured at the river. 'Water monster lives there. Lord will protect.'

Jack shot a look at Rao, who raised his eyebrows. Jack was used to a certain amount of superstition. His own countrymen believed in signs, omens, witches and black magic. But talk of water monsters was something from the distant past. Not even the most gullible in Shropshire believed in those any more.

And he knew all of this would be even stranger to Rao. The Captain was fresh from a life of luxury in Rajthana, where he'd been surrounded by the miraculous avatars of the siddhas. Now he'd been dropped right into the middle of a tribe of primitive people living in the wilderness.

They waded across the river and struck off across a plain. The shadows lengthened, dusk spread across the sky and finally they crested a hill and saw twinkling lights beneath them.

'Village.' Cormac tugged at Rao's sleeve. 'Come.'

As they jogged down the slope, Jack could make out a collection of around thirty huts huddled in an oval-shaped bowl. The buildings looked similar to the shelter they'd spent the night in, but these were larger and better constructed. The stone blocks had been chiselled into more regular sizes and the roofs were topped with well-tended turf. Smoke seeped through holes and tangled into the night. Light spilt out through simple doors made of branches and twigs.

The snow had largely melted or been cleared from the village, apart from where it clung to a few rooftops.

Jack heard the villagers before he saw them. They were chanting in unison, their voices sailing up into the dark.

Cormac led the way through a stand of trees and over the lip of the bowl. And then Jack saw around a hundred and fifty Mar spread out in a semicircle on the edge of the village. They were swaying and clapping in time as they sang, all of them grinning, their teeth brilliant white in the dark. The women's tunics reached to their ankles, while the men's stretched to their knees. Over these, they wore the usual shaggy cloaks – except for the children, who were wrapped in blankets.

As Rao trod out of the darkness, the Mar suddenly stopped singing and gasps rippled through the crowd. They all stared wide-eyed at the Great Shee. Rao coughed, shuffled his feet and fidgeted with his sleeve.

A man carrying a spear in one hand stepped forward from the gathering. He appeared to be at least sixty years old, and had white hair, a large beard and a slight limp. But despite his age, his arms and chest rippled with muscles. He wore a woollen cloak – with blue and purple stripes – which was secured at his neck by an ornate silver brooch.

He stopped around ten feet from Rao and Jack, bowed slightly and then spoke in Gaalic.

'This Chief Domnall mac Giric vic Cormaic vic Arcill,' Cormac said. 'He welcomes you to village, oh Great Shee with the brown skin and the eye that can see far.'

Rao cleared his throat, glanced at Jack, then looked between Cormac and Chief Domnall. 'I thank you for your kind welcome.' He pressed his hands together and bowed slightly. 'Namaste.'

Cormac translated for Domnall, who gave a broad grin. One of the Chief's eyes went moist and gleamed in the dim light. He stamped his spear excitedly in the ground a couple of times.

Next Jack heard a wail. The crowd parted and a hunched figure shuffled forward. It was an ancient woman with thick lines on her face and a swaying wattle beneath her chin. Her hair was wiry and hovered about her head like brambles, while her eyes glinted deep within folds of skin. About her neck rattled numerous amulets and charms, one of which was a large brass cross that was scratched and ingrained with dirt.

Using a gnarled branch as a staff, she hobbled slowly towards Jack and Rao, muttering, wailing and intoning in turn. Finally, she paused in front of Rao and looked up. She shut her eyes, breathed in deeply, nodded, opened her eyes again, and then began chanting in a monotone. She shuffled in a circle about Jack and Rao, crossing herself regularly.

'This seer,' Cormac said. 'She blessing and asking Lord for your happiness.'

Rao rubbed his moustache and scuffed the toe of his boot in the ground. 'Very kind, I'm sure.'

The seer completed three circuits, then raised her hands and gave a loud ululation. The crowd cheered, clapped and broke into song again. Now, all formality seemed to disappear, and the Mar rushed forward and pressed themselves around Jack and Rao. They reached out to touch the Captain, jostling him a little.

'Hold on.' Rao glanced at Jack, alarm in his eyes.

But the Mar took no notice of him. Chanting and laughing, they grasped him and lifted him up on their shoulders.

'What are you doing?' Rao looked about wildly. 'Careful there.'

Jack felt hands slip under his arms and he too was wrenched up into the air and supported by numerous shoulders. Both he and Rao were carried forward as if they were sitting in litters, the Mar singing, dancing and clapping all around them.

'Hah.' Rao's face split into a grin. He began laughing. 'Extraordinary.'

Jack found himself smiling too. The Mar's joy was infectious.

He bobbed along on the sea of people, catching glimpses of huts and byres containing black cattle and sheep. Hounds barked and leapt alongside the crowd.

He was borne into the centre of the village, where a bonfire blazed in the open space before a large, rectangular building with a thatched roof. To either side of the hut's doorway stood stone cairns that were topped by strangely shaped, river-worn rocks. Clearly this was an important building – presumably the Chief's home.

The Mar squatted in a loose circle about the fire. Jack and Rao were lowered and encouraged to sit near Chief Domnall. Villagers scurried back and forth between the open space and a set of smaller fires further off behind a low stone wall.

Cormac sat next to Jack. 'Chief Domnall very happy. Says feast in honour of Great Shee.'

Jack glanced at the Chief, who was smiling and nodding at the

Captain. Jack hoped the Mar would never start to doubt Rao really was a shee. Things could get difficult if that happened. The villagers seemed friendly enough at the moment, but if they found out they'd been tricked they might well kill him and Rao.

Men and women appeared from around the stone wall and carried across wooden bowls containing steaming food. They served the Chief first, then Rao and Jack, and then everyone else. Jack looked down at the bowl. It appeared to contain a pottage of meat, carrots and oats. He tasted a bit and found it bland but hearty enough.

Then he noticed Rao staring at his food and pushing it around with his wooden spoon.

Rao leant closer to Jack and spoke softly. 'What's that meat?'

Jack paused. He was still chewing a portion of the meat and suddenly it dawned on him.

It was beef.

'Lamb, I think.' Jack waved his hand vaguely.

'It doesn't look like lamb. It's beef, isn't it?'

'Might be . . . yes.'

The Chief was frowning and speaking loudly now.

Cormac tugged Rao's sleeve. 'Chief asks why you not eat? You not like, oh Great Shee?'

Rao gave a nervous laugh. 'Of course not.' He shovelled some food on to his spoon and raised it to show the Chief. 'Good food. Hmmm.'

Domnall half smiled and stared intently at Rao. Silence spread across the circle and now the rest of the Mar were gazing at the Great Shee. Their eyes gleamed and their skin flickered in the firelight.

'You're going to have to eat that,' Jack said.

Rao blanched. 'I can't.'

'You have to. Things might turn nasty otherwise.'

'There must be some—'

'Now.'

Rao looked around at the Mar, who all continued to stare at him. He licked his lips and swallowed. Then he breathed in sharply, shut his eyes and spooned the food into his mouth. He chewed slowly and deliberately, fighting to keep the look of disgust from his face.

The Mar cheered and began talking amongst themselves again. Domnall beamed and slapped his thighs.

Rao almost gagged, stopped himself and swallowed the meat.

'Better keep going.' Jack nodded at Rao's overflowing bowl. 'Wouldn't want to disappoint the Chief.'

Rao shuddered and shut his eyes for a second. 'Shiva.'

Then he opened his eyes, glared at the stew as if it were his enemy and began spooning it into his mouth.

He ate almost half his food, before he gagged again, put down his spoon and pushed the bowl away. 'Enough.'

Jack wondered whether Rao had eaten enough to satisfy the Chief, but Domnall was busy talking and laughing with his subjects and paying little attention to the Great Shee for the moment. A Mar woman soon took away the Captain's bowl.

Next, a thin man with a wispy beard strode out into the open ground beside the fire. The Mar quietened and the Chief said a few words to the man.

'This bard,' Cormac said. 'Tonight will tell story of Place of Dead Kings.'

Jack sat up straighter, his interest piqued. He wanted to find out all he could about the place where Mahajan was hiding out.

The gathering was completely silent now. Even the numerous dogs sat still.

The bard looked up into the sky and began singing in a clear voice. Now that Jack listened closely to the native tongue, he was reminded a little of the sound of the language some spoke in Wales.

Cormac translated, explaining that long ago, the ancestors of the Mar, Cattans and other tribes in the region had been extremely

257

rich and powerful. They built huge buildings unlike anything seen in the Highlands these days. They lived in vast towns that stretched for miles and they had huge numbers of cattle and sheep, so that no one went hungry.

Their main town was in the valley beyond the Mountain of the Old Trees, and in the centre of that town was a castle, underneath which they buried their kings. This is why this area is still known as the Place of Dead Kings.

God was very happy with these people. They worshipped him and did not give in to the temptations of the Evil One. But then a king named Matain, who was arrogant and reckless, came to the throne. The Devil sent a serpent to whisper in his ear, telling him he could be greater than all the kings before him, greater even than God himself. With this in mind, Matain decreed that a tower be built – the tallest tower in the world. It would be so high it would reach the moon, and Matain himself would sit at its top and rule the world as God from there.

So, the people began to build the tower. They laboured for years, heaping stone upon stone. And the tower grew until it was taller than any of the other buildings in the land, then taller than the tallest hill and then the tallest mountain. Finally, it reached up into the sky.

Matain climbed to the top of the tower and looked up at the moon. It seemed so close now, he could almost reach out and touch it.

'I will be higher than God once I reach the moon,' he said. 'I will take his place and rule the world.'

The builders continued to work on the tower and it grew higher even than the clouds. But every time Matain climbed to the top, the moon was never quite within reach.

He became angry and commanded his labourers to work harder and faster. He enlisted more workers and drove them to build both day and night.

But still the moon lay beyond his grasp.

One night, at the top of his tower, the icy wind in his hair, Matain railed against God and demanded to be allowed to reach the moon. At that moment the tower shook. A crack ran up its side. The tower had been built too tall and could no longer support its own weight. The stones crumbled and the entire structure collapsed, burying Matain beneath it.

The King had been killed by his own arrogance.

After that time, the kingdom fell into decline. The people realised that in following Matain they had let themselves drift away from God. They stopped putting up huge towers, stopped dreaming of ruling the world and reaching the moon. And so they returned to God and left behind the temptations of the Devil.

When the bard finished, the crowd roared with delight and clapped loudly. Many began singing, while others stood and danced about the flames.

'A strange sort of story,' Rao said to Jack. 'What do you make of it?'

Jack shrugged. 'Just a legend, I suppose.'

Rao rubbed his moustache. 'There's truth in legends sometimes. These people, they once had cities and towns. I read that.'

'I heard that too.'

'This story about the tower. Maybe it's their way of explaining why they stopped building castles and the like.'

'Could be.' Jack yawned. He wasn't much interested in what the story was about. He'd been hoping to learn more about the Place of Dead Kings as it was in the present.

He sat watching the dancing Mar for another fifteen minutes or so, yawning repeatedly. This seemed to set off Rao, who began yawning himself. Noticing this, Cormac asked Chief Domnall for permission for the Great Shee to retire and then led Jack and Rao over to a hut. It was a simple, circular structure, like most of the others in the village. A cairn topped by a river-worn rock stood beside the entrance and a twig had been tied to a stone above the door.

'Rowan.' Cormac pointed at the twig. 'Stop witches.'

Jack glanced at the branch. It was not so different from the charms the English used. Did the Mar burn witches too? Sadly, he suspected they did.

He ducked through the doorway and entered a smoky chamber lit only by a fire in the centre. Two piles of bracken lay on the floor, and while these beds were basic, they looked more comfortable than anything he'd slept on for days.

Cormac crouched beside the hearth, smoothed out the embers with a stick and smothered them with ash and several bricks of peat. The covered embers smoked and glowed through the ash, but the peat didn't catch fire.

'Leave like this.' Cormac pointed at the hearth. 'Will burn all night. Not let go out.'

'Why not?' Rao asked.

Cormac's expression went solemn. 'Very bad luck. Great evil will come.' He gestured repeatedly at the fire. 'Not let go out.'

'All right.' Jack raised his hand. 'We'll leave it like that.'

Cormac nodded, slipped over to the entrance and bowed. 'Good night, oh Great Shee.' Then he stooped, left the hut and scraped the door back into place.

Jack took the scimitar from his belt, levered off his mud-logged boots and collapsed on the bracken. He sighed. 'Think I could sleep for a week.'

'What is this?' Rao was examining the stack of bricks beside the fire.

Jack rolled over. 'Peat. From the ground.'

Rao frowned, picked up one of the black blocks and studied it. 'The ground?'

'Yes. Some people use it in England.' Jack lay on his back again and stared up at the dark roof. 'Dig it up, dry it out and burn it.'

'Never heard of such a thing.' Rao replaced the brick.

Jack pulled a blanket over himself and shut his eyes. Sleep

rushed at him almost instantly, but as he drifted off he heard rustling and scratching nearby. He creaked his eyes open. Rao was sitting cross-legged in a shaft of moonlight that pierced the door. Atri's notebook lay open in his lap and he was scribbling in the back pages, stopping at times to dip his pen in an ink pot.

Was Rao adding to Atri's notes? Did he know more about Mahajan than he'd let on?

'What are you doing?' Jack asked.

'Oh.' Rao pointed with the pen at the book. 'Just writing. Some thoughts.'

'About what?'

Rao gave a slight smile. 'Some notes on the Mar, in fact.' He lifted the page he was working on and Jack could just make out sketches of the natives' amulets, along with lines of spidery writing. 'I've been thinking about it. Apart from Mahajan, no one has ever been here. I've decided to write down my observations.' He lowered the book into his lap. 'Perhaps publish a monograph when I get back.'

Jack rolled on to his back again. Perhaps Rao didn't know much about Mahajan after all. 'I forgot. You're a poet.'

Rao rubbed his moustache and laughed nervously. 'Yes. I told you that, didn't I?'

'Nothing to be embarrassed about. You told me a sad story. About your father, and your sweetheart.'

Rao cleared his throat and fidgeted with the pen. 'I perhaps spoke indiscreetly. I thought I was dying.'

'So did I.' Jack shut his eyes. 'Don't worry about it. For what it's worth, I hope you do get back to Rajthana and tell your father to go jump off a cliff.'

Rao coughed. 'I can't do that!'

'I would.'

Rao paused for a few seconds. 'Yes, I believe you would . . .'

261

But even as Rao was speaking, Jack was already slipping off to sleep.

———◆———

Jack heard a shout. His heart lurched and he sat up. For a moment he couldn't remember where he was, but then he saw a suggestion of the hut's walls in the glow of the buried fire. He heard another muffled cry and what sounded like a scuffle coming from Rao's side of the room.

Christ. They were under attack.

He grasped the scimitar, went to stand and then heard a woman speaking rapidly in Gaalic. As his eyes adjusted, he made out Rao sitting up on his bed. A Mar woman crouched beside him, grasping his sleeve and saying repeatedly in broken English, 'My name Eva. Chief daughter.'

Jack put down the scimitar. 'Looks like you've got your hands full there.'

Rao spluttered. 'I have no idea what she's doing here. I felt her grab my hand and I woke up.'

'Eva, do you speak English?' Jack asked.

'Learn few words.' Eva brushed her long brown hair behind her ear. 'Cormac teach.'

'What are you doing here?'

'Chief daughter.' She pressed her hand to her chest. 'Chief daughter.'

'All right, you're the Chief's daughter. But what do you want?'

'Chief send.' She gripped Rao's sleeve. 'We marry.'

'Shiva.' Rao sprang to his knees. 'No.'

Jack couldn't help smiling. 'You don't want to anger the Chief, Rao.'

'What?' Rao wrestled his arm free. 'No. Look, Eva, I can't. No marry.'

Eva frowned and pouted. She looked about twenty years old, as far as Jack could tell in the dim light.

'No.' Rao struggled to find the right words. 'Don't be upset. You see, I can't marry, because . . . I'm already married.'

Eva didn't seem to understand and grasped Rao's sleeve again. 'We marry.'

Jack thought he'd better come to Rao's aid. 'No, can't marry.' He pointed at Rao. 'Already marry. You understand?'

Eva let go of Rao and stared at him. 'Already marry?'

Rao cleared his throat. 'Yes.'

Eva lowered her eyes, stuck out her bottom lip and nodded glumly.

'I'm sorry,' Rao said.

Eva swept her cloak about her, slipped over to the door, looked back once at Rao and then vanished into the night.

'Shiva.' Rao stared at the door. 'What next?'

Jack did his best to stifle a laugh, but couldn't hold it back.

'You might find it funny,' Rao said. 'But you'll be next.'

'I don't think so. I'm not the Great Shee with the brown skin.'

Rao snorted, shook his head and then chuckled himself. 'What a place. Where on earth have I ended up?'

20

—◆—

'Captain Rao. Jack. Come quick.'

Jack sat up, blinked and saw Cormac squatting in the hut's entrance. Judging by the light outside, it was well after dawn. The fire still smouldered and traces of smoke seeped up from between the peat bricks.

Rao rose and scratched his bare head.

Jack rubbed his face. 'What is it?'

'Cattans coming.' Cormac shifted on his haunches. 'Coming to village.'

Jack scrambled to his feet, yanked on his boots and grasped his weapons. Rao threw aside his blanket and buckled on his belt. They scurried out of the hut and followed Cormac towards the edge of the village.

The day was overcast and the light milky. A dry wind whipped down from the mountains and tugged at Jack's tunic. Many of the Mar were rushing about with anxious looks on their faces, all happiness from the night before gone. The bonfire in the centre of the village had died to a black smear.

Jack jogged to keep up with Cormac's huge strides. 'Where are you taking us?'

'Must hide.' Cormac didn't turn his head. 'Cattans bad men.'

They reached the perimeter of the village, jogged up the side of the shallow bowl and entered a stand of trees. Most of the snow had melted, leaving only a few patches in the deepest shade.

A cry went up behind Jack. He turned and saw many of the Mar gathering in the village centre and pointing up a hill. He stared and saw a party of around thirty Cattans weaving their way down the slope.

'Quick.' Cormac gestured to a patch of brambles. 'Here.'

It was a poor hiding place, but there seemed to be nothing else nearby. The three of them squatted down as low as they could.

The Cattans reached the bottom of the incline and strode into the village. They wore the typical heavy cloaks of the savages, but the sign of the white skull was sewn on to their tunics. Most of them carried spears and bows, but a few had longswords swinging at their waists.

Chief Domnall stood in front of his people. Eva and four other young women stood immediately behind him.

'Those Chief daughters,' Cormac explained. 'Chief have no son. Wife dead. Very sad.'

The village dogs had been tied up, but they barked wildly and strained at their leads.

The Cattans came to a halt and one man, who appeared to be the leader, stepped forward. He wore a chain-mail shirt and a round steel helmet. A sword glinted at his side. He barked a few words and Domnall replied in a clear, calm voice. Whatever the Chief said, it seemed to displease the Cattan because he shouted even more loudly. The Chief then gestured to a few of his men, who disappeared behind a hut and returned with ten cattle, which they led over to the Cattans.

'Tribute?' Jack asked Cormac.

Cormac clenched his teeth. His eyes burnt as he stared at the unfolding scene. 'Aye. Cattans come often. Take food.'

The Cattan leader nodded approvingly at the cattle, then pointed to a young Mar woman standing in the front row of the gathering.

A murmur ran through the crowd. The woman cried out and began sobbing. Chief Domnall's face turned red and he lambasted the Cattan. But the man ignored him and clicked his fingers. Two of his men rushed over and grabbed the woman, who screamed and tried to fight them off. One Mar warrior leapt to her defence, but a Cattan punched him in the face and he fell back. The rest of the Mar waved their fists and shouted at the Cattans.

The Cattans drew their swords and pointed their spears at the crowd. The two men hauled the struggling woman over to their leader. The Mar appeared to be on the verge of rushing at the Cattans but managed to restrain themselves.

The leader swept his cloak about him and led his men back out of the village. Several Cattans herded the cattle, while one man shoved the young woman forward and then dragged her along by the hair. Her cries sailed across the valley.

Rao shivered. 'The brutes.'

Cormac glared at the departing warriors. He'd gripped a piece of the bramble bush so tightly the thorns had dug into his skin and blood oozed out from between his fingers.

'Where will they take her?' Jack asked.

Cormac was silent for a long time. 'They take her Place of Dead Kings.' He looked down, unable to speak for a moment. 'Do bad things.'

Jack put his hand on the tall man's shoulder. 'We'll do what we can to help. But you have to take us to the Place of Dead Kings now.'

Cormac nodded. 'Take you. Soon. We prepare first.'

———◆———

Jack sat cross-legged on the bed in the hut, breathing deeply and letting his mind drift gently towards the spirit realm without entering the trance completely. Thoughts spiralled through his head, but he let them come and go without judging them. Elizabeth was there, as always, and Katelin on her deathbed. He saw Jhala at the battle of Ragusa and Saleem in the hands of the savages.

Saleem. He prayed the boy was alive. He wouldn't forgive himself if the lad died.

He heard Rao scratching in his notebook. It was strange that the Captain had decided to document the lives of the Mar, but it reminded Jack a little of Jhala, who'd had a huge library and read extensively about the customs and history of the English. But Jhala had been born in England, although he'd been sent back to Rajthana for his education. This was Rao's first visit to Britain. It was surprising he was taking such an interest.

Jack opened his eyes. How long had they been waiting for Cormac? They needed to get moving now. He was about to crawl outside to gauge the time from the sun, when he thought he might as well ask Rao instead. 'What time is it?'

Rao studied his watch. 'Eleven o'clock.'

'We've been waiting for an hour now. I'm going to find Cormac.'

Jack stooped and left the hut, but then saw Cormac jogging across to him. In the distance, he heard the eerie wail of pipes.

'Come now,' Cormac said.

'We're going to the Place of Dead Kings?'

'Not yet.'

Jack felt a twinge of irritation. How much more time were they going to waste? 'Listen, we have to go now.'

'Yes, that's right.' Rao ducked out of the hut. 'I command it.'

Cormac bowed his head slightly. 'Forgive me, oh Great Shee. But chiefs come. Many chiefs. They help.'

'Help with what?' Jack asked.

'Come.' Cormac tugged at Rao's sleeve. 'You see.'

More pipes squealed and droned. The sounds were drifting from different directions, some close, some further off in the hills.

Jack felt a quiver of anxiety. He remembered hearing the unearthly wailing for the first time, when savages attacked the expedition. But he and Rao didn't seem to be in any danger at the moment.

They followed Cormac to the centre of the village. Domnall stood outside his hut, holding his spear. Beside him were the wizened seer, Eva and her sisters, and several Mar warriors. The

Chief bowed his head in acknowledgement to Rao, but remained standing where he was.

A procession of ten Mar men, whom Jack didn't recognise, appeared from the trees and filed down into the village. At their head strode a piper blowing a set of bagpipes. Jack recognised the instrument – he'd seen a few in the north of England, although they'd been much smaller and made less of a din. The warriors marched into the centre of the village, the piper stopped playing and an elderly man limped forward, supporting himself with a staff.

'This chief from valley over hill,' Cormac said to Jack and Rao.

Domnall and the visiting chief exchanged greetings and the seer performed her ritual of shuffling about the new arrivals three times. The visitors then seated themselves around the edge of the village centre.

More pipes wailed and a further party arrived from another village, also led by a chief. After them came further groups, ten in all, representing, Cormac explained, most of the villages in the immediate vicinity. Each party was welcomed by Domnall and the seer before sitting down with the others in a wide circle.

Finally, the pipes fell silent and the gathering was complete. Domnall, spear still in one hand, addressed the assembled Mar. Finally, he gestured to Rao.

'Chief asks if you can step forward, Great Shee,' Cormac said.

Rao shot a nervous look at Jack, then took a few paces into the middle of the group. Most of the Mar appeared not to have noticed him so far and a murmur flickered around the circle. Many crossed themselves and some bowed their heads.

Rao rubbed his moustache furiously and fidgeted. He was hardly acting like the Great Shee.

Jack walked across to him and whispered, 'Relax. Look confident.'

'Confident?' Rao hissed. 'I have no idea what I'm doing.'

Cormac stood beside Rao and translated as Domnall told the

other chiefs how the Great Shee had appeared to them in their time of need.

Several chiefs spoke. Domnall replied to them and then turned and spoke to Rao.

'Chief says all chiefs honoured to meet Great Shee with brown skin and magic that can see far,' Cormac said. 'Chiefs say they all live in fear of Cattans and Demon. Sometimes no food. Much suffering. Demon has strong black magic. Has weapons that breathe fire.

'Many say that one will come who also has brown skin. But will be good shee, not demon. This shee will fight Demon and free Mar. Now they ask, is Great Shee the one they wait for?'

Rao gave a small cough, leant in close to Jack and said, 'Fight the Demon? What on earth am I going to say now?'

Jack thought quickly. 'Best play along.'

'I can't do that. We can't fight Mahajan. These savages will soon work that out.'

'Look, we have to get to Mahajan's hideout. Cormac's said he'll take us there. Just tell them what they want to hear and then let's get out of here.'

Rao cleared his throat, straightened his tunic and said to Cormac, 'Tell the Chief I and my assistant will do what we can to help.'

Cormac straightened his shoulders and his eyes went moist. He gave a deep bow. 'I pray for this day for long time. I thank God he send you, oh Great Shee. I follow where you lead. Even to death.' Cormac raised his head again and gave Domnall the shee's message.

A firm smile stretched across Domnall's lips and he stamped his spear in the ground several times. The Mar warriors spoke excitedly amongst themselves. Jack heard the words 'Captain Rao' said repeatedly.

Domnall spoke again to Rao, and Cormac translated. 'Chief asks if you have great magic like Demon. Have fire weapons to fight Demon?'

Rao shot a look at Jack. 'We've only got two pistols and no ammunition.'

Jack was well aware of that. 'Just tell them yes.'

Rao tightened his lips and his eyes flashed, but he turned back to Cormac. 'Yes, I have great magic and fire weapons.'

When Cormac explained this to Domnall, the Chief smiled broadly and many of the Mar warriors cheered and clapped. Several stood now and addressed the assembly in loud voices, shaking their spears.

When the men had calmed down a little, Domnall, through Cormac, said to Rao, 'We are overjoyed Great Shee has come to fight Demon. We will follow. All fight to death to free lands. We only ask if Great Shee can show fire magic. We long to see. It give joy to heart.'

Rao paled and hissed at Jack, 'We've got no bullets. We've got nothing to fire.'

Jack's mind raced. He looked at the circle of savages staring expectantly at them. How were they going to get out of this? 'Cormac, the Great Shee is weary. He will show magic that sees far. Fire magic another day.'

Cormac frowned and looked at Rao.

'Er, yes, that's right,' Rao said. 'Fire magic another time.'

Cormac told this news to Domnall. The smile slipped from the Chief's face and he replied to Cormac in a slightly sharper tone.

'Chief asks if Great Shee will not think again,' Cormac said. 'Of course, is decision of Great Shee, but will bring much joy to see fire magic. Chief ask as very great favour of shee with brown skin.'

Jack's heart beat a little faster. The Mar had welcomed him and Rao so warmly he'd forgotten to be afraid of them. But now he stared at the stern faces of the warriors, many of whom were gripping their spears.

Christ. He and Rao were in a tight spot.

Then he had an idea. 'Cormac, tell them to wait a moment. I'll fetch the fire magic of the Great Shee.'

'What are you doing?' Rao's face was drawn and his eyes wide.

'Calm down,' Jack said. 'Stay here.'

He ran back to the hut, hearing the Mar muttering amongst themselves behind him. He ducked through the doorway, wrenched open the knapsack and pulled out one of the pistols. He gazed at the swirling designs engraved on the weapon's brass side plate.

His plan had better work.

He took out the flask, poured powder into the measuring charger and then emptied this into one of the pistol's barrels. He placed a greased patch of cloth over the muzzle and rammed this down with the rod to hold the powder in place. Then he pressed a cap on to the loaded barrel's nipple.

'You'd bloody better fire.' He kissed the pistol. He didn't want to think about what would happen if it misfired.

He rushed back to the assembly, where most of the warriors were now standing and appearing to argue with one another. Cormac's brow was knitting and he was glancing repeatedly between Rao and the other Mar.

Jack drew up beside Rao and handed him the pistol.

Rao's face lit up. 'You found a bullet?'

'No. Just packed it with powder.'

Rao's mouth drooped. 'No bullet? What good is that?'

'Just fire it. It'll make a noise. Hopefully that'll do.'

'And what if it doesn't do?'

'Just get on with it.'

Rao turned to face the crowd and pointed the pistol at the sky. In a clear voice he said, 'Listen. I will demonstrate the fire magic of the Great Shee.'

Cormac didn't even need to translate. The Mar fell suddenly silent and stared at Rao.

Jack crossed himself.

Rao squeezed his eyes shut and pulled the trigger. The hammer clicked down and the weapon cracked and spat smoke.

The Mar all jumped and gasped. A few cowered, while others stared up into the sky. Then they burst into applause, cheered, laughed and waved their weapons in the air. Domnall beamed and stamped his spear into the ground over and over again. Cormac smiled, his eyes shining.

Jack breathed out and said a Hail Mary in his head. He patted Rao on the shoulder. 'Well done, Great Shee. Looks like we got away with it.'

Rao looked as if he were about to faint. 'I feel sick.'

Jack grinned. 'Something for your journal.' He grabbed Cormac's arm. 'Now, the Place of Dead Kings.'

Cormac nodded and called across to Domnall. The Chief raised his hand to silence the crowd and then gave a short speech.

'Chief say we all march on Place of Dead Kings,' Cormac said. 'Kill Demon with fire magic.'

Jack grabbed Cormac's arm again. Christ, another problem to deal with. 'No. We can't do that yet. We have to scout the place out first.'

Cormac frowned.

'We have to look at the Demon's magic,' Jack said, 'so we know how to beat him. You take us first. We take a look. Then decide what to do.'

Cormac relayed this to Domnall, who nodded and spoke to the other chiefs. There was a short debate between them, but finally Cormac said, 'Chiefs agree with plan. I take you Place of Dead Kings. With few other warriors.'

'Good,' Jack said. 'Give the Chief our thanks and let's get going.'

'Not yet,' Cormac said. 'Tonight.'

'Tonight?'

'Day too dangerous. Many Cattans near Place of Dead Kings. We go night. Better.'

Jack sighed. Why did everything have to take so long with the Mar?

'Makes sense,' Rao said. 'We don't want to run into any trouble. Cormac seems to know what he's talking about.'

'How long will it take?' Jack asked Cormac.

'Not far. One night. That all.'

Jack nodded. He hated the idea of delaying the journey any further. But Rao was right, they couldn't risk getting caught or killed. 'Very well. Tonight it is, then.'

21

'It's getting dark.' Rao set aside the bowl of water and the knife he'd been shaving with.

Jack, who'd been lying on the bracken bed, sat up. Through the hut's doorway, he saw the sky was turning violet. 'Finally.'

Rao mopped his face with a cloth and did his best to twirl the ends of his moustache. 'So, what are we going to do when we reach the Place of Dead Kings?'

'Been thinking about that myself. The way I see it, we're there to get our comrades out. That's all.'

'I agree. That's our main purpose. But the Mar are expecting more than that.'

'There's not much we can do to help them.'

'It feels a little hard to let them down. We've misled them.'

'We didn't have a choice. We'll get to Mahajan's hideout and find out what's going on. If there's anything we can do to help the Mar, we'll do it. But we have to get Saleem and Parihar out above all else.'

'Agreed. I'm not sure that the Mar will think too kindly of us if we don't fight Mahajan, though.'

'We'll have to deal with that problem when it comes. We might find we have to leave Mar in a hurry.'

Rao stared at the doorway. 'Seems we face dangers in all directions.'

Jack paused. He was going to have to broach the subject of the Brahmastra – at least, up to a point. They had to know what they were going up against and Rao had Atri's notes, which might help.

But how was he going to raise the topic without revealing he was a crusader?

He picked up some bracken and twirled it around his finger. 'Look, Rao. We have to be straight with each other about things. You agree?'

Rao frowned. 'What do you mean?'

'We have to be honest with each other about what we know about Mahajan. So we both know what we're dealing with.'

'Of course.'

'Good. Glad you agree.' Jack tightened his lips. Should he continue? 'I . . . heard you mention something to Parihar once. When we were travelling up here. You talked about something called the Brahmastra.'

Rao's eyebrows shot up. 'What? How do you know about that?'

Jack held up his hand to calm Rao. 'I just overheard you talking. I understand some Rajthani. From the army.'

Rao's eyes narrowed. 'What did you overhear?'

'Not much. I just heard you use the word "Brahmastra". I don't know what that means. It sounds like some sort of weapon.'

Rao stroked his moustache. 'You're full of surprises, Jack. I don't know what to make of you sometimes.'

'I'm used to listening to what officers say. How do you think men in the army find anything out?'

'I suppose that makes sense.'

'Look, like I said, we have to trust each other. If you know something about Mahajan that could help us, you have to tell me now.'

Rao nodded slowly. 'Fair enough. That is a reasonable request. The Brahmastra, then. I'm afraid I can't tell you a great deal about it. As I said, I'm not from a priest jati. The odd thing is, until recently I wouldn't have even believed the thing could be real. You see, the Brahmastra is something from myth. It's mentioned in ancient legends, from long before Rajthanan times.'

'But what is it?'

'Well, the stories say it was some kind of devastating weapon. It's said it had the power of the sun and when it was used it would destroy the land for miles around and leave it poisoned for decades afterwards. Nothing could live or grow there. It could strike down whole armies in one go and smash whole cities. No one could withstand it.'

Jack went silent. The wind whined between the cracks in the stone walls. 'Sounds like a useful weapon to have on your side.'

'Indeed.'

'And a bad weapon to have used on you.'

'Yes. Of course. It could destroy a whole people.'

'And this thing is real?'

'I have no idea. I find it hard to believe in it, to be honest. It's mentioned in the legends but it's never been heard of in recent times. If it ever existed, it was somehow forgotten or lost.'

'But your commanders think it's real. Otherwise they wouldn't have sent the expedition.'

'My commanders were as baffled about it as me. There were rumours that Mahajan was trying to build a Brahmastra. But they were – still are – nothing more than rumours. The expedition was to find out what Mahajan was up to, that's all. I'm not sure that many people believed we really would find a Brahmastra up here in Scotland.'

'I suppose the army wouldn't mind getting their hands on a Brahmastra if it turned out Mahajan really did have one.'

'That is probably true.'

Probably? Undoubtedly. The generals would be itching to have a weapon like that. The Rajthanan empire would be unstoppable. 'What about Atri? Did he believe in the Brahmastra?'

'I don't know. I didn't speak to him about it much. He was very secretive about this whole mission, but that's the way with siddhas.'

'What about his notebook? Does he say anything about it in there?'

'This?' Rao took the notebook from the satchel and lifted it up.

'I'm afraid it won't be much help. It's all technical notes. I can't make head or tail of it.'

'The secret siddha language?'

'Yes. Well, secret is perhaps stretching it – knowledge of the language is restricted. But the main problem is it's all so damn complicated. I understand a few of the words, but it means nothing unless you've done years of training.'

Was Rao telling the truth? Probably. There was no point in him withholding anything useful now. 'What about those big sheets of paper Atri left? In the satchel?'

Rao frowned. 'How did you know about those? Have you been going through my things?'

'Yes, I did, actually. After we had that argument. I wanted to see if you had anything useful before I left you there.'

Rao's moustache straightened and his eyes glinted in the dim light. 'You had no right to do that.'

Jack thought quickly. He should try to be conciliatory for the time being. He needed to understand as much as he could about Mahajan, and Rao was the only person who could help. 'Maybe. But I didn't . . . know you much then. I wouldn't do that now.'

Rao cleared his throat. 'Yes. Well. I agree things are a little different now.'

'So, what about those sheets? What do they mean?'

Rao sighed. 'I don't think they will be much help either. They're just maps. Atri was also a surveyor, you see. His task was to map the uncharted regions as best he could.'

'That spyglass on a stand.'

'Yes, a surveyor's tool.'

'Nothing about the Brahmastra on those sheets?'

'Nothing like that. Just standard maps. I've taken a look at them. You know, the usual. Mountains, rivers, towns, sattva streams.'

'Sattva streams?'

'Yes, those are all marked down. Useful information for prospectors. A lot of sattva up here, I'm told.'

Jack hadn't known the Rajthanans mapped the streams. But it made sense. They would have to know where the strongest streams were in order to build their mills and set up sattva links.

But before he could mull over any of this further, Cormac appeared in the entrance, silhouetted against the fading light. He held a bow in one hand, and a quiver of arrows hung from his belt.

'Finally,' Jack said. 'Are we going now?'

'Aye,' Cormac said. 'First blessing from seer, then go.'

Blessing from the seer? Jack was about to protest, but Cormac was already leaving. Cursing, Jack stuck the scimitar and knife in his belt and hurried after the tall Scot. Rao scurried along beside him.

Cormac disappeared into a grove nestling in a gully on the edge of the village. Jack and Rao followed him along a track that was clearly little used as branches snagged them and undergrowth grasped their ankles.

Finally Jack caught up to Cormac. He was about to demand to be taken to the Place of Dead Kings, when Cormac gestured to a clearing ahead and said, 'Here seer.'

Jack stared into the shadowy glade. In the centre stood a hut that was so dilapidated it appeared to be no more than a pile of stones. But the fresh green turf on the roof and a line of smoke escaping from the smoke-hole showed the building was inhabited.

Cormac led them across to the hut. The door slid to the side and light spilt out into the dark. The seer stood in the doorway, blinking at them, her wild grey hair coiling about her head. She grunted and gestured for them to enter.

Jack stooped and found himself in a cramped room. The walls and ceiling were so poorly constructed he might as well have been in a cave. Strange mobiles, made of animal bones and metal charms, hung from the ceiling and he had to keep ducking to avoid them. A peat fire flickered in the centre of the chamber and the acrid smoke hazed the interior. All about the walls stood stone cairns, on top of which were odd assortments of objects: worn river-stones, bones, feathers and coloured threads. Atop the largest cairn stood a simple stone cross, engraved with knotted Celtic designs, and below this a wooden female figurine.

The seer hobbled over to the cairn, dipped her finger in a bowl of what appeared to be milk and smeared this on the feet of the figurine.

Cormac pointed at the statue. 'This St Brigit. Will help seeing.'

'Seeing?' Jack asked.

Cormac nodded at the old woman. 'Watch.'

The seer, still facing the cairn, began swaying and chanting. At intervals she stopped and crossed herself, then returned to her singing. Finally, she began shuffling in a circle about the fire. Rao had to move out of her way. She continued chanting, shut her eyes and repeatedly crossed herself.

Then she gave a sudden shout and slipped to the ground. Jack went to run to her aid, but Cormac held him back and shook his head.

The seer writhed on the ground, foam spilling from her mouth, her eyes opening and rolling white. She gave a series of unnatural groans and muttered what might have been Gaalic words, although they sounded more like animal cries than human speech.

'Shiva,' Rao whispered.

After around two minutes, the seer lay still on the ground, blinked a few times and wiped the drool from her chin. She struggled to clamber back to her feet until Cormac went to her side and helped her up. She limped across to a flat stone and sat on it.

She stared at Rao, her eyes glazed, and spoke in Gaalic.

Cormac grinned. 'It is good. Seer say she see many things. Good things. Great Shee with magic from God will fight Demon and throw back in hell. Free these lands.'

'Yes, well.' Rao shuffled awkwardly and rubbed his moustache. 'I'm sure we'll all do our best.'

The seer stood and gestured with her hand for Jack and Rao to approach. They walked over and she pointed at a stack of stones that reached to the height of her chest. On top of the stones lay what Jack at first thought was a battered cardboard box, until he came close enough to see it was an ancient book.

A book? What was a book doing here?

The seer touched the worn cover with her hand, shut her eyes and breathed deeply. She opened the tome, revealing yellow pages that were worn and warped. The black writing was smeared, the letters bleeding into each other. The illuminated pictures were losing their colour and the detail was blurred.

Cormac stared at the manuscript, his face solemn. 'The Bible.'

'The Bible?' Jack leant closer. The pictures were so ravaged by time it was impossible to make out what they were. But it could be a Bible. 'Can she read it?'

'Read?' Cormac said. 'No. No Mar read. This book of ancients. From time of dead kings who build tower to moon. No read. But gives blessing. Blessing of God.'

'Whatever is he talking about?' Rao asked.

'It's the Christian holy book,' Jack said. 'They've kept it here like a kind of relic. It must be hundreds of years old.'

'Extraordinary.' Rao bent over the book. 'A vestige from another era.'

The seer gripped Rao's sleeve and pointed repeatedly at the book.

'Touch it,' Cormac said. 'It give blessing of God.'

'Very well.' Rao gently rested his finger on a page.

'You also.' Cormac motioned to Jack.

Jack touched the edge of the page and a small piece of the parchment broke free.

The seer closed the book, crossed herself several times and said a few words to Rao.

'You blessed now,' Cormac said. 'Come. We go.'

'To the Place of Dead Kings?' Jack was half expecting some further delay.

'Aye. We go now.'

They walked back through the trees. Chief Domnall, his daughters and many of the Mar were waiting in the village centre.

When she saw Rao, Eva rushed across to him and took his hand. 'Careful, Great Shee.'

Rao cleared his throat and gently removed her hand. 'We'll take care. Don't you worry.'

'You come back?' Eva's eyes glistened.

'Yes. Of course.'

'Then we marry. Forget other.'

Rao gave a nervous laugh and glanced at Domnall, who just smiled back at him. 'Um, I don't think so, Eva.'

But it was unclear whether Eva understood, because she grasped his arm. 'I wait.'

Domnall stamped his spear into the ground and said a few words, which Cormac translated. The Chief wished them success, prayed for their safety and longed for the time when the Great Shee would return to the village.

Jack and Rao said farewell. Then Cormac led them and three Mar warriors off towards the hills.

As they reached the edge of the village, Jack heard singing and a blast of pipes. He and Rao glanced over their shoulders and saw the Mar chanting and dancing in the village centre. The villagers waved, smiled and cheered when they saw the Great Shee look back.

'It really will stick in the throat to let these people down,' Rao said.

'I know.' Jack turned back and marched on after Cormac. 'But forget that for the moment. Right now we have to find our friends and get them out. I've got a feeling that's going to be quite a challenge in itself.'

22

Cormac and the three warriors flew like spirits through the darkness. The moon was faint and often the only thing Jack could see clearly of the Mar was the pale quiver bouncing at Cormac's side.

At first Jack managed to keep up. The pain in his chest was slight, his breathing was clear and his legs felt strong. The wind cooled his face and fluttered his long hair behind his head. He'd left the knapsack behind – he had no use for it at the moment – and was only encumbered by the scimitar swinging at his waist.

Rao also kept up the pace, although perspiration broke out on his forehead and glistened in the pallid light.

All about them, the mountains were hulks against the night, phosphorescent snow crowning the peaks. Jack heard no sound, save for the wind in his ears, the crunch of his and Rao's boots and his own shivery breath. The Mar were silent, even their foot-falls muffled by their hide shoes.

Jack constantly passed through sattva streams, each one seemingly stronger than the last. His skin rippled, his scalp tingled and the sweet scent burnt his nostrils and the back of his throat.

About twenty minutes after leaving the village, they came to a shallow river where the water rushed and danced over stones. Cormac said a prayer to a monster who lurked within, and then they splashed across and set off up a hill. They paused twice in the next hour, once to say a prayer outside a grove of trees and another time to bow and chant to the moon when it sailed free of the cloud for a few minutes.

After an hour and a half, Jack noticed the pain beating in his chest and his breathing growing more shallow. Rao wheezed and tripped at times on rocks and clumps of heather. Jack was considering demanding a rest stop, when the Mar ahead of him suddenly halted, dropped to their knees and slipped behind a gorse bush. Cormac looked back, put his finger to his lips and gestured frantically for Jack and Rao to stay low.

Christ. What now? A Cattan patrol?

Jack and Rao jogged silently across to the Mar. Cormac had already raised his bow and drawn out an arrow.

'What is it?' Jack whispered.

Cormac pressed his finger to his lips again and pointed through the thorny branches of the bush.

Jack stared hard into the darkness. At first he saw nothing, but then noticed a pale wisp flitting across a stretch of open ground. Gradually, he traced the outline of a deer with a white marking on its back.

A deer? Was that it? Why were the Mar hunting now?

Cormac nocked the arrow, drew back the bowstring and stared at the deer, his face like stone. The other Mar watched him intently, their features drawn and grey, as if their lives depended on what happened next.

Cormac took at least a minute to line up his shot. Jack shifted on his haunches. He was about to say they shouldn't waste any more time, when Cormac loosed the arrow. The bowstring quivered and sang, and the arrow whistled through the dark.

The deer jumped, squealed, tripped, then got up again. It tried to run, but kept falling.

Cormac grinned, tossed aside the bow, sprang out from behind the bush and sprinted across to the deer. His comrades followed, smiling and giving little whoops. The creature flailed on the ground, clambered up and ran a few feet further. Cormac charged at the beast with incredible speed, whipped out his knife, dived on the animal and slit its throat. The deer bucked a few times and then fell still.

The Mar gathered about Cormac and appeared to jab the fallen creature with their spears.

'What on earth are they doing?' Rao asked.

'Let's find out,' Jack said.

They walked across and saw the warriors were dipping the ends of their weapons in the dead animal's blood.

Cormac raised a red-stained arrow and beamed. 'Blood give good luck.'

Jack put his hands on his hips. 'Is this going to happen all the way to the Place of Dead Kings?'

'No. Just first animal. See first animal on journey. Kill it. Good luck.'

Jack rolled his eyes and glanced at Rao, who shrugged and said, 'I needed a break anyway.'

When the Mar had finished their ritual, they squatted on the ground and rested for a few minutes. They fingered their amulets, muttered prayers and pointed towards a rocky outcrop about two hundred yards away.

Rao asked Cormac, 'What are you pointing at?'

'Bad place,' Cormac said. 'Evil spirits live there.'

'You see spirits everywhere?'

Cormac blinked. 'Of course, Great Shee.' He waved his arm across the shadowy landscape. 'Many spirits.'

Rao gestured at a grove. 'What about those trees over there?'

'Forest spirit live there. Like old man.'

'And that mountain?'

'Big monster. Lizard.'

'Fascinating. You seem to know every bit of the landscape around here. And every bit is associated with some creature.'

'Aye. Ken all land. All spirits.' Cormac pressed his hand to his chest. 'All land in here. In heart. Long time ago, I go south. No see land.' He opened the palm of his hand as if catching liquid. 'My heart. Like blood.'

'I think I understand. You suffered when you were away from this place.'

'Aye. We call *duthchas*. Not ken word in English. Land in heart. When away from land, heart bleeds.'

Rao sat up straighter and stared into the night. His voice was husky as he spoke. 'Yes, I believe I do understand. When one is away from one's home, one's heart can certainly bleed.'

'I agree with that.' Jack stood and picked up his scimitar. 'But we should get moving again. We have to reach the Place of Dead Kings before dawn.'

———————

They ran on through the night, with the wind streaming over them and the jagged backs of the mountains filing past. In the darkness, the landscape, with its hollows, dells and clefts, seemed to contain endless secrets. As if spirits and monsters really did dwell within the shadows.

At about five o'clock, Cormac paused them with his hand, crouched and led them to a line of rocks running along the top of a ridge. Jack peered over a boulder and spotted dim figures crossing a valley below. He took the glass from Rao, stared through it and made out the white skull on the men's tunics.

'Cattans.' He offered the glass to Cormac.

Cormac shook his head. 'No need. I ken Cattans. Many Cattans here near Place of Dead Kings.'

'How far away is it?' Jack asked.

'Not far. We go slow now.' Cormac went to stand, then squatted down again. 'Bad magic starts soon.'

'What do you mean?'

'This land. Bad magic from Demon. You will see.'

Cormac stood again and led them to the right, staying below the crest of the ridge.

Jack followed, looking about him, searching for any sign of Cattans in the dark.

Bad magic starts soon.

What was Cormac talking about? Was this just superstition or something more?

They jogged into a birch forest, which enclosed them in a mist of naked branches. The trees rattled and scraped in the breeze and the damp mulch of leaves underfoot smelt faintly of wine.

Cormac slowed the pace to a walk and they crept ahead stealthily.

Jack kept glancing around and couldn't get it out of his head that there were Cattans waiting nearby with arrows pointed straight at them. They passed into yet another stream and he sensed the sattva rushing around him. His nose ran as the scent scorched his nostrils.

He noticed Rao sniffing. 'You smell it?'

'Yes,' Rao said. 'It's like the mills back home.'

One of the Mar gasped and sprang away from the track, slapping at his cloak with his hands. The other two warriors cowered beside a birch.

Jack's heart spiked. They were under attack. He tore the scimitar from his belt, slipped to the side of the path and scoured the darkness for enemies. Rao gave a small yelp and scrambled across to him.

But Jack saw nothing. Heard no sound.

Then Rao nudged him and pointed at the Mar. 'Look.'

Cormac stood about twenty feet away, staring at what looked like a tiny star drifting down from the treetops. The speck gave off a silver glow and made a faint tinkling sound as it descended. Cormac's eyes were wide and his mouth half open, while the crouching Mar warriors' faces were stricken with terror. The light made the lines on their faces appear deeper and cast their skin a sickly white.

Jack frowned. What the hell was that?

He took a few steps up the track. The shining dot was now level with Cormac's head. Up close, Jack could see it was like a flake of snow or scrap of tissue. And it smelt so strongly of sattva it made him reel.

The thing spun to the ground and melted into the leaf litter, disappearing completely.

One of the Mar cried out. Another speck had fallen on his cloak and he shook it off. Looking around, Jack saw more of the things twirling down, some overhead, some further up the track, some far off in the depths of the forest, where they lit up the tangled branches and gnarled trunks.

'Bad magic,' Cormac said. 'I see before.'

'I've seen it before too.' Rao's boots crunched as he walked up the track. 'There was an accident at a mill once, near where I lived as a child. I saw these that night. It's a kind of ash.'

'Is it dangerous?' Jack asked.

'I don't think so. We were told to stay indoors and not touch them, but I put my hand out of a window and grabbed them anyway.'

Jack looked up and saw thousands of shining fragments floating down, as if the heavens were falling. 'Looks like we're not going to be able to avoid the stuff anyway. Let's go.'

Cormac led the way on through the woods. The ghostly ash continued to spin down, the Mar flinching each time a fragment touched them. The smell of sattva grew stronger and Jack detected something else – coal smoke.

After half an hour, they climbed out of the forest, clambered up a steep scarp and reached a stand of trees that ran along the summit. The Mar reached the other side of the woods first and stood pointing down the far side of the hill, gasping and talking agitatedly.

When Jack reached them, he almost tripped backwards in surprise at what he saw.

Below him, a slope rolled down to a valley, in the centre of which rose a low, flat-topped hill. A dark building squatted like a spider on the summit. A swarm of turrets and spires jutted up from the structure, while a series of chimneys belched grey smoke and streams of luminous ash. The million pinpricks of light sailed like dandelion seeds across the valley, drifting to the ground or wafting away over the surrounding hills.

Jack blinked repeatedly as a wall of sattva stung his eyes.

The Mar crossed themselves, mumbled prayers and fiddled with their amulets.

Cormac pointed at the building. 'Place of Dead Kings. Under hill bury kings.'

'Shiva,' Rao said softly. 'I wasn't expecting something like that.'

'What is it? A mill?' Jack said.

'I'm not sure.' Rao peered through the glass. 'Something like a mill. Take a look.'

Jack gripped the glass and swept it over to the central hill. A tangle of stonework and blackened pipes seethed before him. The walls appeared to be the remains of an ancient castle, but over these squirmed tubes covered in soot. Jagged towers, also a combination of aging stone and iron, rose from the middle of the building. Clouds of smoke, steam and glimmering ash swirled about the structure, almost completely obscuring it at times.

Jack lowered the glass. 'Mahajan's been busy.'

'Indeed.' A flake of shining ash drifted near Rao and lit up his face for a moment. 'What do we do now?'

'We have to get into that castle and take a look around. Saleem and Parihar must be in there somewhere. If they're not, then I don't know where we'll find them.'

'I could go. Talk to Mahajan.'

'And then you might end up captured too. No, we have to be careful. Sneak in somehow.'

Jack peered through the glass again and searched the valley floor. It was difficult to make anything out, but he did spot pale lines, which appeared to be tracks or roads, with bands of Cattans patrolling along them. He lowered the glass and glanced at the sky. A trace of dawn was spreading behind the mountains. 'It'll be light soon. The Cattans will see us straight away if we go down into that valley now. There's nowhere to hide there.'

'So, we wait until tonight?' Rao asked.

Jack rubbed his chin. 'We might have to. Don't like to leave it so long, though.'

Cormac grasped Jack's arm and pressed his finger to his lips. He pointed into the trees behind him.

Jack peered into the darkness and listened carefully. He saw nothing, but heard the distinct crackle of footsteps on leaves and twigs.

His heart quivered. Had they been seen?

'Down,' he hissed.

They all crouched low.

Jack cocked his head. The footsteps were around twenty yards away. About thirty people. Wearing the hide shoes of the natives.

The Mar inched their way silently to a low boulder and stared over the top. Jack followed, with Rao behind him. The Captain trod on a fallen branch and made a scuffling noise. The Mar flinched and Jack froze. But the footsteps continued as before.

Jack crept up beside Cormac and edged his head over the rock. Below, he saw a short slope, at the bottom of which marched a column of savages. The figures were hard to make out as they passed through the dappled shadows of the woods. At first he thought they were Cattans, but none of them bore the white skull on their clothing and none appeared to be carrying weapons. They wore their cloaks lifted high and folded over their heads like cowls, which made them look strange and misshapen in the dim light.

Jack shot a questioning look at Cormac.

'Not Cattans,' Cormac whispered. He lowered his head and tightened his jaw. 'They Mar.'

'What are they doing here?'

Cormac's eyes flashed. 'Traitors.'

'You said the Mar don't work for the Demon.'

'No. None work. But some now come worship.'

'Worship?'

'Demon say he sent by God. Some begin believe. Every few weeks come castle and worship.'

Interesting. An idea was occurring to Jack. 'Are these worshippers let into the castle?'

Cormac spoke to one of the Mar warriors, then said to Jack, 'He say worshipper go in castle. Met one man once who go in.'

'Good. We'll pretend to be worshippers, then.'

The Mar warrior tugged Cormac's cloak and spoke again. Cormac nodded and said to Jack, 'Dangerous. They search for weapon.'

Jack sat back. 'We'll be careful, then. No weapons.'

'Are you sure about this?' Rao said. 'If the Cattans get suspicious, we won't be able to defend ourselves.'

'Don't see what other option we have at the moment.'

Jack looked down the hill. The light was steadily brightening and it was easy to make out the group of Mar worshippers, who were now almost a third of the way down the incline.

'Look.' Cormac pointed to his right.

About fifty savages were winding their way down another hillside. When Jack checked through the glass, he saw they were also worshippers. He searched and spotted other groups making their way across more distant hills. 'There must be a few hundred on their way. We'll blend in easily.'

Several clusters of Mar had already reached the valley floor. Jack observed them through the glass and saw they were sitting down, as if waiting for something.

'Worship later,' Cormac said. 'Open castle gate when sun going down.'

Jack crouched again. Damn, so they would have to wait for

nightfall after all. But there was nothing he could do about that. 'We'll stay here, then. But later this afternoon we have to get down into that valley. We have to be ready when they open the gates.'

———◆———

They remained hidden through the day, taking turns to sleep and keep watch. Finally, Cormac shook them all awake as the sun was lowering and the giant claws of the shadows were reaching across the valley.

It was time. But Jack knew he couldn't walk into the castle dressed as he was. His tunic was the wrong style and too finely stitched. He could change his clothes, but Rao presented an even greater problem.

'I can remove my turban,' Rao said. 'Perhaps take off my boots and borrow someone's shoes.'

Cormac shook his head. 'Brown skin.'

'He's right,' Jack said. 'There's no way you can pass for a Scot. Even with a cloak over your head.'

'Perhaps Great Shee have magic change skin?' Cormac said.

Jack smiled wryly. 'That would be a good power. But no, unfortunately the Great Shee can't do that.' He turned to Rao and said in Arabic. 'You'll have to stay here.'

Rao's moustache tightened. 'I object. I want to rescue our friends as much as you do.'

'It's impossible—'

'I am in charge of this mission.'

Jack snorted. He was about to say something sarcastic but held back. 'Look, I understand what you're saying, but you'd put us all in danger.'

Rao's moustache rippled and his eyes quivered. Finally, he nodded. 'Very well. I suppose you're right.'

Jack switched back to English and included Cormac in the conversation. 'The Great Shee will stay, plus three others. I want only one person coming with me. We can't risk too many of us getting caught. The rest will stay here and take word to the village if we don't come back.'

'I will come,' Cormac said quickly.

Jack nodded. 'Good.'

Cormac explained the plan to the Mar warriors, who seemed to raise some objections at first, but were eventually convinced.

Jack wrenched off his boots and slid down his hose – he had to have naked legs if he were going to pass for a Mar. He swapped clothes with one of the warriors and slipped on the man's tunic and hide shoes. Finally, he slung the heavy woollen cloak over his shoulders and fastened it at his neck with a metal brooch. The cloak smelt of old sweat and wood smoke. But it was warm. Surprisingly warm.

He handed his scimitar and knife to Rao. He would have liked to take the knife with him, but it would be too difficult to conceal.

He put his hand on Rao's shoulder. 'If we're not back by midnight, go to the village and tell them what happened. Then get back to Dun Fries as best you can.'

Rao stood up straighter and raised his chin. 'I will not leave a comrade behind. If you don't return, I shall come to find you.'

Jack shook his head. 'It's too dangerous for you to go in there.'

'I would reason with Mahajan.'

Jack lifted an eyebrow. 'Somehow he doesn't sound like the type who'll listen to reason.'

'I would do my best.'

Jack took a deep breath. There was no point arguing further. He'd told Rao what he wanted him to do. If the Captain did something else, there wasn't going to be much he could do to stop him.

He lifted the cloak up over his head and the smell of smoke and sweat grew stronger. He turned to Cormac. 'Let's get on with it.'

Cormac nodded. They stepped out of the cover of the trees and struck off down the slope.

The late sun sent golden shafts through gaps in the cloud. The groups of Mar were standing now and walking towards the castle, while Cattans patrolled along the roads.

'You reckon we'll get away with this?' Jack asked.

Cormac smiled. 'Great Shee protect us.'

'I hope so,' Jack muttered.

They reached the bottom of the hill and set off across the open ground. A dry wind plucked at their cloaks and swept the grass in different directions. Ahead, Mahajan's castle rose from the hill, black against a sky tinted salmon by the sunset. It looked larger and more imposing from down in the valley. The hillsides were steep, the stone walls high, and the spires and chimneys seemed impossibly tall.

Jack blinked, rubbed his eyes a few times, then stared at the castle again. There was something strange about the building. It seemed to shift and change subtly, as if it were a picture printed on a rippling curtain. The metalwork in particular seemed to waver and squirm.

Cormac frowned. 'Black magic. Hurt eyes.'

Jack nodded. Even he, who was used to mills and avatars, found the castle unnerving.

About halfway to the hill, they met a group of worshippers – three men and seven women – travelling in the same direction. Cormac greeted them in Gaalic and Jack pulled his cloak closer to his face. He and Cormac joined the back of the group and they all pressed on towards the castle.

A party of Cattans marched past but they only gave the worshippers a cursory look. Jack blended in with the others and aroused no suspicion.

The glowing ash – virtually invisible during the day – increasingly stood out in the dim light. From time to time Jack heard the distinctive tinkle as a flake twirled near to him.

The sattva grew stronger. His eyes ran and he had to wipe away the tears. His chest shuddered and burnt, as if stirred by the powerful streams. At one point the pain grew so bad he stumbled and almost fell.

Cormac grasped his arm to steady him. 'What wrong?'

Jack shook off Cormac's hand. 'I'm fine.'

As the far side of the hill came into view, Jack made out a village of native huts clustered at the bottom of the slope. Smoke trickled from the roofs, and figures moved about between the buildings. No doubt many of the Cattans working in the castle lived in the settlement.

They came to the base of the hill and Jack looked up. The castle was silhouetted against a blast of red sunset and smouldered within clouds of steam and smoke. The walls and towers, entwined by pipes, continued to slip away as he tried to focus on them, the effect making him dizzy.

The portcullis stood open and worshippers were queuing as they waited to be admitted through the giant gatehouse. Jack and Cormac trudged up to the back of the line, inched their way forward and finally came to the entrance. Iron pipes, as thick as tree trunks, twisted to either side of the entryway, steam wheezing from valves and joins in the metal. Ten Cattans stood guard, and Jack immediately noted they were carrying knife-muskets on their shoulders.

So, Mahajan had taught at least some of the Cattans to use firearms.

He glanced up and spotted serpent-headed Rajthanan guns poking out from the battlements. Mahajan's castle was better defended than he'd thought possible up here in Scotland.

Two Cattan guards patted him and Cormac down for weapons, then grunted and waved them in. They followed the other worshippers along the passage beneath the gatehouse, through the open gates and into a bailey. Pipes slithered over the surroundings walls, whistling and pumping out steam. The smell of sattva and coal was so overpowering it made Jack's head spin and even Cormac wrinkled his nose. The buildings wobbled and shifted giddily when Jack tried to concentrate on them. He felt as though he were about to faint again, but shut his eyes for a second and managed to pull himself together.

Cormac hesitated, gave a small hiss and crossed himself. It took Jack a moment to realise why. As he peered through the drifts of steam, he made out a huge metal form embedded high up in the wall on the far side of the bailey. He squinted, trying to make it out clearly, and finally the mist parted enough for him to see. It was a giant skull, at least twelve feet high and made of riveted black iron. The eye sockets were dark holes and the mouth hung slightly open, revealing rusting teeth.

'What is?' Cormac whispered.

'No idea,' Jack said. It might be no more than a strange murti, but he didn't like the look of it.

They shuffled forward to make way for the worshippers streaming in behind them. Cattan guards watched from the ramparts, their white skull emblems shining in the dying light. The Mar stood, with their cloaks over their heads, facing a wooden platform that had been erected beneath the skull. Most crossed themselves, toyed with amulets and muttered prayers. A few simply bowed their heads and waited silently.

Jack and Cormac found a spot to one side of the crowd. Jack didn't dare speak more than a few hushed words to Cormac in case they were overheard using English.

After around ten minutes, a Cattan climbed the steps up the side of the platform and turned to face the assembly. Jack recognised the man instantly – it was the leader of the war party that had captured Saleem and the others. His dark hair was still tied in a topknot and he wore chain mail and a surcoat bearing the white skull device.

A tremor of hope ran through Jack. If this man was here, that meant Saleem must be in the castle. Surely the Cattans wouldn't have taken the captives anywhere else?

The tall Cattan stepped up to the edge of the platform and looked down at the Mar, his top lip raised in a sneer.

'He Nectan,' Cormac whispered. 'Cattan leader. He serve Mahajan long time.'

Nectan crossed himself and began speaking in Gaalic. The gathering fell silent. Nectan spoke for about a minute and then paused. The worshippers bowed their heads and muttered prayers. Then Nectan lifted his hand dramatically and said, 'Mahajan.'

There was a tortured squeal of metal. The worshippers gasped as the jaw of the giant skull dropped open and red flames flickered alight within its eye sockets. The skull gave a shuddering groan and a globe of orange fire burst from its mouth. The Mar flinched and a few ducked, but the flames tumbled high above their heads and soon vanished.

Next the skull groaned again and thick black smoke frothed from its maw. The smoke billowed and swirled and soon filled the bailey. Many of the worshippers coughed as the acrid fog embraced them. Jack could see no more than a foot ahead of him, although the red glow of the skull's eyes still shone through the murk.

Finally, the smoke began to clear and the flames in the skull's eyes dimmed. Nectan had disappeared, but a new figure had slipped up to the stage and now stepped out of the rolling haze.

The worshippers all dropped to their knees and in unison said one word: 'Mahajan.'

23

Mahajan didn't look as Jack had expected. Although Jack wasn't sure what he *had* expected.

The siddha was a Rajthanan of average height in his mid-fifties. He was slightly overweight and his stomach bulged against his clothing. His face was fleshy and his fingers were short and fat. He was balding and what remained of his hair was white and cropped short. His eyes were a dirty yellow and set deep within purple circles.

He was dressed like a savage. He wore a native cloak, tunic and surcoat displaying the white skull. Numerous amulets hung around his neck and jangled when he moved. He carried a simple wooden staff in one hand, although he seemed to have no need for it as he walked across the stage without any difficulty.

He stood on the edge of the platform and surveyed his followers. Sattva – so strong it hurt even the inside of Jack's ears – pulsed out from him in waves. He paused for a moment and then spoke in Gaalic. Jack had no idea whether he was fluent or not, but the worshippers seemed to understand because they stood and bowed their heads. Mahajan paced up and down the platform, shaking his staff and exhorting the crowd. From time to time he went silent and the worshippers said prayers in unison. It seemed Mahajan was leading a Mass, or something like it.

Night had set in completely now. The flakes of ash shimmered as they sailed down into the bailey, evaporating as they settled on the ground or on members of the congregation.

A wave of pain blasted Jack. He shut his eyes and fought to

keep himself from passing out. If he fainted now the guards would no doubt investigate and he would be exposed as an impostor.

He swallowed and managed to pull himself back from the brink. Cormac glanced at him and frowned, but he gave the tall man a tight smile to indicate there was nothing to worry about.

Mahajan continued to rant from the platform.

How long would the unholy Mass last for? Once it was over, no doubt all the worshippers would be ushered back out of the gates. Jack had to work out how he was going to get further into the castle before then. He had to make sure he made use of this one chance.

He cast his eye over his surroundings. Behind the stage stood a wall that blocked access to the inner sections of the castle. To the right of the stage, towards the corner of the bailey, was a set of double doors, but two guards stood beside them. Numerous Cattans, carrying spears and muskets, paced along the battlements above.

Damn. There was no obvious way to get beyond the bailey. The castle had clearly been designed to be defended even if attackers made it through the main gate.

He looked up at the skull. What was the thing really? Was it just some piece of machinery designed to frighten the natives? When Mahajan finished speaking, perhaps there would be another display – more smoke and flame. Yes, he was sure that would happen.

And that gave him an idea.

It was a crazy idea but it was the only plan he could think of at that moment.

He looked sideways at Cormac. The tall man was glaring at Mahajan with cold hatred. Was he thinking how the Great Shee would soon overthrow the Demon? The faith of the Mar villagers was so absolute now, Jack was certain they would follow Rao wherever he went. Jack and Rao had taken advantage of their ignorance of the outside world, and Jack didn't feel particularly good about that.

He made a decision. He wouldn't allow Cormac to follow him into any further danger.

He glanced around. All the worshippers appeared preoccupied with Mahajan, so he tugged Cormac's sleeve and the tall man bent closer.

'Listen,' Jack whispered. 'When this is over, leave the castle without me. I'll join you and the others at midnight.'

Cormac's brow furrowed and he went to speak.

'The Great Shee commands it,' Jack said quickly.

The lines on Cormac's forehead darkened further. He opened his mouth again to say something, but Jack pressed his finger to his lips and gestured to a worshipper standing in front of them. An elderly woman was looking back over her shoulder, perhaps startled to hear words in a strange language. Cormac gave her a smile, crossed himself and bowed his head. That seemed to be enough to calm whatever suspicions she'd had and she turned to face Mahajan again.

Jack motioned with his head towards the front of the crowd and made his way forward, Cormac following. They slipped between worshippers, Jack looking up from time to time at the Cattans observing from the wall. Would he and Cormac arouse suspicion? It seemed not. None of the guards reacted – and in any case, there were a handful of other worshippers moving about the bailey as well.

Jack paused when he reached the second row from the front. He was near to the right corner of the stage and from this angle it was difficult to see Mahajan. But it was the wooden platform that interested him at the moment. It was a solid structure with boards across the front and sides that reached to about a foot above the ground.

Perfect.

He shot a look at Cormac, who was fiddling with his beard. Would the tall Mar try to follow? That could cause a serious problem for both of them. Jack prayed Cormac would do as he was told and obey the command of the Great Shee.

Finally, after around ten minutes, Mahajan concluded the Mass. The siddha stood still on the stage and the Mar bowed repeatedly, whispering their prayers.

Jack's heart beat faster. This might be his only chance to rescue Saleem. His plan had to work.

He looked up at the skull. The great metal head was immobile. Maybe he'd been wrong to think—

Then diseased metal groaned and the iron jaw jolted down. Flames spewed from the mouth, followed by coils of black smoke. The choking fog spilt over the stage, enveloped Mahajan and tumbled out into the bailey.

Jack was plunged into almost complete darkness. He sensed the people around him, but couldn't see them.

His heart slammed in his chest.

Now. He had to move now.

He pushed his way forward between two worshippers, raised his hand and felt the side of the platform. The smoke stung his eyes and the sattva made his head spin.

Concentrate. Don't pass out.

He dropped to the ground and rolled under the stage, just fitting through the gap between the boards and the earth.

His heart beat wildly. Had he been seen? Were guards coming for him? Would Cormac try to follow?

He lay on his back, staring up. The smoke began to clear, although it was so dark under the platform he could barely make out the planks and beams above him. Boards sealed him in on all sides. He half expected a Cattan to peer under the edge at any moment. But no one came.

No one seemed to have noticed him.

He wiped the sweat from his forehead with the cloak, then turned on to his side and squinted through the gap beneath the boards. The smoke was drifting away and he could make out the shuffling feet of the worshippers. Most were turning and ambling off. They were clearly leaving the bailey.

Good. His plan was working, which surprised him. There was still no sign of Cormac and he hoped that meant the Mar warrior was leaving with the other worshippers. With any luck, Cormac would be back with Rao and the others within the hour. By midnight, Jack would get out of the castle and join them.

Somehow.

He kept an eye out for approaching feet. What would he do if a guard stooped down and spotted him hiding? There wasn't a lot he *could* do. He could fight but he didn't even have a weapon. Would the guards kill him? Or would they try to take him alive?

He did his best to stop his thoughts racing. He had to concentrate on what he was going to do next.

He rolled over to the other side of the platform. Peering under the gap, he saw the stone wall immediately before him. He couldn't get out that way. He crawled to the end of the stage and tried to spot the doors in the corner of the bailey. But from this angle he couldn't see them.

Damn. The doors were his best bet for getting deeper into the castle. But he couldn't see whether the guards were still standing beside them.

He lay on his back. Pain stabbed him once more and he winced. The powerful sattva brushed against his face.

How much longer did he have? There were eight days now before Kanvar's cure wore off, but he wondered whether he would even last that long.

By now the worshippers must have all left. The Cattans would have returned to whatever duties they had. But still, he had to wait longer, wait until the guards were preoccupied and less attentive.

He lay under the stage for what he thought was half an hour. Pain jabbed into his chest repeatedly and darkness threatened to swallow him. He gritted his teeth, shut his eyes and tried the Great Health yantra. But, as always, it did nothing.

Damn his weakness. Ever since that fateful day on the battlefield when the sattva-fire had struck him he'd been cursed by his injury. Hadn't he already been punished enough? Hadn't he already paid his debt to God, or karma, or whatever power controlled these things?

He was drifting away. He could feel it. And as much as he tried to hold on, black waves dragged at him, pulling him out into a vast, twilit ocean.

He clutched at the earth beneath his hands as if he could draw himself back somehow.

But it was pointless. Was he going to die here? Underneath a platform in the castle, with whatever secrets Mahajan harboured only yards away?

He wondered whether Mahajan really had found the Grail, whether this castle, this Place of Dead Kings, might not be Castle Corbenic after all.

But then he slipped away completely.

━◆━

Jack glanced up as he walked across the parade ground. Captain Jhala stood staring at him from the veranda of his office.

Why was Jhala watching him so closely? Had he done something wrong? He couldn't think what.

He reached Jhala's bungalow, went up the steps, namasted and handed over an envelope. 'From the Bristol barracks, sir. Just arrived this morning.'

Jhala took the envelope but didn't even look at the writing on the outside. He tapped it against his hand and rolled his tongue around in his mouth. He continued to stare at Jack.

Jack forced himself to look at Jhala without meeting his commander's eyes directly, as he knew the Rajthanans preferred.

What was going on? He was becoming certain he was somehow in trouble.

Finally, Jhala pointed at the parade ground. 'You avoided that corner over there.'

Jack looked behind him. He had indeed swerved around that spot. But what of it?

'I noticed the other day,' Jhala said. 'Every time you walk across you go around it.'

'Sorry, sir.'

Jhala smiled and stared off into space. 'Nothing to be sorry about, lad. It's just strange, that's all. Come with me.' He walked down the steps and across the open ground.

Jack followed but slowed as they approached the far right corner. He didn't like going into that spot but it was hard to explain why.

Jhala stopped and turned. 'Walk over here, Casey.'

Jack didn't want to do it but knew he had to obey. It was a silly thing anyway. He'd been through the Slav War, fought at Ragusa. What did it matter about walking into that spot?

He took two paces forward and felt the familiar tingle on his skin. Sweet perfume touched his nose. He shivered slightly.

Jhala folded his arms across his chest. 'You noticed something, didn't you?'

'What do you mean, sir?'

'When you stepped forward you shook slightly. I could tell.'

'Just a chill, I'm sure, sir.'

Jhala walked closer. 'I don't think so. You smelt something sweet, didn't you?'

'Yes, sir.'

'Smelt that before?'

It was strange to be discussing this with Jhala. Jack hadn't spoken to anyone about it since he was a child explaining to his playmates that he could tell when places were 'haunted'. That was the only way he'd been able to describe the sensation. Some places felt inhabited by ghosts and made your skin crawl, while others didn't.

But he'd never met anyone else who sensed these haunted spots. He'd begun to think it must be in his imagination, or perhaps some trick of the Devil.

And yet Jhala seemed to understand.

'Yes, sir,' Jack said. 'I have smelt it before.'

Jhala smiled slowly. 'Do you know what a native siddha is?'

'Some kind of sorcerer, I heard.'

Jhala snorted. 'Sorcerer? If you like. But a native siddha is much more than that. You may have a power within you, Casey. A power that not even the Rajthanan siddhas can learn.'

Jack frowned. This was the strangest conversation he'd ever had with Jhala. He was just an ordinary soldier. Did Jhala really think he had a special power?

'Meet me at the training tent tomorrow at nine o'clock,' Jhala said. 'You're something special, Casey. I can sense it.'

Jhala walked back to his bungalow with his hands behind his back, leaving Jack standing on the parade ground with his mouth hanging open.

Was Jhala mad?

Jack had heard rumours that Jhala was a sorcerer, but he'd never believed them. Now he wasn't so sure. Perhaps there was more to Jhala than he'd realised.

Jack had the creeping sense that somehow he'd taken a first step into a world that was far larger and stranger than he'd previously imagined.

———◆———

Jack opened his eyes. He'd been dreaming about Jhala – he could tell, even though he couldn't recall what the dream had been about. He'd passed out and then must have drifted off to sleep.

He was staring up at the underside of the wooden stage. He was still in the castle bailey. And he still hadn't been discovered.

The pain in his chest had receded to a dull ache and his breathing was clear and deep.

How long had he been lying there? He rolled over, crawled to the edge of the platform and squinted out. It was dark, although a few lights cast faint radiance across the ground. Occasionally, a flake of glowing ash drifted to the earth and melted instantly. He couldn't see any feet, couldn't hear anyone nearby. The only sound was the occasional puff of steam and the distant, perpetual thudding of machinery.

The worshippers seemed to have all left. The Cattan guards would presumably have returned to their usual duties. No one would suspect he was hiding under the stage.

But what to do now?

The only way he could get further into the castle was through the side doors. But would these still be guarded? If they were, the Cattans would immediately see he was an impostor. On the other hand, there was little reason to guard the doors once the worshippers had left. If he were lucky, the entrance would be unattended and unlocked.

He rubbed his face. Was he thinking straight? What other choice did he have?

He would have to do it. He was going to get out from his hiding place and walk calmly across the bailey. At a glance, he would look like a Cattan – he was dressed appropriately in his cloak and tunic. Of course, he wasn't wearing the sign of the white skull, but it would take someone a few seconds to realise that.

He might just be able to make it.

He took a deep breath and rolled out from under the platform. He stood immediately and blackness reeled about him. He'd forgotten how ill he was. He slammed his eyes shut, managed to steady himself and then looked around. Shadows webbed the bailey and the only light came from a handful of windows in the towers deeper in the castle.

The doors were about thirty yards away.

And they were unguarded.

Without hesitation, he strode across to them.

He half expected to hear someone shout or even shoot at him. But nothing happened. He risked glancing up and saw only a couple of Cattans standing on the wall, both of them facing away from him. He looked across the bailey and noticed a few guards walking about, but none of them paid him the slightest attention.

In the dark he obviously passed for a Cattan.

He reached the doors. His hand shook slightly as he turned one of the ringed handles. Of course, the door would be locked or bolted, and then he would be trapped in the bailey. He would be captured and killed in no time.

Except the door yielded and opened into a passage. He slipped inside, heart pumping feverishly, and swung the door shut behind him. The hall had plain stone walls and smelt of coal. The only light filtered in from an archway at the far end.

He paused for a second. He'd made it this far. Next he had to find Saleem.

He slipped down the passage towards the exit, but then heard voices. Two men were approaching and would turn into the archway within seconds.

His heart smacked harder.

There was a door to his left, just a few feet away. He strode faster, reached it and shoved his shoulder against it. It swung open, but as he went through someone called out in Gaalic. He couldn't understand the words, but he didn't like the sound of the harsh tone.

Had he been spotted?

He found himself in a windowless hall lit by guttering torches set in sconces. Pipes writhed over the walls and ceiling, shifting slightly when he tried to focus on them. Warm air and coal smoke struck him and every part of his exposed skin smarted at the strong sattva. He'd never been in such a powerful stream, had never even believed one like this could exist.

He hurried down the corridor and came to a chamber half filled by a pile of coal. Someone called to him and when he looked back, he saw two Cattans running up the hall, swords swinging at their sides.

Damn. They'd seen him and were clearly suspicious.

He dashed down a further corridor, charged through an arch and was immediately blasted by heat. A row of giant boilers swelled from the far wall of a wide chamber. Men in tunics shovelled coal constantly through hatches to feed the throbbing fires within. A few men glanced at Jack, but most continued labouring, their skin gleaming with sweat and streaked with soot.

He dodged his way through the men, smoke whirling around him and the heat of the furnaces beating on one side of his face.

He heard further shouts behind him. Looking back, he saw the two Cattans were still following.

Damn.

He ran more quickly and bumped into one of the workers, who growled at him. He stumbled on and reached an arched exit. He ran through this and up a flight of corkscrew stairs. His heavy breathing rattled in the stairwell. He heard the scuffle of feet echoing up after him and occasionally his pursuers called out.

He kept going up three flights and reached a thin, gloomy hall that bent away to the right. He left the stairwell, charged down the passage and hid around the corner. He stood with his back pressed against the stone, his chest heaving and trickles of sweat running down his cheeks. The smell of sattva was still strong here, but there were no pipes running along the walls, no sign of any machinery. Tallow candles flickered in brackets along the hallway.

He listened carefully and heard the guards reach the landing, then stop and speak to each other. But there were more than two men now – he picked out at least four voices. Worse, while two now charged on up the steps, two made their way down the hall towards him. He heard the wooden floorboards creak beneath their feet.

How many guards were searching for him now?

He ran down the corridor, stepping as quietly as he could. He tried a door, found it locked, tried another, then gave up and sprinted up the passageway. At the end, he found another stairway spiralling up.

He heard shouts behind him. Looking over his shoulder, he saw two Cattans bounding up the hall towards him.

He launched himself up the steps, his hide shoes scraping on the stone. The Cattans were right behind him – he could hear them panting and calling to him as they clambered up.

He went up three more flights and then suddenly came out into the open. He was on top of a tower, battlements all around him and the night sky arcing above. A colossal chimney reared up to his left, puffing out whorls of thick smoke and glinting ash. Clots of steam whistled from valves and veiled the buildings and towers nearby.

There was no one up here, but no obvious way out.

And he could still hear the footsteps of the Cattans behind him.

He ran to the parapet and looked down. He was six storeys up and the ground far below was no more than a knot of shadows. The walls of the tower were sheer and impossible to climb.

He was trapped.

He ran across to the other side of the roof and this time spotted a balcony jutting out of the wall two floors below. He could try jumping down to that – if he were crazy. If he missed, he would fall to his death in a crevice between the buildings.

Steam hissed from further down the wall and obscured his view of the balcony for a second.

He would have to jump. It was his only chance now.

Without pausing, he turned round, slipped over the wall and hung there, still holding on to the edge. He looked down and his head reeled. He felt sick.

He heard shouting from nearby – the Cattans must have reached the top of the stairs and were no doubt startled to find he'd vanished.

He had to let go. So long as he dropped straight down, staying close to the wall without touching it, he would be all right.

He said a Hail Mary.

And then he released his grip.

He fell so quickly he didn't even have time to think about what was happening. One second he was holding on to the battlements, the next he was rolling across the stone balcony. Pain welled in one arm – he'd hit it on something as he fell. But otherwise he was unhurt.

He glanced up and saw no one looking over the ramparts. Not yet.

A set of double doors stood open before him. Curtains of some diaphanous material floated in the slight breeze, but he couldn't make out anything of the room beyond.

But he couldn't waste any time.

He charged through the curtains, got tangled up in one, thrashed about for a moment and broke free. He had no time to take in his surroundings, however, as he heard someone cry out nearby. He spun round and saw a woman cowering in the corner of the chamber.

An Indian woman.

24

Jack frowned. What was an Indian woman doing out here in the wilds of Scotland?

She wore a red shawl and a green sari that was gathered between her legs to form a pair of loose pantaloons. Earrings glinted in both her ears and a thin golden torc circled her neck. Bangles encrusted her wrists and tinkled as she moved. It was hard to tell her age, but Jack thought she was perhaps in her thirties.

She shook slightly as she huddled near the floor. Her eyes, edged by dark eyeliner, were wide and glassy.

Jack held up his hand and said in Rajthani, 'I'm not going to hurt you.'

She opened her mouth.

Was she going to scream?

'No.' Jack pressed his finger to his lips. 'Please. I won't harm you. I promise.'

She stared at him and chewed her bottom lip. She shot a look at the doors to the balcony, as if she were going to run there. But instead she looked back at Jack. 'What do you want?'

'Nothing. I'm just leaving.' He glanced around for an exit. A series of cane lattice screens blocked his view of the far side of the room. He couldn't see a door anywhere, couldn't even tell how large the chamber was.

He heard a scrape and then footsteps coming from somewhere behind the screens.

'Here.' The woman opened the door of an ornate wardrobe.

He was stunned for a moment. What? Was she trying to help him? Why?

'They'll see you,' the woman said. 'Quick.'

He had to trust her. He couldn't see a way out of the room and there was no point running back to the balcony – once there, he would be cornered.

He slipped into the wardrobe and pressed himself between a row of perfumed saris, shawls and jackets. The woman shut the door and he peered out through a decorative lattice panel. His arm still throbbed where he'd struck it, but it didn't seem badly injured.

A Scottish woman scurried into the room, pressed her hands together, bowed and said, 'Namaste.' She wore the typical ankle-length tunic of the savages, but it was finely sewn and spotlessly clean. Her hair was surprisingly clean too and tied back in a ponytail.

'What is it?' the Rajthanan woman asked.

'They think there's an intruder in the castle, madam.' The Scot spoke Rajthani well but with a thick accent.

'Really?' The woman stared out at the balcony. As she did this, Jack noticed an iron chain secured to her ankle. His eyes followed the chain and found the point where it was bolted to the wall.

The woman was a captive.

'We'd best shut these, madam.' The Scot closed the balcony doors and pulled across the latch.

'I don't think anyone will get in through there.'

'Yes, madam. But the guard told me to. Just in case.'

'Who is this intruder?'

'Don't know. The guard said some strange man was seen near here.'

'A strange man?' The woman gave a wry smile. 'I'll look out for him.'

'Yes, madam. They've put a few guards outside your door for the time being.' The Scot bowed and shuffled away through the gaps between the screens. A few seconds later a door scraped open and then closed.

The Rajthanan woman waited for a moment, then walked around the screens, the chain attached to her ankle clinking. Jack could just make out her flickering silhouette through the dense mesh of cane. Seemingly satisfied there was now no one in the room, she came back to the wardrobe and opened the door.

Jack stepped out. 'Thank you.'

He couldn't quite believe his luck in coming across this woman. He would probably have been captured by now if it weren't for her.

He looked around and took in several luxurious Rajthanan-style cushion-seats, a dressing table, wicker stools, a rug covered in intricate designs and a bed shrouded by silk drapes. A fire crackled in a small hearth and several oil lanterns were dotted about the chamber. He smelt jasmine, cinnamon and lotus, although this wasn't enough to disguise the background scent of coal and sattva.

It was odd to be standing in the private room of a Rajthanan woman. Normally, an Englishman would be executed for that. He felt strangely awkward, as if he'd walked in while the woman was half dressed.

He pulled his hair back, retied his ponytail and straightened his tunic. 'I'll be on my way, then.'

The woman smiled quizzically. 'Don't think you'll get far. There're guards outside my door.'

'Then I'll go back out that way.' He motioned to the balcony.

'You going to climb? It's a long way to fall.'

'I'll have to take my chances.'

'I've got a better idea. Hide here for a few hours. The guards won't stay outside the door long. Most of them get drunk in the evening. Usually there are hardly any of them around at night.'

Jack rubbed his chin. The woman was making sense. He couldn't fight armed guards when he didn't have a weapon. And if the Cattans were mostly drunk, that would make it easier for him to move around the castle.

But still, why was this woman helping him? Could he trust her? 'Who are you?'

'You've just burst into my room and you're asking me who I am?'

He coughed and straightened his shoulders. 'Sorry, madam. I don't have time for niceties.'

Her eyes twinkled. 'My name's Sonali. Who are you?'

Was there any point lying to her? 'Jack.'

'Jack.' She sounded the word out slowly, as if sampling a rare fruit. 'And what are you doing here, Jack?'

As he thought how to respond to this question, the door creaked open again. He heard voices somewhere behind the screens.

Sonali's face dropped and her eyes went dark. 'Back in there.' She pushed him towards the wardrobe.

He slipped inside and she shut the door.

'There you are,' a man said from the other side of the room.

Sonali jumped and turned.

Jack saw a dark figure coalesce behind the lattice screens. He tensed. Who'd just come into the room? Had he seen Jack?

Sonali turned her back on the new arrival, walked across the room and stood before the mirror on top of her dressing table. She brushed her long black hair.

The man emerged from behind the screens.

Jack's heart jolted.

It was Mahajan.

The siddha was still dressed in a Scottish cloak and tunic, but had set aside his staff. 'The guards think there was an intruder.'

Sonali glanced at Mahajan in her mirror, then looked away and continued brushing her hair.

'Did you see anyone?' Mahajan asked. 'He was in this tower.'

Sonali looked at Mahajan in the mirror again and raised her chin haughtily. 'I saw no one. Leave me now.'

Mahajan scowled. A blast of sattva flew out from him, so

powerful Jack had to fight to stop himself from choking. Mahajan strode across to Sonali, grasped her hair and yanked her head back. She cried out and stumbled to her knees. Mahajan dragged her into the centre of the room. She shrieked, struggled to free herself and managed to get back on her feet.

Christ. Jack's heart pumped hard. Was he going to stay hiding and watch Sonali being beaten?

Sonali swung herself round and Mahajan let go of her. She snarled and flew at him, trying to scratch his face. But a glowing, bronze-coloured mantle suddenly enveloped him. She hit the shimmering bronze with a sound like a gong and was repulsed backwards so hard she fell against the dressing table. She slipped to the floor again.

The shield vanished as quickly as it had appeared and Mahajan stood over her. 'Pathetic. Why do you bother?'

Sonali looked up, her eyes both tearful and fierce. She swore at Mahajan using Rajthani words Jack didn't recognise.

Mahajan glared at her, his features twisting. 'Stupid girl.'

Sonali gave a shout, which was cut short almost immediately. She scrabbled at the torc about her neck, trying without success to wrench it off. She made rasping sounds and writhed on the floor. Her face went red. She seemed to be choking.

Jack tightened his fists. He would have to do something. Mahajan was using some sort of power to strangle Sonali and he couldn't stand by and watch her die. He cursed the fact he didn't have a pistol – he could have shot Mahajan in the back before the siddha could even turn. Instead, he was going to have to rush at Mahajan and pummel him with his fists.

Jack steeled himself to move. But then Mahajan took a step back. Sonali gasped and began gulping down air again. The torc was no longer choking her.

'Don't try me, girl,' Mahajan said. 'I will snuff you out one of these days.'

Sonali sat up, rubbing her neck. 'You won't dare.'

314

'I'm tiring of these games. You will change your mind, or I will make you.'

'I never will.'

Mahajan smiled and said in an oily voice, 'We'll see. I might enjoy making you.' He walked to the balcony doors, opened one of them and stood looking out through the billowing curtains. He shivered slightly and rubbed one of his arms. 'It's getting cold. Perhaps it will snow again. I do so love the snow.' He turned and smiled at Sonali. 'It's the wildness of it. It seeps into you, don't you think?' He looked back out of the window. 'Civilisation is so constraining, but out here with the savages . . . we can find the savagery within us.'

'You're insane.'

'Perhaps. But I have never felt more sane. Think about what I've said. I won't delay any longer.'

He left suddenly, making his way through the maze of screens. A few seconds later, the door scraped and then slammed shut.

Jack breathed out. His heart was still beating wildly.

Sonali slipped over to the wardrobe and opened it. 'He's gone.'

'Are you all right?'

She looked away. 'Yes.'

'That necklace.' He reached out to touch the torc. He could see a line of red where it had dug into her skin.

She slapped his hand away. 'Leave it.' She walked across to the balcony and opened both doors wide.

'Only trying to help.'

She stared outside. The wind had picked up and the curtains now lifted and coiled about her. Her face was still. 'No one can help me.'

'You sure about that?'

'You don't understand.'

'I understand enough. I can see you're trapped here with that thing around your neck.'

Sonali stroked the torc with her finger but stayed silent.

'Mahajan controls it?' Jack said.

'Yes.' She looked down. 'If he commands, it'll choke me. He can kill me any time he pleases.'

'And yet he keeps you alive.'

'Perhaps not for much longer.'

'Unless you change your mind. About what?'

'There's much more to this than you know.' She looked at Jack and swept her hair back with her fingers. As she did this, her shawl slipped down and revealed a criss-cross of white scars on her arm.

Jack stepped closer. 'Did Mahajan do that?'

She covered her arm quickly. 'It's none of your business.'

Jack felt heat ripple across his face. 'He tortured you?'

'Forget it.'

Mahajan was an evil bastard. 'I'll get you out of here.'

'I can't leave the castle. Mahajan will activate the necklace.'

'Then we'll get it off.'

Sonali's eyes flashed. 'Don't you think I've tried?'

'There's got to be a way.' He looked around for something he could use to prise off the torc.

'No. Mahajan's a powerful siddha. The necklace can't be broken. Not while he's alive.'

Jack paused. Sonali knew more about all this than he did. There was no reason for him to doubt what she said. But at the same time, Sonali had helped him and he had to return the favour somehow. 'So, if Mahajan is killed, you'll be free.'

'Don't even think about it. He's covered in a shield. All the time. Not even bullets can get through it. Only a powerful siddha could harm him. He's practically invincible.'

'No one's invincible.'

She turned away again. 'There's nothing you can do. Wait for a little longer. Then get out of here. It's for the best.'

Jack sighed. He didn't like the idea of leaving Sonali trapped in the castle. But he also knew she was right – there was little he could do for her at the moment.

316

He slumped down in a cushion-seat and rubbed the back of his neck. Tiredness weighed on him. 'Before I go, there's something you might be able to help me with.'

She turned and sat on a stool beside the dressing table. 'What?'

'I'm looking for four comrades. They were captured by Cattans. They might be here.'

'Three soldiers and a Rajthanan officer?'

Jack sat up straighter. 'Yes. You've seen them?'

'No. But I heard about them. A war party brought them in. Mahajan was very suspicious about what they were doing all the way out here.'

Jack paused, then asked slowly, 'Are they alive?'

'Yes.'

Jack leant forward. 'You're sure?'

She nodded. 'Pretty sure. Mahajan mentioned them yesterday. He said he still didn't know who they were. He said he was going to find out, though.'

Jack said a quick Hail Mary in his head. 'Where are they?'

'In the dungeon.'

'How do I get there?'

'You won't be able to get them out.'

'I have to.'

'There are guards. Locked doors. Bars. I know. Mahajan locked me in there for a while.'

'Just tell me how to get there. I'll think of something.'

'I will. When the guards are gone from the door. I doubt they'll be there much longer.'

Jack leant against the seat's bolster, tilted his head back and shut his eyes for a moment. He wanted to sleep but knew he couldn't risk it. The Cattans would still be looking for him and might come to search Sonali's room at any time.

The fire in his chest shivered. The strong sattva was still making him giddy.

He opened his eyes again and saw Sonali studying him. Her

features were slender and her hair glowed in the firelight. She looked sad and, he had to admit, beautiful.

'Why are you here?' he asked. 'In this castle?'

'I was one of Mahajan's maids. In Rajthana.'

'A maid?' He'd heard there were Rajthanan servants back in Rajthana, but it was still strange to think of an Indian as a servant.

'Yes. I've been to many places with him. The Inca lands, Andalusia, al-Francon.'

'So why have you ended up a prisoner?'

She looked into the flames. 'I told you. I don't want to talk about that.'

He sighed. Sonali was full of secrets. But if she didn't want his help, what could he do? Still, while he was here he had to find out as much as he could about Mahajan. 'Do you know anything about Mahajan's experiments?'

She looked up quickly. 'What do you mean?'

Should he risk revealing to her what he knew? He had to if he wanted answers. 'The Brahmastra. Ever heard of that?'

Her mouth dropped. 'You know about that?'

'A bit. I know it's a kind of weapon. Is it real?'

'Maybe. I think so.'

'Has Mahajan made one?'

'He believes so. He's been trying for a long time. He discovered an ancient manuscript. Or rediscovered it. It was in a private archive, but everyone had forgotten about it. It was in an old, secret language that no one knows any more, but he deciphered it.'

'And that told him how to make a Brahmastra?'

'Yes.' She looked at her hands. 'It's a manuscript of the Kapalika siddhas. It contains many evil things.'

'Kapalika?'

She looked up, her face traced by the firelight. 'They were an order of siddhas who practised . . . unspeakable things. They believed in achieving powers through destroying purity. They tried to defile themselves in every way.'

Jack remembered Mahajan's words earlier. 'Become savages?'

'Mahajan believes that, yes. The Kapalikas somehow stole the secret of the Brahmastra, a long time ago. They weren't meant to have it.'

'And this Brahmastra. Is it really as powerful as in the stories?'

'I hope not.' She shivered.

'Would Mahajan use it?'

'I'm certain he would. He follows the teachings of the Kapalikas. They worshipped death and destruction. Their sign was the skull – that's why Mahajan makes the Cattans wear it.'

'So, who would he use the Brahmastra on? Who's he fighting for?'

'Fighting for?' She snorted. 'For himself. For his own power. He's mad.'

'A madman shouldn't have a weapon like that.'

'No. Perhaps you can help. Can you get a message out?'

'I can try.'

'I've sent word before. Many months ago. A native servant. He said he'd take my message all the way to England.'

Jack sat back. 'Perhaps he made it. The empire knows about the Brahmastra.'

Her eyes widened. 'Really?'

'That's why I'm here. The army sent an expedition to see what Mahajan's up to.'

Sonali gripped the edge of her shawl. 'If they know, surely they'll send another party.'

'Maybe. They aren't sure whether to believe the story.'

'You have to make them believe it.'

'I'll do my best. Where's the Brahmastra now?'

'I've never seen it. But Mahajan spends all his time in a workshop under the inner bailey. It'll be in there somewhere.'

'I'll take a look.'

She shook her head. 'You won't get in there either. There are many, many guards and the doors are locked with yogic powers.'

'You said there weren't many guards at night.'

'There are around that room. And the dungeon. Believe me.'

There was no reason for him to doubt Sonali. She knew the castle well and had done nothing but help him so far. If she'd wanted to, she could have turned him over to the guards half an hour ago. He had to trust her.

But there was one last thing he wanted to know. 'You know anything about the Grail?'

She frowned. 'No.'

'Mahajan's never spoken about it?'

She shook her head. 'What is it?'

'Nothing. Just an old story.' He stood. 'Now, let's see if the guards are gone. I can't wait around here all night.'

25

Sonali slid the door open, peered outside, then turned to Jack. 'It's still clear.'

He nodded. Having seen that the guards had left, Sonali had explained the layout of the castle to him. So long as he could remember her directions, he should be able to find both Mahajan's workshop and the dungeon.

He went to leave, but paused for a moment. He couldn't help looking at the torc about Sonali's neck. It glinted in the dull light and dug slightly into her soft flesh. 'I'll be back in a few hours.'

She frowned. 'You have to get out of the castle.'

'I can't leave you here.'

'Go. While you can.'

He wasn't going to abandon her but there was no point arguing about it now. Instead, he said a curt farewell and slipped out of the door.

The stone corridor stretched in both directions. Candles cast wavering light across the walls, but left large patches of shadow. Doors led off to both sides.

He ran through Sonali's directions in his head again, then struck off to the right, treading softly and listening for the sound of anyone approaching. What would he do if a Cattan appeared? Fight? Run? He would have to gauge the situation when it came and make a quick decision.

He turned into another hall, as Sonali had instructed. He was heading to Mahajan's workshop first – Sonali had said that was closer than the dungeon, and the journey would be along passages that were often empty.

After he'd gone a few paces, he heard footsteps and men's voices behind him, coming from the passage he'd just left. He ran to the end of the corridor, skidded around the corner and pressed himself against the wall. His chest trembled and his head swam. He'd felt better while he was resting in Sonali's room, but now that he was moving around again his injury was worsening.

The footsteps came closer, slapping against the wooden floor and echoing down the hall. Had the men heard him? Seen him?

Then the footsteps began to quieten and recede.

He breathed out. So far, luck was with him.

He pressed on down the passage and hesitated beside a window with a half-open shutter. He listened intently. There were no footsteps. He could risk stopping for a moment.

He eased open the shutter and peered out into the darkness. From this angle he had a good view of the front of the castle. The walls and bastions were outlined by splashes of light from windows, the vague moon and specks of luminous ash. He spied a black expanse that must be the inner bailey, beneath which lay Mahajan's workshop.

He heard voices coming from further down the corridor, so he slid the shutter closed and moved on.

He came to the corkscrew staircase he'd run up earlier in the day. The scent of sattva and coal spiralled up. A tremor crossed his chest, his legs weakened and black spots spun before his eyes.

He shook his head to keep himself from passing out. He had to keep going. He couldn't fail now.

He started down the stairs, listening carefully for anyone coming the other way. Pipes began knitting across the walls, heat wafted up and the distant hum of industry vibrated in the air. Wherever there was metal, he noticed the uneasy shifting he'd seen when he'd first arrived at the castle. Nothing seemed stable and certain. Everything had the quality of smoke.

Blackness hovered about him. He paused and tried to clear his head, but the darkness enveloped him further. He stuck out his hand to steady himself, his fingers finding and then gripping a pipe that was warm and slightly damp to the touch. He felt the faint quiver of machinery through the metal.

Concentrate. Don't faint. Don't fall down now.

The blackness parted and he could see clearly again. He was breathing heavily but the pain in his chest eased a little.

Christ. How much longer did he have now? Days? Hours?

And what about the Grail? Despite his scepticism, despite his lack of belief in his people's superstitions, he'd been hoping the Grail was real, hoping that Mahajan had found it. Even when he'd come to the castle hours earlier he'd let his thoughts run away with the idea that this place was the Corbenic of the old stories. But Sonali had never heard of the Grail. Mahajan hadn't mentioned it.

He had to give up on the idea of the Grail now. If there were any secret in the castle, it would be a monstrous weapon.

Nothing was going to save him.

He swallowed. He was feeling strong enough now to continue and slipped on down the stairs.

He heard voices coming from above, then footsteps in the stairwell. He went more quickly.

And then suddenly he was at ground level. He'd travelled faster and further than he'd realised and lost track of which storey he was on. He was back in the hallway which led to the boiler room. Heat and coal smoke washed over him and in the distance dim figures laboured, their skin shining in the ruddy light. It seemed the men needed to work continuously to keep the castle running.

He headed away from the boilers, turned down a few gloomy passages and finally reached the set of stairs that led to the catacombs. Sonali had explained there was a complex maze of halls and chambers beneath the castle. A few had survived from earlier times, but most had been built by Mahajan.

He looked around. There was no one in the area. No one had

seen him come to this place. So far, everything was going according to plan.

He scurried down the stairs and came out in a hall lit by pale, silvery light that seemed to come from no particular source. Seething tubes encrusted the walls. Steam hissed from valves, water gurgled deep within the ironwork and black ooze leaked out from between rivets. The metal continually shifted and slipped around as he tried to concentrate on it. But like everywhere else in the castle, it was solid when he touched it.

He crept down the passage, took a turning to the left and then to the right. The wheeze of steam and the chugging of machinery grew even louder. The air was moist and warm.

Finally he reached a long hall that Sonali had told him led to Mahajan's workshop.

He heard footsteps echoing behind him. He glanced around. There was nowhere to hide in the corridor, but there was an opening in the wall about thirty feet away. He slipped down the passage and paused by the exit. The room beyond was dark and he could only just see the outline of the metal swarming over the walls.

The footsteps rattled louder. Whoever was coming would soon turn into the hall.

He slipped into the room. The footsteps stopped, then continued. Two people were walking towards him and would soon reach the entryway. If he stayed where he was, they would see him.

He went through an opening to his right and sneaked down a further hall. He was leaving the route Sonali had described to him, but he had no choice at the moment. The light was so dim now he could barely make out the way ahead.

A dense chirping sound grew louder, drowning out the rumble of machinery and the clatter of the footsteps. It became more shrill the further along the passage he walked.

He stopped for a second. The trilling was all around him, seeming to come from the walls only inches away.

He stared into the darkness. He sensed slight changes in the air, as if several small fans were fluttering.

Christ. What was that?

He noticed a light ahead and stumbled towards it. As the glow brightened, he began to make out the walls, which were plastered with the usual contorted metal. As before, the pipes seemed to move. Only now they were shivering rapidly. This wasn't the shifting he'd noticed earlier, it was flickers and ripples, like branches and leaves moving in the wind.

The sizzling noise was so loud now it made his ears ring.

An arch opened to his left – the light was spilling out from the room beyond. He stumbled through the entrance and froze instantly. The hair shot up on the back of his neck.

He was in a small, octagonal chamber, the walls of which were smothered by a quivering mass of steel creatures.

Avatars.

Some of the beasts looked like fish, others like crustaceans, still others like bloated insects. They shuffled wings, wriggled antennae and scraped legs against the stone. At first he thought they were clinging to the pipes, but then he realised they were in fact part of the metalwork itself. It was as though they'd been impaled on the tubes and left writhing in agony.

On the far wall hung a circular metal plaque, on which was engraved the image of a turbaned figure holding aloft a shape that looked like an animal foetus.

Jack's skin crawled. He recognised the design. He'd seen it once before – in an abandoned mill near London. The picture had been on a plate on the base of a device he believed was used to create avatars. He recalled the machine now – it had looked like a five-foot-wide claw of wire and steel, with the plate in the centre.

His breathing was shallow and pain flickered in his chest. Perhaps he shouldn't have been surprised Mahajan had been creating avatars – the whole castle was something like a mill, after all. At least these beasts seemed harmless. They were trapped within the piping and were more part of the castle's machinery than separate beings. But still, he wasn't going to stay where he was any longer.

He stepped out into the dark corridor and made his way back the way he'd come. He was going to return to Sonali's route – there was no knowing what he'd find in the maze if he wandered off any further.

The whine of the avatars decreased as he neared the end of the passage.

Finally, he paused. He could see the way out to the main hall ahead of him. His heart was beating fast, but it was slowing now that he'd left the avatars behind. He listened but could no longer hear the footsteps. He crept closer to the opening and pressed himself against the warm, wet pipes. He still heard nothing.

Whoever had been there seemed to have gone.

He stuck his head out into the corridor and looked both ways. There was no one in sight.

He slipped out the entryway and stole down the hall. He listened carefully for the sound of footsteps but no one came. Eventually he reached the end of the hall and entered a small, gloomy chamber thick with huge tubes. The sattva was so strong it felt like sand floating in the air. His lungs hurt when he breathed and he had to fight back the darkness creeping up from the corners of his vision.

On the other side of the room stood an archway. Sonali had told him the door to Mahajan's workshop was just beyond this. But she'd been adamant there would be guards on duty there.

He crept around the edge of the room, reached the arch and inched his head around the side. Beyond lay a hall that was more than twice the width of the corridors he'd passed along so far. Sinewy pipes glinted in the silver light and sattva buffeted him as it spiralled up the passage. His eyes stung and he had to keep blinking in order to see clearly.

At the end of the hall stood a circular pair of steel double doors.

Outside these were six Cattans carrying knife-muskets and longswords. Some were slouching against the wall, others were talking idly amongst themselves, but all looked sober and alert.

Six armed men. There was no easy way around them. Even if Jack had a weapon it would be difficult to fight against so many. And even if he could get past the Cattans, there were still the doors to deal with. Sonali had said they were sealed by Mahajan's powers. What chance did Jack have of getting through all that?

And yet, it would be hard to turn away when he was so close. Somewhere behind those doors lay the Brahmastra.

If he could just get in there.

But what would he do even if he did get in there? Destroy the Brahmastra? Take it and try to use it himself?

A wave of blackness swept over him. He edged back from the archway, bent over and fought to stay conscious. He muttered a Hail Mary and after about a minute the swell passed over him.

He stood up straight again. There was no point staying where he was. If the workshop were key to Mahajan's experiments, it was unlikely the guards would leave during the night. He would have to come up with a plan to get past them later.

Now, he had to find Saleem.

Following Sonali's instructions, he left the workshop and wound his way through the warren of tunnels. There were few Cattans about and he could move with relative ease. Occasionally he heard voices and footsteps, but he slunk into the shadows and hid each time. Sometimes he spotted guards but he always managed to avoid them.

After around twenty minutes, he reached stone steps that led up to ground level. According to Sonali, the route would now pass through areas where there were more guards. He would have to be cautious.

A pool of darkness spread across his eyes. He put his hand on the wall to steady himself and finally the faintness passed. He gulped down some air, crept up the stairs and came out in a small, empty passage with a trace of light spilling in from an opening a few feet away. He stole up to the exit and looked around the side.

Before him stretched the inner bailey, lit by a hint of moonlight and the orange glow from windows in the surrounding towers. The ground was compacted earth, but across the centre lay a circular expanse of paving stones. Straight across from him rose the wall that separated the inner bailey from the outer courtyard where Mahajan had spoken to the crowd. At various points along the ramparts, pipes and tubes reared up out of the stone like great misshapen fingers. A few Cattans stood guard between these, but most were looking away from the bailey and out towards the valley.

Far above, glowing ash circled in the sky. A few flakes spun down and vanished within the castle walls, but most were swept away by the wind, glinting against the turbulent clouds.

To his left loomed the tower housing the dungeon. It was only fifty feet away, but he would have to cross the bailey to get to it and the guards might spot him as he did that.

He heard voices and shrank back into the passage. A pair of Cattans wandered past, arms about each other and singing. Once they'd gone, he poked his head out again. A few men stood talking far off to his right, a guard strolled along the wall to his left, but otherwise there was no one about.

In the dark, in his cloak, he could pass for a Cattan. It was time to move on.

He slipped out into the bailey and strode towards the tower. His heart sped and he tensed, thinking someone would surely see he was an impostor.

But no one reacted and he reached the door.

He paused. Sonali had told him the tower was ordinarily full of guards, but the dungeon was in the base of the building. He had to go in.

He opened the door and found himself in a small, torch-lit

room. A peat fire, which had almost died, glowed in the hearth, and a few stools stood in a corner. The walls and ceiling were free from the pipes that infested other parts of the castle.

He jumped slightly when he made out a Cattan lying on the floor. He was about to dash back out the door, but stopped when he noticed the man wasn't moving. The Cattan's eyes were closed and he was snoring.

Jack breathed out and crossed himself. Luck was still on his side.

Men's voices sailed through from an adjoining room. He sneaked across the chamber and stuck his head gingerly through a doorway. He saw steps leading down to the dungeon, just as Sonali had described. The voices were rising up the stairwell.

He glanced around. Apart from the sleeping guard, there was no one in this part of the building. For the moment he was safe, but he had to get down those stairs if he were going to find Saleem.

There was nothing else for it.

He took a few steps and listened. The men below continued talking, neither getting closer nor further away. He crept on, placing each foot carefully, listening intently for any sign that one of the men had come to the stairwell.

There was no change in the sound. The men spoke and laughed a few times, but stayed where they were.

Finally, light filtered up the stairs. The wavering light of torches. He could see a stone floor ahead where the steps came to an end. The dungeon was just a few feet away.

Sonali had been convinced he wouldn't even make it this far, but here he was.

He stole to the bottom of the stairs and stood still, straining to hear the guards. He made out eight or nine separate voices. Wooden chairs scraped and rocked against the floor.

He had to look around the corner. He couldn't delay any longer. But he was taking a huge risk.

He held his breath as he slipped his head around the side. In less than a second he took in the whole scene. Before him was a chamber with rough stone walls. Nine Cattans sat hunched about a table, a few sipping from tankards. Beyond them stood a small, barred cell, inside which sat Saleem, Parihar and the two Saxon soldiers. To the side of the cell, an archway opened on to steps leading down into the depths of the dungeon.

Jack slipped back before he was seen. He'd been lucky not to have been spotted – the Cattans were no more than thirty feet away from him. Any of them could have turned at any time.

He shut his eyes for a second. Saleem's face was emblazoned in his mind. The lad had looked gaunt, his skin smeared with dirt. He'd been sitting on the floor with his knees drawn up to his chin and a look of complete dejection on his face.

What had he been through? What had they done to him?

At least he was alive. Jack whispered a Hail Mary. Thank God the lad was alive.

A few chairs squeaked against the stone floor and Jack heard footsteps approaching the stairway.

Damn. He would be seen if he stayed where he was.

He shot back up the steps, wincing at every slight sound his feet made. Footsteps and Cattan voices pursued him. The men were walking quickly and would soon catch up to him.

A film of sweat spread over his face. He ran, taking two steps at a time, throwing all caution aside in his rush to avoid being seen.

Panting hard, he reached ground level.

Which way now?

He went to move towards the exit to the bailey, but halted as the door began to creak open. Someone was coming in.

Christ. His escape route was cut off and the men behind him would soon be at the top of the stairs.

Without thinking, he charged on up the stairway and paused when he reached the next level. The scuffle of footsteps rose up from below. The men were still following him. For a moment he suspected they'd seen him, but then he realised that, as they weren't running or shouting, he was probably still safe.

He pressed on to the next storey and waited again. Surely the Cattans would stop and leave the staircase soon.

But as he stood listening – chest crackling with pain, breathing shallow and the darkness threatening from the corner of his eyes – he heard the men continue up the steps.

Damn. He was trapped in the tower now and running out of luck. He scurried up a further four flights, but the guards continued to follow. Should he carry on up the stairs? Wouldn't he be more trapped the higher he went?

Whatever he did he had to move soon. The Cattans were only a few feet below him and would soon emerge from the darkness.

He left the stairs and charged down a plain hallway where most of the torches had gone out. He stopped at the first door he came to and pressed his ear against the wood. He heard nothing. But that didn't mean there was no one on the other side. Someone could be sitting quietly beside a fire. Or standing on guard.

He tensed his hand. The sound of the footsteps floated down the hall. Any moment now the Cattans would reach the top of the stairs and would be able to see him.

Damn it. He had to go in.

Should he rush in and surprise anyone inside? Should he creep in?

In the end he just pushed the door and strode through as if he were calmly entering his own home.

26

❦

Jack found himself in a small, dark chamber. In the flickering light of the torches behind him, he saw six straw beds strewn across the floor. On two of these lay sleeping Cattans.

His heart pounded. If he stepped back into the hall now he would be spotted immediately. He would have to stay in the room.

Holding his breath, he turned and gently eased the door shut. One of the sleeping men spluttered and turned over, but didn't wake.

Jack pressed his ear to the door. He was sure the men coming up the stairs would carry on to the top of the tower.

But they didn't. Instead, he heard their steps scratching the floor outside in the hall.

Christ. His luck had definitely run out now.

The footsteps drew closer. The Cattans were talking loudly – their voices were loud enough to wake the sleeping men.

Jack looked around the room. A further door stood slightly ajar in the far wall. If he could get across to that perhaps he would find somewhere to hide, or a way to escape. Whatever he did, he couldn't risk staying where he was.

He crept across to the door, avoiding the straw. One of the men grunted but neither woke.

He reached the far side of the chamber, but then heard the handle in the door behind him creak and the latch lift. Christ. The men were coming into the room.

Heart bashing, he shot through the second door and edged it closed. He was in a tiny storeroom lined with shelves. It was almost completely dark in the room, the only light filtering in through the gaps in the boards of a window shutter.

He leant against the door, listening. Sweat broke out on his forehead. He heard the Cattans enter the room and the sleeping men wake. Now all the guards spoke to each other. Were they searching for him? He tried to detect any hint of agitation in their voices, but as far as he could tell they were relaxed. Perhaps they hadn't seen him.

He noticed light slipping under the bottom of the door. The Cattans must have lit torches or candles. What did that mean? That none of them were going to sleep?

He stood listening for what seemed a long time, but must have only been around ten minutes.

The men continued talking and moving around the room. Once, someone left to go out into the hall and then came back again. They didn't seem to be searching for an intruder. They seemed to be talking idly, passing the time, perhaps drinking ale.

How long would they stay awake for? He'd lost track of time but he was certain it must be well after midnight.

What to do? He could stay in the storeroom and wait for the men to leave or fall asleep. But what if one of them came in to get something from the store? What if they didn't leave the other room until morning? It would be difficult for him to get out of the tower during daylight.

The window. It was the only escape route.

He felt around the side of the shutter and found the latch. Should he risk opening it? Would someone notice him looking out and alert the guards?

He had to take a chance.

He crouched, inched the shutter open and peered over the window sill. The cold night air clasped his face and a breeze ruffled his hair. The sky was still pitch black, but speckled with shining ash. Immediately below him ran the castle's outer wall, with battlements to one side and prongs of twisted metal rising at regular intervals along the other. A handful of guns poked out from the ramparts, but no Cattans patrolled this part of the wall. In the distance he made out the edge of the outer bailey.

He was only one storey above the walkway along the top of the wall. He could easily jump down. He stuck his head out further to check the distance and spied a single guard standing right beneath the window, leaning against the wall of the tower.

Damn.

He ducked back inside.

He was still trapped.

Perhaps there was something in the storeroom that could help. With the window shutter ajar, enough moonlight shone inside for him to see the shelves properly. Mostly, they were empty. A few spare blankets lay folded on one shelf, and a set of earthenware mugs lined another. Higher up he saw a stack of bows but no arrows. And then his eyes fell on something he recognised.

He stood up, stretched and took down an ammunition pouch – European Army issue. It must have been one of those taken from the dead Saxons. He lifted the lid and found about twenty musket cartridges inside. He reached up again, felt around and grasped a small satchel. When he opened it, he found a bag of pistol balls – the satchel must have belonged to an officer.

All these bullets would be useful – if he had a firearm.

He hunted around further, checking every inch of the shelves. But he found no pistol or musket or any other kind of weapon.

Damn.

He stuck the cartridges in the satchel with the pistol balls and then slung the bag over his shoulder. The bullets would come in handy if he ever got out of the storeroom. It was no easy feat to lay your hands on ammunition in Scotland.

He went back to the door. He heard a series of clicks, interspersed with cheers from the men. It only took him a second to realise they were playing a game of dice.

He sat on the floor and waited. Occasionally he got up and

peered through the window, but the guard remained slouching against the wall below. Sometimes the man wandered along the walkway towards the stairs down to the bailey, but each time he returned to his position.

Jack considered jumping out and attacking him, but he wouldn't be able to do that silently enough not to attract attention.

He was trapped, and so he waited.

His thoughts whirled. What would he do if anyone came into the storeroom? Should he give himself up straight away? Should he fight to the death?

And what was he going to do if he managed to get out of the storeroom without being seen? There was little point returning to the dungeon. Sonali had been right, there were too many guards there. He could try to kill a Cattan, take his skull tunic and pose as a guard himself. Perhaps he would be able to get his hands on the keys to Saleem's cell. But even if he could do that and free Saleem and the others, they would all be caught immediately as they tried to flee.

What about Sonali? There was no easy way to free her either. But it would be hard to leave her to her fate.

The more he considered what action to take, the more his thoughts revolved around Mahajan. The siddha was the key to all the problems he faced. If he could deal with Mahajan, kill or perhaps capture him, then he could deal with everything else. But Sonali had said Mahajan was constantly shielded by his yogic power. Nothing could get through this defence – not even bullets.

His thoughts wandered, skipping through memories of Katelin and Elizabeth. He recalled happier times when they'd all lived together in Dorsetshire. But the experience was bittersweet. He would never see Elizabeth again, would never hold her in his arms, would never cradle his grandchild.

Then for some reason his mind drifted back to the last time he'd seen Jhala. It had been three years ago at the estate where Jack then worked. He and his guru had sat in the gazebo in the formal garden and Jhala had told him that Elizabeth had been arrested and was due to be executed. Then Jhala had offered him a deal. If Jack hunted down William, Jhala would spare Elizabeth.

The memory was seared in Jack's mind. The world had been turned upside down at that point. Until then, Jack had trusted the Rajthanans, had served them since he was sixteen. He'd thought of Jhala as a friend. But on that day, everything fell apart.

The anger still smouldered within him when he recalled what had happened.

Jhala had forced him to choose between his daughter and his friend. And of course, he'd had to choose his daughter.

Jhala had later been killed by his own men, who'd mutinied against him. But if Jhala had lived, would Jack have hunted him down and killed him? Would he have slain his own guru?

Jhala deserved to die for what he'd done.

In his mind, Jack had killed him many times.

———◆———

Jack stared into the darkness. How long had he been sitting in the storeroom? Two hours? More?

The Cattans were still playing dice, talking and laughing in the next room. He hoped Rao, Cormac and the others had left their hiding place on the hill by now and were heading back to the village. He prayed they were all safe.

He raised himself to the window to check on the guard. A grin slipped over his lips. The Cattan had finally left his post and there was no one else along the stretch of wall immediately below. Jack stuck his head out further and looked around. There were a few guards in the distance, but they were unlikely to notice him if he jumped out now.

Was there anyone else around who would see him? There might be someone down in the inner bailey, or looking out of a window. But he would have to risk it. He couldn't stay where he was.

He crossed himself, drew out Katelin's necklace and kissed it.

Then he opened the shutter fully and swung himself over the window sill so that he was sitting with his feet dangling outside. He scanned the surroundings. He still saw no one and heard no sign that anyone had spotted him.

He launched himself into the air, plummeted down, struck the walkway and rolled forward, his cloak sweeping around him. He shot straight back upright and stood looking out over the battlements as if he were a guard.

His heart beat wildly.

Had he been seen? Would someone raise the alarm?

Nothing happened.

He looked about surreptitiously. A few Cattans still paced the walls in the distance, but none had noticed him jump.

He whispered a Hail Mary, then marched along the walkway towards a set of stairs leading down into the bailey – he had to get out of sight before someone became suspicious. The black metal spikes jutted up beside him at various points, reaching to about twenty feet above the ramparts. Like much of the castle, the structures shifted uneasily between being solid and illusory.

To his left, beyond the wall, he caught a glimpse of the Cattan village at the base of the hill. There were no lights in the settlement and the huts were only suggestions of grey against the black ground.

He reached the steps. Now he was far enough along the wall to see down into the outer bailey. He spotted the dark bulge of the metal skull, the wooden platform where Mahajan had spoken and the muddy ground where the worshippers had stood. On the left side of the bailey, three mule carts had drawn up beside a small, single-storey building. A set of double doors at the front of the building had been swung open and a group of natives were shovelling something from the back of the carts through the doorway. A further two carts were trundling through the castle's main gates, which were wide open.

What was going on?

Jack walked on past the stairs and continued to the wall that separated the inner and outer baileys. Now he could see that the natives weren't Cattans – at least, they didn't have the white skull on their tunics. And they were unloading what looked like coal from the carts into some kind of store.

Interesting. He'd been wondering where Mahajan's supply of coal came from. There must be pits somewhere nearby.

The Cattans weren't taking much notice of the labouring natives. A few guards wandered along the walls and two stood beside the gatehouse. But none of them were even looking at the workers.

And that gave Jack an idea – an escape plan.

But should he leave the castle now? He didn't want to abandon Saleem, but he was certain he'd done as much as he could on his own. He needed help and would have to return with more men.

He just had to pray that Saleem survived until he came back.

He returned to the stairs, dashed down to the inner bailey and strode across to the passage he'd run along earlier that night. He crept down the empty hall and reached the doors to the outer bailey.

He paused with his fingers on the ringed handle. Once he stepped out, the Cattans on the wall would be able to see him. But they hadn't appeared interested in what was going on in the bailey. With any luck, he would blend in with the men shovelling the coal.

He pulled his cloak up over his head and secured it more tightly about his neck. Then he swung one of the doors open, marched straight out and slipped over to the closest mule cart. The men had just finished unloading the coal and were throwing their spades into the back of the vehicle.

No one paid him any attention as the three front mule carts were circled around and taken back towards the gate. Jack trailed behind a group of about thirty men, none of whom looked back once. The party reached the gatehouse and ambled between the two guards slouching on either side. Jack's heart beat harder as he walked past the Cattans. Would they notice he was an impostor? Would they stop him and question him?

But the guards paid him no attention at all and within minutes he was striding down the hill at the back of the group. He glanced over his shoulder once and saw the contorted castle, the black towers, the chimneys and the swirling silver ash.

This was only a temporary retreat. He was coming back to the castle. This wasn't the end.

Dawn was peeling back a corner of the sky as Jack neared the top of the hill. The light pencilled in the trees along the summit. When he looked back, the castle glinted as the sun's rays caught the metal. He'd been in the building far longer than he'd realised. But at least he'd made it out alive.

He trudged into the woods, searching for the place where he, Rao and the Mar had hidden the day before. He wasn't expecting to see his comrades – he just wanted to find their tracks so that he could follow them back to the village.

He pushed aside bushes and brambles, and finally spotted the boulder they'd crouched behind when they first saw the worshippers. He forced his way through dry bracken, and then stopped suddenly.

The tip of a spear had shot out from behind a tree and now rested against his neck. He felt the cold metal on his skin.

'Wait.' Rao stepped out from the side of the boulder. A wide smile crossed his face. 'It's Jack.'

The spear lowered and Cormac appeared from behind the tree, his beard bristling as he grinned. The three Mar warriors paced out from where they'd been hiding.

Rao rushed forward, started a namaste then threw his arms about Jack, slapping him on the back. 'We were certain you were dead or captured.'

Jack hugged Rao back awkwardly. He hadn't expected a

reaction like this. 'I told you all to go back to the village.'

Rao stepped back and put his hands on his hips. 'We wouldn't abandon you. We were all agreed about that.'

Cormac nodded. 'We come. Find you.'

'You were going to try to get into the castle?' Jack asked.

'We had to,' Rao said.

Jack shook his head, but found a smile creeping across his lips. 'You would have been shot in minutes. You're lucky I got back here in time to stop you.'

PART FIVE

27

<hr/>

Cormac squatted in the hut's entrance, silhouetted in the late afternoon light. 'Chiefs come soon.'

'We'll wait here,' Jack said. 'Come and get us when they arrive.'

Cormac nodded, bowed his head towards the Great Shee and slipped away.

Jack sat back on his bracken bed. He and Rao were in their hut in the village, after being greeted joyously by the Mar on their return. Chief Domnall had announced the local chiefs were returning to the village to hear what the Great Shee had discovered at the Place of Dead Kings.

'What are we going to do?' Rao was sitting cross-legged beside the smouldering peat fire. 'They'll expect me to fight Mahajan. They think the Great Shee is here to save them.'

Jack rubbed the back of his neck. 'You'll have to oblige them, then.'

Rao's eyes widened. 'I can't do that! Mahajan's a siddha. You said he has some sort of shield.'

Jack had told Rao everything he'd found out about the castle, including what he'd learnt about the underground workshop, avatars and the dungeon.

'Don't worry. Not you on your own.' Jack looked out the open door. The sounds of the village wafted inside. 'I've been thinking about it. We can't leave Saleem and Parihar behind, can we?'

Rao's moustache stiffened. 'No. This Mahajan seems to be a brute. Before, I'd assumed Parihar would be well treated by a fellow Rajthanan. Now I see I was quite wrong.'

'Right. And we can't leave Mahajan to have the Brahmastra, if he really does have it.'

'Indeed not. The man appears insane.'

'So, as I see it, our only choice is to fight Mahajan and his men.'

'Fight them? With what? They've got muskets, guns. Who knows what powers Mahajan has.'

'I've been talking to Cormac and Domnall. They reckon they can muster three thousand warriors if most of the Mar and a few neighbouring tribes join forces.'

Rao rubbed his moustache. 'That is a large number. If it's true.'

'With three thousand, I reckon we can take the castle. It's not all that well defended at the moment. I had a good look at the place. They can't have more than forty guns and mortars. And I'd take a stab at estimating they have about four hundred fighting men, if that. Apparently another large Cattan war party's just been sent south, but they won't be able to get back to the castle quickly.'

'They have muskets.'

'True, but if we can get inside the castle that won't count for much. In hand-to-hand fighting we'll beat them through weight of numbers.'

'What about Mahajan's powers?'

'That is an unknown. I'll grant you that. We'll have to deal with whatever comes up.'

'And the Brahmastra?'

'Mahajan might not have finished it yet. Sonali wasn't sure. He hasn't used it yet, has he?'

'That's no guarantee.'

'No. But the Brahmastra doesn't sound like a short-range weapon. If it can lay waste to a whole city, you wouldn't want to use it against someone a few yards away, would you?'

'I hadn't thought of it like that. The problem is, we know so little about the thing. This all seems very risky.'

'You got any other ideas?'

Rao rubbed his moustache more vigorously. 'I have to say, I

don't. We can't go back to Dun Fries now. We can't do nothing. We have to act. I fear your plan is the best option we have, but I'm not sure it will work.'

'A little faith. That's all we need.' He had to appear confident in front of Rao, despite the fact he was far from certain about their chances.

'I wish I shared your optimism.'

Jack toyed with a piece of bracken. There was something else he had to talk to Rao about, and it wasn't going to be easy. 'Have you thought what we should do with the Brahmastra?'

'Assuming we actually beat Mahajan?'

'Yes.'

'And he really has managed to build the thing?'

Jack nodded.

Rao stared into space. 'I will put it in the hands of the army. They can decide what to do with it.'

Jack had thought Rao might say something like that. This was going to be a difficult conversation. 'Are you sure that's for the best?'

'Whatever do you mean?'

'The thing is . . . the army might try to use it, mightn't they? Imagine the damage that'll do.'

'I believe they would only use it where necessary, in the service of dharma.'

'Not sure I agree with that.'

Rao frowned. 'What?'

'I've seen the army do some terrible things.'

'Nonsense. I don't think I like the gist of what you're saying, Jack.'

Jack stared hard at Rao. 'That's because you haven't been on the receiving end of what the army can do. You haven't had to face an assault by the European or Rajthanan Army.'

'And neither have you.' Rao paused. 'You haven't, have you? You said you were *in* the army.'

345

'I was. But when the mutiny started . . . well, I found myself on the other side.'

'What?' Rao's voice was no louder than a whisper. 'You're not . . . a traitor.'

'Afraid so.'

'You.' Rao leapt to his feet, his eyes blazing. He pointed his finger at Jack. 'You. Treason! Traitor!'

'Sit down—'

'I will not sit down. You've lied to me and led me astray. Why did I trust you? I must be mad. My father told me the English were treacherous brutes. I should have listened to him.'

'Calm down. Let me explain.'

'I will not hear another word from you. You . . . you've let me down, Jack. You've let me down very badly.'

Rao stormed out of the hut, his turban brushing against the top of the low door frame.

Jack jumped up and followed. The Captain was striding away from the village and up the lip of the hollow. Dusk was approaching and the trees and huts were tinged golden.

Cormac ran across to Jack, a frown locked on his forehead. 'Where Great Shee go?'

'Don't worry.' Jack raised his hand. 'I'll talk to him.'

'There is problem?'

'No problem.'

Jack strode after Rao. The Captain soon vanished into the shadows beneath the trees. Where was he going? He wasn't setting off into the wilderness, was he?

Jack started running. He forced his way through the under-growth and found Rao standing on the far side of the stretch of woods, staring up at the bare slope of a hill.

Jack walked across and stood beside him. What to say? 'Look, I'm sorry.'

Rao's eyes were glassy and his moustache rigid. 'You lied to me.'

'Not exactly. I just didn't tell you the whole truth.'

Rao looked at his boots. 'So, were you going to slit my throat and take the Brahmastra for yourself, then?'

'No. I mean, I wasn't going to kill you. That was never my plan.' He stared up the hill. 'But when I set out, I was thinking to get the Brahmastra for the rebels.'

'I see. You knew about it all along?'

'No. My commanders heard a rumour that Mahajan had some sort of weapon.'

'So, that's why they sent you.'

'Yes.'

Rao stared at him. 'How could you betray your oath? How could you betray the army?'

'It wasn't easy. It took me a while to decide. It was a complicated situation.'

'You have abandoned dharma. You have walked away from everything that's right in this world.'

Jack shook his head. 'You've only been in these lands for a few months. You don't understand. England is my country. The empire has taken it from my people.'

'The empire has brought dharma to this place.'

'You think so? Look at Mahajan. See what he's done here. He's taken these lands from the Mar and enslaved them. All to further his own power.'

'Mahajan is a traitor to the empire too.'

'But it's the same, don't you see? He's come here with his powers and avatars and taken over. That's what the empire's done in England.'

Rao stared into the distance and went silent for a long time.

Finally, Jack sighed. 'Look, we have to plan our next move. We have to work together.'

'And what makes you think I'm going to take part in this plan of yours?'

'We have to put aside our differences. For our friends.'

'And after we free them? What about the Brahmastra?'

Jack scratched the back of his neck. 'We'll have to agree what to do with that.'

'I will not let it fall into the hands of the rebels. I would die to prevent that.'

'I wouldn't expect you to agree to that. The thing is, I'm not sure I want the rebels to have it anyway.'

'What are you talking about now?'

'I've been thinking about the Brahmastra. Thinking about it a lot. If it's real, I don't think anyone should have it. Not the crusade. Not the empire. It's too dangerous.'

'What are you saying?'

'I reckon we should destroy it. Destroy all Mahajan's work so no one can get their hands on it.'

'You are asking me to betray the empire.'

'And I'll be betraying the crusade. But I don't see it like that. The Brahmastra is evil. In the wrong hands it could be devastating. We can't leave something like that in this world.'

'You make a good case for destroying it. I'll give you that.'

'So, we'll put this disagreement aside? Work together?'

Rao straightened his shoulders and lifted his chin. The late afternoon light turned his eyes crystal. 'I'll consider it.'

———◆———

A bonfire blazed in the heart of the village. Chief Domnall sat outside his hut, the red light playing over his face. Eva and her four sisters sat next to him, while warriors from the village were spread out to either side. The local chiefs had returned with their retinues and they all squatted about the fire in a wide circle. Jack and Rao crouched with Cormac in an empty space on one side of the crowd. The numerous village dogs skulked in the dark and watched the proceedings.

Domnall stood and limped forward a few paces. A longsword in a leather scabbard hung at his side. Cormac had explained this was the only sword in the village and had been passed down through the generations since the time of the dead kings.

The Chief gave a long speech in Gaalic, which Cormac translated for Jack and Rao's benefit. Domnall thanked the chiefs for assembling once again, praised the Great Shee and exhorted the gathered leaders to join forces against the Demon. Finally, he turned to Rao and asked him what he'd learnt at the Place of Dead Kings and how they were to fight the Demon.

Jack took a deep breath. He and Rao had barely spoken for the past hour and he had no idea how the Captain was going to respond. Rao hadn't left the village, so presumably that meant he hadn't completely rejected the idea of attacking the castle.

Jack wished he'd had the chance to tell Rao what to say. But he was going to have to leave it up to the Captain to speak in his own words.

Rao cleared his throat, stood up and straightened his tunic. He pressed his hands together and bowed slightly. 'Namaste. You have come to hear the words of the Great Shee. So, I will do my best to explain myself. I have returned from the Place of Dead Kings. I and my assistant have seen the defences. I believe we can defeat the Demon, but only if we all march on his castle and attack him together. If we don't join forces,' he looked down at Jack, 'we will never succeed.'

Once Cormac had translated the words, the crowd leapt to their feet, cheered loudly and broke into chants and war cries. They waved their spears, the firelight casting them red as devils.

Domnall raised his hand and called for quiet. The assembly calmed and the Chief then asked Rao whether he had powers that could defeat the Demon. He solemnly recounted that many said the Demon had great magic. Some even said he could never be killed.

Jack tensed his hands. Rao had to say the right thing now.

Rao coughed, looked at his boots, then gazed at the gathering. 'Yes, with your help, I can beat the Demon.'

The crowd roared with delight at this. Domnall drew his sword and held it up with two hands, the ancient blade rippling in the firelight. He called for the fiery crosses to be lit and carried throughout the Land of Mar.

'This way we call all to fight,' Cormac explained to Jack and Rao.

Ten men approached with wooden crosses on tall poles, which they held in the bonfire until the wood caught alight. They then raised the poles high above their heads, the crosses blazing and sparking against the black night.

Domnall said some final words, and the men ran off in different directions, holding the flaming wood above them. Jack watched as the burning crosses climbed the surrounding hillsides, shining brightly in the vast darkness of the wilderness.

It was strange to think that when he'd first seen a fiery cross a week and a half earlier it had been a sign of savagery and terror, and yet now there was something stirring about watching the men journeying up, up into the mountains to summon the warriors of Mar.

Pipers began blowing their instruments furiously, sending sinewy cries into the night. Other men bashed hand-held drums with sticks. Mar men and women chanted and clapped in time, while the rest danced wildly about the flames. The dogs barked and howled.

Jack patted Rao on the back. The Captain stiffened, but gave Jack a curt nod.

'Thank you,' Jack said.

———❖———

Cormac helped Rao fasten his cloak about his neck with a brooch. Jack shook his head and grinned. The Captain was a strange sight with his brown skin, red turban and officer's boots, all wrapped up in a native cloak that looked as though it had never been washed.

Cormac straightened the cloak and dusted some bracken from Rao's shoulder. He stepped back and smiled. 'Great Shee look good.'

Rao squared his shoulders and raised his chin. For a moment, just a moment, Jack could imagine him as a Scottish chieftain.

Jack pulled his own native cloak tighter about him. Both he and Rao had decided to dress this way in order to disguise themselves. But Jack had to admit, he was finding the native attire more comfortable and much warmer than his English clothes.

Three days had passed since the meeting of the chiefs and during that time Rao had been withdrawn and frosty when he spoke to Jack. But today, for the first time, Jack sensed the Captain was thawing a little.

Cormac led them to the centre of the village, where most of the Mar had gathered to see the war party leave. The Mar and neighbouring tribes were due to muster at a place called the Lake of Shining Water. Almost every man from the village under the age of forty stood ready to march, spears and bows at their sides and knives in their belts.

Chief Domnall was outside his hut. He wore a padded tunic, smeared with grease, as a sort of basic armour. Over this was his blue and purple striped cloak, while his longsword hung at his side.

'The Chief's coming?' Jack asked Cormac.

Cormac nodded. 'Chief will fight.'

Jack raised his eyebrows. The Chief was hardly young, and he walked with a limp.

'Chief say he was in shadow for long time after wife die,' Cormac said. 'He sad he have no son to lead village when he gone. But since Great Shee come, the sun shine on him again. He feel strong now. He will fight for Land of Mar.'

Eva rushed over to Rao and gripped his arm, tears brimming in her eyes. 'Great Shee. Careful. Come back.'

Rao coughed. 'I will, Eva. Don't you worry.'

'Then marry.'

Rao gave a little laugh and prised off her hand. 'I'm not sure about that.'

'I wait. I wait Great Shee come back.'

A piper blasted a series of whining notes and a cheer went up from the crowd.

'Now,' Cormac said. 'We go Lake of Shining Water.'

───────◆───────

Jack heard the chanting long before he saw anything. Night had fallen, the sliver of moon was hidden behind the cloud and the darkness was as thick as soup. The mountains towered all around him, their peaks glowing with snow.

'Can you hear it?' Rao asked as he walked alongside Jack. 'It sounds like there're thousands of them.'

'Hope so,' Jack said.

Beside them strode the Mar warriors from the village, their cloaks swishing and amulets clinking. The party had run for much of the day, but had finally slowed – to Jack's relief – when it grew dark. Chief Domnall had, incredibly, kept up with his men, flying along despite his injured leg.

They rounded the side of a rocky outcrop and a valley opened up below.

'Shiva,' Rao hissed.

Thousands of fires peppered the valley floor. The chanting was even louder now, rolling about the hills and rising up into the brooding clouds. On the left side of the valley lay a long, thin lake, the firelight shimmering on its dark water.

Cormac puffed out his chest. 'Mar come. Many Mar. Other tribe too.'

'Thank God,' Jack muttered under his breath. He hadn't known for certain what kind of army he would find here, but this looked to be more than he could have hoped for.

They marched downhill and after ten minutes Jack could make

352

out the warriors standing beside the campfires. Many waved their spears above their heads, while others bore burning crosses which slashed the dark with bright orange flame. Drums pounded and pipes droned.

A high-pitched ululation spread across the vast gathering and the chant changed. Jack could hear it clearly: '*Cap-tain Rao. Cap-tain Rao.*'

Rao's jaw dropped. 'Shiva.'

Warriors rushed up the hill and flocked around them. They grasped Rao and raised him up on their shoulders, the Captain calling out for them to be careful. Then Jack was wrenched up and carried forward too, while Cormac, Domnall and the others from the village ran along behind.

The singing whirled in the air. Warriors swarmed about Jack, their eyes wild and their teeth shining in the dark. A forest of spears and flaming crosses swayed in every direction.

Jack was borne, as if by an uneasy sea, across to a mound in the centre of the camp. Rao was lifted on to a flat stone slab at the top of the knoll, while Jack was placed slightly lower on the side of the slope.

Jack looked around. A horde of chanting, cheering, waving Mar surrounded him on all sides. The sound of them punched the air and rocked the mountains.

'*Cap-tain Rao. Cap-tain Rao.*'

Rao frowned and looked down at Jack.

'I think they want you to say something,' Jack said.

Rao bent down lower. 'But what?'

'Think of something. You're the Great Shee.'

'Shiva.'

Rao straightened again, rubbed his moustache, pursed his lips and gazed out across the seething throng. He cleared his throat a couple of times, then lifted his chin and said in a wavering voice, 'I am the Great Shee. I have come to you now.'

The crowd quietened slightly and became less exuberant. Jack noticed a few puzzled frowns on people's faces. Was that because they couldn't understand Rao's words, or because he didn't seem like a shee?

Rao looked down at Jack again and made a questioning face.

'Just get on with it,' Jack said.

Rao raised his hand and said in a clear voice, 'We will defeat the Demon. We will cast him down.'

The Mar cheered and waved their spears, swords and burning crosses. They couldn't understand what Rao was saying, but they clearly liked the way he was saying it.

The response must have buoyed Rao because he now shouted, 'I will lead you! I will lead you to victory. The Demon will be slain by the magic of the Great Shee!'

He drew his pistol and pointed it into the air – Jack had loaded the weapon himself earlier in the day using bullets from Mahajan's castle. Rao fired. The weapon flashed, kicked and spat out a jet of smoke. The loud crack fell across the crowd, who gave a collective gasp, paused for a second and then began hooting and whooping with joy. Pipes wailed and the chants of 'Cap-tain Rao' thundered across the hills.

Rao looked down. His eyes blazed and his chest heaved, as if he'd been possessed.

Jack grinned. 'Well done. You finally sounded like a Great Shee.'

———◆———

Twenty Mar warriors stood in a circle, carrying torches that sent flickering light across the bare ground. Jack and Rao stood in the centre of the group with the chiefs of the ten largest sub-tribes around them. Despite leading a minor branch of the Mar clan, Domnall was part of the group due to the huge honour of having the Great Shee stay in his village. The Chief beamed constantly, apparently basking in Rao's glow.

Jack had scratched a rough outline of Mahajan's castle in the earth and now he pointed at it with a stick. He'd seen Jhala do this many times to explain battle plans to the company. Strangely, he was now commanding an army about the size of the regiment Jhala had been leading when he died.

'The Demon has his guards placed on the outer walls, all along here,' Jack said.

Cormac, who stood at Jack's side, translated and the chiefs nodded to show they understood.

'There are fire weapons on these walls too,' Jack continued. 'I saw them along here and here, but they can easily be moved to other positions. The main gate is here. The Demon's defences are concentrated near there at the moment, and I expect it to stay that way. The slope to the rear of the castle is steep and the wall is high. The Demon won't think to place too many defences there.

'Now, I say we do what the Demon most expects – attack the castle from the front, at the main gate. That will ensure he keeps most of his forces around there. In the meantime, we'll send a smaller force, which we'll keep secret for as long as possible, to the rear of the castle. We'll attack there where he'll least expect it.'

'You said the slope was too steep and the castle walls were too high to attack there,' Rao said.

'They're not too steep for an attack, they just make an attack much more difficult. But without many Cattans there to fight us, we can do it. We'll build ladders, run across the valley and be up on the walls before they know what's hit them.'

The chiefs nodded once Cormac had translated. They seemed satisfied so far with Jack's plan.

'Now,' Jack said. 'We need to split the force in two. I will lead the much smaller party that will attack the back of the castle. I'll take three hundred men. No more than that, otherwise we're sure to be spotted.'

'I will lead the main force,' Rao said.

Jack looked up. The Captain straightened his back and raised his chin. His eyes glittered in the firelight. He looked like a man who could lead the Mar to victory. And the Mar were much less likely to falter if they had the Great Shee marching along with them.

Jack nodded. 'Good. You will lead the larger force, with Domnall's help. You'll attack the front of the castle and try to get through the gate. You can cut down trees to use as battering rams. I'll get up on the wall with the others and hit Mahajan from behind before he has a chance to change tactics.'

'Agreed,' Rao said.

Cormac explained the plan to the chiefs and they nodded in agreement and spoke amongst themselves.

Domnall stood slightly to the side and gripped the pommel of his sword. His smile was broad and his eyes glassy as he gazed into the darkness.

He looked as though he'd finally come home after wandering for years in the wilderness.

A shaft of pain struck Jack in the chest. He winced and struggled not to double over. Within seconds the sensation passed, but it reminded him of the desperate situation he was in.

Today was the day Kanvar's cure was supposed to wear off. Today was the end of the two-month reprieve.

And yet he was still alive, still walking and talking and able to prepare for the battle ahead. He was sitting on a rock polishing the scimitar and watching the warriors pack away their things in the fuzzy morning light.

Soon, the war party would separate. Rao, Domnall and the other chiefs would lead the bulk of the men towards the castle. Jack would march his force of three hundred warriors across the hills. They would travel through the night and hide near the castle. Tomorrow, at noon, they would attack.

But would he survive until then? Or would the sattva-fire finally finish him off?

Whatever happened, he knew he would never see Elizabeth again. Even in the unlikely event they were able to defeat Mahajan, he would die soon from his injury anyway. The journey back to Shropshire would take weeks. He would never make it.

For a moment he remembered when Elizabeth was born. It had been in the middle of the night and Katelin had lain on the bed, broken with exhaustion. But he'd lifted the tiny form of his daughter up to the candlelight so that he could stare for the first time at her perfect face.

He wished he could speak to her one last time.

But there was no point feeling sorry for himself now. He had to still the rippling pool of his mind and focus on the task ahead of him.

'Here, take these.' Rao walked across to Jack, holding out the last of the pistol bullets.

'You have enough?' Jack asked.

'Plenty.' Rao patted his pocket.

They'd already shared out the powder, even emptying the musket cartridges Jack had taken from the castle to make sure they both had enough for the assault.

Jack accepted the bullets and put them in his satchel.

'So.' Rao studied his hands. 'This is it.'

'Seems so.'

'I've been speaking to Domnall. We'll be off in a few minutes.'

'Good.'

Rao shivered slightly and hugged his cloak closer.

'First big battle?' Jack asked.

'Yes. If you don't count us being attacked on the way up here.'

'You'll be all right. We'll win this. I'm certain.' Jack was very far from certain, but there was no point letting anyone know that. The Mar had an absolute belief in the Great Shee. So long as Rao believed too, there was a chance they'd take the castle.

'I've been thinking.' Rao stared into the distance. His breath clouded around his mouth. 'About what you said a few days ago.'

'What did I say?'

'You know, about Mahajan taking these lands.'

Christ. Jack didn't want another argument now. 'We can talk about it some other—'

'No, no.' Rao raised his hand. 'I agree with you. This place is the home of the Mar. They know every bit of it. Like Cormac said, it's inside them. If that's how the English feel about England, then maybe the empire wasn't right to annex the country.'

Jack sat back. He hadn't expected this. He hadn't believed a Rajthanan could ever say such a thing. 'You've had a change of heart.'

'You got me thinking. You know, long ago the Rajthanans were conquered. Mohammedans from the north took our lands. But Jaidev Chauhan and the siddhas led us to victory against the sultans. We freed our lands and Rajthana has never been invaded since.'

'I've heard about it a few times.' Jhala had told Jack the story on numerous occasions.

Rao nodded and looked straight at Jack. 'I just wanted you to know. In case . . .'

'It's all right.' Jack patted Rao on the shoulder. 'I understand.'

28

Jack heard the harsh rasp of a crow. He peered through the leafless trees. Thick mist had settled over the countryside during the night and rubbed out most of the world. He could only see clearly thirty feet ahead of him.

The crow cawed again.

The Mar warrior beside Jack cupped his hands around his mouth and gave a return cry that was a perfect imitation of the bird's call. When the crow in the distance rasped again, the warrior grinned, grasped Jack's cloak and pointed excitedly into the mist.

Jack understood what the man was trying to tell him and in less than a minute three Mar warriors materialised in the fog, scrambled down the slope and entered the trees. It was Cormac and the other two who'd gone scouting earlier.

Jack crossed himself and mumbled a Hail Mary. The three of them had been gone for so long he'd started to think they'd run into trouble.

He glanced behind him at the three hundred warriors who crouched in the forest in a scattered line. With their cloaks drawn over them, they were well camouflaged against the muddy earth, rocks and undergrowth. They gripped their spears and stared around them, their faces silvered. Wooden ladders lay along the ground beside them. They'd built these the night before, binding the branches together with whatever they could lay their hands on – rope, vines, pieces of cloth.

Pain flared in Jack's chest. He grunted, shut his eyes, and waited a few seconds for it to recede.

Cormac and the others clambered through the woods and squatted beside him.

'See no Cattans.' Cormac panted. 'Safe to move.'

'Good,' Jack said. 'Looks like we've made it without being seen. And the castle?'

Cormac pointed ahead at the dark smudge of a saddle between the hills. 'Over there. Other side.'

'The castle's on the other side of that slope?'

'Aye.'

Jack looked up. The sun was lost behind the fog, the light diffuse, as if coming from no particular direction. 'You think it's noon yet?'

Cormac looked up. 'Aye. Noon now.'

Jack trusted Cormac's judgement. The Mar were even better at living in the wilderness than he was. They were no doubt used to gauging the time in these conditions.

If it were noon, then it was time to move. All going well, Rao and the rest of the Mar would now be looking down at the castle from the far side of the valley. Mahajan and his men would have seen them massing in the hills, but that was all part of the plan. At Rao's command, the Mar would pour down the hill and rush at the castle gate. Cormac had found another warrior who knew enough English to act as a translator, but it would hardly be necessary. Rao just had to point and say one word: 'Charge.'

Jack couldn't hear the sound of guns or muskets. The attack hadn't started yet. Rao had his watch, so his timing would be precise. But the assault would come soon. In the next few minutes, Jack was sure.

Pain rushed through him again. He twisted his face.

Cormac put his hand on Jack's shoulder. 'Problem?'

Jack did his best to force back the stabbing sensation. 'It's nothing.'

Within a few seconds the worst of it had passed.

Several of the Mar muttered and pointed ahead. Jack looked

up and spotted a flake of glowing ash drifting down from the sky and lighting up the surrounding mist. Further flakes followed. Soon a swarm of the shining dots sailed across the hills, bobbing and dipping before eventually spiralling to the earth.

The wind must have changed direction. He hadn't seen any ash during the journey so far.

The warriors grumbled more loudly.

'They say spirits,' Cormac said.

'Tell them not to be afraid,' Jack replied. 'The Great Shee will protect us.'

Cormac whispered the words to the nearest men, who passed the message on down the line. This seemed to have the desired effect as the warriors quietened.

'Right.' Jack took a deep breath. 'Let's go.'

The men cast aside their cloaks and hid them in the undergrowth. Jack did the same – it would be easier to climb without the heavy garment. A few of the Mar were dressed in padded tunics, but most wore the usual knee-length garb with bare legs.

Yet again Jack marvelled at their hardiness. The elements seemed to have no effect on these people. No wonder Rao had become so fascinated by them.

At Jack's command, they crept forward out of the woods and into the open. Jack and Cormac were at the head of the party, while the others followed in a broken column. Jack had done little planning or given the men many instructions. They were to get over the saddle, charge at the castle, raise the ladders, fight and spike the guns. That was it.

He wondered briefly what tactics Jhala would have used. Would he have approved of Jack's strategy? What other strategy was there? Jack had come up with the best plan he could given the circumstances. It was too late to have second thoughts now.

The scimitar swung at his side as he moved. The pistol and the knife nestled on the other side of his belt.

The mist coiled about him, brushing his face and beading his clothes and hair. The phosphorescent ash fell in curtains. One flake circled close to his face, giving off a faint ringing sound. Another descended on to Cormac's tunic and vanished as it touched the cloth.

This close to the castle, the scent of sattva was strong again. The streams were thick and constantly sent Jack's skin quivering.

Pain stabbed Jack's chest. He stumbled, regained his footing and carried on. Cormac frowned but said nothing.

The scarp loomed ahead. It was a short distance to the top of the saddle, but the incline was steep and smothered in trees. It would be a difficult scramble up . . .

Then Cormac gave a sudden roar that made Jack jump. The tall man raised the side of his tunic. A hole had been torn in the cloth and an arrow now quivered in the ground directly behind him. The missile must have missed his body by an inch.

Jack heard a hiss and a second arrow slipped out of the fog. The metal head and feather flights spun as the missile plunged straight towards him.

Christ.

He dodged to the side. The arrow hummed past and speared the earth a couple of feet behind him.

The air suddenly came alive with whirring missiles. They criss-crossed the mist like flying insects. The warriors behind Jack shouted. One man thudded to the ground and squirmed, an arrow lodged deep in his throat. Another slumped to the side with a missile in his thigh. Arrows danced off the heather and rocks.

Jack scanned the way ahead and could just make out dim shapes moving at the top of the saddle.

Damn. Mahajan's forces had somehow seen them approaching.

Cormac wailed. 'I fail. I look. No see.'

'You did your best. They must have been hiding near the castle and come up after you left. A patrol must have seen us. They knew we were coming.'

An arrow smacked into an ash flake and sent sparks flying.

Another skipped across the ground and slid past Jack's boot.

Jack fought back a rising tide of pain. Retreat wasn't an option. Rao and the others would attack soon and would be slaughtered if Jack and his men couldn't get into the castle and spike the guns.

There was only one thing for it.

He drew his scimitar, raised it above his head and did what Jhala or any other officer would have done – he shouted, '*Charge!*'

Then he was running towards the trees, straight into the blizzard of missiles. Glinting ash sang around him, arrows whined past and the blood roared in his ears. He kept shouting and the sound of his own frenzied voice carried him forward.

Cormac began running a second after Jack, but soon caught up and bellowed a war cry. His eyes bulged, his mouth opened in a snarl and the veins in his neck and forehead stood out like tree roots.

Jack was dimly aware that the Mar warriors were charging behind him. He could hear their shouts, the thud, thud of their feet and the occasional scream as one of them was hit.

A skirl of pipes sailed down from the hills. He was close enough to the slope now to make out the figures massing on the hilltop.

He reached the bottom of the scarp and bolted into the woods. The branches meshed about him, and the undergrowth and vines clung to his legs. He slipped, grasped at the damp ground, regained his footing and charged on.

Looking to the side, he saw Cormac loping uphill, smacking aside bushes that got in his way. When Jack glanced back over his shoulder, he saw the first of the Mar flooding into the forest and scrambling up the incline, with more appearing from the mist all the time.

A storm of arrows pelted the trees and bounced off branches. One pierced a trunk next to Jack. Others stabbed the ground or snapped on rocks. But at least the woods provided a degree of cover.

The slope steepened and Jack had to put his scimitar back in his belt and clamber up on his hands and knees. Mud and dead leaves splattered him in the face. He tasted wet earth in his mouth. His fingers tore at the ground in an effort to stop himself slipping backwards.

The pain beat like a hammer in his chest. He felt himself choking a few times and even thought he would black out.

But somehow he kept going.

A great rumble rolled through the earth. He felt it in his hands as he grabbed at the ground. Two further rumbles followed, the sound clapping between the hills.

Gunfire.

The assault on the castle must have begun.

Cormac stalled and stared up the hill. The Mar warriors also slowed their pace, their mouths hanging open and their eyes white with fear.

'Keep going!' Jack shouted. 'The Great Shee will protect us!'

Cormac took a huge breath and bawled out the words in Gaalic. He shook his spear at the enemy ranged somewhere above. Then he charged on up the hill, the other Mar following.

Jack scrambled to keep up. Cormac was already ten feet ahead of him and other warriors were slipping past him to either side.

A dense crackling erupted further up the scarp. Jack spotted dabs of flame blinking through the trees.

Muskets.

The Cattans had muskets.

Bullets shredded twigs, slashed branches, slapped into tree trunks. The ground ahead of him rippled and kicked up leaves and specks of dirt. Flakes of ash spun and whirled as balls whipped past them. A warrior near Jack gave a choking cry and fell. Another doubled over as he caught a bullet in his stomach.

The muskets spluttered again and hailed more balls down into the woods.

Jack struggled on. He had to get up the slope, get in amongst the Cattans. He would kill them, as many as he could, because now it didn't matter if he died, only that he got to the top of this scarp and took as many of the enemy with him as he could.

He heard chimes of steel, shouts, screams, groans. And then he was running out of the trees and up the final approach to the summit. Many of the Mar were already there and battering into a line of Cattans. Men wrestled, swung swords, and lunged with spears or knives. Jack could barely tell which side was which – only the occasional flash of a white skull on a tunic gave him any indication.

A Mar warrior, with blood covering his face, staggered towards him, then fell to the ground. A Cattan lay nearby, grasping at the air and moaning.

Jack paused to gauge the situation. The Cattans had dropped their muskets and now fought with swords and axes. The Mar had only their spears and knives, but they outnumbered the Cattans by two to one. Now that Jack's men had reached the summit they could win this battle.

He heard a roar nearby and spun round in time to see a Cattan swinging a giant axe at him. He ducked and the blade whistled past just above his head. In a fluid movement, he drew the pistol, cocked it and fired, all before the Cattan had regained his balance. The bullet smacked into the Cattan's stomach and a stripe of blood sprayed Jack. The Cattan grunted and gazed at the wound. Then he looked back at Jack and stumbled forward again, his face twisted with rage.

Jack cocked the hammer, the cylinder spinning, and fired again. Flame and smoke jetted from the pistol and the Cattan's chest spat blood. The man staggered backwards, then lurched forward again and collapsed on Jack.

Jack fell back with the man on top of him. He could smell the Cattan's dank hair and the wet-sheep stench of his cloak. The Cattan gargled, coughed blood into Jack's face, tried to rise, couldn't and finally lay still.

Jack heaved the man aside and scrambled back to his feet.

Cormac ran up to him. 'Hurt?'

Jack shook his head. 'I'm all right.'

Swiping the blood from his face, he looked around. The battle was over. About a hundred Mar and Cattans lay on the ground, some squirming in pain, others still. But the remaining Cattans were fleeing into the mist.

How many Mar were left? From a quick look, he thought at least two hundred stood panting on the summit. Not many, but it would have to do.

Several warriors were giving high-pitched cries and pointing down the other side of the hill. It was only now that Jack took a moment to take in the scene. Below him, a gentle slope slid down into the murk. The rest of the valley beyond was clotted with mist, but in the centre, the dark bulk of the castle rose from the hill. In the fog, the building was hallucinatory, the towers and chimneys wavering and uncertain, the shining ash wheeling about it.

An orange flash lit up one side of the castle for a moment. A boom shuddered across the valley. Two further flashes followed in rapid succession. Each glow was blurred by the mist, as if the explosions were underwater.

The battle for the castle's main gate was continuing. Somewhere on the far side of the hill, Rao, Domnall and the others were attacking.

Jack found himself whispering a prayer for them.

A few of the Mar were trying to tend to their wounded comrades. But Jack knew there was no time to waste. The fallen would have to fend for themselves until the battle was over.

He wrenched out the scimitar and shouted, 'To the castle!'

He sprinted down the slope, smashing through thistles and leaping over clumps of gorse, holding the blade above his head as he'd seen Jhala do so many times. That was the way to lead a company. From the front. Scimitar in hand.

The Mar roared and followed him. He heard the beat of their

feet on the ground and the wild cheering from their lips. Soon they'd caught up to him and a few began to inch ahead.

The scaling parties rushed out in front, bearing the long, roughly made ladders beside them. If they got just one ladder up and secure, that was enough. With one ladder and a few men you could create a breach in a fortress's defences.

The Mar swarmed to the bottom of the hill and charged across the valley floor. The castle was no more than half a mile away, being much closer to the hills on this side of the valley. Gunfire flickered behind the towers, silhouetting the tortured metal and stonework. The pounding noise tumbled across the open ground.

A speck of ash flashed in Jack's face and he spat to blow it away. A ripple of pain made him stumble, but he shook his head, growled and pressed on.

The castle wall reared up ahead. It was only around seven hundred yards away now. Jack flicked a look across at Cormac and the tall man grinned back, his eyes feverish.

They were going to make it.

Then a copper flash burst on top of the wall. Jack heard the telltale shriek of a round shot, although he could see nothing through the mist. More flashes shivered along the ramparts. And then the balls came screaming through the murk. They appeared suddenly, swooping down like hawks.

A ball hit the ground ahead of Jack and bounced up over his head. Another slammed into a warrior just along from him. The man's body flew apart in a cloud of red and one of his arms went cartwheeling through the air.

Jack heard wet thumps and cries all about him as men were struck down.

Christ. There were far more guns on this side of the wall than he'd anticipated. Mahajan must have believed Jack's force was larger than it really was. The only consolation was that Rao's troops would be facing an easier battle on the other side of the castle.

The guns continued to flare across the wall. And now specks of fire arced down through the fog.

Shells.

The first explosion ripped open the mist high overhead. Orange flame, with a white heart, punched the dark. Musket balls and fragments whistled through the air. A second shell slapped the ground several yards ahead of Jack and sent up a sheet of fire and earth. The blast pummelled him with hot air, almost knocking him off his feet, and a shell fragment whirled past to his left.

Cormac growled and waved his fist at the enemy.

The shells and round shot howled all around them. Flashes burnt Jack's eyes and powder smoke stung his nostrils. The wound seethed in his chest and his eyes ran as he charged deeper into the globe of sattva encircling the castle.

Darkness rushed over him for a second. He lost his breath, struggled for air, then said a Hail Mary in his head and pulled himself together.

Then Cormac came to an abrupt halt. Jack skidded, flailed his arms and almost smacked into the tall Scot.

Cormac gave a grunt and took a few steps back. Jack squinted through the mist. A shell shattered away to his right, sending streaks of light across the ground. In the momentary glare, he saw a dark form rising up from the earth. It looked something like a fat locust, only it was the size of a cat and made of iron. Its feelers twitched, its mandibles wriggled and it gave a sharp squeal, which was audible even over the din of the battle.

An avatar.

Ahead, the ground rippled and further beasts clambered up from where they'd lain half buried in the earth. There appeared to be hundreds of them.

The closest creature gave a series of clicks and a tiny jet of steam wheezed from its side. Then it tightened its back legs and sprang into the air, trilling as it flew straight for Cormac.

29

Cormac cried out and stumbled back.

Jack tore out the pistol and fired. His shot was better than he'd expected and the bullet smacked the avatar in the middle of its head. With a metallic whine, the creature flew apart. Shards of metal, cogs and springs twisted through the air and rolled across the ground.

But hundreds more avatars squatted ahead.

Christ. Mahajan had laid a trap for them. But there was no turning back now.

Jack tossed the pistol to his left hand and drew the scimitar. Cormac took his spear in both hands and lowered the tip.

'Demons!' Cormac shouted. 'Evil of Mahajan!'

Jack roared as loudly as he could and charged.

Having continued running, many of the Mar were already in amongst the creatures. One man screamed and staggered about, a beast lodged over his face. Another yelled as he tried to brush away avatars clinging to his tunic. A warrior lay still on the ground, two beasts stuck to his head and pulsing as they slurped his blood. The creatures hopped about like fleas, crouching and then springing forward and latching on to their prey.

An avatar launched itself at Jack. He halted, braced himself, swung the scimitar and hacked the beast in half, the blade squealing as it struck the creature's iron cladding.

A beast leapt at Cormac, but he ducked and avoided it. As he straightened, a second sprang towards his stomach. He growled, swung the spear like a staff and batted the creature to the side.

Jack and Cormac fought their way forward, stabbing and hacking any avatars that came near. More and more creatures flew at them, but they kept fending the beasts off.

Then Jack heard the whistle of a shell. He looked up and saw the black ball plummeting towards him. Everything slowed down. A terrible fascination with the missile seized him. It was so close he could make out its sparking fuse and the light playing over its curved surface. For a second he was certain it would hit him. Elizabeth and Katelin and William and Jhala and his parents raced through his head.

He was going to die. There was no avoiding it.

But then the shell thumped into the ground a few yards away, roared and clapped open. A wave of clods and fire pounded him and Cormac. A shell fragment screamed as it struck his scimitar and smashed it into a hundred pieces. He tumbled backwards, hit the ground and was showered with dirt.

He lay stunned for a moment, out of breath and unable to move. Bright spots swam before him and his ears rang. Then he came to his senses and wiped the dust from his face.

Cormac was already standing over him. 'Hurt?'

Jack thought about it. His hand throbbed, but that was only due to being jarred when the scimitar shattered. Otherwise, he seemed uninjured. 'I'm fine.'

Cormac nodded, extended his hand and yanked Jack up. For a moment, darkness reeled about Jack's head and he had to lean against Cormac's arm to support himself. But within a few seconds the faintness passed.

'Problem?' Cormac shouted.

'No problem.'

Jack glanced at the crater left by the shell. Three half-smashed avatars writhed within the churned earth.

He and Cormac were lucky to be alive.

He spun to face the castle walls. The mist twisted in front of his face, but the grim stonework was close enough now for him to see more of the detail. A first wave of Mar warriors had already reached the base of the hill and had begun clambering up.

He glanced back and saw numerous bodies scattered across the ground, surrounded by feeding avatars. A few men still shouted as they staggered about with creatures attached to them. But it looked as though around a hundred men had survived.

That might be enough.

He prayed it was enough.

Looking back at the castle, he realised something else. Although the guns continued to roar on the far side of the building, here they'd stopped. No round shot or shells rained down from the walls. Mahajan's men must be running short of ammunition – they wouldn't have had huge supplies up here in Scotland and probably never expected an attack from such a large force.

'Come on.' He nodded towards the castle. 'Let's get up there.'

He and Cormac ran towards the bottom of the hill, joining the last wave of warriors who'd escaped the avatars. The scarp here was covered in scree that constantly slid away from under their feet. The men scrabbling ahead kicked small stones back in their faces. Jack caught a mouthful of dust and spat it out as he clambered on.

A skirl of pipes swept down from the top of the wall.

And then the muskets started.

Across the ramparts, firearms spluttered and popped, a huge cloud of white smoke pouring down from the wall. Specks of flame jabbed the mist and bullets teemed in the air. Balls rattled and danced on the scree. Stones screamed, hopped and splintered.

Jack heard a crack as a man near him was hit in the head and fell back. A warrior slipped over as a bullet caught his leg.

There was a myriad of tings, snaps, chimes and thuds as the bullets struck metal, wood, flesh and bone. A ball severed the string of an amulet. Another clipped off a man's finger. A third punctured a water skin.

A musket ball pinged off the head of Cormac's spear. The tall man stumbled, growled, regained his footing and pressed on.

Jack looked up. The wall wasn't far now – only around twenty yards away. But the musket fire was so hot he was unsure how many of his men were even going to make it that far.

A bullet whined in his ear. Another tugged his sleeve.

Just a few more yards now.

The first of the Mar were already at the wall and swinging up the makeshift ladders. The warriors rushed up the steps, the wood sagging and juddering as more and more of them clambered up. They were fearless and would have made good skirmishers in the army.

The Cattans grasped the tops of the ladders and tried to heave them away from the wall. They managed to shove one to the side, the Mar warriors shouting as they tumbled to the ground. The Cattans rammed the butts of their muskets against another ladder and forced it away. The ladder toppled backwards, the men flailing their arms and legs as they fell.

Muskets blasted. Mist and smoke whirled around the battlements and radiant ash spun as bullets scythed past.

Jack's breath was short and the air burnt in his lungs. The pain slammed over and over again within his chest.

Just a few more steps.

And then he was there, at the base of the wall.

Cormac charged up one ladder, while Jack scrambled up another. Jack's feet battered the creaking branches and the ladder wobbled and swayed as the men swarmed up. Bullets buzzed about him like bees. The warrior immediately above gasped and jerked his head. Something warm slapped Jack in the face. The man slipped back, swatting at his forehead, and Jack swung out of the way as he fell.

Jack smelt the iron scent of blood and something sticky ran into his eyes. He stopped for a second, wiped his face and saw a steaming mess of brains and specks of skull on his fingers.

But the warrior immediately below was already pressing up against him. Others further down were shouting, obviously anxious to get off the unsteady ladder. Jack scrabbled on up the rungs, pieces of bark coming free in his fingers and splinters catching in his palms.

He was more than two-thirds of the way up. The climb seemed to have taken only a couple of seconds, but it must have been longer. He had a sense of the wall falling away to either side and the ground reeling below, but he had no time to take it in. From a quick glance, he saw further ladders still leaning against the battlements, with men scurrying up like ants. One ladder tottered back as he watched and warriors spiralled to the ground.

Bullets shrieked in his ears. He felt them fingering the air near to him. One passed so close it burnt his cheek.

Shafts of pain coursed through him. Sweat streamed into his eyes. The sattva was so powerful his skin crawled.

At the top of the ladder, the first Mar warrior had reached the parapet. A startled Cattan, caught reloading his musket, fired with the ramrod still jammed in the barrel. The rod impaled the Mar in the head and he fell off the ladder.

But now more men were tumbling over the battlements and engaging the Cattans in hand-to-hand fighting. Jack dragged himself over the top of the wall, swung down to the walkway and skipped out of the way of the warriors scrambling up behind him.

The Mar fought with the Cattans all along the wall. Swords and axes glinted as they arced through the air. The Mar jabbed with spears and knives. Men grunted and roared. The guns stood silent in the midst of the fighting.

To his left, Jack spotted Nectan, the dark-haired Cattan commander, slicing the head of a Mar in half with a longsword.

Nectan. The man who'd captured Saleem. Jack had a score to settle with him. And more than that, the Cattans might waver if he could kill their leader.

He scurried along beside the parapet and went to grab his

pistol. But Nectan seemed to sense his presence, whirled round and swung his blade, his eyes white and bulging. Jack ducked down beside a gun. The sword clanged and spat sparks as it struck the iron piece. The gun rolled back slightly on its block-shaped standing carriage.

Nectan bellowed and leapt over the gun to where Jack was crouching. But Jack circled under the piece, gripping the swirling designs encrusting the surface. The iron was still warm from the earlier firings. He came up on the other side, face to face with the glaring eye of the gun's serpent-head muzzle.

Nectan sliced his sword sideways, but Jack ducked again in plenty of time and the blade whisked over his head. He wrenched out the pistol, stood and fired. The hammer clicked down.

Nothing.

Damn it. A misfire.

Feverishly, he cocked and pulled the trigger again.

Still nothing.

A score of curses tumbled through his head.

Nectan must have understood what had happened because the expression of shock on his face slipped away and was replaced by a broad grin. His crooked teeth crept into view and his eyes narrowed. He lifted his sword with both hands.

Jack tensed his legs, vaulted over the gun and thumped into Nectan's chest. Nectan wheezed, slipped, tried to regain his footing and fell back. Jack landed on top and had his knife out in a second. But Nectan was strong – much stronger than Jack. He gripped Jack's wrist and forced the knife away towards Jack's neck.

Sweat bloomed on Jack's forehead and the pain welled in his chest. The knife edged towards him, the blade glowing softly in the misty light.

Nectan smirked and his bloodshot eyes glinted. Jack could smell the Cattan's rank breath as he panted.

Jack couldn't force Nectan's hand away. He was going to be stabbed if he didn't do something soon.

He leapt back and on to his feet, yanking his hand free. Nectan, no longer pressed down by Jack's bodyweight, barked in Gaalic, sprang up and flew at Jack. Jack swung the knife, but Nectan deftly stuck out his arm and blocked the blow. Nectan lunged forward and slammed the top of his forehead into Jack's face. A bright light flashed in Jack's eyes and the world reeled about him for a moment. Pain pulsed across his nose. He fell back and knocked his head against the battlements.

Nectan grasped Jack's tunic at the neck and punched him hard in the face. A light flashed again. Feebly, Jack lifted the knife, but he felt Nectan prise the weapon from his fingers.

He found he could only see out of one eye – the other was covered by the swelling from where he'd been hit. But he could make out Nectan standing over him with the knife raised, ready to strike.

The shouts and rings of metal from the fight beat in Jack's ears. The tangled scent of powder smoke and sattva, acrid and sweet, mingled in his nostrils. Everything seemed still. Frozen. In the distance he could hear guns booming and thought vaguely that this meant Rao and his men were still facing stiff opposition.

A flake of ash bobbed near Nectan's face, giving his features a greenish hue.

The knife hovered in the air.

This was the end. Jack was certain of that now. Strange. He'd been sure the sattva-fire was going to kill him. Now it was going to be a savage out in the wilds of Scotland.

Nectan jolted. His head separated from his neck and flew into the air. For a second Jack saw the Cattan's startled eyes staring at him as the head tumbled upside down and spun away over the wall.

The headless body slumped against Jack's chest, spraying him with warm, salty blood.

Cormac stood behind the fallen Cattan, wielding a longsword he must have wrested from one of the enemy. Blood speckled his tunic and the blade was smeared with red.

Jack managed a weak grin, shoved aside Nectan's corpse and accepted Cormac's outstretched hand.

Cormac spat at the dead body. 'Evil.'

Jack mopped blood from his face. 'Thanks for that.'

His legs were shaky and he put his hand against the wall to steady himself. He could still only see out of one eye. When he touched his face he felt the swelling engulfing the left side of his head. Looking around, everything seemed strange and unreal. The ghostly ash, pipe-infested turrets, black chimneys and mist were like a vision from some other world. Everything shifted. Nothing was entirely solid.

Jack swallowed as the floor seemed to buck beneath him.

He had to get himself back under control.

Cormac was staring at him and saying something, but he couldn't hear properly. He blinked a few times and finally the words percolated into his head.

'Finish,' Cormac was saying. 'We finish.'

We finish? What did that mean? But as Jack glanced around he immediately understood. The Cattans defending the castle's rear wall were all dead, fatally wounded or had fled.

Only twenty Mar warriors were left standing, and they were bloody and exhausted.

But they'd taken the wall.

'Great Shee help.' Cormac pressed his fist to his chest. 'Great Shee give us strength.'

The warriors congregated about Jack. He looked at their stern faces through his good eye. They were amongst the fiercest fighters he'd ever come across. Their faith in the Great Shee might be naive and simplistic, but it'd been strong enough to inspire them to take a castle with nothing but spears.

These people had amused him with their lack of knowledge of the outside world. But he shouldn't have mocked them. Their bravery humbled him.

Guns grumbled on the far side of the castle, hidden behind

the convoluted buildings. Flickers of orange light wracked the mist above the towers.

They'd won this initial fight, but the main battle was still raging.

'We fight,' Cormac said. 'We win.' A flake of ash sailed near his head and his eyes sparkled in the glow.

Jack paused. Twenty men weren't enough to take on the remaining Cattans. But Rao and the others needed their help. They couldn't turn back now, even if they were going to their deaths.

He nodded. 'We fight. I agree. We'll go along the wall and get to the front of the castle. As we planned.'

Cormac translated and the warriors gave a cheer, raising their spears and the swords they'd taken from the dead Cattans. Cormac lifted the bloody longsword he'd used to hack off Nectan's head.

'But first we have to spike these guns,' Jack said, nodding at the weapons along the wall.

The Mar cheered again and set to work immediately. They hammered metal spikes into the guns' vents to prevent the weapons being fired, just as Jack had taught them to do the previous night.

Meanwhile, Jack retrieved his knife, then fired the pistol in the air a few times. The caps sparked but the damn weapon still didn't work. Was there something wrong with it? Had the powder got wet?

He had no time to find out the problem. Instead, he picked up a musket lying abandoned on the walkway, slipped out the ramrod and prodded it down the barrel to check that the weapon was loaded. He felt the rod jam against a spherical bullet.

Good. He slung the musket over his shoulder and turned back to the Mar, who had now finished with the guns. 'Right, then. Let's go. God's blessing to you all. And God's will in Scotland.'

30

Jack ran along the castle wall, Cormac beside him and the remaining warriors jogging behind. His face still throbbed, but with each step his head seemed to clear, his breathing grew easier and the pain in his chest, while constant, grew less severe. Occasionally black spots spun before him, but he was feeling much stronger than before.

How much longer would he live? Hours? Days?

He put the question out of his mind and concentrated on the row of battlements leading off into the haze.

Keep following dharma, the rightful path. Keep putting one step ahead of the other.

Jhala's words. Why did his thoughts keep returning to Jhala?

Several of the Mar warriors shouted.

Cormac grasped Jack's shoulder and pointed up. 'Look.'

Jack paused and stared. The mist had lifted slightly but it still veiled the castle's walls and towers. At first he saw nothing untoward, but then spotted a globular form floating between two chimneys. He blinked. Had he imagined it?

Then the shape swooped out from a cloud of smoke and he recognised it instantly – the giant metal skull from the bailey.

Flying.

Christ. What was that thing? An avatar?

Jack slipped the musket from his shoulder. The Mar cried out and shook their spears and swords at the head hurtling towards them.

The light from the guns rippled over the skull's black surface.

It opened its jaw slightly to reveal the rusting teeth within. Its eye sockets were dark at first, but then flame roared alight inside the cranium and burst out through its eyes and mouth. It gave a tortured, metallic screech.

'A devil.' Cormac lifted his sword with both hands.

The Mar wailed and cried out prayers. But, to their credit, none of them fled.

Jack pointed the musket at the skull and stared along the sights. Would a bullet stop the thing? He doubted it but there was little else he could do.

He was about to pull the trigger, when the head changed course, swung upwards again and looped away behind the castle, giving a final shriek as it vanished.

Cormac's eyes were wide and his jaw clenched.

'Come on.' Jack lowered the musket. 'We have to keep going.'

Cormac nodded and shouted the command to the Mar. But he kept his eyes trained on the sky as they jogged along.

Jack glanced up a couple of times himself. How dangerous was the skull? Was it a toy to scare the natives or something more powerful? He tried to put these thoughts out of his head as he ran. He had a feeling he was going to find out the answers soon anyway.

He reached the corner where the castle's rear and side walls met. As he turned, he saw the blurred outline of a column of Cattans charging along the ramparts towards him. Someone must have alerted them to the struggle on the rear wall. He stared into the mist. He couldn't gauge the size of the party, but he and his men had to get through the Cattans regardless of how many of them there were.

He took his musket from his shoulder and held it at his side as he ran forward. Cormac loped beside him and the other Mar padded behind.

The party of guards became clearer – there were no more than fifty of them. When they were about sixty yards away, Jack stopped and raised the musket. He only had one bullet, but perhaps a single shot would be enough to startle them and drive them back.

Before he could fire, Cormac grabbed his sleeve and shouted, 'Down!'

Jack squatted with Cormac. He didn't know why at first, but then saw five of the Mar running up from behind with their spears. They skidded to a halt just short of him and hurled their weapons, which corkscrewed through the mist and plunged into the group of Cattans. One smacked a guard in the chest and bowled him over. Another impaled a man in the head and knocked him off the wall.

The Cattans slowed. A few drew their bows and nocked arrows. Meanwhile a second wave of Mar charged up behind Jack and flung their spears. The missiles plummeted at the Cattans and several more men jolted and fell.

Two Cattans fired arrows, but the shots were poor and the missiles sailed past far overhead.

'Now.' Cormac stood, bellowed a war cry and sprinted towards the Cattans, holding aloft his longsword.

Jack leapt up, released the musket's knife and followed, shouting so loudly his throat ached. He heard the Mar cheering as they ran behind him.

The remaining Cattans faltered. They would be unable to see their foe clearly and might believe they were facing more men than they actually were.

Jack shouted more loudly. Cormac lifted his sword high above his head.

A few of the Cattans turned and bolted back the way they'd come. Seeing this, the others followed.

Jack and Cormac ran side by side, shouting until they were hoarse. The Cattans didn't pause or regroup and instead sprinted on towards the front of the castle. The buildings streaked past to Jack's right, the sound of the guns vibrated through his boots and the mist ahead glowed with gunfire. Luminous ash floated everywhere. He reached the tower where he'd hidden overnight in the storeroom, and now the central inner bailey opened up beneath him. He caught a glimpse of the circle of paving stones in the centre of the bailey and the iron, claw-like protuberances rising periodically from the surrounding walls.

The guns that had previously been stationed along this section of the ramparts had been removed. And still no guards came to oppose him and Cormac. And still the Cattans ahead kept fleeing.

It was all too easy.

Then pain fractured his chest. Darkness closed over him. He gritted his teeth, stumbled, tried to continue and collapsed to his knees. Cormac skidded to a halt and came loping back, while the other Mar clustered around him.

The worst of the pain drained away and Jack managed to stand again. 'I'm all right.'

'Wounded?' Cormac asked.

Jack shook his head. 'Forget it. Let's get moving.'

Several warriors pointed up and cried out. When Jack squinted into the sky, he saw the skull was orbiting above them once again. The creature exhaled a globe of fire, which quickly dwindled to black smoke that trailed behind it like drool. It screamed as it roared past, this time flying low enough for Jack to catch the scent of coal and sattva wafting from it. The beast vanished into the mist again as it headed towards the front of the castle.

Jack was strong enough now to continue, and he and Cormac led the way along the wall. They passed more of the giant metal prongs and came to the edge of the bailey. The wall that separated the inner and outer baileys ran off to Jack's right, further metal spikes rising from it at regular intervals. Beyond the wall, he could see the wooden platform and the open space where he'd stood with the other worshippers more than a week ago. The thick pipes squirming over the stonework wheezed. A few Cattans scurried across the ground, but most were up on the walls.

Ahead along the ramparts, spectral in the mist, scores of Cattans laboured over the artillery, sponging the bores, heaving balls into the muzzles and firing. Someone had trained them well and they showed no fear of the 'fire weapons'. The guns bucked, and flame and smoke spewed from the serpent-headed pieces.

Between the guns, banks of Cattans stood firing their muskets over the wall, thick smoke billowing about them and merging with the fog.

And beyond the wall Jack noticed a suggestion of movement. He stopped and stared. Through the fog he made out the outline of thousands of figures – Rao's forces. They'd reached the castle walls, but had clearly found it impossible so far to either batter down the gates or scale the battlements. If they couldn't do either, they would soon be slaughtered. They were easy targets on the hill and hundreds must have already been slain.

Arrows flickered up from the ground and flew over the castle walls. But otherwise Rao's men had no way of returning fire against their opponents.

Cormac and the other Mar were shouting and pointing. At first Jack thought the skull must be returning, but then he saw what had caught their eyes. On the far side of the bailey, a figure stood balancing on top of the battlements, facing out towards the attackers with his arms raised to the heavens.

Jack stared harder. The figure wore a cloak and held a staff in one hand. Arrows stormed about him, but he showed no fear. Occasionally a missile struck, but each time a bronze mantle flashed about him and the arrow bounced away.

Mahajan.

'Demon.' Cormac crossed himself.

The other Mar hissed and muttered prayers.

And now the siddha swung one arm in a circle a few times, pointed at the sky and flung his arm towards the enemy beyond the gates, as if he were hurling something.

A deep groan crossed the sky. The air shivered and the walls vibrated so much that Jack's teeth buzzed. The skull loomed out of the fog like a metal moon and hovered for a moment above the castle. It grated open its maw and gave a screech that made the hair stand up on the back of Jack's neck.

Then the beast dived towards Rao's men. It opened its jaw wider, bellowed and blasted fire from its mouth and eyes. The flames spewed over the ground, tossing up chunks of earth and what Jack was certain were charred bodies.

The skull shot up into the sky again and circled away into the mist. No doubt it would soon be back.

Christ. The beast would decimate Rao's forces.

But Jack had little time to reflect on this. A musket cracked nearby and he heard the whine of a bullet even over the growl of the guns. A handful of guards along the closest section of the outer wall were pointing their muskets at Jack and his men. The fleeing Cattans must have alerted them to the presence of attackers. The muskets coughed, white smoke blossomed and balls whistled through the mist.

'Down here!' Jack leapt behind the battlements that ran along the dividing wall. Thankfully the ramparts had been designed to defend against a force that made it through the main gate and as far as the outer bailey.

Cormac and the others ducked down in a line beside Jack.

The muskets popped again and bullets screamed against the parapet, chipping off fragments and puffing up dust. A few arrows fluttered past, as if pursuing the musket balls.

Christ. What now?

He inched his head around the side of the parapet and looked along the top of the outer wall. Through the streams of mist, he made out the Cattans. They were raising their muskets and bows to fire again. But soon they would realise how few men Jack had with him. Then they were bound to charge along the wall and attack. That would be the end – there was no chance of Jack's small band defeating such a large number of opponents.

'We fight?' Cormac asked.

'Not sure,' Jack shouted back.

He raised his head over the battlements and Cormac joined him. Mahajan still stood on the ramparts with his hands raised, his shield blinking bronze occasionally and flicking away arrows. Shimmering ash hovered about him. He swung one arm around again and the black skull leered out of the clouds. The creature groaned, plummeted towards the Mar and scorched the ground with its fiery breath.

Muskets spluttered again, and Jack and Cormac ducked down as the bullets whistled past. An arrow threaded through an embrasure, hissed past close to Jack's face and shot down into the bailey below.

The guns still thundered and the booms quivered through the stone behind Jack's back.

Pain welled in Jack's chest and darkness clouded his eyes. He shut his eyelids for a second and gritted his teeth against the burning sensation.

As the worst of the pain receded, he opened his eyes to see Cormac staring at him with a grave look on his face.

'I'm all right,' Jack said hurriedly. He adjusted his position, wincing slightly. 'We have to stop the Demon somehow. We can't get to the guns at the moment. But if we kill their leader the Cattans might lose heart.'

'Great Shee will fight Demon,' Cormac said.

'The Great Shee's magic doesn't seem to be working so well at the moment,' Jack muttered.

'I know what to do.'

Jack jumped at the voice suddenly speaking behind him. He swivelled and jolted when he saw Sonali crouching on the walkway.

Sonali? Christ. What was she doing here?

She'd run up somehow without him noticing. She wore a green sari, gathered into pantaloons, and red and gold slippers. Numerous bangles sparkled on her wrists.

The torc still clutched her neck. She was still under Mahajan's power.

'What?' Jack spluttered. 'How?'

Her brow knitted. 'There's no time to explain. You have to do as I say.'

Musket balls rattled against the masonry overhead.

'What are you talking about?' Jack shouted.

'Killing Mahajan,' Sonali said. 'I'm talking about killing Mahajan.'

31

A blast of gunfire lit up Sonali's face for a moment. She raised her hand and pushed back a loose strand of black hair.

Darkness frosted the corners of Jack's eyes. Pain clutched his chest again and he clenched his fist as he fought to overcome it.

Sonali was like a strange vision. She'd appeared out of nowhere and seemed to be talking about things that were impossible. Was she mad? Was she trying to trick him?

Was he even seeing things?

'A shee.' Cormac's mouth hung open and he bowed his head in Sonali's direction.

The rest of the Mar gazed in awe at the brown-skinned, magical woman.

'Come with me,' Sonali said to Jack.

She went to move, but Jack grasped her arm.

'Hold on,' Jack said. 'What's going on?'

She frowned and shook away his hand. 'Listen to me. I'm a siddha.'

'What?'

'A perfected one. A yogin.'

'I know what a siddha is. How can you be one?'

'Mahajan trained me.'

'Mahajan?'

'Yes, and I know how we can kill him. But you need to help me.'

'How?'

'I've learnt the Lightning yantra.'

Jack's mind flickered. A war yantra. Kanvar had shown it to the pupils in the House of Sorcery. 'I've heard of it.'

'I'll attack Mahajan with it.'

'What about his shield?'

'The shield will stop the lightning. But then it'll vanish for a second. Mahajan will be able to rebuild it, but for a second he'll be exposed.'

'What good's that?'

'You can shoot him. With that.' She tapped the musket. 'Can you shoot straight?'

'Christ. I can try.'

Should he believe Sonali? What else could he do?

He waited until a wave of bullets spattered the ramparts, then peered over the edge. Mahajan still stood atop the battlements, swinging his arm to command the skull. How far away was he? Jack tried to gauge the distance. It looked like more than a hundred yards. A musket could shoot that far, but it was hardly accurate. A knife-musket was a weapon for standing in line with your comrades and battering the enemy with round after round. You needed a rifled firearm if you were going to pick off targets at a distance.

He slid back down. 'Let's go over there. In the middle.' He pointed along the dividing wall. 'We'll be closer to Mahajan there.'

Sonali nodded.

'Cattans come!' Cormac had stuck his head around the side of the wall.

Jack shuffled across and looked around. Cattans, waving swords and spears, were running along the outer wall. They must have realised they were facing only a tiny force.

They would be at the dividing wall in minutes.

Jack grasped Cormac's shoulder. 'We're going to fight Mahajan. The shee woman is going to help.'

'Ah.' Cormac faced Sonali and lowered his head. 'Great Shee, Captain Rao, send her.'

'Something like that,' Jack said. 'Now listen. You lot have to hold off the Cattans for a few minutes.'

Cormac straightened his back, even as he remained crouched. 'We do it.'

'Good.' Jack patted Cormac on the shoulder. 'God's grace to you.'

'And you, Jack, friend of Great Shee.'

Jack paused. He wasn't sure that Cormac and the others would survive. There were hundreds of Cattans along the wall. They would easily outnumber the small band of twenty Mar warriors. He thought he should say something more but there was no time.

'Quick.' Sonali tugged at his sleeve.

He pulled away from Cormac and followed Sonali along the wall, staying hunched below the top of the battlements. Sonali's green sari swished about her legs and her slippers pattered against the stone.

Jack thought of Rao for a moment. Was the Captain still alive? And what about Saleem? Was he still trapped in the dungeon?

So much was resting on him and Sonali killing Mahajan. But he didn't even know whether Sonali was telling him the truth. Everything she'd said seemed unreal.

Pain struck him. He almost fell over, but managed to regain his balance before Sonali noticed anything. He paused, looked over the wall, and saw that Mahajan was now directly in front of him on the other side of the bailey.

'Here,' he called to Sonali. He was surprised by how weak and cracked his voice was.

Sonali spun round, charged back and squatted beside him.

Another wave of pain washed over him and he doubled over for a second.

'What's wrong?' Sonali asked.

He gritted his teeth. 'Nothing.'

He heard shouts and the ring of metal behind him. He glanced over his shoulder and saw that the Cattans had reached the dividing wall and set upon the Mar. The warriors were defending their position, swinging their swords and jabbing with their spears, but several had already fallen.

They wouldn't be able to hold back the Cattans for long.

Jack peered at Mahajan. The siddha was swinging his arm and gesturing at Rao's men again. With a booming roar, the skull emerged from the fog, flame licking from its mouth and eye sockets.

'What is that thing?' he asked Sonali. 'The Brahmastra?'

She shook her head. 'The Brahmastra is far more powerful. We have to attack Mahajan now, Jack.'

'You sure this is going to work?'

'The Lightning attack will work. I tried it once before. Mahajan almost killed me when I did that. You sure you can hit him from here?'

Jack paused. He had a clear shot at Mahajan, but the siddha was moving around and the mist obscured the view. His chances were middling at best. 'I'll do it.'

'You'll only have a second. Then the shield will come up again.'

Jack nodded. 'What about the necklace? Won't Mahajan set it to strangle you?'

'Probably.'

'It'll kill you.'

'If you kill him first, maybe it'll stop.'

'You sure?'

'No.'

He heard a cry to his right. A lone Cattan was charging down from the far end of the separating wall, a longsword in his hand.

Christ. Jack hadn't even considered a threat from this direction. The man would reach them in seconds.

He couldn't shoot the Cattan with the musket – if he did that he'd have nothing to fire at Mahajan. With no other option, he stood and drew the knife from his belt.

'No.' Sonali slipped past him and faced the approaching guard.

Jack was about to pull her back, when she closed her eyes and began muttering words he didn't recognise. She held out her arm and lifted her eyelids again.

The Cattan was less than twenty feet from her, his eyes shining and a hungry look on his face.

She screeched as if she were in great pain and powerful sattva pulsed out from her. Dazzling green lightning snarled from her fingertips, pummelled the Cattan in the chest and plucked him off his feet. The man flew back and landed further down the walkway, smoke rising from his dead body.

Sonali slumped forward and held the parapet to support herself. Sweat glistened on her forehead and she panted with exhaustion.

'Are you all right?' Jack said.

She nodded, went to speak, then gasped and clutched at the torc. The metal was sinking into her neck as if the skin were soft dough. She gave a small moan and looked across the bailey.

Jack stared through the mist. He saw that Mahajan had leapt down from the battlements and now stood facing him and Sonali.

'He sensed me use a power.' Sonali's voice was thin. 'Now. We have to do it.'

She leant against the parapet and mouthed the secret words again, wincing as the torc squeezed tighter.

Mahajan raised his arm. With a deafening rumble, the skull descended and hung in the air above him. The metal death's head opened its mouth and grinned, exposing its jagged teeth. Its blank eye sockets bored right into Jack.

'Quick.' Sonali's voice was faint.

Jack leant against the battlements, raised the musket and stared along the sights. Mahajan circled his arm, but his torso remained largely fixed in one position. Jack could still only see out of one eye, but he only needed the one. Sweat popped on his forehead and his heart hummed.

The guns roared, the muskets spluttered, the mist swayed and the ash spiralled over everything.

Sonali held out her arm and gave a muted shriek.

At the same time, Mahajan pointed straight back at her. The skull growled, quivered and then hurtled across the bailey. Mist streamed over the black iron. Flame throbbed alight inside it. Within seconds it would reach Jack and Sonali.

Green lightning blazed from Sonali's finger, snaked across the bailey and thumped into Mahajan. Mahajan tottered backwards. His shield blinked bright bronze and vanished.

The skull howled through the air.

But Jack didn't look up.

He couldn't.

Because now was his one chance to shoot Mahajan.

One second. That was all the time he had.

With his gaze still locked on the sights, he pulled the musket's trigger. The butt kicked into his shoulder and a jet of smoke burst from the barrel and blurred his view.

His heart seemed to stop. Everything went silent.

He dodged to the side to look around the smoke and saw Mahajan still standing on the walkway.

Jack seemed to wait for a long time, long enough for thoughts to flood his mind. Had his shot gone wide? Fallen short?

Then Mahajan jumped and folded backwards against the battlements.

Jack had hit him.

But even as he registered this, the skull swooped down and blotted out the view. For a moment he was face to face with the evil countenance. Then the beast screamed and red flame erupted from its eyes and mouth.

The heat punched Jack in the face. He cried out, leapt towards Sonali and knocked her down below the parapet. The two of them skidded across the walkway as fire boiled over the battlements and hissed across the stone behind them.

The air was so hot it scalded Jack's skin for a second.

He landed beside Sonali and looked back to see the skull roar past and chip off the top of the battlements, before sweeping up into the sky and wheeling around in a wide arc.

He heard a choking sound. Sonali was writhing on the ground and fighting to pull off the torc. Her eyes bulged and tears ran across her cheeks. She tried to speak, but the only sounds she made were gasps.

Christ.

He squatted beside her and tried to work his finger under the necklace. But it was too tight and impossible to grip. He wrenched out his knife and tried to ease it under the torc. But even that proved impossible without cutting into her neck.

She kicked her legs and thrashed about.

Damn it.

He stood and saw Mahajan was lying sprawled on the walkway with a group of his men gathered about him. At first Jack thought the siddha must be dead, but then Mahajan feebly raised one arm.

Should Jack try to shoot him again? With what?

He heard cries from the end of the wall. Cormac and his men were being overwhelmed by the Cattans. They wouldn't be able to hold the attackers back for much longer.

Jack felt a grumble through the stone, looked over the parapet again and saw the skull had circled back and now hovered above Mahajan. The prone siddha gestured limply towards Jack. The skull roared and launched itself across the bailey once more.

No.

Sonali was still lying on the walkway and struggling with the torc, her face red and swelling. He had to get her out of the way or she would be burnt alive. He grasped her shoulders and dragged with all of his remaining strength. She twisted and turned. Perspiration covered her face and her mouth hung open.

The skull gave a piercing shriek.

He looked up in time to see it plunge towards him. The fire glowed into life within it and its mouth opened wider.

Jack's heart smacked in his chest. Blots of darkness swirled about him.

The skull was about to blast him and Sonali. He couldn't get out of the way in time—

Then the flames snuffed out.

The creature changed course slightly and bowled ahead without attacking. Only now it was heading directly for the battlements.

It was going to hit.

With a last surge of strength, Jack hauled Sonali. Blackness washed over him. He could barely breathe. He was certain he would pass out at any moment.

The skull groaned like a foghorn and smacked into the battlements about twenty feet from Jack. The wall shook and he slipped back. Shards of stone shrieked in all directions and dust bloomed. With a metal squeal, the creature ploughed straight through the masonry and careered down into the inner bailey. It pounded the earth, spitting up a geyser of clods, and buried itself so deeply that only the back of its crown poked up from the ground.

Jack sat on the walkway. The world whirled around him. Cathedral bells pealed in his ears. Dust embraced him and shining ash flakes swooped past like comets. Broken stonework lay scattered across the walkway, spreading out from the large gouge left in the wall by the falling skull.

Everything went dark for a moment. But he shook his head and fought off the dizziness.

Sonali.

She was lying next to him, smothered by dust and absolutely still. Her eyes were closed.

Christ. The torc had strangled her.

He rushed to her side and frantically swept the dirt away from her neck. The torc had vanished, leaving only an indentation in her skin.

Then her eyes sprang open and she coughed, wheezed and gasped for breath, as if she'd been drowning. Jack helped her sit

393

up and she coughed and spluttered some more, her whole body shuddering.

Alive. Thank Christ. He quickly crossed himself.

'Mahajan,' she said, her voice hoarse.

Jack understood and thrust his head over the parapet. The siddha lay motionless on the walkway. A group of Cattans stood nearby, their heads lowered and their arms hanging limply at their sides.

Mahajan must be dead.

That explained why the skull had crashed and the torc had vanished. The bullet had killed the siddha just in time.

Jack crouched down again. 'We did it.'

Sonali looked confused.

He clutched her shoulders. 'Mahajan's dead.'

She touched her neck, stroked the liberated skin with her finger and a slight smile crept across her lips.

Cormac burst through the mist and clouds of dust, leaping over chunks of shattered masonry. He skidded to a halt, squatted and grasped Jack's arm. 'You live.'

'Yes, we live,' Jack said.

Sonali coughed a few more times and wiped her mouth with her hand.

Cormac bowed his head and spoke softly. 'Great Shee woman. I have seen the lightning from your hand. You are as great as the great Captain Rao. You have struck down Demon.' He raised his head and looked at Jack. 'And you too. With fire weapon. I see.'

'We all did our best.' Jack raised himself, pain still lancing his chest.

Five Mar warriors jogged along the wall and came to a halt behind Cormac. Blood smeared their clothes and speckled their faces. A few had gashes on their arms and legs. They were clearly the only survivors from the party Jack had led into the castle. And yet they smiled broadly, their eyes shining.

The guns and muskets had fallen silent. A hush seemed to

blanket everything. Several Cattans still stared at Mahajan's fallen body, but others were now fleeing along the ramparts or charging down the stairs. Cattans ran across the inner and outer baileys, shouting, but seemingly unable to organise themselves to resist the attackers any longer. Without their leader, they seemed to have lost the will to fight.

Jack thought he could hear the faint cheering of the horde of warriors beyond the castle walls.

Then the stone beneath him jolted and a grumble emanated from the earth. The wall rocked and he had to grasp the parapet to steady himself.

It felt like an earthquake. He'd been in one years ago in the Napoli Caliphate.

The Cattans shouted and charged about in all directions.

Cormac frowned. 'Demon. Magic still here.'

'No.' Sonali raised herself to her feet. 'The castle's held together by Mahajan's power. Now he's dead it'll fall apart.'

With a shrill squeal, one of the prongs on the side of the inner bailey buckled inwards, as if being crushed by a gigantic hand. The ground rolled and the roaring sound grew louder. A chimney swayed and toppled over. Falling stones and pipes splattered over the lower buildings and dashed across the bailey.

Sonali leant against the wall, too weak to stand unaided. Sweat and dirt streaked her face and she swallowed repeatedly as though she were about to throw up. Using a power could exhaust a person at the best of times. On top of that she'd almost been strangled.

'We have to get out of here,' she said, her voice rasping. 'The whole place will collapse.'

Jack agreed but there were two things he still had to do. 'You go. I'll send some of the Mar with you.'

Sonali frowned. 'We all have to go.'

'My friends are still in the dungeon.'

'I'll help you get them.'

'You're in no fit state to do that.' This was true, but also, after

395

freeing Saleem, he meant to get into Mahajan's workshop and destroy the Brahmastra. He didn't want Sonali following him into the catacombs while the castle was falling apart.

The ground heaved, as if a wave had passed beneath it. Steam shrieked from numerous pipes as they split open.

Sonali clung to the wall and looked as though she would faint for a moment. Finally, she nodded weakly. 'All right.'

'Good.' Jack patted her on the arm. 'You're free now.' He turned to Cormac. 'Tell three warriors to go with the shee woman. They must go to the back of the castle and get down the ladders. They have to tell Domnall and the others to move right away from the castle.'

Cormac nodded and barked this command to the warriors. Then three of the Mar assisted Sonali as she limped away along the dividing wall.

The ground surged and rumbled. Jack grasped the parapet, as if he were on a boat in a stormy sea. On the other side of the inner bailey a building cracked, tumbled down and puffed out a wide skirt of dust.

'You and the others come with me,' he said to Cormac. 'There's one last thing I need your help with.'

Jack ran along the edge of the inner bailey, Cormac at his side and the two remaining Mar warriors bounding behind. The tower that housed the dungeon loomed ahead. Thank God it was still standing, but how many Cattans were in there?

He spotted two dead guards – who appeared to have been killed by falling masonry – and stopped to grab a musket lying beside one of them. The earth grumbled and tilted. Above him, an iron prong creaked and plunged towards the bailey. He dashed out of the way as the contorted metal smashed across the ground.

He stumbled on to the tower. With Cormac and the others

behind him, he kicked open the door and found the room beyond deserted. He clicked out the musket's knife and headed for the staircase. The building shuddered and the ground rolled wildly. Cracks forked across the ceiling and chunks of stone fell. He staggered to the top of the steps and looked down. The stairwell was pitch black and dust floated up from below.

Cormac and the others skidded over to him and stared down into the depths. Jack noted the looks of concern on their faces.

'I'll go down,' he said. 'You wait here.'

'No,' Cormac said. 'We come.'

Jack nodded, slung the musket over his shoulder and grasped a torch from a sconce. He held the dancing flames ahead of him as he plunged into the dust-filled gloom. His chest throbbed and he felt light-headed. He had to keep blinking and shaking his head to stop himself passing out.

How much longer did he have to live?

The floor lurched and groaned. Cracks fanned across the wall and dust showered him. The torch sputtered and almost went out for a moment. He coughed as the grit clogged his lungs, but he pressed on regardless.

From deep in the earth came the continuous roar of rocks grinding together.

Would the building stay standing long enough for him to find Saleem? He whispered a Hail Mary. Please let him save the boy.

He jumped and recoiled when he almost stood on a hand. A dead Cattan, partially buried by fallen masonry, lay on the stairs. Jack edged past, clattered on down the steps and finally reached the dungeon.

The room was in complete darkness. He swept the torch about him and saw another dead Cattan, scattered stones and a broken chair. He paced further into the chamber, the torch spitting and hissing as he swished it.

And then he stopped.

The ceiling above the far end of the room had caved in

completely. There was nothing but a wall of rubble and rock where Saleem's cell had been.

No.

Cormac ran up behind him. 'Where friend?'

Jack pointed at the rubble. 'They were over there.'

'Ah.' Cormac stood up straighter and shifted his grip on his sword.

'We have to find them.' Jack waved the torch in front of him. 'Saleem!'

Silence.

'Saleem!' he shouted again.

The ground shifted beneath his feet and he had to hold out his arms to steady himself. A piece of stone slapped the ground nearby and shattered. Dust puffed in his face. One of the Mar slipped over and fell on his backside.

'We go.' Cormac grasped Jack's shoulder. 'Dangerous.'

'I can't leave them,' Jack shouted. 'You lot go.'

He ignored Cormac's further entreaties, charged across the room and swung the torch about, searching for a way through the rubble.

Cormac ran across and grasped his tunic. 'We go!'

A wave passed through the ground, lifting Jack up at least a foot, and then dashing him down again. The paving stones squealed as they cracked and splintered. Jack lost his footing and grasped at the rubble to keep himself upright.

'I'm not going!' Jack shouted back at Cormac. 'You go. Now!'

Then he heard a cry from within the fallen stones. It was faint, and only just audible over the background roaring in earth. But it was someone's voice, without a doubt.

'Saleem!' Jack shouted.

Faintly, he heard the voice calling back, saying one word repeatedly: 'Jack.'

Christ. Saleem. Had to be.

He thrust the torch above his head and in the sputtering glow saw there was a small gap at the top of the mound. He jammed the torch between two slabs so that it jutted out and provided light. Then he clambered up, grasped some stones and wrenched them free. Cormac put away his sword and climbed up beside Jack. They both scraped away rubble until there was enough space to crawl through.

The ground bucked again and some of the stones shifted. A huge slab smacked on to the ground.

Cormac frowned at Jack. 'Dangerous.'

But Jack grabbed the torch and handed it to Cormac. 'Hold that up.'

In the light cast by the flames, he dragged himself up the pile of stones, scrambled over the top and found himself in a circular area, about ten feet across, where the ceiling had held. The broken stonework enclosed this space on all sides, but this one spot was mostly clear. He could see little in the dim light at first, but then Cormac climbed up to the gap and pushed the torch through. A yellow glow flooded the small area.

And there, crouching in a corner, clothes torn and face covered in dirt, was Saleem.

The lad's haunted face suddenly split into a smile. 'Jack.'

Jack rushed across, grasped Saleem and hugged him. A Hail Mary tumbled through his head. Thank God the lad was alive. He never would have forgiven himself if Saleem had died.

Blinking away a tear, Jack stood back. 'Are you hurt?'

'Not really. But I'm stuck.' Saleem tugged at a chain secured about his ankle. The end of the chain disappeared under the rubble.

Jack nodded. 'Where are Parihar and the others?'

Saleem's smile evaporated. He pointed behind Jack and his voice was croaky as he said, 'There.'

Jack spun round and saw Parihar and the two Saxons lying half protruding from the stonework. Cormac was squeezing over the top of the rubble, dislodging dust and small stones. He held the torch in one hand, and in the trembling light Jack saw that the faces of the three bodies were as still and grey as the stone that partially covered them.

He ran across and crouched beside Parihar. The Lieutenant's features were twisted and his mouth hung open as if he were about to cry out. His legs and abdomen were crushed beneath the stone. Even before Jack checked for a pulse, he knew Parihar was dead. The two Saxons had also been killed – the side of one man's head had been smashed by a rock, while the other was so buried beneath the rubble only his arm and part of his face were visible.

Cormac scrambled down beside Jack, looked solemnly at the corpses and crossed himself.

Jack stood up. 'Let's get Saleem free.'

They crossed over to the lad, who was pulling futilely at the chain. Cormac gently pushed Saleem aside, grabbed a chunk of masonry, swung it above his head and slammed it down on the chain. The metal rang and the paving stones on the floor gave a hollow crack, but the chain remained unbroken. Jack grasped a smaller rock and followed suit. He and Cormac bashed over and over again at the chain, but it still held firm.

'Hold on,' Jack said.

He stepped back a few paces, grasped the musket and fired at the chain. The metal splintered and Saleem sprang free, a grin on his face.

Then a growl trembled in the earth, the ground swayed and rubble rolled down the slopes. Dust swamped the enclosed space.

'Go.' Jack waved towards the gap at the top of the stones. 'Quickly.'

Saleem went first, Cormac helping him up from behind. Jack motioned for Cormac to follow, but the tall Scot shook his head, grabbed Jack's arm and pushed him up the slope. Jack scrambled over the top and dropped down to the other side where Saleem and the two warriors were waiting. Cormac followed, dust covering every inch of him and even collecting in his beard.

'Out!' Jack shouted. 'Now.'

They all charged to the stairwell. The ground rocked three times as they made their way up. Saleem slipped but Jack caught him and hurried him on.

Then they were at the top of the steps and rushing across the foyer, out of the door and into the bailey. The ground seethed. The perimeter walls had already cracked in many places and chunks of stone tumbled down. A piece of the battlements thumped into the earth near Jack. The metal spikes surrounding the bailey had either fallen or been crushed.

The only Cattans Jack could see were lying dead on the ground.

Cormac stared about him, eyes wide and shining. He pointed to the steps up to the battlements. 'We go.'

'You lot go,' Jack said. 'I've got one last thing to do.'

Cormac frowned. 'We come with you.'

Jack shook his head. He didn't want anyone following him into the bowels of the castle – it was too risky. He, on the other hand, would be dead soon anyway. 'No. Just me. The rest of you get out.'

'What are you talking about?' Saleem shouted.

Jack felt light-headed and pain swamped him. He staggered and would have fallen if Cormac hadn't rushed to his side and supported him. His vision swam. The moving ground, shifting walls, glowing ash and whirling steam all made him faint. He felt as though he were in a fever dream.

He swallowed, pulled away from Cormac and managed to stand upright. 'Listen.' His voice was faint and hoarse. 'There's something I have to do and only I can do it. I might not make it. You lot must go now while you can.'

Cormac spoke quickly to the other Mar, then turned back to Jack. 'Warriors will go. I come.'

Christ. Jack didn't have time for this. 'No. You have to get out. Get a message to Rao and tell him I've gone to do what we agreed.'

Cormac's frown darkened. 'Agreed?'

'Yes.' Jack struggled for breath. Just talking was draining his strength. 'It's an important message. You must go now and tell him. In case I don't make it.'

Cormac bowed his head slightly. 'Will do as you ask. Will take message to Great Shee.'

'But I won't,' Saleem said. 'I'm coming with you, wherever you're going.'

Jack stumbled a little, then regained his balance. Saleem's face whirled before him. Everything seemed strangely dark, as if he were looking through green-stained glass. 'No. Go.'

Saleem shook his head. 'I ran away in Wiltshire. I won't do that now.'

Jack blinked and fought to stay conscious. He knew how determined Saleem could be. The lad would probably follow him no matter what he said.

Jack nodded and said in a cracked voice, 'All right. If you must.'

32

Steam shrieked from burst valves. Jack and Saleem clambered through the jungle of broken pipes criss-crossing the passage. The ground listed and tossed the two of them against the warm tubes. The earth grumbled constantly, the vibration passing through every piece of metal and stone.

'What are you looking for?' Saleem shouted.

Jack peered ahead through the clouds of steam. 'There's something I need to do.'

'What?'

'You'll see.'

He ducked under a vent and stumbled on down the corridor. As in the upper levels of the castle, there were no Cattans. The guards had all either died or fled. He and Saleem had been able to make their way through the catacombs without any trouble. They would have reached Mahajan's workshop already, in fact, if Jack hadn't been so weak.

The ground heaved, bashing Jack and Saleem first to one side of the hall, then the other. Rivets popped and new jets of steam screeched out. The ceiling cracked and a torrent of earth fell to the floor. Slick with sweat and covered in dirt, Jack battled on along the corridor.

He reached the entrance to the hallway that lead to the workshop, pushed aside a knot of pipes and then froze. Ahead, a dark metal form blocked the passage. At first he didn't realise what it was, but then he made out a jaw, teeth and an empty eye socket.

Mahajan's demon skull.

The thing had hit the bailey with such force it had burrowed all the way through to the catacombs. Now it was pressed face down as if trying to bite the floor. A thicket of twisted pipes hung from where it had punched through the ceiling.

'What is that?' Saleem asked.

'Some kind of avatar. As far as I know.'

The floor shuddered and the creature's maw squealed open, then clanged shut. Jack was certain this movement was due to the earth shifting. But then, after the quake passed, the beast ground its jaw open and closed again a few times.

Damn it. There seemed to be some sort of life left in the creature, its mouth working like the spasms of a dying insect.

He approached the trapped beast, holding on to smashed pipes for support. Blots of darkness bled across his eyes. The roaring in the earth was growing louder all the time.

With a rusty grating sound, the skull chomped on the air. The great teeth clamped shut, then squeaked apart, then clamped shut again. The movements were unpredictable. Sometimes the maw would be still for several seconds, other times it chewed constantly.

How to get through? There was no way to squeeze around the skull – it was obstructing the hall completely. When the mouth was open, they would be able to crawl through to the other side, but would risk being bitten in half. He recalled the thing's fiery breath as well. The last place he wanted to be was inside that maw.

'What now?' Saleem asked.

'We have to get through somehow.'

Saleem stared at the grinding creature and chewed his lip. 'Is there another way?'

'Not as far as I know.' Sonali had said this was the only route to the workshop. She'd been clear about that.

The earth rose and threw Jack against the wall. A shaft of pain impaled his chest. It was so fierce it drove the air from his lungs. He slipped to the floor and darkness smothered him. He struggled to stay conscious, but he was floating away.

'Jack!'

He heard a voice calling to him from far away.

'Jack!'

It came again. He recognised it, but couldn't place it.

What did it matter anyway? The last thing he remembered was lying on the floor in the underground passage, pain stabbing him. He must be dead. Was the voice an angel calling to him? Was it Katelin?

Katelin.

He saw her as she'd been just before she died, lying in bed, sweat gleaming on her face, her hair so wet it stuck to her scalp, her skin so pale he could see the blue veins clearly beneath.

Was he going to see her again? After all these years?

'Jack!'

No, that voice wasn't Katelin's. He heard the rising grumble of the earth all around him. He heard the hissing steam.

And now he knew who the voice belonged to – Saleem.

He lifted his eyelids and saw, through his good eye, the lad crouching beside him.

A frown crumpled Saleem's forehead and his eyes were wide and glassy. 'Allah is great. I thought you were dead.'

'So did I.' Jack sat up and winced at the pain boiling in his chest.

'You can't go on.'

'I have to.'

'We need to go back.'

'No.' Jack grimaced as a pulse of pain passed through him. 'You go. I have to get to the end of this corridor. It's near. Just up there.'

'What is?'

'A weapon. Mahajan was building it.'

'The Grail? Is that it?'

'No. It's something evil. I have to destroy it.'

'Won't it be crushed when this place comes down?'

'Don't know. I have to be sure. Make sure no one can ever

405

find it.' Jack tried to stand, but his legs wobbled and he sat back down again. 'Look, I'm dying. I haven't got long now. You have to go.'

Saleem shook his head. 'I said I'd stay with you, so that's what I'm going to do. Since the rebellion started I wanted to be a knight. A knight wouldn't leave.'

Jack tried to protest, but the pain pinned him back against the wall and black spots circled him like crows.

Saleem stood up and approached the skull. The jaw still creaked open and closed.

Jack blinked. What was the boy up to? He watched as Saleem searched the ground and finally picked up a five-foot-long metal strut that must have fallen from the wall. A puff of steam obscured the lad for a moment, and then Jack's worst fears were confirmed when he saw Saleem holding the pole horizontally. The idiot was going to try to jam the strut into the skull's mouth to hold it open. But to do that, he was going to have to stick his head and chest inside and risk being crushed to death.

Jack tried to move. He had to stop Saleem – the fool would kill himself. But he couldn't get up. When he tried to shout, only a thin groan passed his lips.

Saleem steadied himself as the ground shook and then stood poised, waiting for the right moment.

The rusting teeth slammed down, stayed still for a second, then clanged up. Saleem went to lean inside, but then the mouth snapped down again and he jumped back. It was impossible for him to time his move with the jaw crunching at irregular intervals.

Creak-bam. Creak-bam.

Saleem waited. Went to move. Pulled back. Waited some more.

Jack managed to crawl forward a few feet. He had to move faster. Damn his illness. Damn the cursed fire burning in his chest. If he could just—

Then Saleem did it. When the mouth was open at its widest, he stuck his head inside and rammed the bar into position. The jaw went to close, but ground against the strut. The skull whirred and squealed, but the pole held firm.

Jack sank back against the wall and breathed out, almost fainting with relief.

Saleem scrambled over to him. 'We're going through.'

Saleem half lifted, half dragged Jack over to the skull. By the time they got there, Jack was feeling strong enough to crawl between the teeth. The inside of the maw smelt of soot and the roaring in the earth echoed like the sea. It was unnerving to hear the mouth scraping against the pole as it tried to close. But he and Saleem made it safely to the other side and clambered out.

Jack managed to stand and Saleem supported him as he limped towards the workshop. The earth reeled repeatedly and both of them were thrown against one wall and then the other. Jack collapsed several times and Saleem had to drag him some of the way. Stone and dust trickled down as the ceiling fractured.

The scent of sattva grew stronger. Jack's eyes ran, his nose started to bleed and the insides of his ears stung. The sattva was a physical weight pressing on him from all directions.

They reached the chamber at the end of the passage, stumbled through the archway on the far side and came to the wide hall, which was still lit by a silvery glow. Through a flurry of steam, Jack could just make out the steel doors to Mahajan's chamber. They were shut but at least there were no guards around.

Jack staggered ahead, his arm still around Saleem's neck. The ground rolled, stone smashed on the floor and new jets of steam screeched.

The sattva rolled about Jack, almost knocking him over. He had to force himself forward as if through water. His skin felt hot.

Saleem coughed and wiped his eyes – even he was finding the sattva overwhelming.

And then they were at the doors. Jack swayed and darkness smothered him for a moment. Sonali had said Mahajan's power kept the doors sealed, but perhaps they would open now that the siddha was dead. He had no idea what he would do if they didn't.

He reached out and pushed against the steel. The metal felt cold, almost freezing, against his palm.

The door clicked and swung gently inwards.

Thank God. Jack said a quick Hail Mary in his head.

This was it. He was finally going to find out what Mahajan had been working on for years up in the Scottish wilderness.

He limped through the open door, Saleem still at his side.

And then he stopped suddenly.

Sattva blasted him like a powerful wind. His hair fluttered behind his head and his eyes watered. His skin felt stretched and rubbed raw.

Saleem cried out and put one arm up over his face. 'Poison.'

'No.' Jack's voice was cracked. 'It's just sattva.' But he wasn't certain how harmless it truly was.

Blinking, he looked around the chamber. It was less imposing than he'd expected. The ceiling was low, only a foot or so above his head, and the shape was octagonal. The entire room was perhaps fifty feet across. Eight thick pipes, entwined with wires, ran down each of the walls, crossed the floor and melded into a central circular platform that was topped by a sheet of shining steel.

On one side of the room stood a wooden desk, strewn with papers, pens and a few ink pots. Five sculpted slabs of marble lay beside the walls at various points.

It didn't look like a workshop at all.

Was this all there was? Where was the Brahmastra? He'd expected to see some sort of huge device capable of laying waste to towns and cities.

His legs buckled and he sank to his knees. Pain swirled within him and flickered down his left arm. He'd experienced this before, when he'd almost died in London three years ago. He must be near to death now. He could barely move.

Saleem crouched beside him. 'Where's the weapon?'

Jack struggled to speak. 'Don't know. Need to search.'

He grasped Saleem's arm and used it to wrench himself upright. The pain thumped over and over again in his chest.

He glanced at the marble block nearby and now noticed it was a tomb. The top of the slab was carved into the likeness of a knight lying on his back with a sword at his side. Despite the stone being worn smooth by the years, Jack made out armour and what looked like a crown on the figure's head.

A crown.

Of course. He stared at the other four tombs scattered around the edge of the room. All of them were topped by similar carved figures.

Kings.

This really must have been where the Scots placed their dead rulers. Mahajan must have come across these tombs when he was building the catacombs and decided to keep them.

The room swayed and a fissure split the ceiling. Grit and stone fragments flushed down. Jack wiped dust from his eyes.

They had to move quickly. The whole place could collapse at any moment. And yet when he tried to walk he could manage only a painfully slow limp.

Saleem supported him as he hobbled towards the desk. He sensed fluctuations in the sattva. Instead of moving in a uniform pool, he was passing through patches that were slightly stronger and then slightly weaker. It was barely noticeable, but with his special sensitivity he could detect it.

He was walking through successive sattva streams, all of which rushed and swirled towards the centre of the room.

A realisation crept into his mind. This workshop, whatever it was, was a meeting point of numerous streams. They must tumble across the land and collide here. That was the only explanation.

Darkness washed over him. Pain hammered like a second heartbeat in his chest. He fell forward, but he was close enough to the desk now to lean against it and stop himself slipping to the floor.

He panted, tried to catch his breath. Slowly the darkness slid back enough for him to make out several large sheets of paper and a few journals.

'What is all that?' Saleem asked.

Jack shook his head. 'Can't read it. Check the drawers.'

Saleem scurried around to the other side of the desk and pulled open each of the drawers in turn. He shook his head. 'Nothing.'

Damn it.

Jack leant over the table. A drop of sweat ran off his forehead and splattered on one of the sheets. The darkness came and went.

Nothing.

No sign of the Brahmastra.

He managed to push himself upright again and scanned the room. The walls were bare, save for the eight pipes, while the floor and ceiling had no markings on them of any sort. Aside from the tombs and the desk, the only thing in the room was the raised platform, and he could see that was empty.

Nothing.

Jack managed a wry grin. It looked as though Mahajan hadn't built a Brahmastra at all. It looked as though he hadn't even tried. There was nothing in the room – no devices, machines, avatars. Mahajan must have been bluffing, although why was anyone's guess.

All Jack could think to do was take a look at the platform. He doubted it could help him, but it was the only thing left in the room that he hadn't checked yet. Once he'd cast his eyes over it he would know the Brahmastra wasn't here. Never had been.

And then, if God wanted to take him, so be it.

He staggered towards the centre of the room. Saleem rushed around the desk and supported him as he limped. The earth throbbed and groaned. A crack forked across the stone floor. One of the eight pipes fractured and steam screamed from the hole.

Jack sensed he'd stopped breathing. He felt he was falling. But at the same time, somehow, he was still walking. One step at a time. Towards the middle of the room.

The sattva swilled about him. The skin on his face stretched and his scalp crawled. He was nearing the convergence point. The place where the streams met.

He reached the platform, Saleem still propping him up. Everything went black. He was flying for a moment. Then he blinked and pulled himself back.

And then he saw it.

Etched across the metal sheet was the figure of a turbaned siddha holding aloft what looked like a misshapen foetus. Jack recognised it instantly. It was the image the Rajthanans placed on their devices for creating avatars. He'd seen one a few days earlier in the catacombs. But this was much larger, given that the metal plate was at least fifteen feet across.

Why was this image here?

He sensed himself falling again. He realised he hadn't taken a breath for a long time.

He slumped towards the platform and felt the powerful streams washing over him. He was sinking into the blistering point where the streams collided.

Before the darkness passed over him entirely he found himself thinking about the metal claws that surrounded the inner bailey. They'd always reminded him of something and now he knew what – the spikes that encircled the Rajthanans' devices for creating avatars. Only far larger.

And as he fell further, he realised something else. The platform before him was somewhere under the inner bailey and the central circle of paving stones. What if it were directly beneath those stones? That would mean it was in the middle of the bailey. In the middle of the giant prongs.

Of course.

The whole castle was a device for creating avatars. Or creating one vast avatar.

A devastating war avatar?

The Brahmastra?

But he had no time to consider this further as the darkness was rushing over him.

Dimly, from far away, he felt his face smack the ice-cold steel sheet. The powerful sattva streamed over him. He was lying right in the middle of it.

In the middle of Mahajan's machine.

But that meant little to him now. He was fading. He was certain of that. He thought of Katelin again, saw her lying on her deathbed. She reached up to touch his face and her fingers were like wisps of smoke.

Then, as his mind blinked out, it ran through a series of flashing images and memories, including, in quick succession all the yantras he'd ever learnt. They flickered and bounced in the pool of his mind.

Before even these were gone completely.

———◆———

He opened his eyes. He could breathe freely. He took a deeper breath and then an even deeper one. The pain in his chest and arm had gone. He felt strong again.

He sat up.

Saleem yelped and jumped back, eyes wide. 'I thought . . . you . . .'

'So did I.' Jack flexed his fingers, sensing the sattva swarm over him, his skin rippling.

He was better. The injury in his chest had gone completely and the sattva-fire had vanished. He was free from the wound for the first time in twelve years.

And he knew how it had happened. The knowledge was lodged in his mind as if it had always been there. The Great Health yantra – the healing yantra Kanvar had given him – had finally worked. Somehow, as he'd lain dying, he'd recovered his ability to subvert the law of karma and learn a new yantra. His mind had then instinctively smelted sattva and activated the power.

Somehow he'd done it, just as he'd done it three years ago in London. But he still had no idea how.

The earth rolled and a deep pounding and grinding reverberated throughout the chamber. A further crack snarled across the ceiling and dust and splinters of stone gushed down.

'We have to go.' Saleem dragged at Jack's arm.

Jack leapt up. He no longer needed any help from Saleem. He could move as freely as if he were twenty years old again.

But Saleem was right – they had to go. However, he wasn't going to leave Mahajan's papers behind. Mahajan's experiments were still a mystery and he wanted some answers. If it turned out the writings contained something evil, he would make sure they were destroyed.

He charged across to the desk and swept up the papers. The ground rocked and he lost his footing. Slabs of stone fell and smashed across the floor.

'What are you doing?' Saleem shouted over the deafening roar.

Jack scrambled back to his feet and grasped a couple of pages that had slipped from his hands. He nodded to the floor where five folios lay fallen beside the desk. 'Get those. We might still need them.'

Saleem charged across, skidded as the ground bucked again, and grabbed the books.

'Let's go!' Jack ran out of the room, through the steel doors and into the hallway, which was now riddled with fissures. He and Saleem raced through the clouds of scalding steam, the moisture smothering their skin and clothes.

They reached the archway and then the smaller passage beyond. The skull still blocked the hall, its jaw grinding against the pole. Jack paused beside the beast. He and Saleem would have to climb through again and hope the strut didn't slip as the earth shifted.

He glanced at Saleem. The lad's eyes were popping out of his head, but he still gave Jack a firm nod.

They clambered through the maw, Jack going first, with Saleem right behind. The jaw gnashed feverishly but the strut held firm.

They reached the other side and charged on through the catacombs, scrambling through the forest of fallen pipes. They reached the steps to ground level, sprinted up and ran across the inner bailey. The surrounding walls swayed alarmingly. Many towers had fallen and sprayed the ground with rubble.

They made it to the other side of the bailey, went down the dark hall and through the doors at the end. They stumbled into the outer bailey. Slabs of broken stone, lumps of wood and Cattan corpses littered the ground. Jack glanced up at the battlements and saw Mahajan's body lying where it had fallen. On the far side of the bailey, the gates hung askew, leaving a narrow opening to the outside.

They'd almost made it.

With the papers still under his arm, Jack sprinted towards the gatehouse. Stones flew about him and glowing ash flickered in his face. The ground continually rolled. He lost his footing a few times, fell and scrambled back up again. Saleem was beside him the whole way, panting heavily, his eyes shining brilliant white.

To Jack's left there was a giant rumble and a section of the outer wall dropped like a curtain released from a rail. With a colossal bang, the masonry slammed into the earth and spat up stone and dust. A large rock whirled towards Jack, but he and Saleem ducked out of the way in time.

They scrambled on towards the gate.

They were almost there. Just a few more yards remained.

The ground rippled like water. They fell, got up, fell again and then finally reached the gates. Saleem pushed himself through the gap, followed by Jack. They charged down the passage beneath the gatehouse and over the fallen portcullis.

And then they were outside the walls and skidding and slipping down the hill. One of Mahajan's papers flew from Jack's hand, but he let it twist away on the wind. Behind him, he heard the shrieks, roars, squeals and booms of the castle disintegrating. But he didn't stop to look back. He had to get as far away from those walls as he could.

Through the last strands of thinning mist, he saw figures spread out across the valley floor. He stalled. Were they Cattans?

Then someone shouted, 'Jack!'

A man came running up the path towards him.

'Jack!' the figure shouted again.

It was Rao.

The Captain's face was streaked with dirt and his tunic was stained. His trousers were ripped and there was a shallow gash in his right thigh, but otherwise he appeared unhurt.

He beamed and threw his arms about Jack.

Jack hugged him, patting him on the back. He couldn't help smiling. Thank God Rao had survived. The Captain deserved to survive.

Over Rao's shoulder he made out other figures in the crowd now – Cormac and several of the Mar warriors from the village. Sonali stood to one side, wrapped in a blanket.

Jack said a Hail Mary in his head and thanked God so many had lived. He'd been sure at times they were all going to end up dead.

An enormous groan shuddered through the earth. Cormac and several of the Mar were pointing up at the castle. Jack let go of Rao and looked back.

The gatehouse had collapsed and now the surrounding wall was tumbling backwards into the bailey. There was a series of booms, and dust and stone jetted into the sky. Then the remaining walls and towers began crumpling inwards, as if the entire castle were being crushed by a giant fist. Blasts shook the hill, and plumes of fire and smoke shot up. Gleaming ash wove overhead. Stone and metal shrieked and buckled.

There was a final, enormous explosion which sent up a ball of veined fire so hot it warmed Jack's face even as he stood at the bottom of the hill.

The Mar behind him gasped and several ducked, although there was no need.

As the smoke drifted away, Jack saw there was nothing but a trace of rubble where the castle had once been.

PART SIX

33

Jack picked his way around the edge of the rubble, stepping over lumps of stone, scraps of twisted iron, chunks of burnt wood. He stopped when Sonali halted beside him. A cold wind tugged at his hair and he shivered slightly, despite his cloak.

He looked towards the centre of what had once been the castle. The mist had cleared hours earlier, but the sky was still thick with black cloud and the dull light gave everything a mysterious sheen. He could make out where the outer walls had been, and could roughly gauge where the inner bailey must have stood. But little of the castle remained. What flotsam and jetsam there was didn't seem to be enough. It was as though much of the stone and metal had been sucked down into the earth.

'Strange how there's so little of it left,' he said.

Sonali nodded and hugged her cloak tighter. 'The castle was mostly made of Mahajan's powers.'

'He must have been a great siddha. A mahasiddha.'

'I suppose you could say that.' Sonali stared impassively at the ruins.

Jack stepped up on to a broken slab. 'That must have been the centre of the castle there.' He pointed to the middle of the rear section of the ruins, which had sunk into a shallow crater.

Sonali nodded.

He stepped back down and turned to her. 'What was it?'

'What?'

'That force in the middle of the castle, in Mahajan's workshop?'

'It's a place where many sattva streams meet. Many powerful

419

streams. That's why Mahajan built the castle here. He needed fuel for the Brahmastra.'

Jack held out his hand and sensed the grainy texture of the sattva rushing towards the centre of the castle. 'I thought so. I felt it when I was down there.'

Sonali frowned. 'Felt it?'

Jack gave her a wry smile. 'I'm a siddha too. A native siddha, as they say.'

She raised an eyebrow. 'Why didn't *you* use a power against Mahajan, then?'

'I don't know any war yantras.'

She looked back at the ruins. 'You're full of surprises.'

Jack snorted. 'What about you? You didn't tell me you were a siddha.'

'I didn't want you to know about my situation. Didn't want to draw you into it.'

'What situation?'

'With Mahajan.' She pushed back a stray lock of hair and gave a sigh. 'I suppose there's no reason not to tell you now. I was Mahajan's servant for many years. What I told you was true. But he realised I was sensitive to sattva after we got to Mar. The sattva's so strong here I was having fits and fainting spells. He quickly realised.'

'So, he trained you?'

'He taught me a few powers.'

'Like Lightning?'

'No, not that. That one I taught myself. In secret.'

'You stole it?'

'One of the servants got it for me.'

Jack nodded. He'd taken a yantra from Jhala's office himself once.

'I wanted to kill Mahajan with it,' Sonali continued. 'So, I used it on him. Five months ago. That's how I knew it would destroy his shield for a moment.'

'Mahajan can't have been happy about that.'

Sonali looked down. 'He almost killed me. I was certain he would. He was in a rage.'

'Why didn't he kill you?'

'For the same reason he kept me alive all this time. For the same reason he kept me trapped here in Mar.' She looked up and met Jack's gaze. 'He wanted me to command the Brahmastra.'

Jack blinked a few times. 'What?'

'Mahajan was a blocked siddha. He couldn't learn new yantras.'

'Of course – he must have been, if he was using powers.'

'And to control the Brahmastra, he needed to learn a new yantra. He'd worked out the design from the old manuscripts. But he couldn't use it.'

Jack nodded. Things were becoming clearer now. 'So, Mahajan needed you.'

'Yes. He taught me the yantra. I didn't know what it was. But once I'd learnt it . . .' She looked down and clenched the edge of her cloak in her fist. 'It was evil. I sensed it. Like cold metal in my head.'

Jack paused. Sonali looked upset discussing this, but he had to have answers. 'I understand. You refused to use the power, but Mahajan couldn't kill you.'

'Yes. He beat me. But I never gave in. It got worse recently. He was certain he had everything ready. He just needed me.'

'It was deadlock. You against him.'

'That's it. I could break the ankle chain with the Lightning power any time I wanted, but I could never escape the torc. I wouldn't have helped Mahajan, though. The Brahmastra is evil. I'm certain of that. I would have killed myself first. I thought about it many times. For some reason I didn't.'

'You thought you might escape?'

'I don't know. I suppose so. I couldn't completely give up hope. Perhaps I was just a coward.'

Jack cleared his throat. 'I wouldn't have called you that.'

Sonali went silent. Her eyes reddened and moisture crept into their corners.

Jack ran his fingers through his hair. At least he understood things better now.

He recalled Atri's death. The siddha had refused to use a power to defend himself, even when an arrow had hit him. He must have known – or at least suspected – he would need to learn a new power to control the Brahmastra. He must have been determined not to become blocked before he found Mahajan.

'There's still one thing I'm wondering about,' Jack said. 'When I got in the workshop, I didn't find anything. Nothing that looked like a weapon.'

Sonali frowned. 'I never went into the workshop. I don't know what the Brahmastra looks like.'

'Unless it's tiny, it wasn't in there.'

'That is strange. Mahajan was certain he had everything ready. He kept saying that. The Brahmastra must have been hidden in the workshop. There's nowhere else it could have been.'

'I have another idea. I noticed something about the castle. The whole thing looked like a machine for creating avatars, don't you think?'

'I don't know. I saw a picture once—'

'Those metal spikes around the bailey. The circle of stones in the middle. And the workshop underneath. I saw a steel plate in there with a picture on it of a siddha creating an avatar.'

Sonali looked at him. 'Now that you say it. You think—'

'The castle was a machine for creating an avatar. The Brahmastra.'

She shivered. 'Then the Brahmastra would be huge.'

'Bigger than any avatar I've ever seen.'

She nodded slowly. 'It would make sense. The Brahmastra *is* an avatar. I know that much. When I learnt the yantra for controlling it, I understood all the commands, but there was always one I wasn't sure about. It was for "calling" the Brahmastra. Calling

– that could mean creating, couldn't it? Bringing it over from the spirit realm.'

'Seems so.'

'So, Mahajan didn't have the Brahmastra after all. He must have been close, though. He just needed me to call it into life.'

Jack shrugged. 'We'll never know how close he was. And that's the way I want to keep it.'

Someone shouted behind them. Jack turned and saw Cormac running up the side of the hill, calling out, 'Chief dead!'

Jack crossed himself. Domnall had been injured badly during the battle. Although the Mar had tended to him as best they could, Jack had doubted the Chief would survive.

'Dead.' Cormac stood panting in front of Jack. His face was pale and his eyes brimmed with tears.

Jack looked past Cormac and saw the remainder of the Mar clustered in an impromptu camp on the edge of the valley. Many had died, many more were so badly injured they wouldn't survive for long. But, for Cormac's village, the loss of the Chief would be the worst.

Cormac pressed his hand to his chest and cupped it, as if to catch blood flowing from a wound. 'Heart bleeds.'

———————

The seer raised the ancient Bible above her head and intoned slowly. The Gaalic words were at times as guttural as grinding rocks and at other times as whispery as the wind. Her voice seemed to be the voice of the land itself.

Finally, she finished, lowered the holy book and handed it to a Mar girl standing nearby.

A wail went up from the congregation. The entire village had gathered for the funeral and now their cries sailed into the sky. Women shrieked and tore at their hair. Warriors wept and beat their chests with their hands.

In the centre of the group, in a freshly dug grave, lay the body of Chief Domnall. He was wrapped in his striped cloak and his spear lay beside him. His eyes were closed and his face was solemn but calm. His long white hair and beard shone softly in the wintry light.

Jack stood with Saleem, Rao and Sonali. All of them wore native cloaks and stared grimly at the dead Chief. Cormac was directly opposite, his arms hanging limply at his sides and his head bowed. Near to him stood the woman the Cattans had abducted twelve days ago. The warriors had discovered her and some of the other kidnapped women in the village beside Mahajan's castle. At least they were free now.

With great difficulty the seer bent her knees, supporting herself with her staff, and scooped up a handful of dirt. She cast the earth into the grave and it dashed against the Chief's chest.

The wailing grew louder. Eva screeched, pushed past her sisters and collapsed to her knees beside the pit. She sobbed and clawed at the earth, raking up clods and smashing them against the ground. Two of her sisters huddled beside her and tried to calm her.

The seer straightened again and leant against her staff. The rest of the Mar began grasping earth and scattering it over the Chief.

Slowly, the old man was covered over.

An icy wind swept down from the mountains.

The village was without its leader.

'I failed,' Saleem said as he walked up the slope. 'I came here to make up for Wiltshire and I didn't do anything.'

Jack shook his head as he strode beside the lad. 'You did plenty. You helped me fight Wulfric. You survived in Mahajan's dungeon. And you got us past that skull avatar. I never would have made it without you.'

Saleem glanced across at him. 'You think so?'

'I know so. You've made up for Wiltshire. Many times over. You have to stop beating yourself up about it now.'

'Perhaps you're right.' Saleem stared at the ground. 'What about you? And William Merton?'

Jack tensed. It was hard to talk about his friend. 'What about William?'

'You have to forgive yourself too.'

Jack was silent for a moment. He couldn't forgive himself but perhaps he should try. Or at least start to. 'Maybe one day.' He looked up and pointed. 'There he is.'

Above them, on the crest of the hill, stood Rao. He held a burning brand in one hand and the overcast sky swirled behind him. Next to him rose a mound of twigs and branches.

Jack and Saleem trudged up the last few feet to the summit and stood beside the Captain.

'Thank you for coming.' Rao turned and thrust the brand into the pile of wood. The flames crept along the twigs and soon engulfed the larger branches.

The three of them watched as the fire grew brighter and the heat intensified. Soon it was so hot they had to step back a few paces.

Rao gave a loud sigh.

The pyre was for Parihar. It had been impossible to retrieve the Lieutenant's body to cremate it. Instead, according to Rajthanan custom, Rao had made a small effigy out of straw and placed it in the centre of the pile of wood.

Jack had been less than impressed by Parihar. The man had seemed an arrogant idiot during the journey up through Scotland. But he was dead now, and there was no point in thinking ill of the dead.

'It's a hard loss,' Jack said.

Rao nodded. 'More than twenty years he'd been a friend. Since we were this high.' Rao held his hand to his waist.

'Sorry to hear it.'

Rao sighed again. 'Thank you. Both of you.'

'It's nothing,' Jack said. 'We both know what it's like to lose friends. We couldn't let you hold a funeral on your own.'

'No. It's not just that. I meant for everything you've done. Jack, you risked your life to free Parihar. And Saleem, you were with him until the end.'

'You fought too,' Jack said. 'We all tried our best to get him out.'

Rao's jaw quivered slightly but he managed to still it. 'Yes, we did our best by poor Parihar. No one can say we didn't try our best.'

<hr />

Sonali swept her shawl about her and ducked through the hut's entrance. She crouched beside the embers pulsing in the central hearth.

'So, that's all of it.' She nodded at the papers and folios spread out on the floor.

Jack shifted as he sat cross-legged on his bracken bed. 'That's everything we took from Mahajan's workshop.'

Saleem, sitting nearby, nodded, while Rao stared at the papers, rubbing his moustache.

'It's all evil,' Sonali said. 'The work of the Kapalikas.'

'Are there any copies?' Jack asked.

'If there ever were, they would have been somewhere in the castle,' she said. 'They would have been destroyed with everything else.'

'Mahajan wouldn't have stashed copies somewhere else?' Jack asked.

She shook her head. 'There was nowhere else he could keep them. And anyway, he wouldn't dare leave them where anyone else could get hold of them.'

'Perhaps he had a comrade? Another siddha?'

Sonali snorted. 'He worked alone. Believe me. He would never trust anyone else with his secrets.'

Rao cleared his throat. 'So, if I have this right, we have here

426

the only copies of Mahajan's papers. Also, the castle, machine, whatever it was, has been destroyed. There's nothing left of it that would allow it to be rebuilt.'

'I can't see how,' Sonali said. 'I looked at the ruins. There's almost nothing there.'

'I agree,' Jack said. 'There was just a bit of rubble left. Soon it'll be covered over by grass. Nothing there anyone could use.'

Rao nodded slowly and glanced at Jack. 'Then I say we destroy these notes. We agreed no one should have the Brahmastra. If we get rid of these writings no one else will ever be able to build one.'

Sonali nodded. 'Destroy them.' She spoke the words as if she were spitting.

Jack flicked a look at Saleem, who shrugged. 'Whatever you think, Jack.'

Jack paused, then said to Rao, 'What about Atri's notes?'

'What about them?' Rao asked.

'He was researching the Brahmastra, wasn't he? Maybe he wrote something about it.'

'I can't think he would have known anything much.' Rao pulled Atri's notebook and maps out of his satchel. 'But all the same, we can get rid of them too. To be on the safe side.' He tossed the charts on to the pile of Mahajan's papers. Then he tore out the first half of the notebook and held up the pages. 'This is all Atri's. The back part is my own notes.' He then threw the torn pages on to the pile as well.

Sonali looked at Jack. 'So, we'll destroy it all?'

Jack rubbed his chin. 'Yes. We'll burn it. All except for those maps.'

'These ones?' Rao lifted Atri's charts.

Jack nodded and pointed at two large maps he'd found in Mahajan's workshop. 'And those.'

Rao quickly looked over Mahajan's charts and compared them

to the ones Atri had drawn. 'Yes. They all just seem to be ordinary maps. Nothing about the Brahmastra.'

'So, there's no need to get rid of them,' Jack said.

'I suppose not. But what do you want them for?'

Jack paused. He wasn't completely certain himself. He just had a vague sense that they belonged to his people. 'They're maps of Britain. They're records of these lands. The people of this island should have them.'

'You told me your people don't use Rajthanan maps,' Rao said.

'Perhaps we should. My people have to understand these things.' He motioned to the charts. 'We can start with these. I'll take them to the library at Clun Abbey. The monks will look after them.'

Rao pursed his lips. 'Very well, if you insist. There's no harm in your having them.' He pulled the maps away from the pile and set them aside.

'So, Jack,' Sonali said, 'Mahajan's notes.'

Jack stared at the papers for a moment. Within those pages was the key, perhaps, to building a monstrous weapon. A weapon the crusaders could use to free England for ever. Now that it came to it, it was hard to give up on this chance.

But, no. Something like the Brahmastra shouldn't exist in the world.

He nodded slowly. 'We'll burn them.'

Rao gave Jack a formal nod, then plucked up a handful of pages and shoved them into the fire. The paper caught quickly and was soon devoured by the flames. Rao picked up some folios and tossed them in as well. Then he swept up the final papers and fed them to the fire. A few sparks drifted lazily around the room. Black smoke swirled up like an escaped djinn. Jack half expected some sort of evil power to sweep out of the flames. But nothing happened.

They were just ordinary pages of notes. Nothing else.

The smoke thickened and funnelled up through a slit in the stone roof.

Soon there was nothing left of Mahajan's work except ash.

***

Jack sat up and blinked in the dark. He'd heard a cry – he was certain – but now everything was silent again.

By the light of the smouldering fire, he could see the dark curves of Rao and Saleem sleeping on their bracken beds. Saleem snuffled and shifted, but didn't wake.

Jack sat still. Listening.

Was the village under attack? Had the Cattans returned? For a moment he even had the wild thought that Mahajan wasn't dead and had come back for revenge.

But he heard nothing further. He must have imagined it. He lay back on the bed.

Then he heard the cry again – a thin, distinct wail.

Christ. He grabbed the pistol and scurried outside. A cluster of villagers had gathered about the hut next door.

Sonali's hut.

He heard another cry as he ran across to the gathering. The door had been moved aside, but none of the Mar wanted to enter. Instead, they all stood peering gingerly inside. Cormac stepped out from the group as Jack approached.

'What is it?' Jack asked.

Cormac frowned and gestured to the doorway. 'Not understand. Shee woman calls out.'

Jack looked inside and made out Sonali lying under a blanket. Her eyes were closed and her forehead was bunched into a frown. She tossed and turned, then gave a moan.

'Is bad magic?' Cormac asked.

'Looks more like a bad dream,' Jack said.

He stooped and clambered across to Sonali. She began crying out more frantically as he drew closer.

'Sonali,' he whispered.

She thrashed about and shouted.

'Sonali.' He touched her shoulder.

She opened her eyes, shrieked and sprang away from him. He heard the Mar gasp as they watched through the doorway.

'It's me.' Jack held out his hand. 'You're safe.'

She stared at him, her eyes wide and her chest heaving up and down. She glanced at the villagers, then at the fire, and then finally seemed to remember where she was.

'A dream?' Jack asked.

'Yes.' Her voice was cracked.

'Mahajan?'

She nodded, put her hands to her face and began sobbing.

Jack turned to Cormac and the others. 'It's all right. I'll look after her.'

'Great Shee woman is safe?' Cormac asked.

'Yes. She's safe now. She's just been through a lot.'

<hr />

Jack swung the knapsack on to his back, shoved the pistol into his belt and grasped a knife-musket that had been taken from Mahajan's castle. There was still a dangerous journey ahead through the wilds of Scotland before they got back to England.

Rao was armed with a pistol, while Saleem had a musket. Sonali carried no weapon, but with her powers she was probably the most formidable fighter out of all of them. Jack shook his head as he looked at her standing nearby, wrapped in a native cloak. He'd never met a female siddha before, hadn't even known they existed. But why not? She was sensitive to sattva. She'd had at least the basic training – like him. Why shouldn't she use the powers she'd learnt?

And if it wasn't for her, he had no doubt Mahajan and the Cattans would have won the battle. He would most likely be dead by now in that case.

They all owed her a great debt.

Rao squinted up at the sky. For the first time in many days, the cloud had lifted, revealing stretches of blue. The sun even blinked into view at times. 'We should go soon. It's already mid-morning.'

Jack grinned. 'Didn't check your watch?'

Rao smiled and took the watch from his pocket. 'It stopped. During the fight.' He lifted it to his ear and shook it. 'Sounds like it's broken.'

Jack glanced up. 'Mid-morning. You're right. Well done.'

'Been practising.' Rao eyed the centre of the village, where many of the Mar had gathered. 'What are they up to now? We have to make a start.'

The villagers had promised to send some warriors to guide Jack and the others back to the border. But now the Mar were no doubt engaged in some sort of ritual and wouldn't travel until an auspicious moment.

'We can't go without them,' Jack said. 'I'll go and find Cormac.'

He went to take off the knapsack, then noticed the crowd leaving the centre of the village and walking towards them.

'Ah,' he said. 'Looks like we'll be off soon.'

The Mar approached Jack and the others, clapping their hands and chanting. Soon they were pressing in around the small group.

Eva rushed to Rao's side.

The Captain flinched. 'Now, look here, Eva. I'm—'

'Great Shee.' Eva hung her head. 'I sorry. We no marry.'

'What?'

'I marry other.'

'You marry . . . Oh, I see.' Rao gave a sigh of relief. 'Well. Good.'

Eva looked up. 'You no angry?'

'Of course not. I wish you and your future husband all the best.'

Eva gave Rao a broad smile and bowed.

Rao glanced at Jack and raised his eyebrows.

Jack grinned and then turned to the assembled Mar. 'Thank you, friends, for your hospitality. We will always remember you. But now, it's time for us to leave.'

'You leave,' Eva said. 'But first, Chief speak.'

Jack frowned. 'Chief? I thought there *was* no chief?'

In answer to his question the Mar parted and a man walked forward from the back of the crowd. He wore a striped woollen cloak and Domnall's ancient longsword hung at his side.

Cormac.

Rao gasped and a smile crept across Jack's face.

'We marry.' Eva went to Cormac's side and took his arm. 'We lead village.'

Jack felt emotion well within him. In a husky voice he said, 'I'm sure you'll lead your people wisely.'

'This is splendid.' Rao beamed. 'Simply splendid.'

'I serve people as best I can,' Cormac said. 'We weep for Domnall, but we also have joy in heart. We free. I thank you Great Shee with brown skin and eye that can see far, and Jack, friend of Great Shee, and Sonali, Great Shee woman. You have saved our lands.'

A huge cheer went up from the Mar, and the sound seemed to lift Jack up for a moment. The villagers sang, swayed and clapped in time. Pipes droned and several men bashed hand-held drums.

Cormac motioned to the five warriors who were to accompany Jack and the others on the journey. The men stepped forward, carrying spears and bows.

Jack gave the crowd a final glance and then turned and left with the rest of the small party.

The Mar continued to sing and cheer. No doubt they were praising the Great Shee and his companions.

Rao turned to Jack, his eye glinting. 'They are a remarkable people. Truly remarkable. I'm so glad they are finally free.'

Jack nodded. They were indeed remarkable. And if they could free themselves from Mahajan's rule, maybe there was still hope for the English yet.

34

Rao stood on the brow of the hill, a slight breeze ruffling his native cloak. He peered through the spyglass, his face pinched in concentration.

He lowered the glass and pointed to the west. 'I can just make out Dun Fries over there.'

Jack gazed across the grey, folding landscape. The day was murky and he couldn't see the town or even a trace of smoke.

They'd reached the border of Scotland and said goodbye to their escort of Mar warriors an hour ago. Now they were back in England. They were on their way home.

'So,' Jack said. 'You'll go to Dun Fries?'

Rao nodded. 'I'll report to the army and ask to be posted back to Rajthana.'

'They'll agree to that?'

'I'm sure I'll be due some leave after everything I've been through.'

'And then? When you're back?'

Rao gave a slight smile. 'There's a young lady I have to see.'

Jack grinned. 'You'll defy your father? Your jati?'

'They can all jump off a cliff. I've been a fool. Damn them. Damn their wretched conventions. I'm my own man now. I'll make my own decisions.'

'Pleased to hear it.'

'And you? You'll go back to Shropshire and your daughter?'

Jack nodded.

'I've a lot to thank you for, Jack.'

433

'It was nothing,' Jack mumbled.

'No. You saved my life when those wolves attacked us.'

'And you stayed with me when I was freezing to death. I would have died otherwise.'

'Yes.' Rao looked into the distance. 'I did that, didn't I? We helped each other. That's the way it was. We helped each other and we did our best to help our friends. We followed our dharmas, I believe.'

Jack paused. He and Rao had been through the fire of battle together. They'd trudged across endless miles, faced dangers and hostile forces. He couldn't just part ways with the Captain now without saying something. But what? He'd never been good at this sort of thing.

He held out his hand. 'God's grace to you, Rao. Best of luck.'

Rao looked at Jack's outstretched hand, puzzlement snaking across his forehead.

'We shake hands,' Jack said. 'It's our custom in England. Remember. When we were camping that first night.'

'Oh, yes.' Rao smiled, took Jack's hand and shook it firmly. There was a trace of a tear in the corner of his eye. 'Jack, I don't know what to say.'

'It's all right. You don't have to say—'

'You've been like a brother to me.'

Jack was stunned. 'I . . .' He spluttered, lost for words. He'd never heard a Rajthanan say such a thing to a European.

'I mean it.' Rao shook Jack's hand more fervently. 'Brothers.'

Jack fought back the tears and gripped Rao's hand tighter. He felt something open inside him. 'Yes. Brothers.'

◆

The crossroads stood before them. It was just an ordinary meeting of two dirt roads. One route coiled away across the flats towards Dun Fries. The other curved to the south-east, following a line of hills before plunging directly south.

'So, this is it,' Jack said.

'Indeed,' Rao said. 'This is where we part.' He turned to Sonali. 'I'll make sure you find passage back to Rajthana from Dun Fries.'

'I'm not sure.' Sonali toyed with the edge of her cloak. 'I have some relatives in the south. In Dorsetshire. I was thinking of going there.'

'Very well.' Rao nodded. 'I'll make sure you get passage there.'

'Maybe . . .' Sonali's voice trailed off and she glanced at Jack.

Jack stalled. Sonali had mentioned a few times that she was thinking of travelling south with him and Saleem. He wasn't sure why.

She'd said there was nothing for her in Rajthana now. She'd said she had to start again. As much as anything, she seemed in a daze and still recovering from everything that had happened to her.

Ordinarily he would have said no straight away. They still had many miles to travel, through difficult and sometimes dangerous country. She would be far safer travelling on a Rajthanan steamship.

But on the other hand, if anyone could take care of themselves in a tight spot, it was Sonali.

And there was something else. Just the hint of an idea at the back of Jack's mind.

Sonali was a siddha. She knew yantras he'd never learnt. Maybe she could be persuaded to stay a while in Folly Brook and help him at the House of Sorcery.

'If you want to travel south with us, you're welcome,' he said to Sonali.

Rao frowned. 'Are you certain of this, Sonali?'

She nodded. 'I am.'

'Very well,' Rao said. 'If that's what you wish.' He turned to face Jack and Saleem. 'Well, my friends. I don't know when we'll see each other next. If at all. But I will always remember you and our journey to Scotland.'

Jack patted Rao on the arm. 'And we'll remember you too.'

Rao unfastened his cloak, swung it from his shoulders, folded it and tucked it under one arm. 'I'll be back in Rajthanan society soon.' He smiled. 'It won't do to be dressed like a savage.'

Jack pointed at the cloak. 'But you're still taking it.'

'Oh, yes.' Rao tapped the shaggy pile. 'It'll be a souvenir. A reminder of my time over here.'

'Well, then,' Jack said. 'God's grace to you.'

'Thank you.' Rao stood taller, lifted his chin and straightened his tunic. 'And you too.' Then he spun on his heel and walked steadily away down the road, his boots kicking up clods of wet earth behind him. His red turban bobbed above his head like a beacon shining in the dun landscape.

For some reason a memory of Jhala circled in Jack's mind. He recalled the day he'd left the army. His old guru had come to wish him farewell. Jack still remembered Jhala's words – they were seared in his memory.

'You have been my best disciple. Farewell, Casey . . . Jack.'

Jack was certain Jhala had meant those words. There was no other reason for him to say them, no reason for Jhala to have even come to see Jack off.

There must have been a bond of some sort between him and his old commander, despite what happened later. Despite Jhala forcing him to capture William in order to save Elizabeth.

There was good in the Rajthanans. In some of them at any rate. He would remember that from now on.

He turned to Saleem and Sonali and took a deep breath. 'Right. Let's get going.'

35

<hr/>

Jack saw Elizabeth first. Many of the other inhabitants of Folly Brook were nearby. But Elizabeth was all he could see in that first moment.

She was crouching outside her hut, and when she saw him she leapt up, swept her dress around her and charged across the grass towards him. The other villagers stood by and watched as she ran into his arms so hard he tottered backwards for a second.

She hugged him tight. 'You're alive.'

Jack smiled, stepped back and held her by the shoulders. She looked well. Healthy. And he could see the trace of a bump in her belly. 'Yes, your old father's still alive.'

'What about your injury?'

He pressed his hand to his chest. 'Healed.'

She frowned. 'Completely?'

He nodded.

She beamed, her cheeks flushing. 'Thank the Lord. I thought . . . I might not . . .'

'Don't you worry. It's over now.'

'But how? The Grail?'

'No. The yantra Kanvar gave me worked. Finally.'

'You worked it out?'

Jack scratched the back of his neck. 'I don't know how I did it, to be honest. It just happened.'

'You're here. That's all that matters.' She looked over his shoulder at the two figures standing behind him. At first her face lit up and she said, 'Saleem.' Then her smile suddenly withered. 'Oh.'

Jack turned. Sonali still wore a Scottish cloak over her sari. Her lips were tight and she stared like a cornered cat at the villagers.

'This is Sonali,' Jack said. 'We met her in Scotland. She's going to stay for a few weeks. She's going to help me at the House of Sorcery.'

'A Rajthanan?'

'Yes.'

Elizabeth raised her eyebrows. 'A Rajthanan's helping us?'

'It's a long story. I'll explain later.'

And now the other villagers were crowding around him and Elizabeth, talking excitedly, slapping him on the back and shaking his hand. Saleem's mother and sisters came bustling from Jack's old hut and Saleem rushed across to meet them. Mark and the apprentices from the House of Sorcery were there. Old Mary. Tom the blacksmith. All of them.

Jack clasped Mark's hand. 'Any sign of Kanvar?'

Mark shook his head. 'He never came back.'

Jack frowned. The Sikh had promised to return. But Jack was too happy to worry about this for the moment.

Then someone nearby said, 'It's a pleasure to see you again, sir.'

Jack turned and saw Godwin standing stiffly behind him. The lad was wearing the white reeve's surcoat, and the oversized longsword hung at his side.

'I've done my best to look after the place while you've been away,' Godwin said. 'I hope you'll be satisfied.'

Jack grinned and patted Godwin on the arm. He looked across at the village huts, the emerald grass and the dark hills beyond. 'Just as I remembered it all. You've done well. Son-in-law.'

'No Grail.' Henry's face soured and he leant back in his chair. 'That's all you've got to tell us?'

'That's right.' Jack put his hands behind his back as he stood before the councillors. 'We found Mahajan, but there was no Grail.'

The seven representatives of the Crusader Council shifted in their seats and muttered. They'd gathered in this chamber in Lord Fitzalan's castle to hear Jack's report. Sir Alfred, with his pure white beard and long silver hair, sat in their centre, while Lord Fitzalan himself sat to the old man's right. Henry wasn't a Council member, but Newcastle-on-Clun was his manor and he'd arranged this meeting.

Henry slammed his fist on the table. 'Five men dead. Three missing. And you've got nothing to show for it.'

'If you'll remember, I said the Grail wasn't real from the start,' Jack said.

The Council members muttered louder.

Alfred raised his hand. 'Quiet, gentlemen. Quiet.'

A hush fell over the others.

'We always knew this mission was a gamble,' Alfred continued. 'We knew there was only a slim chance, at best, of finding the Grail.'

'But, sir,' Henry said. 'How can we be certain Casey's telling the truth? I don't trust—'

'He's done nothing to make me suspicious,' Alfred said. 'There's no reason for us to doubt Jack's commitment to the cause.'

Several councillors nodded and mumbled their agreement.

Henry scowled and a few other councillors appeared unhappy with Sir Alfred's words, but none challenged the old man.

'Now,' Alfred said. 'What *did* you find, Jack?'

Jack cleared his throat. 'As I said, we defeated Mahajan and I got into his workshop under the castle. But he didn't have a weapon there. He was working on it, but he didn't have the power to create it. There was no Grail either.' Jack paused for a moment. 'There was one thing, though.'

The councillors shuffled in their chairs and eyed him closely. Henry crossed his arms, while Alfred stared at Jack with watery, red-tinged eyes.

'It's hard to explain,' Jack said. 'It was a meeting point of sattva streams.'

'What devilry are you talking about?' Henry said.

'Not devilry,' Jack said. 'It's like a sacred spot, you could say. A place where yogic powers are strong.'

'A place of black magic by the sound of it,' Henry said.

'Silence,' Alfred snapped. 'Go on, Jack. Tell us about this sacred place. Can it help us?'

'I don't know,' Jack said. 'Possibly. Something strange happened to me in there. I was able to use a power I couldn't use before. That's happened to me another time, but perhaps the strong sattva there helped.'

'What power?' Alfred asked.

'It was a healing power.'

A mutter ran through the small group and several of the councillors spoke softly to each other.

'The Grail is said to heal all wounds,' Lord Fitzalan said.

'Perhaps this sacred place *is* the Grail,' another councillor said.

'Is that possible?' Alfred asked Jack. 'Could the sacred place be the Grail?'

Jack hesitated. It was a strange thought, but then no one knew for certain what the Grail truly was. He'd always been quick to dismiss his countrymen's superstitions. But as Rao had said to him in Scotland, there was truth in legends sometimes. 'It's possible, I suppose.'

Several of the councillors grinned. Others said they should send another expedition.

Jack held up his hand. 'Hold on. I'm not certain about all this. I suppose it could be the Grail. But if it is, I don't see how it can help us. It's strong sattva and I could use a new power. But that's all. I couldn't say how we could use it, even if it was the Grail.'

Alfred nodded slowly. 'I understand, Jack. It's a mystery. For now, at any rate. But it shows that there's hope. Perhaps we'll learn more about it. Perhaps it will turn out to be the Grail after all. Perhaps then we'll be able to use it to free our lands.'

The councillors nodded approvingly.

'We need hope now more than ever,' Alfred continued. 'Vadula's army is said to be preparing to march from Worcestershire. Our spies say it will head here to Shropshire in the near future. An advance party under a general called Jhala is said to already be on the move.'

Jack's heart quivered. 'Jhala? Did you say Jhala?'

'I did,' Alfred said. 'What of it?'

'What do you know about him?' Jack asked. 'Was he once commander of the 2nd Native Infantry?'

Alfred shrugged and glanced at one of the other councillors, a thin man with long dark hair.

The thin man sat forward in his chair, rested his chin on his hands and narrowed his eyes. 'Yes. Our spies tell us Jhala once commanded that regiment. What do *you* know about him?'

The room dropped an inch and Jack felt light-headed. 'I thought he was dead.'

'Yes, he was reported dead during the first crusade,' the thin man said. 'It was thought his men had killed him when they rebelled. But he survived, apparently. He escaped.'

Jack went silent. He couldn't think what to say. Jhala was alive? It seemed incredible, but now that he thought about it, Jhala had only ever been *reported* dead. There could have been a mistake.

'You look pale,' Alfred said. 'Are you all right?'

Jack pulled himself together and squared his shoulders. 'I'm fine. It's nothing. It's just . . . I once served under Jhala, that's all.'

Alfred lifted an eyebrow. 'Interesting. You will have to tell us all you know about him. But in the meantime, there is little point in this meeting continuing. We've said all that needs to be said. Now we must prepare.

'The Rajthanans are coming.'

Acknowledgements

The Place of Dead Kings was, of course, inspired by *Heart of Darkness* by Joseph Conrad, *King Solomon's Mines* by H. Rider Haggard and *The Man Who Would Be King* by Rudyard Kipling.

I would like to thank my agent, Marlene Stringer, for all the work she's done on my behalf, and my editor, Carolyn Caughey, for her wise guidance. Thanks also to Francine Toon and everyone else at Hodder & Stoughton for all the time and effort they have put into this book.

Thank you to Chip Tolaney at Ganesh Mall for advice about Ganesh statues, Randy Wakeman for help with nineteenth-century firearms, Robert Fuchs for information about parchment and medieval manuscripts, Dave King for his feedback, and Dilraj Singh Sachdev for advice about turbans and other matters.

Thanks to my friends, who have encouraged me over many years.

And thank you to my family – Gail Tatham, Harry Wilson, Edward Wilson, Anita Hrebeniak, Blue Quinn, Molly Flowers and Jet Quinn – for their unwavering support. Most of all, thank you to my wife, Helena Quinn, who has done so much to help me during the long months it's taken to write this book.